MY CHEROKEE ROSE

REBA RHYNE

To: Lynn

Jenni needs answers.

What will she find?

Reba Rhyne

ISBN: 978-1-945975-81-3

This is a work of fiction. Names, characters, businesses, places, events and incidents are either the products of the author's imagination or used in a fictitious manner. Any resemblance to actual persons, living or dead, or actual events is purely coincidental.

Cover by Ken Raney.

Background Cover Photo by Robin Rhyne Greenlee of Wonderful Blessings Photography. Looking toward Cherokee from Newfound Gap, Great Smoky Mountains National Park. Blount County, Tennessee

Published by EA Books Publishing a division of
Living Parables of Central Florida, Inc. a 501c3
EABooksPublishing.com

Dedicated to the Women in my Life
All who were and are known to me.

Nancy (Nan) Susanna LeQuire Tipton
My Great, Grandmother

Melvina (Mellie) Lucinda Tipton Whitehead
My Grandmother

Margaret Naomi Whitehead Rhyne
My Mother

Melissa Lynn Meiller Belandres
My Daughter

Other Special Women Near and Far

A local newspaper columnist, Sam Venable, encourages families to write down their life experiences or a memoir to be saved for future generations. Events can be earth-shaking, funny, unhappy, valuable or just plain ordinary. Friends, places and happenings are valuable for future reference and to know the person's life.

Some years after my father died in his seventies, I asked my mother to write her remembrances. For years, she was a well-known genealogist in our neck-of-the-woods. People came from Texas, California and other states to stay and talk ancestors with her. I learned to drive ferrying her to cemeteries and older people's homes to get information on our former relatives.

While reading her memoir, about her growing up years and life, and her job teaching in our school system, I learned about a romance she had before she knew my father. She and a friend went to Cherokee to wait tables during the summer break from school, and this is where she met her first love. Her mother and sister thought she would marry this man. The ring in the box on the back cover is the one mentioned in the book.

My Cherokee Rose is a totally fictionalized story coming out of her comments.

CONTENTS

Foreword	i
Chapter 1	1
Chapter 2	11
Chapter 3	19
Chapter 4	25
Chapter 5	31
Chapter 6	35
Chapter 7	41
Chapter 8	51
Chapter 9	55
Chapter 10	61
Chapter 11	65
Chapter 12	71
Chapter 13	77
Chapter 14	85
Chapter 15	93
Chapter 16	99
Chapter 17	105
Chapter 18	113
Chapter 19	121
Chapter 20	131
Chapter 21	141
Chapter 22	149
Chapter 23	157
Chapter 24	163
Chapter 25	171
Chapter 26	175
Chapter 27	183
Chapter 28	191
Chapter 29	199
Chapter 30	207
Chapter 31	213

Chapter 32	225
Chapter 33	235
Chapter 34	243
Chapter 35	251
Chapter 36	259
Chapter 37	271
Chapter 38	275
Chapter 39	283
Chapter 40	289
Chapter 41	293
Chapter 42	299
Chapter 43	305
Chapter 44	311
Chapter 45	315
Chapter 46	321
Chapter 47	327
Chapter 48	331
Chapter 49	337
Chapter 50	341
Chapter 51	345
Chapter 52	347
Chapter 53	355
Chapter 54	359
Chapter 55	365
Chapter 56	369
Acknowledgments	376
About the Author	377

FOREWORD

Reba Carolyn Rhyne Meiller has completed a task all of us should undertake: She has written her family memories.

Carolyn's book is a work of fiction, Christian-oriented with names changed, yet it chronicles fascinating events from before her birth. Her project underscores the importance of interviewing family members before it's too late. Otherwise, many stories can be lost. In reading her mother's life account, Carolyn learned details that were new to her.

A family history can be as simple as a hand-written notepad or as sophisticated as a published book. The hardest part is getting started. Carolyn did. Now it's your turn.

Sam Venable

Columnist and author

God pity them both! and pity us all,
Who vainly the dreams of youth recall.
For of all sad words of tongue or pen,
The saddest are these: "It might have been!"

An excerpt from Maud Muller
A poem by John Greenleaf Whittier

(Public Domain)

1

Maryville, Tennessee—Monday, March 22, 2006—Jenni

Some grandmothers die easily.

Mine slowly shut her eyes. Her breathing became shallower, until no movement of her chest told the story. For many years, I'd witnessed her preparations for this moment.

"She's gone," my Uncle Jerry said. He sat by her bedside, holding her hand. His usual calm face was racked with grief.

I looked at my watch—11:36 a.m.

"Strange how life brings death and life again," Uncle Stan said quietly in my ear. He stood with his arm around me—eyes moist with tears. He knew, as I did, we'd see her once more.

I nodded, turned my head from the bedside scene, and gazed outside her large bedroom window. It was framed with designer, baby-blue curtains folded in graceful scallops. Untypical of her, blue and scallops. Grandma being a hands-on, physical woman. Not stylish or neat.

The opening showcased the bright sun shining on new-born leaves moving gently with the wind on the tall hickory trees. Because the weather was unusually mild for the end of March, yellow buttercups and pink hyacinths bloomed at the end of the front concrete walk—placed there by her hands. The paper tube and mailbox sat in convenient proximity. The box with the red flag up, representative of her extensive correspondence with her many friends.

Uncle Stan followed my gaze and thoughts. He murmured in a low tone, “She loved reading the newspaper and writing her acquaintances. We won’t be kidding her about reading the junk mail anymore.”

Needing to be alone, I nodded and moved into a corner of the bedroom next to the cherry dresser, where a photo of my grandparents sat in their checkered, polyester best. From both sides of the room came muffled sobs in the crowded space where the family was gathered.

Leaning for support against the piece of furniture, my thoughts ran skipping in all directions—skipping in and out of the present to sweet memories moving about and through my mind.

I didn’t cry.

After the previous week of sitting at her bedside, my emotions were exhausted. The hardest part had been knowing that at any hour my mother and I would need to call the family, let them know she was close to the end.

At exactly eight this morning, my mother had opened the door for the hospice nurse. Mrs. Craig carried a small medical bag into the sickroom. She took my grandmother’s vital signs. Fifteen minutes later, my mother and I called her brothers.

Mom phoned Uncle Jerry, who was staying with his family at a local motel.

I punched in Uncle Stanley’s number.

“Hi, sugar,” he said. Uncle Stan called all the girls in the family “sugar.”

“It’s Grandma . . .” I choked up and couldn’t say another word. The tension and stress of seven days of tending to her nightly needs flooded from my aching heart.

“Is it time?”

After the initial shock of hearing those three words for the second time in two days, I answered, “Yes. The hospice nurse said to call you.”

“I’m on the way, sugar.”

I shook my head at the memory of the short-lived conversation and shuddered at the finality of her passing. It didn't seem possible, after the many years she and I worked, traveled, and played together, five of them with my Grandpa before he died.

Some immeasurable minutes later, I heard Uncle Jerry say reverently, "Someone get the hospice nurse." At sixty-two he was the oldest child and still her baby.

Uncle Jerry's words became the signal for most of the family to leave the room and congregate in the large den down a long, shadowy corridor. I left with the rest, passing a hall mirror, which revealed the dim reflection of a young woman with short brown hair and brown eyes. Not exactly the spitting image of a young grandma, but close enough for my mother to say so.

My mother and Uncle Jerry stayed behind to talk to the nurse. As the executor of her will, Uncle Jerry immediately took charge.

In the den, no one sat in my grandmother's lift-chair. I saw Uncle Stan take a sidewise glance, but he bypassed the dark-blue, over-puffed giant for the comfortable, cushioned couches nearby. Sitting down heavily, he leaned into the striped, green-and-blue seatback and closed his eyes. "Mom both loved and hated her chair," he said to no one in particular.

He was right. She loved it because the electric controls allowed her the freedom to get up and down without aid. Hated it—yes. After losing her mobility and sitting much of the time, she found no comfortable position within its foamed frame.

Arthritis, the Great Robber, stole away easy movement, and with difficulty she hobbled along behind her walker, until during this last year she *graduated for the third time*, she told me, with a grin and a chuckle, *to a wheelchair*.

Comments in the room jolted me back to the present.

"She looked so peaceful."

"I thought death was supposed to be hard."

"She smiled at me this morning after I arrived."

"I wonder if she read the obits today."

Someone in the room chuckled at this, recalling her daily habit.

I wanted to block my ears from these old-hat comments. My Grandma could no longer carry out or bring about things she loved to do. Today she chose to die. I should pass into heaven with such dignity.

I sat staring at the floor, listening as they talked quietly, albeit superficially, about the multifaceted woman who, after ninety-two years on earth, must be laughing in heaven with her extended family. Maddie Whitehead Ryeton, noted genealogist and mother of three, would never research another file. Now she knew everybody in her family and everything about each one. I grinned—a short, brief movement of my mouth, realizing her researching days were over.

Popping noises interrupted my musing and drew my attention to Uncle Stan. He sat opening and closing the "reacher" he'd pulled from the side pocket of her lift-chair. How many times I'd watched as she pulled the gadget out to grab an errant piece of paper saying, "No, don't get up. I can reach it," and then, with me halfway out of my chair, she'd catch the object with those open jaws and smile at proving she could accomplish at least this little task.

Just three days ago she'd sat in that chair looking out the double windows at the snow-covered foothills of the Great Smoky Mountains and said to my mother, "When I was young, we had knee-deep snow, and walking to Maryville College presented a real challenge." Turning to me, she continued, "Jenni, did you know I graduated from there in 1936 during the Great Depression? Worked in the school's maid shop sewing clothes to help pay my tuition."

I could have told her yes, many times.

She didn't speak another word, becoming lost in thoughts of her own.

Later, in the dwindling sunset, she got up awkwardly, graduating again from the chair, to her walker, to her wheelchair. She turned to look at her beloved mountains. In her bent-over position, she forced her head sideways and smiled at the rose and gray hued clouds resting on the hills. "I've always been proud of my family's roots here in East Tennessee. If only the hills could talk. What stories they'd tell about the folks who lived here," she'd said.

She never looked through those windows again.

Her words started me thinking. I'd heard enough stories to fill several books. Authorship—the tiny ambition veiled in the back of my mind stole timidly to the forefront. Why shouldn't I tell those stories?

No one would guess that after being married to my take-charge-and-control-everything Grandpa Charles for over fifty years, Grandma would be so independent, but she was. Independent, I mean. After he died, she never asked her children for help, preferring to pay her bills and run errands on her own until she decided her driving was unsafe.

My mother, Karen, the middle child, always complained about her mother's nose being stuck in a marriage or family record when she visited. I'd tried to organize these scribbled-on books with pages of notes tucked inside. Records and sheets of paper were stuck in the cubby holes of the desk next to her chair, in bookcases across the room, and on the nightstand in her bedroom, where she now lay motionless in her hospital bed. The enormous collection included three books she'd written about her family tree.

Sitting in this den watching her write with ballpoint pen and erase with the white stuff she'd sent for from the drugstore had always reminded me of a verse from the Bible she'd loved so completely. The last verse in John said, *Jesus did many other things as well. If every one of them were written down, I suppose that even the whole world would not have room for the books that would be written.* I know my grandmother couldn't rival Jesus, but John had nothing on her. Her writings were inexhaustible.

Yesterday, as Mom and I stayed with her, she continued to scrawl, in handwriting hardly legible, her thoughts on the newspaper obituaries she'd read that morning. Worn out from this small effort, she let the book, ballpoint pen, and sheets of paper fall to her chest.

She looked up abruptly, straight at my mother. "Is it time?"

My mother slowly nodded and leaned forward saying gently, "Yes."

Startled at my grandmother's question, I went from the room with tears streaming down my face.

"Yes, Mom. It's time." I heard my mother say again.

I turned at the door, saw her hand the book and paper to my mother and smile at nothing in particular. "I'm cold," she said, pulling the pink fleece blanket up to her chin, pushing her thin, bruised arms underneath.

Sobbing, I hurried to the den and sat down, exactly where I sat now—the warmest place within the chill of the room.

Pop. Pop. The sound of the reacher brought me back to the present.

Uncle Stan continued to open and close the tool until his always angry wife, Marilyn, reminded him the movement irritated everyone in the room. "At your age, you ought to know better," she continued to harangue.

He glowered at her, shoving the metal utensil with a short jab back into the lift-chair pocket. Getting up, he left the room.

Uncle Stan never called Aunt Marilyn sugar.

Unperturbed, she patted her partial beehive hairdo, reminiscent of her bleached-blonde, beauty queen days in high school. Her head, with its thinning strands pulled back over her ears and held in place with combs, bobbed as she looked over at her two misbehaving grandchildren. The fraternal twins picked at each other on the floor next to the brick fireplace. "*Chiiildreeen*, you need to be quiet now. This is not the time for roughhousing," she said with her usual strained smile and something masquerading as affection in her tone.

She turned her disapproving look on her son Steve, the twins' father. He was sprawled on a couch nearby.

"*Steeeve*," she said with her customary whine, nodding toward the fireplace.

Steve glanced briefly in her direction, the childrens', and then ignored both.

"*Pleeease* children," she persisted in complaining.

Not obeying their grandmother's complaints, Tyler and Tamara followed their grandfather from the room. I could hear them continuing to poke at each other in the kitchen.

I wanted to shout at my aunt. Don't be yourself. Not today.

I noticed Uncle Jerry's wife, Bonnie, dressed in her New York designer suit, turn her well-bred nose up at her sister-in-law, sniffing at the air as if some horrible stink resided in the room. Her three children with spouses and six grandchildren sat like angels in the midst of the commotion. This included a grandchild—the six-month-old baby girl, a cherub with pink hairbow, rosebud lips, and closed eyes—resting in a new pink car carrier on the floor. No garage sale or used stuff for her.

My eyes continued to wander around the room filled with the work of my Grandma's hand. Every piece told a story. Afghans covered the tops of the couches. Crocheted dollies lay under the glass lamps, and the candy bowl filled with hard spearmint candies sat on the end table. Scrapbooking supplies, a new hobby of the last two years, appeared contained in a box on a bookshelf under the TV next to videos for her grandchildren and a checkerboard and checkers stuffed somehow to the side. Everyone played the game with her. Unlike my grandfather, she let you win.

Uncle Jerry came into the room. All eyes turned in his direction. "We've called the funeral home. They should be here at any moment. You may want to go outside or move to another room in the house." Several nodded their heads and got up, eager to leave. "Oh, before you go, let's have lunch at Cracker Barrel. Make some plans."

"Might be quieter at China Cuisine," his wife suggested. "They have a back room."

"Sure, sure." He nodded. He might have been a successful executive, but Aunt Bonnie ruled at home.

A short consultation among those present revealed some could stay. Others wanted to return home or to work. My mother entered the room.

"Jerry, Mrs. Craig says our cars must be moved from the driveway so the men from the funeral home can back up the sidewalk."

"Okay, Karen. Everyone outside. Pull into the front yard or along the road," he commanded in an authoritative voice, then walked from the den. Several of those in the den didn't want to pull their vehicles on the road's narrow shoulder, and there wasn't enough room under the hickory trees in front of the house. This solved the problem of staying or leaving. The room emptied.

My cousin Steve left to move his truck. The screen door slammed shut behind him. Already parked in the front yard, my mother's sedan didn't need to be moved. She came over, sat down, and put her arm around me. "Are you all right, honey?"

I drew a deep breath, letting the air gush out of my mouth. "I'm okay, Mom."

"Good." She looked up as Uncle Jerry quietly reentered the room. He never let the door slam shut behind him.

"Looks like a mass exodus out there," he observed. "I started to direct traffic, but no one wanted to take orders." He sat down, leaned back, and closed his eyes, his face sallow. He looked exhausted. "Let me have peace," he said, raising his hand and letting it fall to the couch.

No one spoke a word until Uncle Stan and Aunt Marilyn returned from moving their car. I couldn't help but smile at the thought of her directing her spouse from the driveway. I whispered in my mother's ear. "They don't look very happy."

"What else is new?" she said into mine. "At least we haven't had any major squabbling fits."

Aunt Bonnie followed close behind them. She took one look at her husband and immediately went to the kitchen, the muffled thump of her perfect, two-inch, square heels sounding on the hard linoleum surface.

I heard her open a cabinet, get a glass, and run water from the refrigerator. She came back into the den and handed Uncle Jerry the glass.

"Where's your medicine?" she asked him.

"In my coat pocket—living room," he indicated, pointing with his finger. Aunt Bonnie left the room to retrieve the pills.

The front door banged shut. Steve and the twins rushed loudly into the room. He stretched out in a rose-colored armchair. His legs pushed out in front and his back in an awkward arc in the corner of the chair, arms hanging limply off each side. The twins returned to their former position on the floor.

"*Steeeve*, can't you sit up straight," his mother said in her singsong voice. "Remember your back." I saw Steve adjust his position enough to say he'd moved. His children pulled the checkerboard and checkers from the television stand. The first squabble started over whether to put the checkers on the red or black squares.

Aunt Bonnie returned to the room with a prescription bottle. "Jerry, I told the children to go back to the motel or go home. We don't need them here." She looked pointedly at Steve with a hint in her demeanor. There was an awkward silence as he stared back at her.

"Marilyn, where's Stan, Jr.? I thought he'd be here this morning." My mother knew better than to ask Uncle Stan. My aunt answered most of his questions.

Surprisingly, he responded. "Well now, sugar, Junior's working construction in Crossville. We couldn't reach him. Left a message on his cell phone though. I'm sure he'll be here for the funeral."

I wondered if working construction meant opening a beer can, having a hangover, and lighting a cigarette. Mondays aren't good days for a divorced drinker. I checked out his brother, Steve. The answer was revealed in his face of disgust.

The doorbell chimed, and people moved out of the den. My mother left the room to open the front door. From the murmur of men's voices, the creak of the screen door, and distant movements in the foyer, I knew my grandmother would soon leave her home for the last time. She'd pass the beautiful rose garden she had planted as shrubbery in front of her large picture window. *Beauty at the back and front*, she'd told me, meaning the mountains and the flowers.

My cell phone rang. The display said "B.J." I moved to the empty kitchen, then pressed the green button. "Hey, B.J."

"Jenni." Her voice sounded in my ear. "Thought I'd check in during lunch. How's Grandma?"

"She's gone. Almost two hours now."

"I'm so sorry."

"Me too." My voice was unsteady, full of emotion. "Aren't you taking a late lunch?" I managed to say.

"We're busy. Lots of clients today. Jenni, how are you?"

"I'm doin' okay."

"You'll miss her. I know I missed Grammy after she passed. Do you know anything about the arrangements?"

"No. Except she'll go over to Bolivar's. They're here to take her now."

"When you find out, will you let me know?"

"Sure, B.J. Thanks for calling." I hung up the phone, grateful to have her as my best friend since grade school.

What now?

I looked around. The kitchen was a mess. I loaded the dishwasher and ran water into the sink, glad for the noise this made. The bubbling sound covered up the men's voices coming from the foyer.

Welcoming this moment of solitude, my tears dropped with the running water as I washed, rinsed, and dried the dishes. Finished, I wiped tears from my cheeks and walked to the den. For some reason, I couldn't believe this was the end of my grandmother's impact on my life. She'd hinted for several days at—

"Jenni," my mother called. "We're going to eat."

"Okay. I'm coming."

2

When the graveside service ended, most of the Ryeton family headed for the bank of cars parked nearby. A few friends came up to offer condolences. My Uncle Jerry, distinguished in a stylish navy suit with red-and blue-striped tie and red pocket handkerchief, stood in the middle of the cemetery where my grandmother waited to be interred.

After taking one last look around the grassy area and thanking the minister, he walked with my mother toward her car. B.J. and I, arms linked, followed discretely behind.

"Karen, I'm staying in Maryville the rest of the week to work on the estate."

"That's probably a good plan," Mom replied.

"Bonnie and Joey head on to Nashville. The others to Knoxville. I can't see a reason for them to stay. I'll take a weekend flight home. Do you have time to help me with Mom's affairs?"

"My real estate office will give me all the time I need. I'll reduce my schedule and fit helping you in between contacts. Could we by any chance read Mom's will before everyone disappears? Now would be a good time."

My almost-sixty-year-old mother pulled a light jacket around her shoulders. Her long dress swished when she walked—the color, a deep purple she and my grandmother loved. Prematurely gray in her forties and a little on the plump side, Karen Loften's face was devoid of wrinkles. With makeup expertly applied, I called her lovely.

"I'm thinking the same thing. Let's talk to Stan and see if he can meet us at Mom's. I took the will out of her bank lockbox yesterday and looked over the document."

They walked toward Uncle Stan. All the Ryeton sibs had the same head shape and facial features—a rather modified square jaw and high cheek bones. These came from the Tipton side of my mother's family.

It was easy to compare the two brothers as they stood discussing the meeting. Uncle Stan was tall and rotund. Uncle Jerry, tall and thin.

Until two years ago, Uncle Stan sported a partially bald head. Over my aunt's loud objections, he shaved the remaining hair. His pate, as smooth as a watermelon's rind, glistened in the March sunlight. I watched him nod his head and say something to Aunt Marilyn. Waving her hand in the air, she answered him with several short sentences.

Junior stood behind his father, grasping the door handle with his right hand. He didn't seem happy and kicked impatiently at rocks in the cemetery road. His shirttail had escaped his belted pants and was now draped over his beer belly. A partially smoked cigarette hung from the fingers of his left hand. A disappointment to his mother, his father patted him on the back, as he loaded up with them to leave.

Steve, a local contractor, herded his clan into his shiny, black, four-door Chevy truck—*nouveau riche and in debt* written all over them.

Uncle Stan led the way to the main road. Behind him, Uncle Jerry drove his Mercedes with an assortment of SUVs filled with his extended family following.

My mother returned to where B.J. and I stood. "We're going down to the funeral home to pick up the potted plants and vases of cut flowers. Stan says his church sent some specifically for their family. Then we'll go to Mom's and read her will."

"Jenni, let's get together and have dinner tomorrow night. We'll go to Knoxville—take in a movie." B.J. stood looking down at me, expecting an answer.

Mom replied, "That's a wonderful idea, B.J. These last few weeks—well, let's just say different surroundings will be a good change for my daughter." She gave me a hug, headed for the car's driver side, opened the door and got in.

"I'll go. Call me?"

"You bet."

B.J. walked to her small car. "Talk to you tomorrow."
I watched her ease her curves onto the passenger seat, bumping her blonde, short haircut on the door frame. For the life of me, I couldn't figure out why she bought such a small car. She looked like a gangly giraffe, folding, tucking its legs to sit down. Through the windshield, I saw her smooth the rumpled hair. As the car glided past, she waved and flashed a white grin. "I'm going on to work," she called to me.

Mom and I drove across town to the white-columned mortuary. Inside, the director of our service led us down the hall to the mementos and flowers waiting for pickup.

There weren't many. My grandmother outlived most of her friends, and our family wasn't large. They came from businesses where her children worked, their churches, and a few extended family members. One remembrance seemed particularly puzzling.

Uncle Stan picked up the bud vase containing a single red rose and wisp of fern. He walked over to me. "Jenni, I believe you should have this one," he said, holding the flower out to me. I'd hung back during the selections, figuring Mom would let me have one of her pots. "Just your size, isn't it?" he grinned, showing his dental work—two newly capped front teeth.

I took the glass container from his hand. Tied with a red ribbon, a card hung from the rose.

"Who's it from, Uncle Stan?"

"I have no idea."

Holding the vase up to eye level, I looked at the card. "Says Mrs. Joseph Milbern."

He turned around and asked in a loud voice, getting everyone's attention, "Anyone know a Joseph Milbern?"

Uncle Jerry looked up. "No, I don't know anyone by that name."

The others shook their heads.

"Could we have gotten the flower by mistake?" I asked, since we didn't have any other information.

"Let's ask the director as we leave," Uncle Jerry suggested.

"There's another possibility." My mother's comment turned all eyes on her. "Mrs. Milbern may have been someone with whom she corresponded on genealogy questions."

"Hmmm, entirely true. But let's consult with the director to cover all bases. Perhaps he can get an address," Uncle Jerry said. He was an executive who went everywhere with a legal pad full of notes, attended meetings hourly, and was punctual to a fault. I guessed this thoroughness the primary reason for his promotion as senior producer at Bemis Production Company—the most famous commercial, documentary, and movie producing facility in Nashville. Married? Yes, to his job.

"We'll need addresses to send thank-you notes," Aunt Bonnie informed everyone. "My suggestion is if you take the flower or plant, you send the note."

"Are we ready to leave?" Without waiting for an answer, Uncle Jerry picked up a small planter, flicked off some unwanted, microscopic dirt, and walked toward the mortuary entrance.

"*Staaan*, get the peace lily," Aunt Marilyn commanded, holding two vases of cut flowers tightly to her ample chest. From her pinched face, I could tell her flat feet were hurting. If we didn't leave soon, she'd demand a chair to sit on.

Aunt Bonnie strolled after her husband. I watched her go, not sure if her low-heeled gait along with her willowy, bean-pole figure could be called a walk. Her saunter looked more like a warm, slim, gummy bear breezing along.

I giggled at my observation.

"What's so funny, sugar?" Uncle Stan's inquiring face was close. His foot tangled in mine.

I grabbed his arm as I stumbled over his large wingtip. *"Ooh!"*

With sweat on his brow, my pot-bellied Uncle Stan carried a huge, heavy, potted plant with shiny green leaves. He staggered and juggled the black container with contorted motions as the monster almost fell to the floor. I held his arm to steady him.

After he recovered I said, "I wonder how the florist gets the leaves so shiny."

"Wesson oil," he said, without skipping a beat, then burst out laughing.

I noticed the pot fit perfectly over the lump of his stomach. He hugged it tightly to his chest and peered through its foliage, making faces at me. I'd bet ten bucks he didn't hug his wife in the same manner.

I giggled again, louder this time.

Aunt Marilyn threw me a disapproving scowl. She aimed a thunderbolt at my uncle. "*Thiiis* is a place for dead people. *Weee* must be respectful," she scolded in a forced whisper. She squared her shoulders and limped away.

With great effort and puffed out cheeks, I held another giggle.

"How's your love life," my uncle whispered. "Any prospects?"

"About the same, and no," I answered.

"Sugar, I still wish you'd let me set you up with the young man I've been tellin' you about. He's a church-goer and a real catch—lots of money, good job, and good-looking. He's interested in meetin' you. What more do you need?"

"Uncle Stan, you're my favorite uncle. Do you want to remain so?"

"Of course, I do."

"Then drop the subject of a boyfriend. When God gets ready to provide a knight on a white horse, I'll be ready."

"Are you sure you'll be ready?" I knew he referred to my mother's dysfunctional marriage. Everyone agreed, if my father hadn't died, they'd be divorced by now. What Uncle Stan didn't know, and what I didn't tell him, included my perspective on the rest of the family's marriage relationships. They didn't encourage me either. From my observations, love flew out the window as soon as the honeymoon ended.

I had to tell the truth. "I can't be sure about anything."

"*Staaanley*, catch up." Aunt Marilyn called, ending the conversation.

The family followed Uncle Jerry, stopping at the front door and waiting in a group while he questioned the man who coordinated my grandmother's funeral. Finally, satisfied with his answers, he returned. "Karen, he'll call you with the addresses. And yes, the card had Mom's name on it."

As we walked out of the building, I whispered to Mom, "I didn't mean to stir up a hornet's nest."

She patted my arm. "It's okay, honey. I'm with you. I find a vase with one rosebud and an unknown name very interesting. Mysterious." She carried a small potted azalea. Stan's adoring grandchildren followed her with two more.

The ten-year-old twins often stayed the night at my mother's, preferring the quiet of her household to the constant power struggle at their father's and grandfather's homes. I realized their fancy for my mother couldn't sit well with their grandmother.

Steve's wife didn't care. On the occasions I went with my mother to get them for an overnight stay, she'd rushed the two out the door as soon as my mother drove onto their driveway.

We arrived back at Grandma's, and Uncle Jerry ushered the family into the living room. "This won't take long. Mom's will is simple." He cleared his throat, and I listened to the short legalese of bequeaths my grandmother intended to be made.

Her estate, divided equally between the three children, contained special donations to the grandchildren. Uncle Jerry read my name. My ears perked up. "To my beloved grandchild, Jenni, I leave a box stowed in the bottom drawer of my dresser. Thanks for all the wonderful times we spent together and for your help during these last years of my life. The contents are yours to do with as you choose."

A box in her dresser? I couldn't wait to hurry to the master bedroom, but I lingered until my uncle was finished with the reading of the will.

"One other thing. She left letters for each of her children. Karen." He handed my Mom a white envelope. "Stan."

"What's this all about?" Stan asked, turning the envelope over to examine the surface.

"I have no idea. I found them in her bank box." Uncle Jerry stuffed his in a coat pocket.

In the discussion following, my uncle told everyone he'd proceed with probating the will. "I'll email you to set up a date to start the process of clearing the house to sell."

"Now, if each of you will help your children and grandchildren secure the items mentioned in the will and take them from the house, our meeting is over."

Mom went with me to Grandma's bedroom. The hospital bed's sheets and blankets lay neatly folded with the pillow atop. On the dresser, my grandma's well-used matching brush and mirror set rested in a discolored, glass-bottomed tray. The type women loved in the fifties.

I looked at my mother. "Why don't you open the drawer?"

"No, the box is yours. You open it."

The faint smell of lilacs wafted from the dresser drawer. Inside, in the midst of her old socks and hose, a partially hidden and previously used parcel post box looked out of place. "Jenni," in large, black script and clearly my grandmother's distinctive, slanted handwriting, jumped out at me from the package's white surface.

"Jenni, the box is almost sacred."

I nodded, retrieved the rectangular carton and a mesh bag of potpourri tied with a ribbon and taped to the box. She loved making the smelly balls. The aroma of lilacs grew stronger. "I wonder how long it's been here?" I gently closed the dresser drawer, stuffing the small bag in my black pants pocket.

"I don't know, honey."

I gave the cardboard carton a little shake. "Mom, do you have any idea . . ."

"No, I'm wondering like you."

"I seem to be the recipient of mysterious objects today."

"Makes life interesting, doesn't it?" She headed for the door, stopping just inside. "Do you want to have an early dinner? How about Mexican? I'm hungry."

"Yes. Do we need to do anything else here?" I walked over and stood looking around the familiar room, realizing the furniture and other furnishings would be sold.

My mother guessed my thoughts. "Our lives will be different from now on. We won't be coming here for meatloaf and mashed potatoes. The geraniums won't grow on the front porch. Mom and I won't argue over whose chicken and dumplings are the best. I'll miss her." She put her arm around my shoulder. "It's you and me, sweetheart. Promise me, nothing will ever come between us."

I gave her a hug. "I love you, Mom."

"I love you too. Let's tell the others goodbye." We walked down the hall together. She cleared her throat and added, "I can't wait to see what she's left you."

"Me either."

Leaving the rest of our family didn't take long. I wedged the bud vase and box in the front seat of my car, turned the key in the ignition, and pulled out of the driveway. Mom fell in behind me.

I glanced over at the box and vase riding securely on the passenger seat, and then turned my attention to the four-lane heading into town.

I don't know why I didn't double check for traffic at the new stop light, installed only a month earlier at a major intersection on the road—an act I usually preformed. Drivers often ran the light, unaccustomed to the signal. Maybe I had Grandma's death on my mind, or the mysterious vase and box in my front seat. Were they connected in any way?

All I saw was a flash of red, and I heard the sharp sound of metal crashing into metal. My head hit the car's door frame. The air bag exploded in my face, and I lost consciousness.

3

One hour later, I woke up in the emergency room at our hospital, my head pounding. I put my hand up to find out why. "Ouch!" A large swelling was on the outside, and pain bounced around inside my skull. The stringent smell of hospital disinfectant invaded my nostrils.

The sound of low moans caused me to look to the left. Whoever or whatever made those pitiful sounds was behind a pulled curtain. The sight of hospital equipment made my head ache even more, and seeing stretchers wheeled quickly past the open door at the foot of my bed didn't cause a warm, fuzzy feeling.

I noticed movement to my right side and felt a gentle hand on my shoulder. "Jenni, it's Mom. How are you feeling?"

"My head is splitting. W-what happened?"

"There was an accident, and you got banged on the head. Does it hurt terribly?"

"Yes, it hurts. I remember a red flash and metal crunching." I paused as she nodded her head, encouraging me. "You were behind me?"

"Thank God, you don't have amnesia, sweetheart."

"My car, how bad is it?"

"Not good, I'm afraid. The other driver had insurance. I'm sure you'll have a rental car and yours will be fixed."

"How about me? Will I be fixed?" I experimented with moving my extremities. Everything seemed to work okay.

"You haven't lost your sense of humor either." She laughed. "The doctor says no cuts or broken bones, thank God. He had another emergency. We're waiting on him to come back and tell us the prognosis."

"Speaking of doctor, he's here." A young intern said as he entered the room, a stethoscope hanging from his neck and a chart in his left hand. I noticed he sported no wedding ring. "Sorry to take so long. Our emergency room is full. Wednesday's aren't usually this busy." Flipping pages on the chart, he asked, "Ms. Loften, how long has she been conscious?"

"Actually, she just came to."

He noted this on the chart and continued writing.

My hurt head didn't keep me from checking him out. Chlorine-bleached, brown hair, deep blue eyes, and a well-trimmed mustache rested above his sculpted upper lip. The good-looking doctor came to stand by my bed. I managed to focus my eyes on his name tag—Johnstein.

He pulled a gadget from the pocket of his white jacket. "Are you having trouble with your eyes?"

"A little."

"Doctor, what have you decided?" My mother stood up, stretching her taut shoulders.

Johnstein glanced at the chart. "To be on the safe side, I've decided to keep Jenni overnight. We need to monitor her for twenty-four hours, make sure she doesn't have anything more than an MTBI."

"What's an MTBI?" my shocked mother asked. I wanted to know too.

"Oh." The doctor chuckled. "Sounds like something serious, doesn't it? In most cases after a head injury, there is mild concussion to the brain, hence mild traumatic brain injury or MTBI. Most injured patients wake up quickly, say within thirty minutes after being knocked out. Jenni didn't come to for an hour. Keeping her in the hospital is only a precaution. But if she should develop other symptoms, the staff will notice and response will be immediate."

Even though I felt as if my head might crack open, I turned as each of them spoke. Now, I asked the question. "What other problems?"

"Commonly with head trauma such as yours, the patient can experience nausea, amnesia, which you don't seem to be having, double vision, or even convulsions. In a worst-case scenario, intracranial hemorrhage may occur. It's the most serious."

"What are the chances she'll develop any of these?"

"Not high. Twenty-four hours should rule out most, but she'll need to rest and be monitored for a few days, even when she gets out of the hospital. Does Jenni live with you, Ms. Loften?"

"No, she has her own place, but I'll take her home with me."

"Does this mean I'll get out in the morning?"

"Yes, you can leave after I make my rounds. Provided no other problems occur." He turned back to my mom. "Ms. Loften, I wouldn't come before noon. Discharge papers are a bear these days."

"Will she be on medication?"

"Aspirin—follow the instructions on the bottle for headaches, and no alcoholic beverages."

"My daughter doesn't drink."

He nodded. "I think I'll find someone to take Jenni upstairs to her room. I'll see you both tomorrow."

Fifteen minutes later, a dark-skinned orderly came into the room. "Are you ready to go for a ride, young lady?"

"Only if you can use marshmallows for wheels," I said ruefully, grimacing in pain.

He gave a big belly guffaw and busied himself with pulling up the bed rails, getting me ready for transport. "I'll try to give you a *smooooth* ride," he said as he banged the door casing. "Oops, sorry."

We got off the elevator on the third floor, bumping over the threshold and heading down the hall. At the nurse's station, we picked up a CNA, and my ride ended as he wheeled me into a private hospital room.

I'd always been fascinated by the procedure for moving a patient from stretcher to bed. But not this time. I rolled my eyes at Mom, pleading for help. Two minutes later, clasping my head to keep it from moving, I slid through the air and onto my new-sheeted resting place. The orderly disappeared with my bumpy ride.

"Where does it hurt, honey," asked the nurse's assistant, trying to make me comfortable and pushing the hospital tray over my bed.

Physical harm entered my mind, but only briefly, as I looked at her pleasant, smiling face.

"Her head hurts. MTBI, you know," Mom offered, savoring the new acronym. "Car accident."

Those eight words said everything.

The CNA mashed the buttons on the electric bed, moving me from a flat position to a reclining one. Normally I would have nodded my head to dismiss her. Instead, I made motions with my hands, waving her an okay and out of the room. Before she left, she raised an erasable maker to a white board and noted those on duty for this shift.

"Push the button if you need anything. I'll bring some ice water."

Silence reigned.

"Mom, I'm not up to small talk."

"I understand. I'll walk to the nurse's station to see if they've got a newspaper." She followed the CNA out of the room.

I breathed a long sigh and settled into my pillow and bed. What a day. After my Grandma's funeral, the morning had gone from plain and ordinary to complicated and abnormal. The mysterious rose appeared from almost nowhere, and a strange box entered my life.

Uh, oh. Where were they?

I'd ask Mom when she returned.

I closed my eyes, thinking I'd shut out the world. Did the darkness make my head hurt less?

"Dinner's here." The smiling nurse on duty woke me from my sleep, set the tray down, and left. The food smelled delicious, and I realized I was hungry, and my head hurt less.

Mom stood and approached the bed. "Sweetheart, this week's been an emotional rollercoaster. I'm heading home to relax, if that's possible. You're in good hands."

"You'll be back tomorrow?"

"Yes, I'll come after lunch, give you a chance to rest in the morning." She leaned over the bed and kissed my forehead—the side without the pump-knot.

"Oh, Mom, find the bud vase and my box. I can't lose them."

"Already in the front seat of my car. I'll take both by your condo in the morning."

"Okay," I said. She waved and I picked up my fork, tasting the mashed potatoes on the tray.

"And, Jenni," Mom stuck her head in the doorway to add. "Your Uncle Stan may visit later. He's really concerned about you."

"I'll look for him."

"Mom, call B.J. about tomorrow night."

"Sure. I'll take care of it. See you tomorrow."

The food tasted good, but I wasn't as hungry as I thought.

4

"Mom, I'll be glad to get home. This week's been horrific." At least my head wasn't hurting as bad, but my side ached, something I hadn't noticed before.

We were headed down Broadway in her sedan. A red light stopped our progress. She turned and looked at me. "I know what you mean, sweetie. The stress and pressure from Mom's passing, and then your wreck . . ." She shook her head. "Whew! I'm ready for a vacation."

"Why don't you take off for a few days? We'll hang out, eat hot dogs, and watch old movies. I could use your company."

"How I'd love to do just that, but I have several deals working and a customer coming from Kentucky. Everyone seems to want to move to East Tennessee." She followed a long line of traffic down the street.

"And why not. We have a good economy with all the auto related industries. Still, see if you can get off a day or two."

"I'll see. Stay at my house until Monday. Maybe by then you'll have a rental car and your life will settle down to normal."

I couldn't help but wonder if my life would ever be ordinary again. Something nagged me—something saying life was changing.

My mother turned into the entrance of her subdivision. Being a realtor enabled her to buy a two-story, red-brick rancher on the number nine hole of the only golf course in town.

"I'm going to expect you to pamper me. Seriously, there's a bruise on my side to match the one on my head. My body hurts when I move."

"Did you show that to Dr. Johnstein?"

"I didn't know I had it until I put my clothes on to come home. Guess my hurting head took precedence over my body."

"Should I call him and take you back to the emergency room?"

"No. I'm moving. I think I'll live."

We pulled into her garage and the door closed behind us.

"I'll get you settled in your old bedroom. I have to meet Jerry at the courthouse."

We lugged a small suitcase into her kitchen. The one mom filled at my condo on the way to the hospital. "When are you going to get rolling luggage?" she complained.

"Don't carp on me. Mine's perfectly good. Be glad I'm thrifty with my money. Ooor you could put it on your list for my birthday or Christmas."

"Now that's an idea," she said, moving on down her hall.

"I'm going back to the den and lounge on your couch. Is the TV playing?" My mom's television had a penchant for laying down on the job.

She passed the den, coming from the bedroom.

"Has it been that long since you've been here? I had a new forty-eight-inch flat screen installed—digital too."

"Nice." I raised my eyebrows, feigning astonishment at the new appliance hanging on the wall. Several family pictures hung beside the silver-rimmed television. One of Mom and my father caught my attention. I glanced quickly away from the image and headed for her couch. Seeing the picture brought back memories that hurt.

Noises came from the kitchen as I settled on the couch with a mint-green fleece blanket I'd grabbed from her linen closet. I pulled the cover up to my waist. Seizing the channel control, I found a classic station and snuggled in to watch *Dr. Zhivago*.

"Here's a diet cola and some snacks." Mom set a tray with chips, cheese, and dip on the coffee table. "I'll pick up something for dinner. I won't feel like cooking after running around with your uncle all afternoon."

"Don't get too much. I'm not very hungry"

"You rest," she flung over her shoulder as she disappeared down the hall. From a distance, the garage door opened and the car started.

I burrowed into the blanket, shutting my eyes as warmth enveloped my body. Peace? No nurses. No doctors. No hospital noises. Only the sights and sounds of the Russian Revolution.

I awoke to Dr. Zhivago clutching his heart as Lara walked out of sight. The cola's ice had melted, and water puddled in the coaster where the glass sat. My cell phone rang.

"Hello?"

"Hey, girl. How are you feeling?" B.J.'s voice sounded happy.

"Much better. At least my head doesn't hurt as much."

"I'm going to miss going to eat tonight."

"Me too. How about Wednesday?"

"Oh, I can't. Troy will be home, and I'm sure he'll call. What about Thursday night? We'll meet in K-town, eat somewhere, and go to the movies. You pick the place."

"Okay. It's a date."

I watched B.J. as she threaded her way between the tables and toward me. The overhead lighting danced among her blond highlights and made her dark, cherry-red business suit appear lighter, richer. She carried a black clutch purse in her left hand and waved the red-lacquered fingernails of her right as I acknowledged her.

Since she worked as a receptionist for a Knoxville lawyer, meeting close to her work area at a small Italian restaurant we both loved seemed reasonable. The theater could be reached within minutes off Interstate-75.

Checking me out with her brown eyes, she scooted into the navy, cloth booth opposite me, drew in a deep breath, and let it out in a rush of Spearmint-scented air. "Whew! The traffic is awful. I think I'll move south to Sweetwater. How long have you been here?"

Sweetwater was a private joke between us. We'd gotten lost on the small town's curvy roads looking for a wallpaper outlet when I replaced the outdated floral design in my condo. "About ten minutes. I don't like Knoxville traffic either. Maryville's quieter—but not by much."

The waitress came for our drink orders.

"The food smells delicious, and I could eat a horse. I know what I want."

"Me too." I responded. B.J. and I ordered unsweet tea and our usual entrees.

"It's hilarious how we end up with the same food choices at different restaurants."

"Why order anything different if you like a particular item?"

"Exactly." B.J. unwrapped her napkin and placed it in her lap. "Are you all right?" Her voice became serious as she checked my hairline. "Part of your face is black and blue."

I put my hand up to feel the swelling. "It's gone down and doesn't hurt as much."

"And your grandma."

"Better than I thought I'd be." I drew in a short breath and let it out, making a soft whoosh sound. "I'm sure there'll be times Grandma's passing will rush back at me. Times I'll cry. Times I'll laugh at her antics."

She nodded her head. "The hurt will ease off. It did with Grammy."

I decided to change the subject. "Your day busy?"

"Yes." She leaned forward to talk confidentially. "We've taken on a new client. Do you remember the man who supposedly killed the couple last June? They were parked on a lover's lane near the French Broad River."

"Seems to ring a bell."

"He's fired two legal teams, and now we've been hired to represent him. I saw him for the first time today. Sent a chill through me. You know how I've got a sixth sense about these things. I don't like him." She motioned with her hand. Something flashed in the lamplight at our table.

I squealed. "B.J., show me your left hand. Is that what I think it is?" I pulled her hand toward me to check out a large diamond in a white gold setting.

She grinned. "Troy."

"When?"

"Friday night. Of course, I knew . . . I felt like this would happen." She looked down at the diamond solitaire. "Feels strange on my hand."

"You didn't tell me."

"Jenni, you had enough on your mind, and I decided to surprise you."

"You've done just that. Have you set a date?"

"Yes. We decided on everything—afternoon wedding, June fifteenth, Ridgeview Baptist. Troy's going to take his two-week vacation for our honeymoon to the Mexican Riviera. Can you believe it? Will you be my maid of honor? You're my best friend. I wouldn't want anyone else but you." She reached both hands across the table.

I put mine over hers. "I'd be really upset if you didn't ask me. I can't believe you're engaged."

"That makes two of us. I'm going to ask Stella Jensen to be a bridesmaid."

Stella was another high school chum. "Do you think she can come in from school?"

Before she could answer the question, our food arrived. The waitress filled our glasses and left us alone.

B.J. leaned forward, unwrapped her napkin, and tasted the chicken alfredo on her plate. "Ummm, you know, you're not gettin' any younger. Aren't you looking?"

"Looking and doing are two different things. I find myself checkin' out guys. Maybe even dreamin'. My Uncle Stan says I'm as skittish as a young colt when it comes to men and marriage."

B.J. giggled. "I can't wait to get married. I want you to be happy too."

"My family history doesn't encourage me to take the plunge. Mom wed a man who ended up slapping her around. Statistics say I'm subject to doing the same. My Uncle Jerry and Aunt Bonnie have three children. For the life of me, I don't know how. They seem standoffish when they're together with very little affection between them, and he's married to his job. And then there's Uncle Stan. He and Aunt Marilyn argue all the time. No, the prospects of ending up like them scares me to death." Sarcasm laced my words.

"Not all marriages end up akin to your grandma's children. I can't see Troy and I coming close to disintegrating to the level you describe. Good communication—give and take, that's what being married is all about."

"I'll tell you what marriage consists of B.J. Giving sharp barbs back and forth, taking your frustrations out by using blows to diminish your short comings, each partner going in opposite directions because they can barely stand the other's presence, cheating. That's what gives me chills." I shuddered, thinking about this prospect.

"Jenni, not every marriage is like the ones you describe." Hurt by my biting words, she pulled back in the booth.

"I'm sorry B.J. I'm sure you and Troy are different. It's just—well, everyone I'm surrounded with is like that, even many couples in my church. Definitely not good role models to follow."

"I predict someone will show up in your life, and you'll have to unlock the chain you've put around your heart or become a bitter, unfulfilled old lady."

"The apostle Paul says I don't have to marry. I'm holding on to his statement."

"Mark my words." B.J. was adamant.

"You sound like my grandma."

"Have you looked to see what's in the box she gave you?"

"Tomorrow morning. I plan on taking the day. I'm almost sure there are pages to read, so I'll take my time to digest them. I go back to work next Monday."

We ate our food, paid the check, and headed for the movies.

5

I closed the fridge door. The smell of bacon, eggs, and toast was still strong in the kitchen of my two-bedroom condo. Picking up my glass of cola, I strolled out of the room toward the master bedroom and bath.

My bedroom furniture consisted of hand-me-downs from my mother. Dressing the bed was a beige coverlet with coral-pink flowers and wispy green fronds, made-up and expertly tucked under the pillows with shams on top. The dust ruffle was green—a color matching one in the mottled Berber carpet running throughout the house. A collage of paintings from travels with my grandma rested on the walls of the room.

Mom had a flair for decorating. We'd had fun going to garage and estate sales picking up items for practically nothing to furnish the rest of my home. We laughed and poked fun at each other as, pushing and tugging, we tied the pieces in the back of my rattletrap SUV—the one I'd driven before my wrecked car. Although some of my furnishings were used, they combined with the newer pieces to make a rather tasteful arrangement.

I loved my bathroom. The room contained separate double sinks, large tub, and a marbled shower you could get lost in. The sinks and countertops were beige and the fixtures gold. A border around the top of the walls, bought in Sweetwater, pulled together the coral and green, and added blue and gold to the interior decorations.

I stood in front of a large, gold-trimmed mirror hung over the washbasins and combed my short, dark-brown hair, still damp from my earlier shower. The face looking back at me sported luminous brown eyes, the pupils showing flickering gold highlights. *Grandmother eyes*, my mother called them. Turning my face from side-to-side I saw the brown mole next to my hairline and a matching one on my cheek, sorta like an Elizabeth Taylor beauty mark, but not so dark. The nose rather small and pointed. The jaw, a modified Tipton—square with a short chin jutting out in the middle. Not ugly, but makeup brought out more of the image's beauty. With a final pat to my hair, I left the bathroom, walked through the bedroom and down a short hall lined with bookcases full of books to my great room. No living room for me. I wanted a huge open den—a movie room to be exact.

My own purchase and gift to my home included the room's furniture, strategically placed in front of the gas logs in the fireplace. The sectional couch contained two cozy corners where I reclined in comfort while reading the newspaper, watching TV, or running through the day's mail. A large flat screen television hung over the mantel.

The TV blared with the latest weather. I clicked the squawk box off.

Grandma's gift sat on a nearby navy-blue cushion. I reached down and scooted the used USPS carton to my favorite corner.

Restraint tempered my actions concerning the mysterious parcel, putting off the inevitable and prolonging the exposure of the secret within. Would this be my last cherished, personal contact with her?

She'd taped the ends closed with cellophane tape—something she always did to envelopes and packages. Using my letter opener, I picked at one end, and soon the carton opened to reveal a stack of spiral-bound school notebooks. I counted six. A small, teal, velvet-covered box. And a stained, white, lumpy envelope with the flap tucked inside.

Unusual. Not taped. My heart beat faster.

When I shook the box, a smaller crystal case joined the other articles now resting on my couch cushion. Turning the cardboard box and looking within, I could see that nothing else remained to be removed. The end. I rattled the box, wishing to be wrong, hoping the contents were never ending.

The spiral notebooks were numbered. Scrawled on a sticky note on the first one, my grandmother had written in her distinctive slanted handwriting:

> *My dearest granddaughter,*
>
> *For years you've ridden with and driven me to visit and talk to old people about our Tipton kin. My, what stories we've heard. In the last few years, you've begged me to write my memoir. I think you'll be shocked and happy at the story you'll find in this box. I've never told the details to another soul, certainly not to your grandpa. Before you continue, read the letter in the first notebook.*
>
> *All my love, Grandma.*

6

Jenni,

I've struggled with the idea of telling the story included in these pages. Oh, there's nothing I can't be proud about, but since no one has an idea these things happened, except my mother and sister, who are now gone, I find myself a little nervous about putting them on paper—better to let sleeping dogs lie.

I've decided to start with my last year in college—a time of happiness and great loss in the Whitehead family. A time I look back on with love. Once you read the story, you'll know why I say this.

Granddaughter, during our time together, we've heard interesting stories about our ancestors, tales which I think should be fictionalized into books. Remember the Tipton ancestor who supposedly came to the New World in a barrel, or the one who got into a fight with the first governor of Tennessee, or the one who raced his horse against Andrew Jackson, or the set who moved to Missouri, or Texas, or . . .

So many stories to be told.

Sweetheart, you've always had a way with words. I've read many of your school papers and some of your creative writings. What do you think about putting these stories on paper? Not necessarily to be published, but for the preserving of family history—for your children and grandchildren.

I know how you feel about marriage. I'm praying for the handsome knight to come and sweep you off your feet—carry you away to a wonderful life even you can't imagine. God works miracles.

Besides our familial connections, there is another I find more important. That is our connection to Christ's family and our hope of eternal life in Him. Never fail to bring out our Christian ancestry should you go on with this project.

You have my permission to do whatever you wish with the story you're about to examine.

Since you are reading this letter, I am gone, but I know we'll see each other again. You've been my favorite granddaughter. Don't tell the others I said this, but you have been and still are.

I love you very much,

Grandma

I clutched the letter to my breast and felt two warm tears roll down my cheeks. I'd known opening the box would be a trying and poignant experience. I leaned back into my warm corner, pulled my knees up to my chest, and released the last few emotional weeks in a flood of tears. She was gone. I couldn't bring her back—or could I? I looked at the empty box, the notebooks, and the other articles on the couch cushion. She would be close during the time it took to rewrite her memoirs. I wiped my tears on my shirt sleeve, picked up the first notebook, and started to read.

My cell phone ringing startled me. After finishing my grandmother's memoirs, I'd fallen asleep on the couch. The caller ID said "Mother."

"Hello, Mom."

"You sound sleepy, honey."

"Yes. I opened Grandma's box. Sleeping helped to relieve the stress I felt from examining the contents."

"I knew this would be hard on you." I heard B.J. Thomas singing "Raindrops Keep Falling on My Head" coming from her car stereo.

"Do you remember me bugging her about writing her life story?" I sat up on the couch, placing the notebooks back into the open box.

"Yes. I do. Was that in the box?"

"And more. You're not going to believe what happened to her. She wants me to write a book about her experiences." I looked at the clock—noon and I was famished.

"What do you think about her suggestion?"

"Do you think I could? Write, I mean. I'm not sure I have the talent."

"I believe you do, and she sure thought so."

"Then I'd like to at least try. The problem is, I have a job, and to really do a first-rate book, I need to travel and meet the people involved. I may need to go to writer's conferences and read more books on writing. All this takes time."

"I'm coming over. Do you remember the letter your grandmother left each of her children?"

"No. When?"

"When Uncle Jerry read the will. Maybe the crack on the head caused you to forget. Anyway, she left instructions for me to follow. I'll tell you when I get there."

More mystery. "Okay."

"Are cheeseburgers all right? I'll stop on the way."

"Sure. Thanks. My stomach's growling."

"See you in a few."

The phone clicked dead in my ear. What did Mom mean by my grandmother's instructions? I got up from the couch and went to the bathroom. Running water into the sink, I grabbed my face cloth from the shower door handle. Clouds of steam came from the basin as I plunged the cloth into the hot water. I squeezed out the excess. My face felt good as the warmth settled into my skin.

I combed my hair and headed for the kitchen.

When Mom arrived, glasses of ice with unsweet tea sat on my kitchen counter. We plopped down at my bar, unwrapped the burgers, and ate.

"This has been a bear of a day," my mother exclaimed. "First, my nine o'clock didn't show, and then, at eleven, the office secretary called to say a customer I've been working with for three months backed out of her contract. She's got a new boyfriend and plans to move in with him. I decided a hot and juicy cheeseburger would solve all my problems. What do you think?"

I laughed. "Sure won't hurt." My stomach had quit growling.

"Jenni, what did your grandmother say in her letter?"

"How did you know there was a letter?"

"Because my instructions said so." She pulled an envelope out of her pocketbook, which sat on top of the bar. "Here. Read what she said."

I took the inside sheet out and skimmed the words, sucking in my breath with shock. "Fifty thousand dollars!"

"That's what she wrote. You know, she's been giving her children ten thousand dollars each year since Grandpa passed, and there'll be a lump sum once Uncle Jerry settles her affairs. So . . ." She handed me a checkbook. "It's in both our names. Your grandmother wants you to quit your job and concentrate on your writing. That is, if you want to write."

Again, tears filled my eyes. "Mom, are you okay with this? I've saved some money since school." I sat looking at the names on the checks.

She nodded her head. "I am if you'll commit yourself fulltime to the project. You can always go back to work should you need to."

I threw my arms around her—cheeseburger and all. "I'll tell you a secret. I've always wanted to write, but the direction never was clear. Now I know how to proceed. I'll be on a personal mission."

We finished eating and Mom left. I cleaned up, then paced the floor. Where would I start? So many things needed to be done.

The bud vase with the red rose sat on my kitchen counter. I stopped and put out my finger to touch a soft, silky petal. After reading the six notebooks, I knew how the flower fit into my grandmother's life. In the lumpy, stained envelope lay a single rose—a dried replica like the one I touched.

The teal, velvet jewelry box resting on the couch cushion contained a tiny engagement ring with three small stones. The gold circle fit my pinky finger.

From the crystal container, I pulled photos, brochures, and other items from a busy past—a time when a relationship other than my grandfather's claimed her attention. But Grandma insisted I know the other side of the story. This meant a trip to another state.

Author. The name sounded wonderful. I went to my favorite couch corner, picked up a legal pad, and made a list of things to do. Give my notice at work. Drive my rental car to Kentucky. Meet the Milbern's and Abbot Kendall. Check on writer's conference in Asheville, North Carolina. See my creative writing teacher at college. Take night class on writing. I was sure I'd left off several items, but it was a start.

The cell phone rang again. The caller ID said "Withheld."

"Hello?"

"Jenni, this is Peter Johnstein. I wondered how you were doing."

My mind flew around in a circle. I couldn't remember anyone by that name. "I'm sorry, I—"

"The doctor at the hospital. Dr. Peter Johnstein. I must not have made much of an impression." He laughed—a small embarrassed chuckle.

"*Oooh.* I can only blame my amnesia on the MTBI." Now I was laughing.

"At least you remembered my diagnosis. So how are you feeling?"

"I don't seem to have any residual effects from the accident."

"Remember to keep taking it easy. That was some bump you took to your head."

"I won't forget the wreck or getting walloped any time soon."

"Good. There's another reason I'm calling. I wonder if you'd like to have dinner one night next week."

"Do you follow up on all your patients by offering dinner?"

"No. Just the beautiful ones. How about it?" I heard the hospital intercom in the background.

This man flirted with noticeable experience. "I really don't know you."

"You won't get to know me without seeing me."

"Maybe lunch would be better. Less intimate. In the hospital cafeteria."

"You are an interesting young woman. Friday at noon?"

"I'll be there."

"See you then."

I shut my phone wishing I'd not made the date. "You'll go Jenni Loften, and that will be that."

7

On Thursday, B.J. and I had lunch. "I can't believe you quit your job," she exclaimed, as we sat in a corner booth at Sub Shop. "Start from the beginning. Tell me what's happening."

I bit the corner off my six-inch sub. The sweet sauce flooded my mouth. "Teriyaki chicken. I love it."

"I'm not interested in teriyaki or chicken. What's going on in your life?" she demanded as she unfolded the paper from her sub and opened her chips.

"I told you about grandma's gift. Well, I opened the box on Friday." I took another bite and wiped sticky stuff off my face with a napkin.

"Go on. Go on."

"You're so impatient." I grinned at her. But, instead of keeping B.J. in suspense, I put down the sandwich and related the short version of the last few days' events, ending with the unexpected monetary gift.

"She's financing your writing career?"

"Looks that way."

"This is so exciting. I may know a future author. Will you write your grandmother's memoirs?"

"Not exactly. Grandma wanted me to use the information and write a book of fiction based on her experience. No one knew this part of her long life. I think I can tell her story in such a way most women will want to read the novel and at the same time preserve a little bit of our family history."

"Jenni, I'm so thrilled and happy for you. When will you start?"

"I'm going to call the Milbern lady on Saturday—set up a time I can visit and meet Abbott Kendall."

"Now who's this Abbot Kendall?"

"The other man in Maddie Whitehead Ryeton's life."

"Other man. You're kidding me. Your grandma went to church. A more devoted servant of God I can't imagine. Another man?"

"She knew him before Grandpa Charles in Cherokee, North Carolina."

"How . . . or for what reason did your grandma go to the Indian Reservation?"

"She had a high school and college friend, Sybil Blackman, who persuaded her to go and wait tables in the summer recess. Happened after she graduated from college. They used the money for fun things—like travel."

"That means we're talking about a summer romance?"

"I think the acquaintance lasted much longer than the summer. But you'll not get any more information than what I've just told you."

"Aw, come on. You've only whetted my appetite for more."

"Good. I've accomplished my purpose. Now, you'll have to buy and read the book."

"Where does Abbot Kendall live?"

"In Meadowview, Kentucky—about thirty minutes from downtown Lexington—race horse country."

"How exciting. Does he race horses?"

"I don't know. If he did, he's too old now."

"What age is he?"

"I'm thinking early nineties, but I'm guessing."

"Will you get your car back before you start your travels?"

"I talked to the insurance adjuster. He's totaling it and sending a check. With gas prices going up, I'm thinking hybrid for my next vehicle."

B.J. nodded her head. "Troy has one. He likes the car." She started clearing the table.

"Girlfriend, there's something else I need to tell you."

"I don't know if my feeble mind and heart can take more news." She clutched at her head and chest.

"You'll be excited to know I have a date tomorrow for lunch."

"What! A real date? With a guy?"

"All right, don't make such a big deal of the meeting."

"Who is this tough man who fears nothing?"

"The doctor from the emergency room when I went to the hospital."

"I'm going to faint. A real doctor?"

I shook my head. "Come on. Let's get out of here."

We left the eatery and stood by our cars as a city cruiser with blue lights flashing raced down the road.

"Where do ya suppose he's goin' in such a hurry?"

"He's heard I've got a date and he's clearin' the street for tomorrow." I gave an impertinent wave of my hand.

"Jenni, you're full of surprises, but I love you anyway. Call me Friday night with all the details."

"I will," I promised as I entered my car and traveled behind the cruiser.

I took the elevator to the second floor of Blount General Hospital and followed the signs for the cafeteria. Except for my brief stay after the accident, I hadn't been in the building since my father Walter Loften died in the CCU.

My father, the charmer of women, had a twist of anger which exploded at any moment and for the strangest reasons. He hit my mother. Not often, but enough to keep her off balance. Made up with a box of candy or roses or tears.

He managed to conceal his darker side from most everyone who knew him. I thought him handsome and loved him until a chance encounter changed my opinion. He didn't see me, but I saw him—with her. Rumor became fact.

He owned a used car lot and made a decent living. Being the principle salesperson afforded him the opportunity to stay long hours—to have many liaisons. The last one, I remember very well. He moved out of our house for her. My mother, fed up with his infidelity and anger, filed for divorce. I applauded her for finding the intestinal fortitude to make the move. He passed of a massive heart attack before the first court date.

I'd gone to the hospital to tell him goodbye. Trussed up in tubes, wires, and unconscious, doing so was impossible. With a bit of affection left over from the past, I touched his hand. Memories came flooding back—riding a bicycle, swimming in the mountains, and fishing in Tellico Lake. Things he taught me. So many words we needed to say. No response.

The intercom above my head blared and brought me back to the present. Ducking into a convenient lady's room, I plunged my hands into hot water in the sink. My idea—to wash the emotions away. Coming to the hospital was a mistake.

Dr. Peter Johnstein stood outside the cafeteria. He smiled as I approached and came to meet me. I thought he intended to shake hands. Instead, he put his arm around my shoulders and guided me into the short line making its way along the rows of food items.

"I worried you wouldn't show up." Under a full mustache, his open grin showed even, white teeth standing out in stark contrast to his dark, suntanned skin. Chlorine-bleached hair spoke of hours spent poolside, and well-defined muscles, time pumping iron in a gym. Blue eyes—made bluer by colored contacts, twinkled in the cafeteria's fluorescent lights. Gorgeous was the word that ran through my mind. What more could a woman want?

A table of nurses gave us the once-over as we passed near them. Their low chatter made me uncomfortable. I fiddled with my over-the-shoulder purse.

"I keep my appointments, Dr. Johnstein." My answer seemed short and stiff.

He turned his head and looked at me in surprise. "Peter, please. Call me Peter. Did I do something to offend you?"

"I'm sorry. Coming here brings back . . . well . . . memories."

"Some you'd rather forget?"

"Yes. One for sure."

We picked out a salad and meat. A server asked about vegetables.

"Are you passing the desserts? They make the best fruit cobblers." Peter grinned at the attendant behind the counter. She melted down to her boots. He chose peach cobbler and placed the dish on my tray.

At the cash register, he held up two fingers. "Lou, there'll be two on my ticket."

"Dr. Johnstein, how are you today?" The older man with a dark, slightly-askew toupee asked—his fingers busy on the keys. He handed over a red-streaked piece of register paper, and my date pulled a bill from his white coat pocket.

"Busy day in emergency," said Peter, waiting until the attendant finished his sale. Holding my tray, I moved out of the way.

"This morning's fog?" The man handed back change for the ticket and paused to hear the answer to his question.

"Yes. People tend to drive way to fast. We triaged a four-vehicle pileup on Alcoa Highway. One driver slowed to crossover the four-lane to a car dealership on Airport Motor Mile, and the rest is history. Guess he needs a new car now. Thanks, Lou."

Peter shepherded me to a table near the window. Bright sunlight illuminated the part of downtown Maryville I saw in the distance.

"Is this okay?" He indicated the table.

"Perfect." I sat my tray down and raised my eyebrows as he held my chair and then sat opposite me.

"How's the pump knot?" He reached across the table and pushed my bangs aside. I started to recoil but decided his gesture meant physician rather than an imposition on my personal space. After all, we hardly knew each other.

"Much better. Only a little bruising left. The swelling is gone."

"I'm a miracle worker." He grinned. My heart beat faster. Deep dimples showed in his cheeks.

We arranged our food trays and unwrapped the silverware.

"Are you a native of Blount County?" he asked, pulling his chair closer to the table, scraping the black and white checkered floor.

"Born and raised here. Went to Heritage High School. How about you?"

"My parents lived in Germany where I was born. They moved to Clarksville, Tennessee. Dad retired from the Army's 101st Airborne Division fifteen years ago. I was an Army brat."

"Screaming Eagles, huh?"

"Hooah." Another toothy grin worked at the process of softening my heart. "I don't remember much about those days."

"Do your parents still live in Clarksville?"

"No. They bought a home in Gatlinburg—one of the reasons I decided to do my residency here in East Tennessee."

"Will you be a doctor who specializes in trauma care?"

"No—a pharmacist."

"I guess the next obvious question is what are you doing in an emergency room?"

"What's the old army slogan—be all you can be? I'd like to know as much as I can about the many areas available to a physician."

"A noble and intensive undertaking, I'm sure."

"Doesn't leave much time for a personal life at present—lunches in hospital cafeterias," he chuckled, jabbing his fork in the air to punctuate the sentence. "But, what about you? Did you go to college after high school?"

"I followed the family tradition and went to Maryville College. My grandmother and mother both graduated from the school—Bachelor of Science for me."

"You're a research assistant at the University of Tennessee Medical Center in Knoxville?"

I chuckled. "You read my chart."

He nodded. "Of course. You were my patient."

"I was a captive of Petri dishes, microscopes, and centrifuges. In fact, I love being involved in experimenting or researching drugs for the cure of diseases, especially cancer. But I've quit my position. I'm taking a sabbatical for a year or two. Circumstances may necessitate I go back."

"Really? You've got my attention. What are you going to do?"

"Write."

"Write?" He pulled his neck and head backward and stared at me. "Write about what? Novels or newspaper articles or . . ."

"Historical novels. I intend to write about former residents of the Smoky Mountains—the Tiptons and their kin. A series I think."

"I'm curious. How does being a research assistant prepare you for putting pen to paper and," he shook his head and frowned, "writing novels?"

"I'll write about disease-infested historical places." I gave a two-chuckle laugh as I leaned forward. "No, I'm kidding. One of my grandmother's many hobbies included research into family history. She left me her memoir and lots of information she gleaned over decades of study and travel."

"Quite an undertaking I'd say."

"I can't wait to tackle the first book. I've made an outline. Next, I flush out the story."

"Good luck with that. I find it hard to write prescriptions and fill blanks in hospital paperwork—such boring jobs. Guess that's the reason for loading small bottles with pills—good money made easy." He cocked his ear as his name came over the hospital intercom.

"Dr. Johnstein to the emergency room—stat. Dr. Johnstein to the emergency room—stat."

He groaned. "Guess my lunch is over. Are you ready to go?"

"Sure, and you were right about the cobbler."

"I told you." He combined our dishes, rattling them against each other, and headed for a sign saying LEAVE TRAY HERE. A conveyor belt carried them out of sight.

"Come on." He grasped my elbow. "I have to use the elevator too."

He hurried me down the hallway to an empty elevator and punched the G button to the ground floor.

The elevator started with a jerk and stopped with one. The door opened.

"Jenni, I'll call you." I watched him disappear in the direction of the emergency room his white medical coat flapping as he hurried away.

"Gosh, was I that bad." I murmured at his abruptness. I headed for my car.

Later, I called B.J. "My big date's over."

"What did you think of him?" I heard noises coming from her television.

"He's interesting, confusing, and very busy."

"Okay. I sense a note of disappointment. Interesting I get, but what do you mean by confusing and busy?"

"He left without so much as a goodbye, I enjoyed your company, or making another date to see me."

"What exactly did he say?"

"Oh, very original stuff like, I'll call you."

She started laughing. "Maybe he will."

"And maybe he won't, B.J. You and I both know in male talk that's a brush-off."

"Give him a few days to call," she encouraged.

"Sure, I can do that. Confusing—I need more time to form an opinion."

"Let's change the subject. Saturday week I have an appointment to look at wedding dresses. Mom's going. Can you go?"

"Of course. What time? Do you have any idea how many hours I've spent looking at wedding dresses?"

"No."

"Zilch. Nada. What fun we'll have."

"Mom's going to spring for lunch. I hope that works out. You know how compatible we are these days." I heard mixed hurt and sarcasm in her voice.

"You guys have another blowup?"

"Nothing more than usual. I'm thankful for you, girlfriend. And Troy. Without both of you, I'd be a basket case. Oh, Jenni, getting married is so exciting. I can't wait. June will be here with a snap of your finger."

B.J. and I chatted several more minutes before I headed for my bath.

One of my favorite undertakings is standing under a hot shower with water coursing in rivulets down my body—relaxing to the sound, feel, and warmth. Almost as much fun is drying off with a soft towel and putting on my "long-tailed gown" as

Grandma called my slinky rayon night clothes. I remembered hers as cotton or flannel. She called us twins on the occasions I stayed all night, and there were many times.

She'd gotten me into the habit of snacking before bedtime. We'd sit in front of the television—munch popcorn, candy, or spoon a bowl of ice-cream.

I saw no reason to change my routine now. After my hot shower, I headed for my nighttime soul food—the perfect period to end each day.

Call mom, a voice urged. We'd last spoken on Sunday. I dialed her number, but she didn't answer, so I left a voicemail.

The clock in the kitchen said ten o'clock. I pulled a can of cola out of the fridge and poured chips out of a bag into a bowl. In my great room, I clicked on the television to catch the local news, snuggling into a convenient couch corner with my chenille throw.

A few sips of cola later and my cell phone rang. No one called me late at night. Not even my mother. I thought the worst. "Hello?" I waited for the hammer to drop.

"I told you I'd call you," Peter Johnstein said.

A jolt like an electric shock ran over my body. "Yes, you did. Are you still on shift?" My red throw got warmer.

"No. I just walked in the door of my apartment. I can't wait to shower and crawl into bed. I'm bushed. Is this too late to call?"

"Not really. I'm having a snack and watching local news."

"I wanted to apologize for leaving you standing at the elevator. When the intercom says stat, I scoot to the ER on the double. Might be the difference between life and death to someone."

"Apology accepted. I hope the emergency didn't mean someone died."

"No. A knife fight and lots of blood. One would think there's a full moon outside. This phenomenon tends to bring out the beast in people. Werewolves—things like that. *Brrrr*, makes me chill thinking about hairy animals." His voice said he was smiling.

"The weather lady did say freezing tonight. We'll have frost in the morning."

"Speaking of morning, I don't go into work until ten. How about breakfast? At IHOP?"

"I don't usually eat early." This guy was moving too fast. Could he be a love-'em-and-leave-'em-quick kind of man?

"Ms. Lofton, don't you know breakfast is the most important meal of the day? You need protein, pancakes, and lots of sugar to establish a foundation to confront the day's joys and problems." Another smile.

"My grandmother and mother have harped on the subject."

"I'm joining them. Shall I pick you up, or do you meet me at the restaurant?"

I relented. "I'll meet you."

"Good. I'll truck on over to the hospital after we eat. Eight thirty-ish?"

"See you then."

I finished watching the news with my eyelids dropping, my head nodding. I couldn't remember a thing the commentator said. Exhausted, but relaxed after my long day and hot shower, I needed to hit the bed. No need sitting half-asleep. I got up and turned off the TV.

In the kitchen, I threw my empty drink can in the trash and cleaned my chip bowl. Tomorrow I had a breakfast date, and I intended to call the Milbern's in Kentucky. I left the room realizing Saturday would be another emotional day. I set my alarm clock and crawled into bed.

8

Peter wore gray sweats to breakfast. "I hope to get in some time on the elliptical machine at the hospital gym before my shift," he explained. "I'm too tired after working all day."

Although the line ran to the door, the hostess seated us within minutes. I slid onto the booth's cushion. The waitress wasted no time, standing at Peter's elbow before he was comfortably seated. "What would you like to drink?" she looked at me expecting an answer.

We gave her our drink and meal orders. I watched as she disappeared in the direction of the kitchen, ripping our order from her ticket book as she went.

"You're as beautiful at breakfast as you are at lunch."

His words shocked me. "I—uh, thank you." What else could I say? I couldn't meet his steady gaze. I leaned back into the booth and looked away—heart doing pitter-patters.

"I didn't mean to embarrass you." He reached across the table for my hand. "You take my breath away." He waved his other hand as he tried to explain. "There's something. I don't know—from within. A joy coming or bubbling to the surface." He shook his head as he talked. "I can't explain the phenomenon. You're different."

Instead of addressing his comment directly, I said, "Of course I'm different. Genetics proves your statement."

"I don't think its genetics," he said raising his eyebrows. Peter let the subject drop and let go my hand. "What's on your schedule today?"

"Go to the grocery, do a little house cleaning, and call some people my grandmother knew. I need to visit them."

"Why?" He sipped his milk.

"They're connected with her past history. She wanted me to get to know the family, especially Abbot Kendall. She knew him before she married my grandfather."

"Ah. A secret romance, no doubt. Is this the disease-infested historical novel you intend to write? Sounds more like a love story."

"No. It's the historical novel I'm getting ready to research, and the storyline will be a mixture of both—a love-history if you will."

Our food arrived, and we chatted about hospital happenings. We were finished with our meal when he asked, "What are you doing tomorrow?"

"Church," I answered. "I go morning and night and meet Mom for lunch."

"Oh, so you're busy. I don't go to church. My parents never went, so I didn't get into the habit."

"Church is not a habit. It's something you do if you love and follow Christ."

"I see." The way he answered me, I knew he didn't understand at all. My faith in Christ didn't interest him. "I'm off a little early tomorrow afternoon. I guess six isn't a good time for dinner."

"I'll still be at church services."

"What do you think about breakfast on Wednesday? I work the afternoon shift next week—not off until ten or later every night."

"Sure. We can do breakfast."

Peter paid the check as we left the restaurant. We lingered by my car. "Thank you for my meal."

"Money well spent I think. I enjoyed your company." He reached out and gave me a hug. Looking at his watch he said, "Need to go if I'm to make the gym and shower before work." He opened my car door. "See you Wednesday."

"Same time and station?"

"Yes." He ran for his small truck and waved goodbye, leaving the smell of his aftershave on my cheek. "I'll call you."

While weaving through traffic on my way home, I thought about his lack of enthusiasm when I mentioned church. I wondered if any of his family went.

My family's background included Christ-followers as far back as I could remember—in several denominations. I praised God for the faithfulness of my ancestors, many of whom lived in Cades Cove. There, in the scooped-out mountain valley, going to church and belief in a Heavenly Father, Son, and Holy Spirit was deep-rooted, like the knowledge of growing a garden or hunting animals in the forest. All were important to sustaining life.

A voice I recognized cautioned me. *Jenni, be careful. Peter is every woman's dream, but if your relationship goes deeper with him, his lack of spiritual roots will become a roadblock to any commitment.*

9

I decided not to call Abbot Kendall. My grandmother had written his numerals on the bottom of her letter. Still, there were many reasons not to call him.

He might have passed on.

Not likely, since the red rose turned up at Grandma's funeral.

He might be hard of hearing or incapacitated in some other way.

I found Joseph Milbern's telephone number on the Internet. Around two o'clock, I pulled my cell phone to my lap. Drawing in a lungful of air, I let it gush from my mouth and punched in the numbers.

"Milbern's residence," an official female voice answered.

Surprised, I returned, "May I speak to Mrs. Milbern?" and held my breath.

"I'm sorry, but she's in town at present."

"When do you expect her to return?" I squirmed in my cozy couch corner as my voice took a formal tone like the one on the other end.

"Later this afternoon. May I take a message so she can return your call?"

"Yes, of course. Do you have a pen and paper?"

"I'm ready. Please proceed."

"My name is Jenni Lofton." I spelled my name. "My home is in Maryville—uh, Tennessee. I believe she knows my grandmother, Mrs. Maddie Ryeton."

"Yes, ma'am. I'll give her the message as soon as she returns."

"Thank you, so much."

Gosh. Who had I called? Were these people prosperous enough to employ servants? I was both intrigued and intimidated concerning the conversation.

I called my mother. "Hey, honey," she answered.

"Thought I'd check in. See what's goin' on."

She laughed. "Real estate people never quit. We just keep on selling. Sorry I missed you last night. Hazel and I got together at her house to watch *The Magnificent Seven*. We ate popcorn and drooled over Yul Brynner and Steve McQueen."

"Mom, aren't you a little aged for slobbering over screen idols?"

"They were called movie stars in my day. And no, Yul never gets old. To use language from the twenty-first century, he's drop-dead gorgeous—dreamy material."

"Take an aspirin and get five winks on the couch. This'll settle your fever."

We both laughed.

Mom spoke next. "Humans never quit dreaming about the young and beautiful on the screen or off. Appreciate, but don't touch is my motto. *Beauty is only skin deep* came from someone's bad experience."

"Gee. You're getting morbid."

"Yeah, and I don't know where the morbidity came from. Next week we'll do *Zorro*. Antonio Banderas is just yummy."

"Talking about aspirin, I saw Dr. Johnstein from the emergency room this morning."

"Really? Where?"

"At IHOP."

"What were you doing at IHOP? You don't eat breakfast."

"I did this morning—with him."

"Daughter, what are you keeping from me?"

"Nothing. I'm telling you right now."

"How long has this been going on?"

"Yesterday and today. If you'd answered your cell last night, we wouldn't be having this conversation."

"I'm . . . flabbergasted, thrilled, and speechless. So, what's your opinion of him? Do you like him?"

"He's in the same category with Yul . . . drop-dead gorgeous. Guess I haven't formed an opinion as yet." What had Mom said—*look but don't touch?*

"Will you see him again?"

"Wednesday."

"I hope this one works out for you."

"God is in control." I changed the subject. "Mom, I called Mrs. Milbern."

"What did you two talk about? Did you make arrangements to visit Mr. Kendall?"

"She wasn't at home, but I left a message."

"Honey, I'm getting another call. I'll see you at church tomorrow. Lunch, as usual?"

"Yes."

I folded my cell phone closed.

After finishing the conversation with my mother, I decided to wash my kitchen throw rugs and clean around the fridge. I'd almost completed the task when the phone rang.

I got up from the floor and hurried to dry my hands. The dryer buzzed in the utility room. My rugs were dry.

I ran for the phone on the couch. "Hello. This is Jenni."

"Jenni, this is Kathryn Milbern. I'm so happy to get your call."

"Do you know me?"

"Yes, of course. Your grandmother often wrote and spoke of you. I'm so sorry about her passing. I know you'll miss her."

What were the words my mom had used earlier? Flabbergasted, thrilled, and speechless? "My grandmother wrote you?"

"Not exactly. She wrote Pops, and he let me read her letters. Such a wonderful, knowledgeable lady. She loved you very much."

"Who is Pops?"

"Oh, my father, Abbot Kendall. Everyone in the family calls him Pops."

"Mrs. Milbern—"

"No. Please call me Kathy. I insist."

"Kathy, you must realize, our family didn't know anything about my grandmother's relationship with your father until the bud vase appeared at the funeral."

"Per her instructions, Jenni. Pops corresponded and called her on the phone, but she insisted her connection with him be kept private."

"This is all so fascinating."

"I hoped you'd call. When I came back from Lexington and saw your name, I told Sarah all about you."

"Who's Sarah?"

"She helps around the house on Wednesday, Friday, and Saturday. You'll meet her when you come to visit."

"That's what I called about." Shock and amazement in my voice. She expected me to come?

"Pops can't wait to meet you. You're goin' to write the book, aren't you?"

My bewilderment over the developing conversation increased. These people knew everything. My grandmother had prepared the way. What a *schemer* she'd turned out to be—even now! The silence, as my mind wrapped around the conversation, stretched longer than I intended.

"Jenni. You are, aren't you? Write the book I mean?"

"Yes. My grandma wanted me to tackle the project. So, I'm gonna try. When would be a good time to visit and meet your father? I need to interview him."

"Pops birthday is Tuesday, the twenty-fifth of April. Why don't you come and join us? He'll be ninety-four years young. He uses a walker to get around, but his mind is sharp. Let me look at the calendar."

I could hear her flipping pages. "Come on the twenty-fourth of April. That's a Monday and stay until May eighth, another Monday. Will these dates fit into your schedule?"

No need in telling her I'd already quit my job and didn't have anything else to do. "That's two weeks from Monday?"

"Yes. Can you come on such short notice?"

"I'll drive to Kentucky and be there in the afternoon. Is there any type of clothing I should include when I pack?"

"Hmmm . . . our place is a working farm. I can't think of anything special—for sure jeans, dress pants, and something pretty for church. Our church is a little old-fashioned. We haven't gotten used to wearing pants. Some of the women still wear hats. Not me. At least, not to church."

"Is your church in Meadowview?"

She laughed a short, tinkling sound. "If you knew our town, you wouldn't ask such a question. No. We drive about fifteen minutes toward the suburbs of Lexington. Heritage Chapel isn't the largest church around, but the people are friendly. The Kendall family has gone there at least sixty years."

"I can't wait to come. And I can't wait to talk to your father. I've been working on an outline for the book and a list of characters. Mr. Kendall can help me flesh out the individual peculiarities of the main people in the story."

"Jenni, I don't want to go, but I hear my husband calling my name. I'll call you next week with details about your travel. I'm thinking Pops will want you to stay with him. He has a smaller home here on the property. But we'll see."

"I'm excited about everything. I'll talk to you soon."

Fifteen minutes later, I sat with my phone in hand, thinking about my conversation with Kathy. *What about Grandma?* After making the decision to write her story on paper, she had plotted a course to ensure her idea came to fruition.

What more did Kathy Milbern and Pops Kendall know about me? About my family? Only one way to find out.

I scrambled through the newspaper. Where were the pesky coupons for the shops in the mall? If I planned to travel to Kentucky, I needed a few new things. Time to spend some of Grandma's money.

10

"B.J., that dress is *sooo* beautiful." Her mother and I sat in fake gilded-gold chairs with beige satin cushion and back. Along the sides and across the back of the narrow store hung a hundred wedding dresses and veils.

B.J. pirouetted in front of a full-length mirror ten feet away, turning to see each facet of the long, flowing dress she wore. She smiled at her reflection amidst the white, lace, and pearls.

"Do you think so?"

"Yes, dear. We do," replied Mrs. Raymond, urging her daughter to make a decision. She glanced at her watch for the tenth time.

"I love it too. This is the one and no alterations. How about that?"

"I'd say the fact that the dress fits confirms your decision." We'd sat through ten dress changes, and her Mom's statement and attitude meant she'd seen enough.

B.J. drew in a tiny sigh. "Okay. Wrap this one up," she told the sales lady. Both disappeared into the fitting room.

"I wonder why she couldn't have put the last one on first? She liked it the minute she picked it from the rack. I'll never understand her." Mrs. Raymond rose to pace the floor.

"I'd probably have been the same way—always making sure my intuition is right. Too many choices." I waved my hand down the dress-crowded aisleway.

"Back when my mother got married, women often made their dresses—simple but sweet. I have Grammy's packed away in her traveling trunk along with her wedding picture in black and white. Things have changed since the thirties. Since the depression years."

A smiling B.J. appeared with a large white box. "Is anyone hungry?"

Her mother and I looked at each other and then at B.J. "Yes," we said in unison.

"Let's go."

West Knoxville's traffic lived up to its name—cars packed the four-lane. B.J. drove at a snail's pace down Kingston Pike, not realizing an accident at West Town Mall made our drive even worse than usual. "Do you ladies have to eat in Knoxville? I can turn here and take the back roads to Pellissippi Parkway, and we can eat at The Barrel in Maryville."

"Suits me." I agreed from the back seat.

"Mom?"

"Bertie June, I had my heart set on fish at that new place in Turkey Creek, but . . ." She continued in a disgusted tone, nodding her head for emphasis. "Trying on so many dresses took *sooo* long, we're in the midst of the lunch crowd, sooo I'm ready to go home too." I saw B.J. cringe at hearing her mother's caustic response. She disliked her first name. Her mother knew this and used it only when she wanted her daughter to recognize her annoyance.

B.J. wrenched the car into the inside lane and turned left toward Maryville. We drove on in silence.

"Mom, I'm *going* to take you home."

"I'm sorry, dear. Arthur, you know."

"What I know is you have no patience. Don't blame your shortness toward me on arthritis." I saw B.J. clamp her lips shut. Silence. She wanted to say more and did. "Today was supposed to be enjoyable—a fun day not subject to rushing. I'm driving. You don't have to do anything but sit and enjoy the ride."

Her mother wore a strained smile. "I said I'm sorry. Go on to the restaurant, and we'll eat."

I looked at B.J. Her lips continued in a tight line.

Minutes later, we pulled into her mother's driveway. The brick house had slate-blue shutters. It sat in a middle-class neighborhood on the north side of Maryville. Extensive landscaping surrounded the home.

"I wish you wouldn't be so touchy, Bertie June." Mrs. Raymond jerked open her car door and gingerly put a foot on the ground. "Will you call me later?"

"Maybe tomorrow."

The door slammed shut. I watched B.J.'s mother walk up the driveway and disappear into a side door. Her daughter pulled in a lungful of air and exhaled in a forceful stream. Her hands gripped the steering wheel. She leaned forward to rest her forehead on them. "Jenni, do you want to sit up front?"

I moved from the back seat to the passenger seat.

"I don't know why she has to be so demanding—that's not true. She ruled our home with an iron hand. Pushed my father around when he was alive." Another sigh. "She'll never change."

"I understand what you're saying. I see the same struggles in our family. I'm sorry this happened. Today of all days. We had fun with the dresses."

"Do you suppose she gave me the name Bertie June so she could use it in a condescending tone every time she wanted to punish or make me unhappy?"

"What I suppose or propose is we continue on with our plans to eat."

B.J. sat up straight. "You're right. Continue on, we shall." She put the car in gear and backed out of her mother's driveway. At the end of the street, she turned left toward town.

"I have another date tonight with Peter."

"Jenni, are you getting serious about him?"

"He's handsome and attentive, but for some reason I'm hesitating."

"Here we go again—careful, cautious, and prudent."

"I can't help being careful, and you know why."

"Jenni, you're going to have to trust someone . . . someday. Give the man a chance." She took one hand off the steering wheel and waved it in the air. "I know. Let's go on a double date. Troy and I would like to meet him. We'll do it before you go to Kentucky. How about next Saturday?"

"There you go. A little bit of Mom coming through."

"I'm sorry. You're absolutely right. Do you think we can get together before you visit Kentucky?"

"Peter works odd hours. Doesn't have much time off. I'll see."

B.J. maneuvered into a parking space at The Barrel. "Let's go eat."

11

Interstate 75 North flirts with downtown Knoxville. When first built through K-town, truckers called the notorious interchange Malfunction Junction. Traffic tie-ups lasted for hours, especially when bad weather, wrecks, or breakdowns occurred. Major construction changed this.

Today the cars didn't slow down as I drove onto the ramp leading north out of the city. I knew the route well. My grandparents and I traveled the road several times to Corbin, Kentucky. Another of Grandma's college friends, Rachael Wilson, lived there. She had passed, but her daughter, Rachael Poole, and granddaughter remained. Beyond Corbin, I'd be in virgin territory.

Going north, I passed the exit for a museum, where my mountain ancestor's way of living is chronicled and depicted by enthusiasts for preserving the old ways. My mouth watered as I remembered the wonderful smell of wood smoke and sniffing apples laced with cinnamon, which bubbled in a large, iron kettle over an open fire. The museum's founder, became a good friend of his neighbor, who wrote the famous historical novel of his African family, *Roots*. Might I join the ranks of such an illustrious wordsmith? I laughed out loud at such an absurd notion.

Still . . .

The somber, gray sky didn't dampen my enthusiasm for the four-hour drive to Meadowview. A quick check of the weather indicated I'd run into rain around Jellico—a small town sitting on the Tennessee-Kentucky line. Years ago, the last segment of Interstate 75, which was built, replaced the snaky, narrow, uphill section that once sent cars into this friendly coalmining settlement. The new section completely bypassed the scary curves and the town, running the tops of ridges and providing a panoramic view of the western Appalachian foothills. Evidence of the local and lucrative strip mining industry—patches of green grass and newly planted seedlings—appeared at some distance from the road.

Trees beside my path sported the year's new growth of brilliant green leaves, unspoiled by drought or blight. I found it hard to imagine elk and buffalo cavorting beneath tall oaks and maples. They roamed the surrounding mountains and lowlands over two-hundred-fifty years ago. According to Grandma's genealogical records, the first Tipton to the colonies came decades before this.

My first stop in Kentucky was at the welcome center. I needed a new map. Before leaving the building, I checked my route and made notes for the journey from Corbin. I called Grandma's friends, and we made plans to meet at Colonel Sander's first restaurant—downtown.

The rain held off until I pulled from the parking lot. Not a hard rain, but misty and bone chilling. I turned the car's air on defrost and warm.

My car was not a hybrid. After checking prices, I'd decided on a hatchback with all the trimmings. I liked the rear door cargo area and fold-down rear seats. B.J. laughed at me. I didn't blame her after the teasing she'd taken over her small car. Course I wasn't nearly as tall as my basketball-playing friend.

CORBIN. The name appeared on the exit sign. The miles had rolled by fast. Pulling off the interstate, I followed the signs for Kentucky Fried Chicken. None of us had been to see the Poole's for five years—the last time Grandma, Mom, and I had made the trip. I recognized their car parked in front.

"Jenni." Rachael's daughter rushed from the entrance. She threw her arms around me in a bear hug, her long, bleached-blond hair flying over my shoulders.

"Sharon. You haven't changed a bit." I looked into blue eyes shadowed with long, black lashes.

"You haven't either."

We walked arm-in-arm into the restaurant. Her mother's greeting was more reserved.

"Come on girls. We'll order and then talk." Dressed in a gray pantsuit, Mrs. Poole escorted us to a table, and the waitress took our selections from the menu. "Jenni, I'm sorry about your grandmother's passing. You'll miss her."

"Thanks. I already do."

"How's your mother? I hoped she'd come with you." Mrs. Poole squeezed a lemon slice and stirred sweetened iced tea in her glass. The spoon clinked as she moved the amber brew.

"Mom's fine. Working hard. I'm sure she would've come, but I'm planning on staying two weeks with new friends in Meadowview—too long for her to be away from work."

"I don't know Meadowview. Is the town in Kentucky?"

"Yes—a little east of Lexington. Small, I'm told. Grandma's friends." I turned palms up, offering the information.

"I declare, your grandmother musta known people from all fifty states."

"Well, not all fifty. Genealogy breeds friends. She had lots of pen pals."

Sharon sat enjoying the conversation. "Why are you stayin' so long in Meadowview?" she asked.

The waitress arrived with a tray full of food. "Ladies your food is hot. Be careful." After she serviced the table, I explained my grandmother's wishes about the novel—all except for the money.

"Are you going to do it—write a novel?" Sharon asked as she forked a bite of the hot mashed potatoes. Her mother concentrated on a crispy drumstick. I cut into edible chunks of grilled chicken thigh.

"That's my intention. Grandma wanted me to meet the Kendall family. I'm headed to their home now."

"Jenni, I hope you're a great success. I know Maddie," Mrs. Poole paused and smiled, "and your mom support you fully." She wiped her mouth and hands on her napkin.

"You don't realize how much." I thought about the money in my bank account.

"I want to be the first to know when your book comes out." Sharon looked at her watch.

"You'll be among the first, but don't hold your breath. I've talked to several people who had books published. After writing the story, if you can get an agent and publisher, two years may pass before your book gets to print." I ate as I talked, trying not to be bad-mannered. The food on my plate rapidly disappeared.

"Why so long?" asked Mrs. Poole

"I don't know all the details. Just what I've heard. Ask me again after I've gone through the process once." I grinned.

"Once? That means you'll write more than the story Maddie suggested?"

"I'll tell you a secret." I laughed. "My dream is to do a whole series."

"A series?" Mrs. Poole cocked her head and looked at me. "Sounds like an ambitious agenda. I can't imagine anyone dreaming up numerous situations to fill one book let alone several. Takes a creative mind—a daydreamer," she suggested.

"Guilty as charged. But my grandmother has chronicled several unique people in our family. The Tipton's history is full of interesting characters—entrepreneurs, politicians, pioneers—who helped establish America and moved west with the frontier . . . and—oh yes, land speculators. Did you know the speculators bought land in advance of the frontier and sold to people wishing to fulfill their dreams of a better home with good soil to grow luscious crops and raise cattle?" I paused to gulp air.

"Jenni, if enthusiasm will write books, I believe we'll see several," Mrs. Poole observed, pushing away from her finished meal.

"Gosh. I've got to go back to work. My hour's almost gone." Sharon erupted into a flurry of sipping the rest of her tea and wiping her mouth. She pulled her sweater over her shoulders and buttoned it. "It's gotten colder this morning," she explained. We stood, paid our bills, and went outside into the mist.

"Jenni, we didn't even ask about a boyfriend. And you didn't notice my ring." Sharon shoved her hand in my direction.

"Oh. What a gorgeous setting?" The ring's single diamond sat in a swirl, making me wonder what the wedding ring looked like.

Another bear hug and Sharon rushed to the passenger side of her mother's sedan.

"I can't talk now. Call me when you get back to Maryville. Or, better still, stop on your way home. I'll fix dinner and you can meet my future hubby. He's a dreamboat. Mom, we need to go." She opened the car door, waved, and disappeared inside.

"Jenni," Mrs. Poole gave me an arm hug. "Be careful. The roads will be slick." She looked at the leaden clouds threatening to drop buckets of water at any second.

I waved as they left.

Within minutes, I drove onto the entrance ramp to the interstate and continued north. According to the Kentucky map, I'd leave the four-lane at Boonesborough and travel across country.

A brochure from the welcome center said Boonesborough thrived as the old fort established by Daniel Boone. His movements and life confirmed my conversation with Sharon and Mrs. Poole about my own family, exemplifying the frontiersman's advance west through courage and ingenuity.

For a brief moment, I thought about stopping at the fort; instead I crossed the Kentucky River and continued driving east toward Meadowview.

12

Kathy Milburn's laugh came back to me as I drove through Meadowview. My grandmother would've called the town a podunk—one of those don't blink your eyes settlements.

The brick post office was the biggest and, from the looks of the other buildings, the newest one. Not that the town seemed dilapidated. No. The six or eight stores offered the look of well-kept early nineteen-hundreds. If I shut my eyes and used my imagination, horses and buggies would be traveling dirt roads with women in bonnets holding parasols against the bright sunlight. Wonderful to imagine.

I leaned forward over the steering wheel and looked at a patch of blue sky. The rain had stopped and the sun shone through a break in the clouds.

I drove main street Meadowview and took the first road to the right. My instructions from Kathy told me to go one mile, turn left on Cameron Lane, and look for the first house on the left—gray stucco with white trim.

I made the last turn, expecting to see the residence looming before me. The countryside alternated between wooded acres and pastureland. Black Angus cattle grazed in herds behind the black board fences lining the road on both sides.

A narrow lane turned off the road. Through maple trees bunched at the small, nondescript entrance, I saw the partial side of a brick colonial home. Sheltered in tall oak trees, the enormous residence looked elegant with multiple white columns in front—straight out of Margaret Mitchell's, *Gone with the Wind.* The dwelling did not fit Kathy's description. I continued on. The fencing soon turned white.

I'd driven several hundred feet when I decided to return to Meadowview, sure I'd missed the entrance or taken the instructions down wrong. Up ahead, a slight curve made the road wider. I'd turn there.

I slowed and pulled the steering wheel left. Something red flashed beside the road ahead. A mailbox? I whipped the car back right, hoping no one saw me, deciding to check this last possibility. Yes. The postal box read MILBERN.

"Whew. Am I ever glad you've got the right name on your side," I gushed, relieved to find the place.

The box sat to the front of a stacked stone flower bed. Multi-colored pansies cheerfully nodded as drops of water from a white pine hit their petals. Behind the white fence, a large sign read MEADOWVIEW STABLES.

I turned left, my eyes following the driveway. The sight ahead took my breath away. Although a stand of trees surrounded the stacked stone flowerbed and fence, the house sat in a raised open area, unhindered by tall trees. From what I could see, the residence presented a stucco outer surface with white trim, but that wasn't all it offered. Nathaniel Hawthorne's fictional *House of the Seven Gables* had nothing on this flowing, multi-faceted exterior. The double-tiered main home—traditional and modern in every way—sported two wings, each with gables. I could only imagine an exquisite interior.

"Jenni, what have you gotten yourself into?"

I made my way along the curving, concrete driveway lined with graceful elms.

At the end, the road circled around a fountain. Water poured from three urns held by sprites into a pool of water below. Trimmed landscaping shrubs grew between the pool and the concrete drive. The fountain's theme and surrounding grounds seemed more suited to Biltmore House, the French Renaissance Castle in Asheville, North Carolina. Someone who lived here liked European gardens.

I pulled to the front door, wondering where Pops Kendall's home might be in the sprawling acreage I was sure made up the bulk of Meadowview Stables.

Exiting my car, I stepped onto a stamped concrete driveway—the irregular brickwork mottled gray and edged by a contrasting straighter design. The short sidewalk to the front door was one brick higher than the drive. As I reached for the doorbell, the front door opened.

"Jenni. Welcome to Meadowview." The lady in front of me had on a white shirt and gray slacks. Her salt-n-pepper hair, pulled back in a French twist, had bleached highlights around her face. She stepped aside to let me enter and gave me a hug. "Come in out of the rain." She laughed and shut the door.

"I almost didn't find you. I passed another house on your road and thought I'd made a wrong turn."

"Oh, dear. I keep forgetting about the Masons' home. Its entrance is actually not off Cameron Lane but further out of Meadowview. But you're here and safe. I kept praying you'd not have problems driving in the rain."

"Safety is my motto after being hit by a driver that ran a red light six weeks ago. I spent one night in the hospital with a concussion."

"You hadn't told me that. Are you okay now?"

"Yes. Where's Mr. Kendall's home? I didn't see another dwelling from the road."

"Not far from here. He's expecting you." She laughed. "And so excited at your coming. But first I want to show you around. Pops will take dinner with us in the house tonight. You will too. Otherwise, we deliver his meals."

"Doesn't he have a kitchen?"

"He does, but he's never cooked a meal. My mother cooked, and he washed dishes. Seemed to work well with them."

"How long has your mother been gone?"

"Twenty-four years. Breast cancer."

"A terrible way to go."

She nodded. We stepped into the main living room. Overhead, a railing ran around a balcony.

"I thought you must have two floors in the main house."

"We do. The house is much too big for Joe and me since the children are gone. We live in the east wing and rent the main house as a bed and breakfast for those visiting during horse races in the area. We have stables to board horses and riding trails around the property. Come on. I'm going to give you the grand tour." She started out of the living room. "I miss children's laughter echoing down these halls."

We walked the full length of the house while Kathy introduced me to the rooms. I could see why she and her husband moved to a wing. Their section included a sitting room, separate bedroom, and huge bathroom with large walk-in closets. Comfortable upholstered furniture, dressed in pale yellow and purple with multi-colored pillows, sat before a wood-burning fireplace.

"Joe likes yellow and I like purple," explained Kathy.

Turning around she gestured to a set of French doors leading to the patio with table, yellow umbrella, and chairs. Within a few steps, one could take a dip in the heated pool.

"It's heated?"

"Yes. We're all swimmers. Our oldest son won medals. Almost made the Olympic team. Therefore, we swim in the winter. Do you swim?"

"Dog paddle." I grinned. "Little River in the Smokies is cold even in the summer. Does a Red Cross training class count?"

"Sure. We're all for the program. Our children were all instructors." She gave me another mini hug. We stepped through the French doors to the patio. Rain water puddled on the flagstones around the pool. Motioning with her arm she said, "The other wing mirrors this end. Our children use it when they visit." She linked her arm with mine. "Let's go upstairs."

Getting back into the house wasn't hard. Several doors led to the patio, including French doors from the formal dining room. We peeked in as we passed. "We'll eat here tonight around six."

A circular staircase led from the foyer to the upper level. Four separate living units held down each corner around the open railing I'd seen from the living room below. In the center at the back, a theatre room and small workout room finished the floor. A cabinet with DVDs and video cassettes was full.

I looked over the outside acres from the single window in the workout room. Kathy came to stand beside me.

"Pops's home." She pointed to a cottage within calling distance of the patio—a white-framed house of wood. "He refuses to move in here. Wants his independence. I can't blame him."

"Did he build the house?"

"That's another story. Did I tell you he was the pastor of Heritage Chapel?"

"A pastor? No. I had no idea." My grandma's writing didn't mention this fact.

"Thirty-five years. Retired in nineteen-eighty-five. Three years after Mom died."

"Did my grandma know?"

"She knew."

"She never mentioned his being a pastor."

"Probably thought Pops needed to tell you."

"I can't wait to get started."

"Then let's go meet him. We'll drive your car around to the garage and walk to his home."

She insisted I park my car in the five-car garage on the west end of the swimming pool. From the trunk, we pulled two suitcases.

"I forgot your luggage needed to go with us. Come on."

We walked to a covered work area at the end of the garage. Two golf carts sat in front of shelves filled with boxes and tools. "Instead of walking, let's use one of these. Let it be the bellboy." She unplugged the cart and climbed aboard. "Our visitors use these to travel over the property and to the horse stables."

"Where are your stables?"

"You'll see them from Pops's back porch.".

13

Pops Kendall was elegant. I suppose most people would say regal. Like the well-clipped estate he lived on. Of course, property and home can have style, but wood or stone is lifeless.

As he came toward me in the living room of his cottage, I tried to understand my first impression of him. His face fascinated me, showing no hint of unpleasantness, no hidden animosity. Its warmth spread throughout the room like an open fireplace—like the infectious smile he showered on me.

The love of his Savior shone from his countenance with tenderness I'd never experienced. This man, with his handsome head of white hair, knew peace.

Strength. Yes. His body showed the ravages of time, but his spirit exuded and exalted in his hope for tomorrow. Like Paul, he'd run the race. He waited to reap the rewards.

Putting aside his walker, he greeted me with open arms. "Jenni, I've wanted to meet you for so long. I hoped you'd come."

He gathered me in his arms—white hair touching my brown waves. I loved this old man at first sight, trusting him with my whole being.

I kissed him on the cheek and pulled to arm's length. "Mr. Kendall, I—"

He held up his hand. "There is no Mr. Kendall here. The name is Pops. It's been Pops since my first child could talk." He grinned. "Come, Jenni. Please sit down."

"Pops, I'm going back to the house. I'll send someone to get you and Jenni for dinner."

I'd forgotten Kathy, and the two suitcases were gone.

"Thank you, dear." He waved his daughter out the door.

She winked at me and disappeared.

Pops motioned to a love seat. Using his walker, he came to sit beside me. "I believe you have your grandmother's eyes," he said softly and smiled, making deep furrows at the corners of his light brown ones.

I laughed. "Not the first time I've heard that."

He reached for my hand. "Jenni, you'll never know how delighted I am to have you here. I hope Kathy explained you're to stay in the cottage. You'll have one side, and I'll have the other. We'll meet in the middle—right here." He patted the couch. Pops sat straight as an arrow, looking me directly in the eye.

"She did, and I'm so thrilled to be here and meet you. I've tried to imagine what you must be like."

"How do I—I think the younger generation would say—stack up?"

I tossed him a grin. "You're not even close to the picture I had in mind."

"Would you like to go through some of my albums? I have several." He pointed to the coffee table three feet from us. "Good way for you to get acquainted with my family."

"Yes. I would. But first I'd like to unpack my bags, wash my hands—just take a few minutes to familiarize myself with my new surroundings. A breather, as the younger generation would say." I teased back. "Is this okay with you?" I stood and looked down at him.

"I'll show you the way."

He pushed to the edge of the couch and, using the walker, pulled himself to a standing position.

I reached out to help him.

"No, Jenni dear. I decided a few years back to keep active. Strive as much as possible to complete my daily routine."

We walked down the hall to a large bedroom. My suitcases sat on the floor near the bed. "What a beautiful room." Windows on two sides, the room was done in lilac, rose, and slate blue. A lilac-and-blue afghan lay across an arm chair next to a table with a lamp. The crocheted piece reminded me of one my grandmother had made on a trip we'd taken west to Texas.

"Kathy has wonderful taste. She's the decorator of the family. My other daughter Vivian is an accountant like her husband. Couldn't care less about home decor. We kid her about seeing only black, white, and red. You'll meet everyone tomorrow at my birthday party. Come back to the sitting room when you're finished."

I watched him turn and shuffle down the hall. Sadness settled over me as I recalled my grandma's last trip with her walker—a short, painful trip to the bathroom. Much like Pops Kendall, her strength came from a character forged by the Great Depression, the slow rebuilding of America's economy, and World War II.

"Jenni, sit down. We have some minutes before Kathy comes to get us." Pops sat on the love seat with four picture albums piled beside him. "Time for you to get acquainted with my family."

We leafed through the first two and I met his wife—a smiling brunette with bright, blue eyes. "She died about nine years before your grandfather, Charles."

"Did you know my grandfather?" I asked in surprise.

"No—only of him. Maddie and I talked about their life together. She said he was a good man, strong of character." He looked at me, wanting my opinion.

"He qualifies for her description. I've been thinking about his persona. Grandma said his childhood included many hardships with a widowed mother too busy and tired making a living to show her children much love. Charles Ryeton quit school after his sophomore year at Maryville High School. He carried newspapers and worked in a knitting mill until he and his brother scraped enough money together to open a local hardware store on West Broadway."

"A successful businessman your grandmother said."

"Small at first, but the business took off. Then Grandpa quit and went to war. Drafted, you know. He didn't stay long before being medically discharged. Instead of making him strong, the deprivation of his childhood caused several medical problems. I don't know all of them. He clerked again at the hardware when he got released from the Army."

"I know all about the draft. The long absence overseas—I think Maddie and I lost touch when I left for Europe. But we'll talk about those days later." He returned to the albums.

"When I come back to visit, I'll bring Grandma's pictures."

"I've seen them."

"What! You have?"

"Yes. Twelve years ago, I went to Maryville to see her. Kathy took me."

"She didn't tell a soul."

"No. I believe you and your mother were gone on vacation."

"Why? Why did you come?"

"That's part of the story." Pops Kendall grinned but added not a word.

We kept turning pages. I saw Kathy's face looking at me along with her husband Joseph Milbern and their extended family. Her sister Vivian and her husband Paul Clarke occupied several pages of another grouping. "Irene and I had a son, but he died of scarlet fever when he was six." He pointed to a blond-headed boy with the Kendall smile sitting on a pony.

"You had two girls and one boy?"

"Yes. There's no one left to carry on the family name."

"Is Kendall Irish?" My face seemed locked in a perpetual smile while talking to Pops—reflecting his own.

"Yes." He looked at me. "Do you have Maddie's penchant for genealogy?"

"Only so far as writing about her Tipton ancestors. I'll do lots of searching within this individual family."

"I wish I were younger. I'd help you."

"And I'd be glad for your help."

"Have you started writing your book?"

"Not yet. I'll start when I get home. I wanted to get as much information from you as possible. I do have a rough outline." I could have added and *a definite idea of where I want to start.*

Pops closed the picture book and put it aside. He glanced at an atomic clock on the wall next to the entrance door. "Jenni, Kathy will be here momentarily to pick us up for dinner. The most important album is here." He tapped a thin book on his lap. "When I kept an office, this one remained in my bookcase away from the others. Not even my wife knew of it. Several years after Irene passed, I shared the pages with Kathy." He held the book out to me. "Take it to your room. The pictures are labeled. If you have questions, we'll discuss them tomorrow and start talking about Cherokee. Tonight, I want you to meet everyone and have fun.

Joe Milbern was an easy-going man with a quick laugh. He had a habit of running his fingers through his hair, which I supposed might be part of the reason for his receding hairline. During the conversation at the table, I learned he had something in common with my father.

"What kind of cars do you sell, Joe?"

"I have a Ford dealership outside of Lexington. We'll pass it on the way to church Sunday."

The large dining room's mahogany table seated twelve people. One chair with a place setting remained empty.

I looked at Kathy. "Are you expecting someone else?"

"Yes, Abbott's coming—our son," she explained.

Huh . . . their son was named after his grandfather.

"He works at the dealership with me," Joe continued. "Last minute deal. He'll be here soon. He and the customer were signing paperwork when I left."

Pops, Kathy, and Joe continued to discuss the day's activities. This gave me a chance to look around the room. A large buffet rested under a gilt-framed picture of horses running in an open field. In the background, clouds gathered and rain dropped from their dark gray underbellies to the ground. I could imagine a flash of lightning and thunder frightening the horses into running at breakneck speed away from the sound. On the opposite wall, louvered doors hid the contents of shelves inside and a glassed china cabinet held matching pieces of the dishes we ate from.

"Hello, everyone. Sorry I'm late."

I looked up to see a young man about my age—the spitting image of a younger Pops Kendall. His full head of dark hair waved slightly. No hint of a receding hairline here. Striking brown eyes with a bit of tan, a well-defined chin, and even teeth flashed in his open smile. A hint of dimples framed his mouth. But the shoulders—one marvelous characteristic everyone must notice—*broad as a barn door*, my grandmother would have said. Mr. Abbott Milbern either worked out or worked hard at something. Then I understood—swimming.

"Abbott, this is Jenni Loften. Jenni, my son Abbott," said Kathy.

Abbott gave a slight bow. "I'm happy to meet you, Jenni," he said as he pulled his chair from the table and sat down.

I felt flushed, and warmth flowed throughout my body as he gave me the once over. I managed to say, "Pleased to meet you." I hoped he wouldn't hear my heart beating, and I wondered what he thought of me.

Abbott turned his attention to his father, explaining the sale he'd made.

I sat looking at my plate, picking at my food, shocked at my reaction to him. Something about Meadowview Stables and its inhabitants was tearing down my resistance to men.

". . . Saturday's race at Churchill Downs." I caught the last part of the sentence.

"Churchill Downs is this weekend?" My shocked comment sounded shrill to my ears. My head dipped on the last word.

"No, the following weekend, and you're going," said Kathy. "Don't worry. I'll make sure you know the protocol. You'll be okay."

"But, but I knew nothing about going to the race," I blurted, frustrated.

"It's a surprise," said Abbott, giving me another once-over. "I'll chaperone you." Tickled at my discomfiture, his eyes twinkled in the lights of the overhead chandelier. I looked away from his handsome smile as his father spoke.

"The house will be full of people starting Thursday week, and you'll see some nice horse flesh in our fields. None running the race, but bred for show."

Pops put his hand on mine. "Don't worry, Jenni. You'll be fine."

"I've been meaning to ask why so many horses are raised here—in Lexington, I mean."

Abbott answered. "Two words—blue grass and calcium."

"I know this is called the Bluegrass Region because your grass is luxurious and thick. And calcium makes strong bones. Is there a lot of calcium in the soil?"

"Bingo. And water. The water runs through the limestone under the soil, leaching the calcium. Horses drink the water. Thus, our horses are stronger, making the best racers."

"Abbott, some breeders might disagree with you. I can think of another state or two where exceptional horses have been bred and trained," Joe Milbern countered.

"Dad, you're not a Kentucky partisan when it comes to thoroughbreds?"

"I just don't totally agree with you. Are we finished with dinner?"

"Yes, dear. I think we are." Kathy raised her eyebrows. "Living room or poolside?"

"No poolside for me," said Pops, still holding my hand. "In fact, I think I'll take my new girlfriend back to the cottage. My guess is she's tired after her drive."

"Isn't she a little young for you, Pops?" asked Abbott, looking from me to his grandfather. "More my age, I think."

"Not a bit," I said rising and pushing back my chair. Everyone rose with me. "And Pops is right. I am tired."

"I'll drive you to the cottage," said Joe.

"Is there a drugstore nearby?" I asked.

"Sure. On the road to Lexington," responded Abbott. "Dad, I'll take Jenni to the store, and you can drive Pops home."

"I need my purse at the cottage."

"I have money. You can pay me back. Okay?"

I nodded my head.

14

Abbot opened the door to his SUV and I climbed into the passenger seat. He moved smoothly around the front of the car—the muscles in his body working in tandem—effortless, graceful as one of the race horses seen at Churchill Downs.

We drove down the driveway to Cameron Lane, into town, and across Main Street.

“I didn’t mean to interrupt your evening.” My tiredness vanished, body on alert.

“No problem. To tell you a secret, I need to buy Pops a birthday card for tomorrow. I always put off buying cards till the last moment.”

“That’s what I’m going to buy.”

We laughed together. “Could I ask you some questions?”

“Only if I can answer them.” He said smiling.

“How did Pops get his estate? I can’t imagine a minister being able to buy such a large piece of valuable property.”

“Did mom tell you Pop's spent most of his working life as the minister at Heritage Chapel?"

"Yes, she did."

"Pops served the church for years. He became a fixture like the pulpit or a pew. Everyone loved him—men, women, and children.”

“I can see why.”

"I see you've noticed the aura surrounding him." Abbott turned his face in my direction.

I nodded, moving my hands, trying to explain my thoughts. "The feeling or impression of warmth or tenderness—I don't know how to describe the sensation. I've never been around anyone like him before. He exudes love and all that love entails." I raised my hands palms up and moved them in short jerky punctuations to my sentence.

Abbott turned his attention back to the road and gave a two-chuckle laugh. "Expressing the many facets of love is hard. What did the famous English poetess Elizabeth Barrett Browning say when she tried to explain her love to Robert? *How do I love thee? Let me count the ways. I love thee to the depth and breadth and height my soul can reach."*

"Well, go on." I urged.

"I must confess, I don't remember the rest except in bits and pieces."

"Neither do I, but the last part goes, *I love thee with the breath, smiles, tears, of all my life!—and, if God choose, I shall but love thee better after death."*

"I like to think the depth of love Pops radiates is found in following Christ and shines through to all who know him. His church congregation felt its glow." Abbott's voice was hushed and reverent.

"Yes. That's the cause, of course—his deep love for Christ."

"Back to your question. One of the deacons, who devotedly served the church and my grandfather decided upon Pop's retirement to gift him with Meadowview Stables."

"He must have been a very rich man—the donor I mean."

"He was and is. He used Meadowview to raise horses. Race horses. Won races too. Not any major ones. I believe he made his money in coal and oil. And you're right. Pops could never afford such a vast piece of property."

"Did Pops build the house?"

"No. The smaller house sat on the property. Pops couldn't afford to pay the taxes on the land, so he deeded some acreage to Mom and Dad, and they built the home I grew up in. My father takes care of all the property. He can afford to."

"I love the grounds. The front landscaping reminds me of Biltmore Castle in Asheville, North Carolina. Have you been there?"

"Yes. As a matter of fact, the whole family went several years ago. I remember mom gazing in awe at the different kinds of shrubbery and flowers. Maybe that's where she got ideas for ours."

“Does she love flowers?”

“Yes. Starts hers in the greenhouse next to the horse stables. You’ll have to come back in the summer and look at her kaleidoscope of colors.”

Twilight descended as we drove toward Lexington. More houses crowded the road, and we passed several mini-marts advertising gas. The drugstore appeared on the right. My companion turned from the blacktop and pulled into a parking space.

"Here we are. Ready to go inside?"

I started to open the door, but Abbott put out his arm. “Wait. I’ll come around and open the door. Pops never let my grandmother get out of the car without performing this act of courtesy.”

I laughed as he raced around the car to let me out. “Grandpa Charles wouldn’t have thought of such a thing. He wasn’t subservient to anyone or thing—except his garden . . . or football,” I added as I stepped out and he shut the door. “While he lived, his blood ran Orange, through and through.”

“He rooted for the Volunteers?”

I nodded. “Rabid fan.”

“Don’t let him get around my father,” Abbott teased. “We might solve the problem between the Wildcats and Old Smokey once and for all. Course you guys usually beat the socks off us. *Buuut*, one day the tide will turn, and I don’t mean the Crimson Tide.” Abbott held the drugstore door open. “Do you like sports?”

“I watch when the football team plays, and I watch the Lady Volunteers. Pat Summitt is a legend.”

“Yes, she is.”

We were standing in front of the long rack of birthday cards.

"Guess this is where we part ways." Abbott grinned at me and looked up and down the rows of cards. "Ah, there's mine." He pointed to the men's section. "I see friend on down at the end."

I stood leafing through numerous cards, finally choosing one that said something about just meeting you, but feeling as if I've known you for years. The last two lines said, *I hope our friendship will continue to grow as we examine thoughts and feelings from long ago.*

"Did you find one?"

"Yes." I handed the card over. His close proximity unsettled me.

"Very appropriate. Might apply to more than one acquaintance." He looked at me and smiled—an intimate, warm glance.

I looked away but felt my face warm and my insides squirm under his pointed gaze. Jenni, what's wrong with you? Buck up. Be strong. Avoid men like the plague. You can handle this one.

Abbott covered my awkward moment. "Pops has a weakness."

"He does?"

"Maple nut candy." He turned, grabbed my hand, and steered me to the candy aisle. He pulled two bags off a metal spine.

"Get me one."

He held the two bags out to me. "I did."

"I believe you've done this before."

"Every time there's a special occasion. Pops shares with me. I like them too."

We walked down the candy aisle to the checkout.

"Hello, Abbott," a twenty-something reached out blood-red nails and took our purchases. She started entering them into the cash register while darting glances at him from under long lashes heavy with mascara. Bangs fell almost to her grayish eyes.

"Hi, Mandy. How's your father?"

"He's better. You haven't been to see him lately."

"No. The car business picked up. I'm working longer hours each day." Abbott tendered money for the cards and candy. "Thanks, Mandy. I'll see you later."

I felt her eyes follow us as we exited the store. The car's locking system chirped. He opened the door, handing me the sales bag as I slid in. "Old girlfriend?"

He stood in the doorway and answered. "You figured it out, huh," shaking his head. "She and her father attended Heritage. He got sick, and I'm on the committee for visiting our ill members. I chose him. Mandy got the wrong idea, so I rotated my visits with another member. She never became a girlfriend, although I'm not sure what she thought. I didn't encourage her."

He closed the door, walked around the car, and got inside.

Driving back toward Meadowview, I asked, "Do you have a steady girlfriend?"

"Not really. How about you?"

"There's a guy who calls. We go out—date, I mean. I can't say I'm serious about him. He's a little pushy for me."

"Will you get serious?"

At this point I explained my reason for never getting married and ended with, "Falling in love will not be easy for me. I've set my sights really high."

"I guess it's the knight in shining armor, riding a white horse?" he said, using the old cliché. "I might be able to come up with the horse." He laughed.

"I'm looking for someone who's a one-eighty to the men in my family. So far, he's not crossed my path. What are you looking for?"

"Many years ago, I went forward at a church young people's retreat and pledged not to get involved with anyone the Lord didn't lead me to. He hasn't grabbed me by the ear and pushed me in her direction—up 'til today." I knew from the sound of his voice, his head was pointed in my direction.

A flash of lightning lit the SUV's interior. I rolled down my window partway and waited, counting. At twenty-one, muttering thunder rumbled from my right.

He laughed. "You use the count the second's method to determine how far away a storm is brewing?"

"Yes. Don't you?"

"Pops, taught me to count."

"My Grandma taught me. Do you think we'll have more rain?" I asked, raising the window.

"The local news said to the south. That's getting close." Abbott pulled his head down and looked out the window in my direction. "But not near enough to keep me from eating ice cream. How about it? Mom didn't have dessert."

Before I could answer, he swerved left down the main street of Meadowview and braked in front of a tiny walkup store sandwiched between two of the taller buildings. "Friends of mine. They need the business. Vanilla, chocolate, or strawberry?" he said as he hopped from the car.

"I, uh . . ."

"They don't have 'I, uh.'"

"Strawberry then."

We ate the ice cream as we drove back to Pops's home. Abbott parked in front of the cottage with the motor running.

"Do you ride horses?"

"Never. Our family prefers bicycles and four-door trucks."

"We need to rectify a serious lack in your childhood education. I propose an afternoon ride over the farm—sometime this week. Are you game?"

"Sure, if you'll teach me."

"Private lessons. *Pro bono*."

"Free of charge, huh?"

"Yes, my dear. Lessons from the best instructor around. I'm not sure of the day. I need your cell phone number so I can call you." He pulled a small notebook from his shirt pocket and handed the pad to me.

I raised my eyebrows and looked at him.

"Are you thinking black book?"

"Looks suspicious to me."

Abbott laughed as his eyes teased me. "Customers, Jenni. Only prospective car buyers, except for your number." He handed me a pen. "How about inside back flap," he suggested. "I can find it faster there."

I put the last bite of cone in my mouth, wiped my face and hands with a napkin, and wrote my number as he indicated. I opened his car door. "Wait, and I'll get your money," I said as I slid down to the ground.

"You just broke the cardinal rule," he said ducking his head and bumping his hands on the steering wheel.

"What?"

"You left my vehicle without letting me hold the door. This is very important, Jenni."

"Why?"

He grinned. "I'll tell you later."

I went into the house. The lights were out except for a night light in the hallway to my room.

Pops must turn in early, I thought.

My purse rested on the dresser. I opened the latch and took out a bill, heading back to the front door. Abbott was gone. As I looked toward the main house, its lights shining in the darkness, I wondered at his comment. *I'll tell you later*. What did he mean by this?

The night air proved damp and chilly as the lightening flashed to the south. This time I counted to ten. The storm had moved closer to Meadowview Stables. A bird in the shrubbery nearby chirped in alarm, disturbed by movement I couldn't see or hear. A raindrop splashed on my bare arm. Time to go inside.

Back in my bedroom I took the photo album to a sitting chair near a floor lamp, turned on the light switch, and opened the book to the first page. Two separate pictures were placed in small corner tabs on the leaf. One showed my smiling grandmother in a pose I recognized as she stepped across rocks midstream somewhere in the Smokies. The other was of Abbott Kendall, his foot propped on a rock and his arm on his knee. He smiled down at whoever took the picture.

My observation at the dinner table proved correct. Abbott Milbern looked exactly like his grandfather when he was thirty.

15

Pops Kendall rose early each day, as I found out on Tuesday morning when he tapped on my door to announce the morning's meal.

"Jenni, are you awake? Breakfast will be here in fifteen minutes."

"Thanks for telling me. I'll be there." I threw the sheet and quilted spread back, slid to the mattress edge, and yawned. Grabbing my slippers, I put them on and headed for the bathroom.

Ugh. The mirror revealed the need for serious work. Time for repairs wasn't on my side. I brushed my teeth, washed my face, and combed my hair, deciding to eat in my nightgown and robe.

Padding across the room, I opened my bedroom door. The delicious smell of bacon and eggs greeted me. Where would I find the kitchen? Two doors led from the sitting room. I went left. Food smells seemed stronger from this direction.

Good guess. Another large atomic clock on the kitchen wall announced the time as six thirty. Pops sat at a small kitchen table pulling wheat bread from its plastic wrapper.

"Sorry, Jenni. I didn't tell you the time for breakfast." He looked up and smiled. "Did you sleep well?"

I nodded. "Like a rock. My mattress is firmer than the one I usually sleep on at home, but I like it."

"A firm mattress keeps your back straight. My wife insisted on one."

"Do you always eat at six thirty?"

"Always. Lunch is at eleven thirty, and dinner at five. Keeps the body regulated. At eight, I have devotions, and I'm in bed by nine. When I pastored at Heritage, I spent the hours after breakfast studying for each Sunday's lesson. The afternoon's, I visited patients or homes or ran errands."

"A pastor's life is a busy one."

"Yes. There's coffee on the counter." He pointed to an enclosed nook next to the oven. "Would you pour some for both of us? Cups are in the cabinet over the pot. And get the butter and jam from the refrigerator." He pushed the toaster button down until it clicked.

"Did we have rain last night? When Abbott and I came from the drugstore, I felt a drop on my arm." I poured the coffee and took the full, steaming cups of black brew to the table, realizing the package of birthday cards and candy remained in his grandson's vehicle.

"Storm woke me about twelve o'clock. Rained hard for a few minutes and then slacked to a drizzle."

I looked out the kitchen window. The sun's new rays peeked between the trees. In the misty distance, I saw the ragged outline of the horse barn silhouetted on a small hill, its cupola standing above the trees. The greenhouse didn't appear visible.

The shelves of the fridge contained almost no food supplies. I pulled the butter and jam and went to the table. "Do we need anything else before I sit?"

Pops looked over the table. "I don't think so. Be seated, and I'll return thanks." His prayer wasn't long. "I'm afraid your food's getting cold," he explained as the bread jumped up in the toaster.

Our food came in covered dishes much like the ones hospitals use to serve meals. Pops opened his lid. "Did you and Abbott enjoy your trip to the pharmacy?"

"Yes, we did, and I learned a secret about you?" The eggs and bacon were yummy. A small dish of red raspberries with granola sprinkled over them sat in the larger plate. I used my spoon to taste one. The delicate berry flavor filled my mouth.

"Well, if you know and Abbott knows then whatever he told you is no longer a secret. Right?" Pops cocked his head, looking at me as he ate a piece of precooked bacon, which crumbled as you chewed.

I laughed. "I hadn't thought about a secret not being a secret if told."

"What did he confide to you?"

"That you like maple nut candies."

"Ah, he's right, and being a good grandson, he often buys me bags of these sweets. Now I'll tell you a secret. At my age, maple nut candies are hard for me to chew." He wiped his mouth and leaned toward me. "I save them for him." Pops laughed. "I haven't eaten one in years. But don't you tell him." He waved his fork at me.

Our laugher filled the room.

"I won't. We'll have a two-person secret," I assured him.

"Abbott's never gotten married." He put butter on his toast and smeared on jam.

"I asked him about his singleness. He talked about a vow to wait until the Lord leads him to the right woman. Sounds like a good idea to me." I put butter and blackberry jam on my bread.

"I held the retreat or youth camp specifically to alert our young men and women to the necessity of making the right choices. I fear the intention when people get married today is to test their compatibility—some only cohabitate without being legally joined. Divorce is too common in today's society. Too easy. Even in the church."

We were almost finished eating and sat sipping our steaming cups of coffee. "My sentiments exactly, although there's more than one reason I've not taken the plunge."

"Do you mind telling me the cause?"

I sat the cup down and related the same information I'd told Abbott the night before. "I'm not sure I'll ever get married." My last bite of toast and jam crunched in my mouth.

"I'll pray for the right man to appear." He moved back in his chair. "Are you ready to wash dishes?"

"Sure." Taking a last gulp of coffee, I stood to help.

We cleared the table and worked side-by-side, washing and drying the tableware.

"Irene always cooked our meals, and I helped clean up afterwards," he reminisced, rubbing the cloth over a fork.

"You loved your wife very much."

"Yes. The Bible talks about a helpmeet. She was mine in every way. We meshed. We completed each other."

"Yet, you loved my grandmother?"

He stopped drying and looked straight at me. "The heart is a big place, Jenni. It can handle more than a single person without being a traitor to the one you marry."

I stood, trying to digest this bit of information.

Pop continued. "A Russian Catholic exile to Paris, Anne-Sophie Swetchine, once said, *To love deeply in one direction makes us more loving in all others*. Our own Henry David Thoreau penned, *there is no remedy for love but to love more."* My first love taught me to love more."

"I believe I'm starting to understand."

"Maddie took my breath away. She was my first love. Even though circumstances caused us to part, there remained a place in a nook of my heart for her. She's enshrined there, and I visit from time to time." He stood gazing out the window. "I never look at roses without thinking of Maddie—she loved them so much." He continued in a voice filled with emotion. "My Cherokee rose, that's what she was to me."

"My grandma loved every flower she saw. I once gave her a tea rose. The plant is small and delicate. She placed my offering by the front porch so she could see the fragile blooms when she went to get the mail in late spring. It disappeared long ago."

"Spring is my favorite time of year," he said looking out the kitchen window. "The newborn leaves on the trees are an indescribable green. And that old oak tree," he pointed to a tall sturdy one with thick trunk, "just stays rooted in the same spot, producing new ones every year. Guess I'm reminiscing about my birthday today. I'm adding a year."

"You'll be ninety-four?"

"Yes. God has given me ninety-four wonderful, experience-filled, exciting years."

"I'm looking forward to hearing about them."

Pops turned around and gave me a hug. "Time to start?" He tugged at his walker.

"Give me about thirty minutes to get a bath and clean up."
"I'll meet you on our loveseat." His eyes twinkled.
I gave him a quick kiss on the cheek and left the room.

16

"Jenni, I think I'll start with growing up in the mountains of Eastern Kentucky."

"Good. I'd like to know some of your history." After finishing breakfast, I'd rushed to my bedroom, taken a shower, and changed clothes. I sat beside him, makeup on and notebook in hand. Pops handed me a pen from his pocket.

"Thanks. I'll need one."

"Because bootlegging of moonshine became a part of my legacy, I've studied its history." Pops pulled out several sheets of paper from a manila folder in his lap and began to read. "The year was nineteen hundred nineteen. My family lived several miles southeast from Meadowview Stables toward Hazard, Kentucky. I'd turned eight years old when Nebraska completed the ratification of the Eighteenth Amendment and alcohol became illegal. Kentucky's ratification happened the year before.

"At first, my father showed great disdain for those participating in the illegal production of alcohol. He should have since his father preached in a local community church, speaking against drinking alcohol of any kind. Of course, all the hill folk used spirits for medicinal purposes. Then my grandfather died in a flu epidemic in the summer of 1925."

"There were flu epidemics in the twenties?"

"Oh, yes. There've been flu epidemics as long as I can remember."

"My grandmother lost two siblings because of measles with complications of pneumonia."

"Yes, I know. She told me."

"Losing your grandfather must have been hard."

"It was. He and my Pa worked together to support our two families, partly with funds from his pastorate. People often gave him produce from their gardens, chickens and eggs, and even pigs to repay him for his service to the church.

"My family didn't have money. After his father died and my grandmother moved in with us, my father worked our hillside farm—very poor soil and dreadful crops. He struggled terribly as his young family slowly starved. So did his brothers and sisters.

"In the Depression, starting at the end of the roaring twenties with the Wall Street stock crash, jobs and money were even scarcer. As a young man with responsibilities, the making of illegal alcohol or moonshine meant money for food and clothing. I don't know how we would have survived without this income flow. Making shine became a family business."

"Did you help him?"

"Yes. I'm not proud of my part in breaking the law. My brother Frank continued sick throughout his teens. I'm certain he would have died without the cash to buy his medicine. This is my only excuse for helping my father. We needed the money to survive. I learned to drive, racing down the mountainsides to customers in several states."

"I understand." But did I? Starvation hadn't plagued Maddie's family. Farm animals, a large garden, and her father's work as a police officer supplied every need of the Whitehead family during the Depression.

"Pa became one of the biggest producers of shine in the Kentucky hills, running his supplies clear to Knoxville not far from where you live. His reputation for the highest and best proof remained legendary for many years after he quit."

"He never got caught?"

"No. Not being a greedy man, he willingly shared his money. Bribes to local law enforcement ensured a safe passageway through the hills, but I must give him another credit. He often walked into a widow or disabled man's house to lay twenty dollars on a kitchen table."

I nodded. "A lot of money in the thirties."

"Staples for a month and more," he agreed and continued.

"There were tense moments. The Ku Klux Klan became big in the temperance movement. They looked for stills in the vastness of the Kentucky mountains.

"Pa turned our old plow horse into his ride to work with me sitting behind him until he could afford other animals. Those distant hills surrounding our old farm became as familiar as walking to school each day. He nor his brothers ever took the same route twice, winding up valleys and across hilltops, and we moved the copper vats on a regular basis."

"Were you scared?"

"We lived in constant fear. My mother and her children awoke one night with a cross burning in our yard and white-hooded, robed men standing by the flaming wood—a warning to Pa to quit. He didn't. Another time, we got wind of a roadblock planned to stop our run to Virginia. Changing roads, we avoided a confrontation with the Klan. Only God's mercy kept something bad from happening to our family.

"At seventeen I graduated from our local high school with a reputation as a good student with a promising future. Moonshining didn't fit into the picture I painted for my life: teaching school somewhere far from the dirt-poor farms of Eastern Kentucky and the making of illegal alcohol. My father's business wouldn't support further education, but I'd heard of a college in Berea, Kentucky where you could study and work your way through. I determined to go."

"Where exactly is Berea, Kentucky?"

"You passed the town and school on your way here."

"I thought I recognized the name."

"In 1927, after graduating from high school, I persuaded Pa to let me visit Fort Boonesborough, as I had an avid interest in history. Visiting the fort became the excuse to cover my ulterior motive. One of my cousins went with me. He became my confidant and helped me keep my ambitions for furthering my education from my family. With a copy of my high school records secured in a saddlebag, he and I rode our horses around eighty miles to Berea College."

"Tell me a little bit about the school."

"In the 1850s and 60s, Berea College consisted of grades up to twelve and preparatory classes for college. The school held classes for people of every color."

"Unusual before the Civil War."

"Yes." Pops nodded his head. "It was. If I remember my history, during its first years Berea Literary Institute had a rough time staying open. The locals objected to the interracial nature of the college. The school closed during the Civil War. Sometime after the conflict ceased, the Institute added a college department. When I enrolled, the percentage of black to white people startled me. Half of my classmates were black. I soon got used to rubbing elbows with students sporting skin much darker than mine—something my Pa probably wouldn't have approved. His only trip to the school occurred when I received my diploma from our school president, William Hutchins. Prohibition ended the same year, and my father turned fifty. He continued to make illegal moonshine because he didn't pay taxes on the bottles we smuggled into Virginia and Tennessee."

"Receiving a diploma must have been a wonderful accomplishment for a boy who made shine in the Kentucky hills." I put my hand on his arm, and he covered it with his.

"And not an easy one, but I enjoyed every minute of working hard and filling my mind with advanced studies. Going to Berea made me an avid reader—something I take pleasure in to this day."

"As did my grandmother."

"Maddie started college the year I finished."

"Did you have a teaching job waiting when you graduated?"

"I did. In Lexington. But I lacked tenure. The downturn in America's economy caused the elimination of my position. The mid-thirties found me without a job. I would have joined the Civilian Conservation Corps, but my cousin, the same one who kept my secret about college, persuaded me to form a construction team. We roomed together and somehow, with odd jobs, made ends meet." Pops smiled, remembering good times. "Occasional runs of prohibition alcohol helped pay our expenses."

"You and your cousin enjoyed working together?"

"Yes. His name was Harry—Harry Kendall—a really funny guy. He loved telling jokes, but around other people besides those in his family he remained shy and reclusive—hard to get to know. He died several years later in a horrific car accident coming off the mountain close to our old home place. Brakes on his first car gave out. I can hear his laughter even now—a deep belly laugh. It shook his whole body."

"I've never had anyone close to me die—unless my father qualifies."

"Jenni, you sound like you didn't love him, your father?" Pops looked at me, shaking his head. "What happened, child, to cause this?"

"You mean my grandma didn't tell you. She seems to have told you everything else." I feigned surprise along with lightheartedness.

"No." said Pops, his voice serious.

I pulled in air and let it pass through pursed lips. "Pops, can we talk about this part of my life some other time? I'm more interested in what next happened to you."

"We'll go on, but plan on having this discussion later, before you leave." Pops shuffled the papers on his lap and placed some back in the folder. He took one and looked at it. "In 1938, a married college friend, Wilson Platters, told us about making excellent money working the vacation circuit in Gatlinburg, Tennessee and Cherokee, North Carolina. We applied to a local restaurant in Cherokee. A return letter offered two positions. Harry and I didn't hesitate. In early May, we packed our bags, caught a bus, and headed for the Cherokee Indian Reservation in Western North Carolina. Waiting tables with big tips sounded as good as the '49 Gold Rush to California. When we arrived, we found the positions had been taken. Our acceptance letter hadn't arrived. A souvenir store called White Feathers was stocking shelves and rotating inventory. They hired us to help and we stayed for the summer. Not exactly the glamorous jobs we were expecting."

"What products did White Feathers sell?"

"Authentic Cherokee crafts, including moccasins." Pops smiled and laughed. "Don't let me forget to tell you about my first encounter with Maddie."

The cottage door opened, and Kathy walked toward us. “Lunch is served,” she said. “And I’m going to stay and eat with you.” She disappeared into the kitchen.

I looked at my watch. “Where has the time flown?”

“I often think the same thing. The days pass too quickly for me.” Pops stood to his walker. “Young lady, are you ready to eat?”

He followed me to the kitchen.

17

After lunch, Pops pushed his papers back into the folder. "Jenni. Here." He held the printed sheets in my direction. "We'll start again in the morning. Old men need an afternoon nap, especially since my birthday dinner is tonight. Your afternoon is free time for you to explore or read or rest. I'll see you around four."

He did look tired after our long morning. "Next time we won't sit so long," I promised.

I watched as he turned his walker and headed for his end of the house. He walked in his blue house shoes, placing one foot in front of the other. He didn't hobble as my grandma did, but his steps were slow and measured. My chest heaved, and a sad, sorrowful sigh pushed from my lips. We'd only just met. I realized our friendship would be a short one.

Watching television seemed a good option. I started for my bedroom. My cell phone rang. I flipped it open.

"Jenni, I miss you," Peter Johnstein said. "Aren't you missing me?"

"Oh, Peter. I've been *sooo* busy."

"I'll take your answer as a no," he returned, disappointment in his voice.

"Honestly, I haven't had a minute to even think about home—any part of it."

"That makes me feel a little better. Are you making progress on your interview?"

"Mr. Kendall and I spent the morning together. He's a very interesting man."

"Should I be jealous?"

I laughed. "We *are* sharing a loveseat, but at ninety-four he's not looking for another wife. I've never met anyone like him. He's knowledgeable and easy to be around. I enjoy listening to him talk." I didn't feel comfortable mentioning the fact Pops Kendall was easy to love. I didn't want to give Peter an opening or reason to associate the word with me.

"We're still on for the Wednesday you get back, aren't we?"

"Yes. Lunch at the hospital." I heard hospital noise in the background.

"Gotta go. Duty calls." He paused as if pondering his next words. "Jenni . . ."

"I'm here."

"I really do miss you."

He wanted a reply.

"The time will pass fast. I'll see you soon."

I couldn't tell him I missed him. I didn't. I hadn't wished for home one time since coming to Meadowview Stables.

Pops's birthday party went off without a hitch. He and I arrived early, giving us a chance to interact with Vivian and Paul Clarke. The couple had driven from north Lexington through rush-hour traffic.

The four of us stood under the sparkling, glass chandelier in the entrance foyer. The crystal light with its multiple tiers of cut glass hung twenty feet from the vaulted ceiling. Instead of a ball, the last shape of blown liquid glass having the form of a horse dangled from the bottom.

Vivian hung on to her father's arm. "Pops, Paul and I are thinking about retiring to the country. We're tired of driving in bumper-to-bumper cars on the freeway." She laughed as she gave him a bear hug. As she handed him a gift, I noticed her manicured nails with clear polish and white tips—perfect nails for an accountant. She wore her hair in a fluffed, modified page-boy, which suited her long v-shaped face. I figured the shape must be from Irene Kendall's side of the family.

She turned to me. "Jenni, I'm pleased to meet you." We shook hands. "Are you enjoying your stay on the farm?"

"I am. Pops is a wonderful host, and Kathy and her family make me feel very welcome."

We chatted with Pops until two of the Clarke children came bouncing through the front door with spouses and children of their own—five girls in all.

"One of Vivian's children won't be here," Pops whispered in my ear. "She's in the Kentucky Legislature and had a committee meeting this afternoon. You may meet her at Churchill Downs."

"Does she have children?"

"Two boys and two girls. The boys are adopted."

"Kendall descendants seem to produce girls," I observed, as the noise level rose in the room.

"If you want me to tell you why, I can't."

The room continued to fill with Pop's relatives.

Joe Milbern came toward us. "What are you two whispering about?"

Pops answered. "We were discussing the proportion of females to males in my extended family."

"Wait until my crumb snatchers get here, Jenni. The ratio changes a little. Kathy and I had two boys—Abbott you've met, and Earl. Earl went back to our roots. He lives between Hazard and Pikeville, Kentucky. Pops gave him the old home place to tend. He loves being in the mountains. I expect him to arrive any minute. He and his brood will stay tonight and go home tomorrow—and no he doesn't make moonshine."

"What does he do?"

"Oil. He has five wells drilled on his two hundred and twenty acres. All he does is fill out paperwork and deposit his checks."

I looked at Pops and shook my head. "Your family lived atop the land starving to death when black gold rested under the surface."

"Irony of ironies, isn't it? Joe, I believe I'll go sit at the dining table. Get ready for the cake," he joked and grinned. He moved his walker in the direction indicated. His son-in-law and I followed.

"When I think of your state, coal comes to mind rather than oil production."

Joe continued. "Coal is mined in many areas, but our farm is more remote, and the expense of extraction is prohibitive. There's no indication black veins lie underground on our property,"

"Do you like trivia, Jenni?" asked Pops, as Joe pulled his chair from the table.

"I love history and trivia is history."

"Wyoming produces more coal than Kentucky."

"Yeah, yeah," said Joe, "and Texas more oil." He looked around as the front door opened and closed. "Here comes Earl now."

I looked across the room at a tall, lean man dressed in jeans and red flannel shirt carrying a child of about five. Earl Milbern appeared several years older than his brother. The hair on his partially bald head was trimmed short and he wore a fashionable, scruffy beard. His shirt bulged where it crossed his shoulders. What had Kathy said about him? Almost made the Olympic swimming team?

"Hey, Dad. James isn't coming, but I brought Lily. Phil should be here soon with his family." Earl embraced his father, who took the young girl from his arms. He walked across the room and kissed his mother on the cheek.

"Jenni, will you help me."

I'd forgotten Pops, who'd sat down. He was working hard at trying to scoot his chair underneath the table surface. I moved behind him. Neither of us could push, pull, or lift the chair.

"Pops, I can't budge it."

"Here, let me help."

I jumped at the unexpected voice behind me.

"Touchy aren't you." Abbott placed his warm hands on my shoulders and moved me from my working space. He grasped his grandfather's chair. "Lean forward, Pops, with your elbows on the table." Abbott took care of the problem without great effort.

"Thank you, son. Old muscles aren't what they used to be."

"Maybe that's what grandsons are for." He gave his grandfather a hug. "Jenni, I need to see you."

"Pops, I'll be back." Following Abbott, I pondered the obvious affection and love this family unabashedly displayed. My family lacked any resemblance of the same.

As Abbott and I walked away, Pops turned to greet his grandchildren and great-grandchildren. "Your grandfather is blessed." I indicated the group around him, where Lily sat on his lap playing with a pen she'd taken from his pocket.

Abbott looked over his shoulder. "Yes, he is. I should be so lucky some day."

"I take it you do plan on getting married?"

"I'm more sure than ever of not escaping the surly bonds of matrimony."

I laughed. "You liken getting hitched to flying or going into space."

"I can't imagine any activity more wonderful or exciting." His eyes, looking into mine, didn't waver.

I looked away. " I'm impressed. I saw the news that day. My mother cried. Do you think marriage is a disaster or worse?"

"Ms. Loften, I believe I'll be fascinated and gratified by the experience," he teased, flicking a finger at the lapel of my blouse. "And now, let's get down to more mundane activities." He pulled a wrapped gift from a thin plastic bag. "Will this do?"

I looked at the square box covered with blue and silver paper. The words *Happy Birthday* scrawled in gold script, and gold ribbons stamped in abandon over the surface. "Not bad. Our maple nut candies?"

"Yes. Ready to go. Here's your card and a pen."

"You're very efficient, Mr. Milbern. Like your grandfather." I took the pen, wrote a few words, and signed my name.

"I'm always well-organized, habitual, and, most of the time, prompt. Good qualities in a husband, I think."

"How did we get on the topic of marriage?"

"You started the subject."

"Then I'll end it."

But I didn't. Kathy did. She called us to dinner.

The next morning, Pops and I set up a work schedule. We would go over his experiences for two hours after breakfast, take a short break, and continue until lunch. The afternoons were free time to walk, work on my notes, or read.

As we progressed during the week, he supplied more detailed information about his summer at Cherokee. Remembering my grandma's notes, I began to understand why he didn't become my grandfather.

Peter didn't call again, but my mother did one afternoon. We had a long conversation about the Kendall's and the Milberns. I called B.J. on Thursday night.

"I miss you, friend."

"Jenni, I'm sitting home tonight since you aren't here. How's your interview going?" She sounded happy.

"Pops Kendall is an adorable man, but fragile. We work together each morning and spend the afternoon doing other activities. He takes a nap, and I've been using the time to study notes and read my book on creative writing. I've also signed up for a writer's conference in May."

"Have you given any thought to the outline of your future novel?"

"I've changed my arrangement a little. My first instincts were mostly correct. Knowing I can trust my intuition is important. I've written several lines for the first chapter."

"I can't wait to hold a real book in my hand. What about Pops's family? Are they interesting?"

I filled B.J.'s ear full of my opinions regarding the Milberns and the Clarkes, saving Abbott for last.

"Joe and Kathy's son, Abbott, promised to show me around Meadowview Stables on Friday."

"How old is he?"

"Old enough to know better." The phrase my grandmother used when she heard about troubles in our family.

"Come on. Tell me the truth."

"He's two years older than me."

"Is he single? What's he look like?"

"Never been married, and he's actually pretty good-looking."

"Jenni, he's perfect. And . . ."

"Okay, brown hair and eyes—hair's wavy. Broad shoulders like his brother Earl, who, by the way, was a champion swimmer. Abbott loves to tease me."

"Where does he work? Does he have a steady job?"

"Works with his father in the Ford dealership near Lexington. I'll see the lot on Sunday when we go to church at Heritage Chapel."

"Jenni, your life is so exciting."

"I forgot to tell you the most exciting part. I'll be going to Churchill Downs Saturday week. I've never been to a horse race before. For that matter, I've never been to any kind of race."

"Don't the attendees wear hats to horse races?"

"You're right. I hadn't thought."

"You'll need a hat."

"I'm sure Kathy realizes this, but I'll mention I'm hatless tonight at dinner."

"Mom's coming. She's buying me dinner. Call me first of the week."

"How are things going with her?"

B.J. lowered her voice and spoke her words faster. "She could make my life much worse. I've been working longer hours at the office. Keeps us apart and out of each other's hair. Plus, the extra money helps with expenses associated with the wedding.

"Your law office is busier?"

"Bustling. We're picking up more cases because of the publicity associated with the trial I told you about. Here she comes. See you, Jenni," she whispered.

"Later, B.J."

18

"How about dinner?" Sheepish and apologetic, Abbott stood inside a stall with his horse's reins in his hands. After an hour of riding around the property, I'd asked to return to the stables. My hips ached and my legs refused to work.

"Ooh. I don't know if I can do this," I told him as I pulled my leg over the saddle horn.

He extended his arms and caught me, holding me tight to his body to keep me from falling to the ground. The unexpected and quick sound of his heart beating in my ear, unnerved me more than the faint, manly smell of aftershave. Many years had passed since I'd heard another human's heartbeat.

He pulled me upward until his cheek touched mine. I thought he might kiss me. For some seconds, I forgot my aches and tightened my arms around him, dreaming—excusing my lack of control as necessary.

Abbott put his mouth close to my ear, his voice low and husky. Intimate. "Move your legs. I'll hold you."

"I'm—I'm embarrassed," I managed to say, stuttering—surrendering.

"Don't be. I should have known better. You're not used to riding. Go ahead. Take some steps. I won't let you fall. I'm holding you."

I started testing my legs, moving them back and forth, still locked in his arms. Jenni, what's gotten into you? Where's the iron gate protecting your heart?

He turned sideways and, hip-to-hip, we stepped along the stall out into the main passageway of the stables. We walked until I could stand without his assistance. He held the reins to both horses. They followed us. "Ms. Loften, what's the verdict? Dinner?"

I turned toward him, noticing his brown plaid shirt matched his eyes. "Maybe I'd better go back to the cottage. Pops will want me to eat with him." I needed some time to weld pieces over the gaping opening to my heart.

"If that's your only excuse, I'll take care of the problem. We'll take Pops along. It's settled."

A dark-skinned, gray-haired stable hand appeared. "Mista Abbott, is you finished ridin'."

"Yes, we are, Caleb. Will you tend to the horses?"

"Sure thing." White teeth gleamed for a second.

Abbott turned over the horse's reins, and we walked from the stables. He paused. "I intended to show you Mom's greenhouse. Some other time. Pops likes to eat early. Keeps him regular, you know." He turned and grinned at me. His eyes warm, exposing his heart. Did he feel the same emotions I felt? "Let's head for the cottage," he said, starting in its direction.

I shook my head in an almost imperceptible motion and closed my eyes. Could this be happening? I remembered B.J.'s words. *Someday, someone will—* Taking a step forward, I stumbled.

"Jenni." Abbott steadied me. "Looks like I need to take better care of you." He reached for my hand. "Your hand is cold."

We walked to the cottage, hand in hand.

Horse Hair Café might have been called Horse Haven or Horse Heaven because the walls showcased pictures of famous horse flesh back to the twenties—all Kentucky Derby winners. On

Friday night, the place filled early, but we managed a seat in the corner. We placed our orders.

"Pops, I'm going to show Jenni some of the main attractions."

"Go right ahead, son. I see one of my former parishioners coming this way. I'll be busy."

Abbott articulated his expertise as we walked around the restaurant looking at framed photos of thoroughbred race horses. "That's Black Gold. Not much money in racing at the beginning, but in 1924 he did win the fiftieth running of the Kentucky Derby."

"You didn't attend that one," I teased.

"No. I didn't."

"Sure is a beautiful black horse."

We continued our walk, passing horse after horse. Some black and some a reddish-brown.

"In 1948, Citation won the Derby, Preakness, and Belmont races. He was from Calumet Farms and was trained by Ben Jones. Citation became the first horse to win a million dollars."

Abbott pointed to another picture. "There's a movie about Seabiscuit. He's not the only horse Hollywood has chosen to immortalize on film. I did go see the movie. Starred Toby McGuire, alias Spider-Man."

"I don't remember seeing the film. Has it been out long?"

"Yes. I'll rent the DVD. We'll watch it next week. Good preparation for the Derby."

I didn't hesitate. "I'd like that."

"Secretariat." Abbott bent to read the type-written information. "He won the year before I was born. Eddie Maples rode him in his last race."

We walked to another picture. "Whirlaway won the Triple Crown. He's another horse owned by Calumet Farms and trained by Ben Jones."

"Abbott, I believe our salads are sitting on the table."

"Seen enough of horses, huh?" Abbott laughed, commandeering my hand for the second time today. He squeezed it.

I nodded. "For today."

At eight o'clock Sunday morning, we left Meadowview Stables for Heritage Chapel. Church school started at nine and the worship service at ten fifteen.

Joe drove and I sat beside him in the front seat of their van. Kathy and Pops sat in the back. I'd chosen my round-necked, navy-blue suit with the same color shoes and purse. Dangling, multi-colored necklace and earrings completed my outfit.

"Jenni, you look smashing," Pops had commented when I appeared in his living room.

"Your opinion is most valued, kind sir." I bowed to him.

We'd driven twenty miles toward Lexington when Joe said, "Jenni, look to your right. You'll see Milbern Ford dealership."

Car upon car sat in neat rows, some with yellow-lettered price signs in the windows. The sales building, a large square with a high façade and a multitude of tall windows, sat in the midst. The blue sign proclaiming the business name stretched across the front, just under the roof overhang.

"Joe, you have a large inventory of cars."

"Yeah. Do you need a new one?" he joked.

"Not now. How are sales?"

"We're doin' well. Abbott's our top salesman this month."

"A chip off the old block," offered Pops. He continued, "Jenni do you see the tall spar in the distance?"

"Yes."

"Look for the chapel on your left."

I leaned forward and looked through the window as we topped a hill.

I don't know why I expected a small church. Maybe the word chapel had thrown me. Sitting in a large open area, Heritage Chapel imposed its presence on everything around.

"The parking area holds several more vehicles than my dealership." Joe laughed. "Pops had the parking lot expanded. Most of the buildings were built while he was pastor. The newest, finished twelve years ago, is the youth facility." He pointed to a large building.

"Looks like a gymnasium."

"There's one inside. Classrooms are upstairs circling the court. Underneath them are the bleachers. The building doubles as our new fellowship hall with full cooking facilities and storage for a hundred tables and chairs. The design is rather unique." Joe pulled into a parking space next to a side door. "This is the old people's entrance." He chuckled.

Before he could leave the car, a middle-aged man rushed to open Pops's door.

"Good morning, Pastor Kendall." He helped Pops from the car and brought his walker around to the side.

I whispered to Kathy. "Pops is much respected here."

"Yes. God brought him to this church. He'll tell you the story, I'm sure."

Joe came around the car. "Are you girls ready to go?"

"We sure are." Kathy turned to me. "Jenni, you go with me." She linked her arm in mine. "We'll see you guys in the auditorium," she tossed over her shoulder at Joe.

I caught glimpses of classes, the choir room, and a large assembly area as we walked down the main hall behind the sanctuary. A glassed library and media room appeared at the end of the hall. We turned left to another impressive and open entranceway with circular stairs leading to an upper story framed by an iron railing.

"That's our class." Kathy motioned toward a room halfway down a hallway radiating off the upstairs balcony. Several women came to greet us as we entered and took a seat.

The method for teaching the group's lesson differed little from my home church. After a while, the bell signaled the end of our class. Those who came to say goodbye extended an invitation to come back next Sunday.

"We'll be in Louisville and go to church there," answered Kathy, then whispered in my ear, "unless plans change."

The auditorium contained several rows of pews and a balcony holding four or five hundred. The stage had a single, simple stand for the pastor's Bible and notes. Behind him a choir loft stretched to the ceiling, and, to the left side, an imposing orchestra with several participants tuned their instruments.

Kathy and I approached the altar area and sat in the second pew back from the front of the podium. "We always sit here," she explained. "Jenni, I see a lady who's been sick quite a while. I'm going to go greet her. Joe and Pops will be here soon."

"Go ahead. I'll look at the bulletin." I watched her cross the aisle and walk back to a white-haired woman sitting with a younger man. Her son, I supposed. I turned to the bulletin and had only read the names of the pastors when Joe and Pops arrived.

"Hi, Jenni. Do you mind if two good-looking gentlemen sit with you?" Joe beamed and slid in beside me. "Pops likes to sit at the end of the pew, and, to tell you the truth, I'm happy to let him. His admirers hang over me and muss my hair." He rubbed his bald pate as he put his Bible in the songbook rack. "Half the church will be over here before the service starts. Look at that."

Several people were bunched around the former pastor.

Kathy came hurrying back. "Let me in before Pops sits down."

Joe exited the pew, and she scooted in beside me. Joe managed to pry Pops loose from his devotees. He sat at the end but continued to talk to his friends. The church filled with people, and several chose the pew next to me. The organist started to play the opening song "*Holy, Holy, Holy,*" and the other musicians joined the music, which swelled to the rafters and filled my heart.

When Abbott appeared, very little space was left on the bench, but he inched his way down the pew. Everyone pushed together to make room. He sat down and put his arm around me, giving me a little pat on my shoulder. Leaning over, he greeted his mother and father.

His suit was a camel color with a striped, brown-and-navy tie. He wore a beige shirt and brown penny loafers. So good-looking, he could have stepped out of a Sunday paper sale insert. "I'm sorry I'm late," he whispered in my ear.

"I didn't think you were ever late. Not a good husband characteristic," I whispered back.

He squeezed my shoulder again. "A wife would probably penalize me," he suggested, his lips close to my ear.

Thank goodness, the choir stood to sing.

I turned my attention to the service, but the faint smell of aftershave and his distinctive voice during the music service made me acutely aware of his presence.

"You have a beautiful singing voice," he whispered, as the choir prepared to sing the morning's special song.

His eyes turned toward mine as I answered, "Thanks, so do you."

After church, we ate lunch in Lexington, and later Kathy and I went to buy a hat. This didn't turn out to be hard since every store had them. Back in the car, Joe headed for Meadowview Stables, leaving Abbott in Lexington.

Later, at the cottage, as Pops headed to bed, I told him, "I find it interesting none of your grandchildren followed you to the ministry."

He looked at me and smiled. "There may still be a chance." He put up his hands and cocked his head, indicating no more questions about this statement.

19

Our mornings during my second week of stay had been very productive. Each day after our session, I'd go to my room with my notes and his written material. The stack grew higher, and my book chapters increased in my laptop. Writing Maddie's story proved to be easier than I'd thought possible—the words flowed from my mind to the screen.

Thursday morning, we sat together on the loveseat with cups of steaming coffee.

"Pops, what about Sybil Blackman? What was she like?"

"Maddie didn't tell you about her?"

"There's material about their high school and college days and the teaching period following. She includes some information of the Cherokee months, but nothing of Sybil's personality or what happens after the summer is over. I found this rather strange after being best chums in school. Almost as if their relationship changed."

"Maybe Maddie didn't want to judge a friend, or a former friend. I can only imagine what must have transpired between them."

"I need to know if I'm to write her true character."

"Sybil Blackman must have been the pampered, protected girl in a family of boys. Never denied a material possession, she saw her arrival in Cherokee as a way to flaunt the loosening of her bonds—especially with men."

"Wow." I interpreted his words as a delicate way of saying she ran after men.

"Yes. Wow, indeed. And there were men available."

"Not a very good recollection. Did my grandmother follow Sybil in this regard?" I knew my opinion, but I needed to hear his.

"Oh, no. Not at all. Maddie's reserve and shyness—no, not shyness . . . maybe reticence is a better word—toward men stood out the minute I met her. Drew me to her. She wasn't like her friend at all."

"But my grandmother did like everyone she met."

"Women and men, Jenni. There's a difference, and people know the distinction. Maddie loved serving her customers and received good tips. Her wide smile and those deep dimples charmed everyone—including me." Pops leaned back into the couch's cushions, remembering the past. For the next hour, we discussed the people in my grandmother's life. A clearer picture emerged of her interaction with those who became her summer friends.

Pops took his afternoon nap, and I decided to walk about the farm. Horse trails circled and crisscrossed the area. I started toward the horse barn, but veered left, determined to take a different direction into woods on the northwest side of the cupola-topped shelter—an area I hadn't been in before.

I walked along, enjoying the day's warmth and the rat-a-tat of a distant woodpecker. Anyone looking at me saw a young woman dressed in knit fuchsia pants with a toned-down top containing the same color—bright, cheerful hues buoying my spirit and speaking of inner happiness bubbling from the soul. I often dressed in the two. Today I wore them for a different reason. They hid an inward need, pushing to the surface of my consciousness. A deficiency in my life I didn't want to recognize struggled to be acknowledged. The satisfaction of this lack fought to be known.

The trail wrapped around me like a comforting blanket.

A slight opening up ahead revealed a flowing, gurgling stream of water—not wide. I stepped across and sat on a large, flat stone, which seemed positioned for such an activity. A peaceful cathedral in the green forest. Laughing, I put my elbow on my knee and rested my chin on my partially closed hand, taking on the serious repose of Rodin's The Thinker. The statue depicting man's inner struggles. Why did this come to mind?

What struggles, Ms. Loften?

Without warning, tears rolled down my cheeks. What on earth is wrong with you, Jenni? The sobbing continued with deep, body-shaking movements and floods of water Hoover Dam couldn't hold back.

Struggling with emotions I didn't recognize, I sat with my hands clasped together. What had happened? The iron gate, the one I'd been fighting to weld shut since coming to Meadowview had left in a flood of tears. Love for Abbott Milbern came inside. He'd called every night since Sunday. We'd discussed politics, the Kentucky Wildcats, and our belief in God.

I wanted to love this man. The discovery left me breathless with wonder. Happiness filled the hollows of my heart.

I went to my knees beside the rippling stream, recognizing something sacred about this place.

Jenni, pray, a voice seemed to say.

And so I did.

Father, thank you for this unspeakable joy. For taking away my resistance to love. For being my salvation in so many ways.

I continued to pour out my heart, asking His blessing on any future with Abbott. Surely, if God brought about this miracle of opening my heart to love, He had some intention or plan to complete. Later, sitting on the stone in this quiet place, I felt the peace of God. I rose to my feet and headed home.

Steps as light as a feather guided me back to the cottage. I heard music coming from the main house as I approached. Someone was playing the lonesome, crying saxophone.

I stood outside on Pops' porch and listened to the mournful sound as the tune rose and fell. Was the music innately sad or did the person manipulating the keys pour forth an unsolved problem? The sound touched my new sensitive heart, which understood the player's need.

The movement of tires on gravel, suggesting the arrival of the golf cart at the porch, caught my attention. Someone knocked. I got up from the couch, knowing Kathy couldn't be delivering dinner. She always let herself in thru the cottage door.

I opened the door. "Abbott. I didn't expect you."

"A pleasant surprise, I hope." Smiling, he carried a tray of food to the kitchen and returned. "Pops up?"

"No," I answered, dropping my eyes—unable to think of other more expressive words. My heart's new revelation made me even more sensitive to his presence—the awakening still raw and exposed.

"I'll go wake him." Abbott disappeared toward his grandfather's bedroom.

Was the door of my heart open? Could he see the truth enthroned there? Why did I feel the need to hide the love I felt for him? I sat on the loveseat and closed my eyes, putting all thoughts of Abbott Milbern from my mind.

The rolling creak of the walker meant the two were coming. I headed for the kitchen, laying out three dinner meals. The smell of garlic floated past my nostrils. Spaghetti and buttered Italian bread. Yum. Apple cobbler completed the meal.

"You'll need to put the bread in the toaster," Abbott said.

I did as he instructed and poured tall glasses of sweetened iced tea. The three of us sat at the table. I didn't realize how hungry I'd gotten from walking the trails of Meadowview Stables.

"Jenni, I came earlier and no one answered the door."

"I went walking."

"I looked for you. Where did you go?"

"Over the meadow and through the woods." I rendered a line from a song my grandmother taught me. "Through the trees on the left of the stables, Mr. Milbern."

"A favorite place of mine. There's an opening next to the warbling creek where I sit on a large rock and think. Solve many earth-shaking problems there. Did you find the grassy area?"

I looked from my empty plate into his eyes. Was he toying with me? Had he followed me? Did he see my heartfelt sobs and hear my thankful prayer? "I-I did."

He answered my questions with his next words. “I haven’t been to my beloved rock in a while. Too busy.”

“Does this mean you’ve solved all your troubles?” I flirted with him. Flirting, an act to draw men’s attention, wasn’t an accomplished phenomenon with me since I kept the opposite sex at arm’s length. Abbott’s status in my life had changed this afternoon.

His smile was wry. “I wouldn’t go that far. Maybe I need a good session at the rock. Although,” he put up his forefinger, making a point, “one problem may have been solved rather lately.” He looked pointedly at me.

Pops had remained quiet through this exchange. “Children, we could all use a good session at the Rock. Jesus handles all kinds of situations.”

“Amen,” responded his grandson, brought back into his grandfather’s presence.

“Jenni, will you sing the rest of the song? You started with the first line,” Pops said.

“Do you know the melody?”

“Yes. Maddie sang the tune for me. Said she required her students to memorize the lyrics and music.”

“Then I will sing if you help me.” Self-consciousness didn’t normally plague me, but Abbott’s gaze made me nervous.

I went around the table and put my cheek on Pops’s. He sang in a wavering tenor voice, and I in soprano.

Over the river and thru the wood, To grandmother's house we go;
The horse knows the way to carry the sleigh,
Thru the white and drifted snow, oh!
Over the river and thru the wood, Oh, how the wind does blow!
It stings the toes, And bites the nose,
As over the ground we go.

“There’s more, Jenni.”

“Yes, I know, but I don’t remember the rest.” I straightened my back and raised my arms to the ceiling, drawing in a lungful of air, letting it rush from my mouth.

"That's beautiful." Abbott cleared his voice and shifted around in his chair. "Who wrote the lyrics?"

"I don't remember. Pops?"

"I did know. Abbott will find the person on the Internet."

Abbott stood. "Let's wash the dishes. I brought Seabiscuit to watch. Pops, you go sit in the living room. Jenni and I'll take care of this chore."

Pops headed for the other room. At the doorway, he stopped, then turned and winked at me.

I squeezed the dish detergent into the sink and ran hot water. "Speaking of music, I heard some coming from the main house—a saxophone I think."

"Abbott plays the sax. Takes after his grandfather." Pops kept standing in the doorway watching us. "He plays very well."

"I marched in the school band. Thought about joining a local jazz group. Didn't work out. Did you take music?"

"Piano lessons, but don't ask me to tickle the keys. I can read music. That's one good thing to come of my parent's money."

"Did you know a sax has keys, and sometimes they're topped with ivory."

I laughed. "You're kidding."

"No, I'm not. And there's also an embouchure. Bet you never heard this word before."

I laughed again. "You're right. What's an embouchure?" I tested the word.

"An embouchure is the mouthpiece of a wind instrument where the lips and tongue touch and adjust when playing a song. I'd go into more detail, but I'm afraid I'd bore you."

"Thanks for not boring me."

"The word can also be applied to the mouth of a river or where a valley spreads to become a plain," said Pops, who'd stayed to hear our conversation. "I've used the word when preaching. Course, I explained the word to my audience."

We turned to look at him.

"Pops, go sit down. You'll get tired," exclaimed Abbott. "I don't want you going to sleep in the movie. We're ready to start the DVD."

I opened the strainer. The water gurgled as it swished down the drain. Abbott dried the last piece, placing the glass in the open cabinet. He closed the door, picked up the delivery tray, and took the round circle and plastic serving dishes to the golf cart.

When I entered the living room, Pops was sitting in his lift chair. Abbott was kneeling before the television, shoving the door closed on the DVD player. He stood. Turned off the lights and approached the loveseat.

"Which side do you want?" He grinned.

"The one I use when Pops sits with me."

From the corner of my eye, I saw Pops smile.

Turning into a matchmaker, huh. I had a feeling my loveseat partner knew this too.

I sat down, and the three of us turned our attention to the movie.

"I think some of the language is a little rough," Abbott warned.

Seabiscuit started with an explanation of the Ford car and the assembly line.

"I thought you said the movie was about a horse?" I teased.

"Patience. Keep watching." Abbott whispered, and opened his hands in a hang-in-there gesture. He leaned toward me on the couch and relaxed.

I watched the story unfold, jumping from one scene to another. Owning a car dealership, Californian Charles Howard becomes a wealthy man who loses his young son in a tragic truck accident. His wife, because she can't deal with the son's death, leaves also. The stock market crashes. Families start living and working from their cars.

Red Pollard's family lives in Canada. Seeing a chance for Red to use his natural ability in working with horses, his father leaves him at sixteen in the care of a horse trainer. The young boy grows older and cynical, becoming a loner, boxer, and jockey.

The principles in the movie end up in Mexico where gambling and horse racing is legal. Howard meets his second wife. She loves horses, but he hasn't ridden in years. They go riding.

I whispered to Abbott. "Did I understand her to say riding will come back to him?"

"Yes. Like pedaling a bicycle. You don't forget."

The next scene flashes to Howard and his new wife who take off running on their horses.

"I can't do that."

"S-s-sh." Abbott brushed my arm with his left forefinger. His right arm slides behind me on the back of the couch.

I looked at him.

He tilted his head in Pops direction. "He's asleep."

Pops sat with his head down on his shoulder—eyes closed.

Howard puts together a racing stable with a trainer named Smith, Red Pollard, and Seabiscuit—an unlikely crew to turn out a winner.

Seabiscuit is a sickly colt, small with a gentle nature. The horse loves to snooze in the pasture and put on the feed bucket. Biscuit doesn't have the spirit of race horse material, but bred from Man-o-War, another famous racer, there's a possibility he can become one.

Trainer Smith has a way with horses and people. The tension builds as he pairs Red and Biscuit. They both need extensive healing and training. Maybe between them both…

The movie started slow, but as Seabiscuit and Red interacted to become a team, I began to root for the duo. One-by-one, the obstacles are overcome.

But, old habits die hard.

During their first race, I watch as Red's old nature and temper gets him into trouble with another jockey. He loses a race he should have won.

Reprimanded and chastened, Red follows the trainer's exact instructions during the second race.

I sat to the edge of the couch. There's a moment of silence. The crowd roars as the horse's lunge from the starting gate. Bunched up, they round the first turn. On the back stretch, Red holds Biscuit until the right moment. Around the last curve, the horses thunder on, the crowd jumps to its feet. Red gives the horse his lead and urges him on.

I jumped to my feet, “Come on, Seabiscuit! Come on. Run.” The horse pulled away from the others and crossed the finish line. Two tears ran down my cheeks.

From my left, Pops’ chair moved to lift him to a standing position. He chuckled. “Enough noise to wake the dead.” He pulled his walker toward him. “Jenni, give me a goodnight kiss.”

I walked over and did as asked. “Goodnight, Pops”

“Goodnight, dear girl.” He put one skinny hand to my shoulder. “Tomorrow, God willing, we travel to Louisville to watch a real race. I promise to stay awake for the Running of the Roses. Goodnight, son.”

“Pops, I’ll help you to your room.”

“Not necessary. I manage every night by myself. Watch the rest of the movie.”

We kept standing until the old man disappeared down the hall.

Abbott motioned to the couch. “The movie’s only half over.”

I didn’t find the rest of the movie as exciting as the first part. I did root for Seabiscuit when he beat the Horse of the Year, War Admiral.

“Do you drive to Lexington tonight or stay at the main house?”

Abbott knelt to take out the movie. “To town. My suitcase is in my apartment. You guys pick me up on the way to Louisville.” He moved toward the door and turned the knob.

I followed him. “I’ll see you tomorrow.” The light from the porch shadowed his face.

He stood in the open door. “Jenni, I . . .” He took a step toward me and circled my shoulder with his arm, pulling me to him. “Do I get a goodnight kiss like, Pops?”

I moved to kiss him on the cheek, but he turned his head and kissed me lightly on the lips.

“Goodnight, Jenni. I think you’ll enjoy the race.”

He disappeared into the darkness outside. I heard the golf cart crunch the gravels in the path toward the main house.

Friday afternoon, we drove to Frankfort, Kentucky. Abbott decided to drive his car, so we didn’t stop to pick him up.

20

Kathy and I stood under the gold letters of the Gate 17 entrance waiting for Abbott to appear. He'd called her hotel room to say he needed to run an errand. Not to wait. He'd meet us at Churchill Downs.

In front of our position, a sea of cars filled the parking lot. Most of them had been there since early morning, when the first races started. Although police directed traffic, vehicles clogged the street with bumper-to-bumper drivers. Every lawn advertised parking, and most were filled.

"Where is he? He said three thirty."

"How will he get a parking place in this mess?"

"We've been parking at the same house for years. Pay in advance. He'll have a place—it's the traffic getting there."

"How many people attend the Kentucky Derby?"

"At least a hundred and fifty thousand today. Most of them in the infield. Forty dollars will get you standing room on the grass. Most of the infield crowd comes to socialize and get drunk—not to watch the race. Those in the stands and in the boxes are serious about horse racing."

Behind us a loud bell rang, and the unseen crowd roared.

"Did a race start?"

"Yes. Several races are scheduled today. The derby is the last on the program. I wish Abbott would come. Our reservations for Matt Winn Dining Room are for four thirty."

"Did someone say something about eating?" Abbott touched my elbow, sending a tingling sensation to my shoulder. He carried a backpack.

"Son, I'd almost given you up for lost."

"I'm here. Shall we go through the counters?" He leaned over and whispered to me, "I know. I'm not good husband material. It's your fault I'm late."

"I don't understand."

"You will."

Beyond the entrance and above our heads hung an enormous glass chandelier with leaf-like, multi-colored parts. "How beautiful," I exclaimed.

"Made here in Louisville by a glassmaker who's been in business as long as Churchill Downs," Abbott explained.

The rectangle turnstiles were marble. We walked thru and headed for a set of elevators.

"Everything looks new."

"It is. Completed last year."

"What's that?" I stopped walking. In a dim room, banks of tiny booths with computer screens filled a large area. An excited crowd of people waited to enter the busy spot as others exited. Television monitors with speakers blaring hung from the ceiling.

"Booths to place bets on races."

"Do you bet?"

"No. I don't buy lottery tickets either."

"Hurry, you two." Kathy held the door of the elevator. "Pops and Joe will be wondering where we are."

The two men sat at a round table in a glassed-in, air-conditioned room overlooking the race track.

"I'm glad you got here, son." Pops waved as we approached.

"How much time before dinner?" Abbott asked his dad.

"Reservations at four thirty. Not long."

"I'm going to show Jenni the rest of Millionaires Row. We'll meet you at the entrance."

"Don't be late," Kathy called as we walked through the glass doors into the outside air.

Several people stood around the railings with binoculars and mint juleps. They were watching the activities going on toward the starting gate. Down below, the view afforded a panorama of the oval-shaped, dirt track. I saw the bleachers for regulars and standing admission. Across the racetrack, the winner's circle for the last race contained hundreds of rose bushes in a sea of red.

"Do all of today's winners get to go to the rose area?"

"No. Look down below us. The winner's circle for the other races is not nearly as elaborate."

"What time will the last race take place?"

"The Run for the Roses is at six fifteen."

"I understand your mother's comment on the infield crowd." Packed elbow to elbow, the mass of humanity seemed to flow in one continuous motion. "How can they enjoy the races?"

"Let me assure you, at this stage of the day, no one on the other side cares about races, horses, or roses."

"Why do they come?"

"For most, coming to the derby is a tradition carried through multiple generations—sorta like genetic characteristics."

"I understand the transfer of genes. What about the extended Kendall family? Why do they come?"

"We come for Pops. The church member who gave him the farm invites him and seven of his family to fill one of the tables on Millionaire's Row each year. Who comes with my grandfather is rotated so every member of our family has a chance to be special and enjoy the race in comfort. Do you see the gentleman in the top hat? The one in the navy suit and red tie?" Abbott pointed discreetly to the other end of our perch.

"Yes."

"He pays for two tables in the room behind us."

"How much does a seat at the table cost?"

"Don't ask. Be thankful for his benevolence. When Pops is gone, none of the family will come back." Abbott reached for my hand. "Come on. We don't have much time before dinner. There's something you need to see." We walked back through the glass doors of Millionaires Row to the elevator.

When we walked from the elevator, the dining room appeared on the left. "We'll eat here. The seating is members only—membership in the Turf Club. What I want you to see is at the other end of the hallway."

Behind glass panels, an artist had constructed a miniature model of the race track and stands, using myriads of colors—the whole thing in glass. A hundred or more three-inch, blown-glass figures cheered a race, and horses pounded down the track. "How beautiful," I exclaimed as I walked from one end to the other.

"You're beautiful." Abbott said, his eyes following me. "I love your outfit."

"Thank you." I looked down at my simple black dress with white trim and buttons. Kathy had advised me not to wear heels, saying my feet would be sore the next day. I'd put on black flats and carried a black purse.

"I especially like the black hat. Make it white and you'd have a halo around your head."

I turned from his gaze. The glass panels reflected the hat. Its felt body covered my head, rimmed my eyes, and partially covered my ears—perfectly offsetting my square, Tipton jaw. A rhinestone band, accented to one side by filmy feathers and ribbons, wrapped around the hat's body. Starched, mesh fabric with tiny ribs radiating from the top went to the brim's stiff edge. In white, the whole affair *could* pass for a halo.

I nodded my head and smiled as he came to stand behind me. "You're right."

"I like women who wear hats." His meaning was unmistakable.

"Abbott, Jenni. Are you ready to go into dinner?" The rest of the Milbern's stood behind us.

The spell broken, we both laughed.

Weep no more, my lady,
Oh weep no more today!
We will sing one song for the old Kentucky home,
For the old Kentucky home far away.

The strains of *My Old Kentucky Home* died away. The horses were readied behind twenty gates.

"Jenni, try these on for size." Abbott handed me a pair of binoculars. "They're yours—and the reason I didn't get here on time."

We stood at the rail outside of the glassed-in room. Pops sat in his wheelchair beside us along with the rest of the Milbern family.

"You didn't have to." I protested as he helped me adjust them.

He pulled another pair from his backpack. "I use them on the backstretch. Coming toward the finish line, I prefer the naked eye."

"Who's the favorite in the race?"

"Several of the horses are very good bets on winning—Brother Derek, Lawyer Ron, and Barbaro."

"Who are we rooting for?"

"I've been looking at Barbaro. He's undefeated coming into the race. Edgar Prado from Peru is his jockey. Prado rides winners."

"What color of silks is the jockey wearing?"

"Green body, blue sleeves, and blue hat." He looked through his glasses. "They're all in the gates."

The bell sounded. "They're off!"

The instantaneous roar from the crowd drowned out the blaring loud speakers for a second. I watched as the horses bunched together close to the inside rail. Clods of dirt flew into the air from the thoroughbreds hooves. They thundered down the first stretch, past our position in the boxes above, heading for the first curve.

"Barbaro's fifth," said Abbott. "See his colors on the outside."

I thought I saw his colors but couldn't be sure. "Who's in front?"

"Keyed Entry with Sinister Minister a close second. Listen to Durkin. He'll keep you informed better than I."

The derby announcer, Tom Durkin, kept up a running commentary on the race. "They're rounding the first curve with . . ."

I looked through my binoculars as the horses rounded the second curve and headed down the back stretch. The field positions of the leaders hadn't changed.

"They're rounding the third turn . . . Barbaro's making a move on the outside, comin' up fast. As they round the final curve, Barbaro take's the lead at the top of the stretch." The crowd roared approval.

I could see the magnificent bay horse in the lead. The three-year-old colt thundered down the stretch toward the finish line.

I jumped up and down, screaming like everyone else, cheering for Barbaro, oblivious to everything except the horse. "Go! Go!"

The electricity became contagious as the beautiful horse opened up a six-and-a-half-length, effortless lead and crossed the finish line. The millionaires along the rails congratulated each other. "What a race. What a race." I heard their exclamation again and again. Even Pops pumped his fist in the air.

Tears ran down my face. Peering at me, Abbott offered his handkerchief.

I bent down to talk to Pops. "That was some race."

I wasn't the only one in tears. I gave him Abbott's handkerchief. Could this be his last Kentucky Derby? I wondered if this thought made him sad.

Abbott insisted I ride back with him to Meadowview Stables. "We'll tour some more of Churchill Downs while the traffic thins a bit." We sat at our round table waiting for the others to exit the room. Because Pops rode in a wheelchair, the other occupants in the room let him go first.

"Won't you get to your condo really late if you take me home?"

"Home, Miss Loften?" Abbott raised his eyebrows.

"You know what I mean."

"I'm sure Pops would like to keep you." He grinned, showing his almost dimples.

"He's a sweet man. I love him dearly."

"I see." Abbott cleared his throat and took my hand. "Let's take a last look at the track before we try the elevator."

"Are you killing more time?"

"Yes."

We rose, went out the glass doors, and watched the crowd for several minutes as it disappeared under us. A lone hawk flew into the rafters above the moving mass. I pointed to the gray bird.

"Sad part of nature. Birds of prey love doves and other feathered creatures. If you stay here long enough, you'll see a dove caught in the claws of a hawk," Abbott said.

The bird left its perch among the rafters, catching a current of air and soaring above the track.

"Amazing something so deadly could be so graceful when flying."

Abbott nodded. "Okay. Let's try the elevator."

We left the elevator in front of the Horseshoe Bar. "I'm going to take you to the schooling stalls. We passed them as we came in earlier."

He explained that the twenty horses, their owners, trainers, jockeys, and support people were the only ones allowed in the rectangle where the horses grouped to be led to the race track. Around the closed off area, thousands milled and gawked at the horses and celebrities before the animals were led through a tunnel to the race track.

We took escalators upstairs to the room where jockeys weighed in. Abbott peeked into the room next door. "Come. Take a look at the jockey room. Here they change into their silks."

"Do they race in more than one each day."

"Jockeys can ride in every one, changing silks for each horse ridden." We walked around the room. "Would you like to visit the gift shop before we leave?"

"Sure."

Down the escalators and a short walk across the courtyard brought us to the glass doors of the shop. "Take your time. Traffic will be much better the longer we wait."

When we came out of the gift shop, the sun hung low in the west. "Jenni, would you like something to drink. We'll take it with us."

"A cola would be great."

We sipped our drinks as we exited the race course gates.

Three blocks from the entrance to Churchill Downs, Abbott's SUV sat parked in the yard of a row house. We waved at the homeowner, got in, and, bouncing over the curb, drove onto Central Avenue. A right turn on Third Street and several blocks later, we made our last cut onto Interstate 264, heading east from Louisville.

"I love this time of year and this time of day," Abbott said as we breezed along. "Right about now, I'd be walking around my condo's greenway. Next to swimming, walking relaxes me—keeps me from wondering about life and what's around the corner."

"It seems to me your life is pretty well set. I can't imagine what you'd be concerned about."

"I do a good job of appearing established, settled, under control." He paused.

"What distresses you?"

"I haven't been able to put a finger on what's eating me. Or maybe I'm in denial. Possibly I do know the problem—just don't want to admit it."

I felt his inward struggle. "Have you talked to Pops? He's a wise old man."

He nodded his head, agreeing with me. "You're right. I should talk to him." Abbott changed the subject. "You leave tomorrow?"

"Yes. I'll find going hard. Your family has welcomed me with open arms. I've not had time to think about home."

"You'll forget your Kentucky friends when you leave."

"No. That's not going to happen, but I will be busy. B.J.—my best friend—is getting married in a month. My Mom and I plan on giving her a shower before the wedding." I told him all the details of B.J.'s romance with Troy and her wedding plans.

"You're her maid-of-honor?"

"Yes." I drew in some air and let it out slowly, realizing the day had taken its toll on my energy.

Abbott reached over and turned on the radio. Barbra Streisand's sultry voice came from the speakers singing, *The Shadow of Your Smile*. The song continued with Abbott joining the famous singer on the last few lines.

Abbott reached for my hand. "Are you tired?"

"A little."

"The seat leans back. We're still an hour from home."

I pulled off my hat and put the seat back. I looked out the side window. The warm lights of houses moving beside the road were mesmerizing. I dropped off to sleep during the last fifteen minutes of our drive.

"Jenni, we're here." Abbott was gentle as he helped me from the car to the door, which stood open. "I'll see you in the morning. Go on in."

"You aren't going to work tomorrow?"

"I'm going in at noon."

I stepped through the opening and he shut the door quietly behind me.

I stood on the other side, realizing that Abbott intended to tell me goodbye. What other words would he speak? I walked down the hallway and got ready for bed. Sleep didn't come easy.

21

Streaming rays of the sun came through the windows of my bedroom the next morning. Monday. The day I would head home. Rubbing the sleep out of my eyes, I blinked at the bright light.

I looked at the clock—seven thirty. I'd overslept. Forgotten to set the alarm. What would Pops think? I hopped out of bed, slipped my dressing gown over my long-tailed nightgown, and headed for the bathroom. Brushing teeth, washing face, and combing my hair were completed in record time. Pops was sitting in his lift chair reading the morning's paper. He didn't usually sit there.

"About time you got out of bed." He laughed, looking over the top of his paper. "Abbott and I thought you'd sleep all day."

"Abbott?" That answered my unspoken question. My senses went from almost calm and peaceful to on the alert.

"Yes, Abbott." His voice from the kitchen. Then he appeared holding an egg turner and grinning from ear-to-ear. "I almost came to see if you'd expired overnight—maybe the Churchill Downs experience proved too much for you. But I heard you in the bathroom."

"I did forget to set the alarm, something I don't do very often—and on my last day. I'm so sorry." I went over to kiss Pops on the cheek.

"The bacon is frying, Ms. Loften. How do you want your eggs?" Abbott disappeared into the kitchen, and I followed him.

"Do you know the difference between sunny-side up and over easy?"

"Yes."

"I'm impressed," I teased him.

"Well?" He turned the bacon in the pan, splashing grease on the stove, which he quickly removed with a swipe of a wet dishrag from the sink. "How about your eggs?"

"Over easy—no runny whites, please."

"My sentiments exactly, but I believe that's over-medium." Abbott maneuvered the turner, moving the bacon from the skillet to a paper napkin. He cleaned the pan, melted butter, and added two eggs. "Bread is toasting in the oven."

I turned around and saw the table set for one. He'd eaten with Pops.

I ate by myself in the kitchen. The drone of the men's voices came from the other room. When I finished, I washed the dishes in the sink and left them on the countertop to dry.

"Guys, I'm going to get dressed. Shouldn't take long."

I returned to the living room in a navy, knit pants suit—one I decided would be comfortable on the return trip home. Behind me in the bedroom, my suitcases waited to be closed after a last inspection of my end of the house.

Abbott stood as I entered. "I believe you left this in my vehicle." He held out my black hat.

"Yes. I did." I took the hat, placed it in the middle of the hall leading to my wing.

"What time are you leaving?" Pops asked.

"Before lunch. I'll eat on the road. I feel like I've been gone a year."

"I can't tell you how I've enjoyed having you. This old house will be so lonely without my Jenni."

I went to him, my heart swelling with emotion. He leaned toward me as I knelt on the floor before him. His thin arms drew me to him and mine curled around his neck. "Oh, Pops. I'm coming back to see you, and I'll call every week to check on you—maybe more than once if I get bogged down in my writing." Tears welled in my eyes.

"Then I pray you'll stay in the bogs. Come soon and stay another two weeks." He patted my head and kissed me on the cheek.

"Okay, you two. Enough mush. I brought my sax to cheer you up."

I turned around and sat on the floor at Pops's feet, still holding his hands.

Abbott raised his instrument from the floor beside the television and tore into his rendition of *Yakety Sax*, using gyrations of the hips and jerking shoulders to match the music. Pops and I went into gales of laughter at his antics. When he finished, we all gasped for air.

Pops made the first statement. "Boots Randolph's most famous composition. I always loved to hear him play."

Abbott patted his saxophone. "I'm going to put 'er in the car." He hurried through the front door, leaving it open.

"Pops. There's one more question I need to ask you."

"Go ahead, child."

Abbott returned as I asked, "You said something occurred during World War II that changed the course of your life. What happened?"

"Abbott knows this story well. In the late thirties, Europe's continent turned upside down with Hitler's invasion of Germany's neighboring countries. Our country remained out of the conflict until the invasion of England seemed imminent. Nothing our allies threw at the Nazi's stopped them. If America helped, more men needed to be trained for combat. The United States started the draft. I decided to volunteer before my number came up—summer of 1940. I've never been known as much of a letter writer, so when I went into basic training, my letters to Maddie were sporadic, but I did write."

Abbott added, "Pops signed for three years in the infantry. Congress kept extending the service times and finally declared war in December 1941. After the declaration, volunteers or draftees were required to stay until the conflict ended."

Pops continued. "I entered the army because I hoped teaching positions would be available after I served my three-year tour of duty. That's what I wrote to your grandmother."

"My grandmother wrote you letters?"

"Yes. Then they stopped, and I didn't know why. I couldn't find out because my unit was sent to Europe."

"You came home in 1945?"

"I served five years." Pops nodded and continued. "December three years after volunteering found me at the Battle of the Bulge. I should have been mustering out, but, instead, my one responsibility in life had changed to killing people. Survival—the uppermost word in my mind. I got lost in a world of blood and death as our field artillery unit and the infantry shot their way across Belgium.

"I'll never forget the town of Malmedy. About one hundred men of Battery B of the 285th Field Artillery Observation Battalion advanced south of this small town in Belgium. Being the last of my former unit, I joined with this great group of soldiers. We were warned of Germans in the area and urged to detour, but our captain and command decided to continue with their orders and not revert from the road we were on.

"We came under the fire of a large Panzer Division. They were on the move west toward Allied lines and commanded by Joachim Peiper. We returned fire about Baugnez Crossroads—just southeast of Malmedy. Outnumbered by thousands of Hitler's elite personal guard, we surrendered.

"What happened next is much disputed, but I'll tell you my story. We were herded into a field surrounded by hedgerows. The snow came to my boot tops and the cold wind caused as much shivering as our situation. The German troops kept tramping toward the bridges they'd been ordered to secure and hold, passing our position until the last unit stood before our one hundred or so men. We'd heard of atrocities associated with Peiper's troops. They didn't take prisoners.

"With the first bursts of machine gun fire, several Americans broke from the huddled men and ran for the hedgerows, providing target practice for the Germans with rifles. Others started falling around me. One, a tall, heavy sergeant, staggered backward, knocked me down, and fell on top of me.

He died. Another man fell over his legs. Two more fell like cordwood beside him. I became lodged under the dead and dying men—hidden and pinned in the snow with one arm free enough to move the cold, wet fluff from my nose and make a hollow for my face.

"When I lifted the jacket sleeve of the dead sergeant, the eyes of a fellow soldier stared back at me. He curled his mouth into a slight smile.

"'Are you hurt?'" I whispered to him as volleys of gunfire continued. 'Side and leg, I think.' He groaned and moved his legs. I put my finger to my mouth. 'Be still. We might get out of this. I'll help you.'

"German soldiers moved through the downed men. I heard single gunshots. They grew closer. My friend jerked in a spasm. A dark shadow covered him, and the butt of a gun came crashing down on his head—once, twice, three times.

"I closed my eyes to the sight of blood spurting from his head. Tiny, red droplets in the snow. I thought I was next. Then I heard orders shouted from the road. The crunch of receding feet. When the sound of grinding tanks and truck motors could no longer be heard, I pushed myself from under the man who'd saved my life. Two men came from the hedgerows several feet away. We checked those lying in the snow. Two more had survived. After raiding the disabled mess truck assigned to our battery and stuffing our pockets full of food, the five of us started for our lines."

"You came close to dying." I reached for his hand and squeezed hard.

"Yes. While walking back to the American lines, I remembered sitting under my Grandfather Kendall's preaching. He often said God pulls us through certain death because He has something else needing to be done. I hadn't thought much about religion or Jesus Christ for some time—since Maddie witnessed to me at Cherokee. I told you that story. On the way west, across the rolling hills of the Belgian countryside, I accepted His salvation and whatever plan He had for me. God had rescued me from certain death. I owed Him my life. A changed man came back from the war."

"That's the understatement of the year, Pops." Abbott stood from the loveseat and stretched his arms over his head. "God called you to the ministry."

"Yes, He did." Pops looked at me. "Once on American soil, I went to see Maddie. She had two small children with her husband Charles—Jerry and your mother Karen." He turned his attention to Abbott. "Then I headed on to seminary. Met your grandmother and got married."

His grandson walked over and put a hand on the old man's sunken shoulder. "God has used your experience to bring many children into his fold."

Pops crooked his neck to see Abbott's face. "Wouldn't be surprised if He isn't still using me today." Pops turned his eyes on me. They were full of meaning.

"Are any of the men who escaped with you alive at present?" I asked.

"No. I'm the last one."

"May I help you up, Jenni?" Abbott held out his hand.

I scrambled to my feet. "The company's wonderful, but if I'm to get home before dinner, which my mother's cooking, I need to be going. Abbott, can you take me to the garage to get my car."

"I'll do better than that. If your bags are packed, we'll put them in my SUV and I'll drive you to yours and help you with the transfer."

"Okay. Give me a sec to check my bedroom for stray articles, and I'll have them ready." I almost stepped on my black hat on my way down the hall. "Here's your first passenger." I held my chapeau out to him.

Telling Pops goodbye wasn't easy. The tears rolled down my face as Abbott helped me into his passenger seat. "Here." He held out a handkerchief. "That makes two you have."

"I'll wash them and mail them to you. Why do you keep handkerchiefs on you? I didn't think men carried a hanky these days." I dabbed at my eyes.

"My family's full of weepers. They come in handy."

We pulled behind my car and transferred the luggage. The next moments turned awkward. My throat constricted. "I guess this is goodbye."

"Jenni, I'll never say goodbye to you, and don't you say it to me. Call me when you get home. The plan is to know you arrived safe and sound." He held out his hand.

I put mine into his.

With a sudden movement, he circled me in his arms, pulling me tight into an embrace. His low, gruff voice whispered in my ear, causing my aching, traitorous heart to yearn for—yes, declare him its ruler.

"Oh, Jenni. I feel like I've known you forever. These two weeks have been the best of my life. I'm going to miss seeing you—miss knowing you're only minutes away."

"Leaving is hard on me too."

"My feelings might be more than friendship. How would you feel about that?"

His carefulness touched me. He didn't want to get hurt. Neither did I, after guarding my heart for so many years. "Abbott, I feel the same. My heart hurts when I think we might never see each other again."

"Then we'll have to see each other again."

"Yes. When?"

"Two weeks, maybe three?"

"We'll talk on the phone."

"Everyday?" he asked.

"Yes. I'll call tonight."

He kissed me, his lips lingering on mine and then moving with small delicate kisses to my forehead, eyes, and cheeks—returning to a mingling of our lips together.

"I'm already waiting for your call." He grinned, showing his almost dimples.

"Silly, let me go."

Another dip of the head and short touching of lips and Abbott opened my car door. "I'll see you soon."

I turned to slip inside, glancing toward the cottage through the trees. I could have sworn I saw the front door shut. Had Pops seen our kisses?

22

May 18, 1939—Maddie

I looked over my darkened, third-grade classroom. It was the last day of the school year, and my students—twelve boys and sixteen girls—were crowded together in a makeshift room only large enough to hold twenty.

Outside, the rain came down in a deluge. The mountain storm dropped buckets of water and overran the gutters on Walland School. The lightening, which had taken out the electricity, popped and roared over the protruding hillside. The branches of a tree scraped the side of the white-frame building, and the flashing light display threw shadows over the opposite wall.

"Hey, Maddie. Whaddaya think about this?" Sybil's unexpected voice at my elbow caused me to jump.

"You scared the life outta me." I turned and looked into a set of baby-blue eyes.

"Sorry. I thought you heard the door open. You moved." Sybil spoke quietly, her mouth pulled into a pout at my scolding.

"I moved because the lightnin' musta hit a tree outside or somethin'. What are you doin' here? Your students will be runnin' around like monkeys."

"You know I don't like storms. Especially when the power goes."

I put my arm around her shoulder. She pulled her arms across her chest and clasped her hands under her chin, hugging herself. This wasn't the first time she'd run to my room for moral support during a storm.

"There's an extra chair next to my desk." I used my arm to guide her there. "Sit here." I gently pushed her down to the flat-bottomed, straight-backed seat identical to the one I utilized and patted her strawberry-blonde hair. She tugged at a curl behind her ear.

I knew Sybil shouldn't stay away from her classroom. One of the rules our school principal posted conspicuously in his office read *NEVER* LEAVE YOUR STUDENTS ALONE. She often stretched that rule.

"Children. Put your heads down, and let's have quiet time. The storm will pass. School will be out in an hour."

They did as told. I smiled, realizing some of my students hadn't always obeyed. Even Matt McDonald's head rested on his hands. I walked over to him. "Matt. Please watch over the others. I'm going to walk Miss Blackman back to her class."

"Yes, ma'am. You can count on me."

I couldn't always depend on him. At the start of the school year, Matt proved to be the oldest, tallest boy in class—and the biggest problem. His reputation preceded his red head. Among his greatest joys were picking on the younger children and disrupting class. Those first weeks, slithering snakes, a jar full of grasshoppers, and bats joined the students in my classroom. When he realized his antics didn't upset me, I gained his respect.

"Come on, Sybil. I'll walk you to your room."

"Can't I stay here?" she pleaded, getting up from her chair.

"No. The principal may check to make sure we're safe. You don't want to get written into his daily logbook."

"Aw, he wouldn't do that. My father would have a short talk with him."

"Come on. Fathers can't solve all problems." I gave her a nudge out into the hall.

We walked four doors down a narrow hallway to a spacious corner room with windows on two sides—one of the most desired in the building. The Blackmans pulled strings to get their daughter a teaching position after she graduated from Maryville

College. I think I may have been included in the deal. We both came to Walland.

The sound of running feet and scraping desks emanated from the room. Flushed faces and anxious eyes greeted us upon entering.

Putting my hand up to my mouth, I said to Sybil, "Think they had a guard posted?"

"I wouldn't be surprised."

We walked in the open door. "Your students can still see to read or study," I observed.

"Yes, but the lightning flashes."

I shook my head and grinned as I stepped to the front of her room. "Some people want the moon too," I muttered to myself. My best friend could be so exasperating. I turned to the students. "Everyone, please." Sixty eyes turned in my direction. "Pull your desks away from the windows and up toward teacher's desk." More scraping of desks and excited movement of bodies.

"Maddie, what are you doing?" Sybil asked.

"Don't you have a book you can read?" Fourth grade students loved a good story, and our small library had several books containing short stories. "I'd be reading to my class if my room wasn't so dark."

She went to a tall shelf behind her desk and selected a blue book with gold lettering. "I don't know why I didn't think of reading." Going to the front of her desk, she leaned back against the edge and turned to a page.

Pausing in the doorway to her room, I heard her expressive voice start the story. Sybil excelled at our college drama productions. I turned to walk down the hall and met the principal coming toward me.

"Miss Blackman. Is she all right?"

"Yes, sir."

"Knowing her unease when storms blow through, I came to check on her." He often socialized with the Blackmans in Maryville.

"She's reading to her class."

As we approached my room, a flash of light lit up the dark hallway. "This is a bad one," he said.

"Yes. The worst in the three years I've been here. Do you agree?" We stood at the door to my classroom.

"I think the lightning struck something. Hope its aim wasn't at a house in the vicinity. Hate to see a student's home destroyed by fire."

I nodded my head and peeked in my room. My students were still having quiet time. "Sorry I left."

He waved his hand in a gesture of dismissal. "Miss Whitehead, I appreciate you helping Sybil. I understand why you left, and you weren't gone but a few minutes." His deliberate look I understood. My name wouldn't be entered in his daily notes. He turned to leave.

"Thank you, sir."

"Matt informed me of his duties while you were gone. Did a good job too." He waved at the young man who raised his hand.

I nodded, then returned to my classroom.

I walked to my desk and sat down, needing some quiet time myself. My arm looked inviting, asking me to rest with my students. I didn't. I looked over my classroom, thinking this was the last day they'd be in my class. My students. I'd grown to love each of them—to know this cove they lived in, respect it and their families.

Each year, Smoky Mountain storms released pent-up anger on the mounts and valleys of East Tennessee. Trees whipped in the wind and rain lashed houses and land. The water washed the air, clearing the sky of dust, making the landscape vivid, bright, and expectant.

Years ago, I had dubbed Little River the storm's cousin. It received the torrents of water raging between its banks, roaring as the watercourse ejected the stream onto the Tennessee Valley flatlands clear to Chattanooga. Days later, the torrent would settle—timid and contented as a sheep in a fenced, green pasture. My students lived in this environment that alternated between explosive and serene, accepting the good and bad as part of life.

The small town of Walland was a river community, stretching two miles along the waterway in each direction and into the coves from the school. Once a flourishing company town, now the men caught buses long before the sun rose over Chilhowee Mountain and rode to work at the Aluminum Company of America, twelve miles away. The day shift returned before school let out in the afternoon.

After the Civil War, the ravaged South didn't bounce back. Emotions ran high when northern businesses tried to locate in the lower states. But East Tennessee, mostly pro-union, welcomed businesses from the North. With hydraulic power in plentiful supply, the turn of the century brought the lumber trade, dams on the Little Tennessee River, and Alcoa. Money and schools raised the quality of life in the mountain communities.

"What Depression?" my policeman father often said to Mama. We had fat cattle in our fields, egg-laying chickens, and an acre planted in vegetables for the winter. Didn't the Bible say, *by the sweat of your brow?* Everyone in our family worked hard. If there was a depression, our family scarcely knew it. This was not true for some of the river people.

Walland Primary and High School received the children from the families living along Little River and in the coves. A few, rooted in the shallow soil found in some areas, struggled to make ends meet. Matt McDonald's family was one of them.

Our county educational system encouraged visiting each student's home. Not until I visited Matt's did I understand his aggressive, but not destructive, behavior toward his peers. Until then, I'd wondered why he wore the same clean, ironed shirt and britches each day to school.

His father had worked at Schlosser Leather Company until a fire destroyed the facility. The stock market had crashed two years prior, and the owners decided not to rebuild. While working at the tannery, Mr. McDonald and his family enjoyed a good living. On Saturday, he'd sell honey from his beehives at a stand along the rock road from Walland to Townsend. My father often stopped to buy a jar, saying his bees made the best in the area.

To visit many of my students, I walked swinging bridges across Little River. These were plank affairs with one-and-a-half-inch cables slung in an arc over the rushing water. Large lintels with support posts on each end held the walkways. To get home, some of my students would trust their lives to one of these pathways. I wouldn't want to cross one with raging water rolling downriver underneath.

On the occasions I visited my students, I stayed overnight at Chilhowee Inn. The columned residence had attached a framed, two-story sleeping building on the main road through Walland. Put up by the tanning company to house the mill's visitors, the lodge now served customers coming to vacation in the Smokies. It was here that I ate my evening meals, if not with a student's family.

"Teacher." Matt's tap on my arm brought me fully awake. I'd dozed off after putting my head down with the rest of the class. The lights were back on.

"Yes, Matt."

He pointed to a large clock on the wall. "Teacher, school's out."

I grinned at him. "Thank you, Matt. I'll miss you this summer."

He smiled back. "Yeah, you will. I've helped you a lot this year."

"You sure have. I wish you could be in my class next year, but Miss Blackman will appreciate having your help. She's looking forward to your assistance."

"She said that?" Matt's eyes and face lit up with pleasure.

"Guess we'd better get everyone ready to leave."

Matt started back to his desk.

"Oh, Matt. I have a bundle for you in the clothes closet. Be sure and get it when you leave."

"Yes, Miss Whitehead."

I gave my farewell speech. Several of my students appeared close to tears as we gathered books, papers, and pencils. "Come and say hello next year."

The final bell rang on my third year at Walland School. Tomorrow, Sybil and I would come and straighten our rooms, celebrate by eating lunch at Chilhowee Inn with the other teachers, and start preparations to travel to Cherokee, North Carolina—our fourth year of waiting tables at the Waltzing Bear Motor Inn and Restaurant. But this year our work schedule would be interrupted about half way through. We'd planned a trip to the 1939 New York City World's Fair. King George and Queen Elizabeth were visiting. I was excited on both accounts.

23

"Maddie, your ride is here." Edie poked her head into the bedroom we shared. My sister and I were exact opposites. Edith Whitehead had blond hair and blue eyes. My face, framed by short, dark-brown waves, held brown eyes. Her side of our clothes closet looked neat. Mine jumbled. She excelled in sports. I liked French and English. And at twenty-five, I bested her by six years.

"Here. Carry my large suitcase. I'll get the smaller one, my hat box, and my train case."

"Does this bag go?" She pointed to a leather bag next to our dressing table.

"Yes, my shoes." I checked out my navy traveling suit in the mirror, which was fastened to the back of the bedroom door and pushed my blue, straw hat with yellow daises and band firmly on my head. The navy, tie-up shoes with short, square heels were practical and new. A quick glance around the area, and I walked into the living room.

Edie preceded me. "Ugh. What do you have in here? The kitchen sink?"

I giggled. "No. Hurry silly. Don't want to keep Mr. Blackman waiting."

"I wish I could go to the World's Fair. I'd love to see the Empire State Building and the Statue of Liberty."

"I'll send you a postcard from New York."

Mama stood outside talking to Mr. Blackman. She opened the screened front door for us and we stepped out onto the wooden, wrap-around porch of our Union community home. It was located three miles from downtown Maryville and two miles from Maryville College, where Sybil and I had graduated three years ago. The screen door slammed behind us.

Mama wiped her hands on her flour-sack apron. Her brown shirt dress with white polka dots came down below her knees. She looked a lot like me, but her dark hair had turned gray at the temples. "Here she is, Mr. Blackman." She took the largest suitcase from Edie and picked up a market basket from the seat of a wicker chair on the porch. A dish towel covered the contents. "Food for your travels, Maddie," she said.

"Thanks, Mama." She never failed to send enough for us all.

I stepped off the porch and waved at Sybil who sat in the backseat of Mr. Blackman's black sedan. The car stood under a huge oak on the circular, gravel drive at the end of our flagstone walk. She waved back as her father approached me. He wore a black suit and felt hat. "Maddie, do you have more luggage?"

"No, sir. That's all."

Edie, Mr. Blackman, and Mama lugged my suitcases to the car. I followed behind, carrying my coat and purse. The odor of something delicious came from the basket.

"Maddie, you'll be in the passenger seat."

I nodded and turned to my mother as my luggage disappeared in the car's trunk. "I'll miss you, Mama."

She put her arm around me and gave me a quick hug. The smell of the morning's fried bacon drifted from her clothes. "Three months will go by fast."

"I promised Edie a postcard from New York. I'll send you and Daddy one too."

"Don't worry about the postcard, although I'd like to get one. Keep yourself safe. Don't get into any dark alleyways or go into places where you might get into trouble." Her brown eyes snapped as they always did when giving orders. She reached up to pat one of my short stray waves into place.

I knew she didn't worry about me frequenting places where trouble could brew. My mother and father trusted me, raising me by biblical principles, which I honored. Sybil might be another matter, and she knew this.

I looked at her and smiled. "I understand your concern. I'll do my best."

"God go with you Maddie." Another quick hug and she turned toward the house with Edie on her heels. My younger sister couldn't wait to get me out of the house. We loved each other—we'd fight anyone threatening the other—but the prospects of a bedroom of her own for three months overjoyed her each summer.

Mr. Blackman started the car. "Are you ready to head for Cherokee?"

"The question is are they ready for us," said Sybil laughing.

He maneuvered the vehicle down the driveway to the main road, where we turned left. I looked past him at my home sitting under the tall oak trees with their huge trunks and long branches. These aged guardians of our farm, rooted long before our family existed, were the envy of our neighbors. As the car went forward, the morning mist and the rising bank blocked the sight. I turned my attention to the curvy road in front of us. In six hours, our group should arrive in Cherokee, North Carolina.

We made small talk as Mr. Blackman drove the snaky road through Hubbard community and Walland.

"Wave goodbye to school, Maddie." Sybil waved and laughed as we passed the cutoff road leading up the hill. The prospects of getting out from under her parents' watchful eyes always made her happy.

One mile above the school, we rounded a curve. Being Saturday, Matt's father sat by his honey stand, near a swinging bridge over Little River. Mr. Blackman slowed, pulled past the stand, and stopped.

"McDonald has the best honey in Blount County. I need to buy now. Dark'll set in before I come through tonight."

"That's what my father says too." I hopped out to greet the older man. Matt and his mother came across the swinging bridge. Two days after Thursday's raging storm, Little River still ran swiftly, but within its banks. Mrs. McDonald carried her husband's breakfast and lunch.

After depositing her basket of food inside his booth, Matt's mother came to stand beside me. She spoke in a soft whisper. "Miss Whitehead, thanks for your bundle. I'm already making good use of the items." She swished the tail of her skirt, and I recognized the cloth my Mama had sewn last week on her new sewing machine. She'd made her a brand-new skirt instead of sending her a used article. "Your mama's a good'un."

"Yes, she—"

A whine from down the road we'd come on made everyone turn to stare. A van truck swayed around the last curve, kicking up a cloud of dust from its rear wheels. Black letters on the side read RYETON BROS. HARDWARE.

Mr. McDonald spoke first. "It's the travelin' hardware van from Ryeton's. The brothers decided to try the same idea of a rollin' grocery store. See if'n they can make enough money to be profitable."

A tall, thin, dark-headed, young man jumped from the cab and came around the front to shake McDonald's hand and Mr. Blackman's.

"Charles, how are you? Let me introduce you to my daughter, Sybil, and to Miss Whitehead."

I looked into clear-blue eyes set in a long, thin face. He smiled slightly as I greeted him. "Pleased to meet you, Mr. Ryeton."

"Girls, we'd better go if we're to make Cherokee this afternoon." Sybil's dad steered us back to the car. He shut the door after we climbed inside.

"He's cute, Daddy."

"And eligible. He and his brother seem to be doing well with the hardware store."

"He looked like he could use a good meal." I volunteered. Mr. Blackman climbed in the driver's side and started the car.

"Daddy, let's take him out to eat when I get back after summer vacation."

"We'll see," he said, letting the brake off and continuing up the road.

At Townsend, we passed the office and almost empty buildings of the Little River Lumber Company. The company sold around seventy-five thousand acres and miles of discontinued railroad bed to the new park.

From Townsend, the road took us up the dismantled train track's bed. The gradual incline made a wonderful, graveled highway into the new Great Smoky Mountains National Park, saving the nation several thousand dollars and much labor.

The road followed Little River under Indian Head to Elkmont where the intricate stonework of the Civilian Conservation Corps covered the stream's turn to the right. If not for the meal Mama fixed, I'd have suggested turning and eating a delicious dinner at the Wonderland Hotel.

We passed through busy Fighting Creek Gap. Several cars in the parking lot meant people were hiking to Laurel Falls. On our last trip, Mama packed a picnic basket, and my family sat on the slippery rocks, craning our necks to watch the white shimmering water gush over the upper edge and fall in glittering droplets into the pool below, only to plunge again into a deep ravine and disappear. The roar was deafening.

At Sugarlands Visitor Center, Sybil's father pulled off the road and parked in front.

"You have ten minutes for the comfort station, and this bus'll move out of the parkin' lot without you," Mr. Blackman threatened. "We'll stop again at Newfound Gap and eat our lunch. I sure hope traffic isn't lined up clear to the Chimneys. Saturday's are always subject to tie-ups."

Compared to the outhouses most people still used in Blount County, the indoor plumbing of the park's new comfort stations were a wonderment. The Blackmans had an indoor bathroom. We did not. Sybil and I stood before the white sinks to wash our hands.

"Charles Ryeton is a swell-lookin' fella."

"Sybil, all you think about is men."

"Not true. I think about other things."

"Like what?"

"Like we'd better hurry back to the car or my father will be gone without us." She flew out the bathroom door, and I took off behind her. We raced for the sedan, laughing as we went.

The traffic snaked up the road a mile from the top of Newfound Gap. Part of the trouble came from a bear with two cubs, who'd displayed her foraging skills by turning over a park trashcan and strewing its contents over a roadside picnic area. Gawker's pulled off the road and blocked cars coming from both directions. A park ranger broke up the jam.

Another hold-up occurred at the gap. CCC workers in blue denim, along with various pieces of equipment, cleared part of the parking area to erect a permanent stone dais for the park's dedication next year. President Roosevelt intended to come.

We ate Mama's lunch sitting on the stonework rimming the parking area, our feet dangling over nothing below. The view of layer beyond layer of blue mountains made our chicken salad, celery sticks, and fried pies taste much better.

"I declare, Maddie. Your mother is the best cook in Blount County. If she wasn't already married, I'd marry her." Mr. Blackman wiped his mouth on a napkin from the basket. "And, she thinks of everything." He waved the cloth in the air.

"She learned cookin' from her mama. Grandma Nan lives at Chilhowee. She still cooks on a woodstove. Says she doesn't want to change."

"Could I send my wife up there for lessons?"

I laughed. "She'd have to learn to clean rooms plus cook. Grandma runs a boardin' house. The revival preacher always stays with her."

"Sybil's mom could use a bit of teachin' in that direction too."

"Dad. Wait till I tell Mom what you said."

"No use stirring up trouble, girl."

The steep trip down the mountain from the parking lot proved to be as bad as the one driving up. We stopped often to let the brakes cool.

24

Cherokee Indian Reservation runs the length of the Great Smoky Mountains National Park on the eastern side. The only access to the park is at Oconaluftee. Mr. Blackman bypassed the comfort station at the park entrance.

"Girls, it's only minutes to the lodge," he explained.

Waltzing Bear Lodge and Restaurant sat under the shadow of huge sycamore trees next to Oconaluftee River. A rambling edifice of huge building timbers and well-known cuisine, the summer months saw the rooms and restaurant full to capacity.

Its owner, Johnny Raintree, a full-blooded Cherokee, could pass for a much younger man than his forty-eight years. He stood on the porch in front of check-in as we pulled to the curb. "Look what the cat's drug in," he exclaimed, his grin wide in his handsome face.

"You better be glad Jack caught us." Jack, the old tomcat struggled to his feet from his basket on the porch. He stretched his front paws and headed straight for Sybil and me, purring as he approached.

"This place couldn't run without this duo working here in the summer," Sybil retorted, patting herself on the chest.

I picked Jack up. "Who's been feeding you? You're heavy as lead." I scratched his furry head.

Mr. Blackman busied himself with putting luggage on the wooden boardwalk. Johnny went to help.

"Guess you can take care of the girls from here." He shook hands with the owner. "Sybil, give me a hug goodbye."

Sybil preformed the duty as asked.

"I'll come and get you when summer's over. Give your Mother and me a call from time to time. You know how she worries when you're out of sight." Mr. Blackman started the car and waved as he left. We watched him drive out of view, then turned around to talk to Johnny.

"Girls, I believe you know the system here. You'll start work in the morning, but, now, take the rest of today off."

"Is our room the same one?"

"Yes," he nodded. "Your uniforms are labeled in the back closet."

"Start at five in the morning?"

"Not a minute after."

Sybil and I shared a couple of twin beds in the attic of Waltzing Bear Lodge and Restaurant. The walls were finished head-high. Gables with windows on each end of the open area served to let the cool night air move from one end to the other. I placed my purse and coat on a chair next to the door, unpinned my hat, and looked around. Two small dressers and one full-length mirror made up the rest of the furniture. Pieces of wire strung between rafters served to hang clothing. The other six waitresses, all non-natives, had similar rooms in different sections of the lodge buildings. Those who serviced the guest bedrooms were employed from the residents of Cherokee.

Our bathroom necessitated a walk down the inside back stairs to the first floor where we and the other girls had the use of a large private room with tub, commode, and washstand. Separate, locked cubbyholes for personal items let us leave supplies downstairs.

I walked to my dresser and placed my hat on top. The room looked the same as last year. A bird singing outside the attic window caused us both to turn and grin.

"Looks like Mocker made it through the winter."

Sybil laughed. "Maybe he'll be too old to keep us awake singing half the night." The mockingbird's habit of a long, nighttime serenade kept the residents and attic sleepers from much needed sleep.

"We're goin' to find out. Think we should go ahead and make our beds?" I asked, turning from the window. I'd finished hanging clothes and filling my dresser with underwear, socks, and other necessities.

"No. Let's get out of here. Maybe Johnny will let us borrow his new Chevy convertible. I'd like to see what main street Cherokee looks like this year."

"What you really mean is check out the swells—see if any are interesting."

"Maddie, why don't you like men?"

"I do like men."

"You don't act as if you do."

"Come on." The best way to shut Sybil up proved to be immediate action.

Our joy ride down Cherokee's main street in Johnny's new car satisfied my companion's mind. Choices would be plentiful this year. She seemed intrigued by several men working four doors down the street from our restaurant.

"Stop here, Maddie. Let's see if any of last year's employees returned."

The store, White Feathers, contained every Indian craft known in the Cherokee nation—some expensive, handmade items, some manufactured, cheap junk.

We walked inside, I to look around, she to ogle and flirt with the salesmen. These were the times I was embarrassed to call her my friend. I steered away from her and nosed around in the leather moccasins.

"May I help you?"

His brown eyes were breathtaking—the color of sweetened ice tea. His dark, wavy hair, strong chin, and well-defined mouth were overshadowed by the broadest shoulders I'd ever seen. He smiled with a hint of dimples to the sides of his mouth.

"May I help you?" he repeated.

"I, uh, I'm only looking. House shoes, maybe." I didn't need house shoes. I'd brought two pairs in my leather bag.

"Moccasins do make nice soft ones. I've a pair myself. What size do you wear?"

"Eight, eight-and-a-half."

"You have big feet."

"What!" I never got angry, but this man's comment piqued and upset me. My feet weren't tiny like Sybil's, who often reminded me of this fact.

"Oh, I didn't mean—uh, that is to say . . ." He started laughing. "Let me explain. I work the children's sizes. Compared to them, you do have bi—*larger* feet."

I couldn't smile at his remarks. "Well, Chief Big Foot, I'll collect my friend and go." I walked stiffly over to Sybil, grasped her arm, and towed her through the entrance door. My forcefulness caused her to stumble on the one step into the street.

She corrected her staggering balance and called back to one of the men. "I'll see you tonight at the restaurant."

"Sybil, what have you done?" I asked when we got into the car.

"I have a date for supper, and he has a car. We're going riding after we eat."

"Do you know this man? Know anything about him?" I asked as I watched passing cars, preparing to back onto the street.

"How bad can he be if he works down the street from us? Anyway, I'm not a child. I can make my own decisions and see whom I wish."

I backed the car into the street.

"Sometimes I wonder."

"Wonder about what?"

"If you can make adult decisions."

"Oh, shush. You're such an old fuddy-duddy."

"Eat with him, but don't go riding until you know him better. Please consider my advice. Let's go back to the room. I'd like to stretch out before supper."

My afternoon nap left me refreshed. "Sybil, the clock says five. We need to clean up and go to early supper."

Sybil stretched and yawned. "What time?"

"Five."

"Oh dear, I told Ray I'd meet him at five thirty." She slung her long legs over the edge of her bed and headed for the stairs.

"I'll see you in the dining room." She started down the wooden stairs and called back, "Maddie, I won't go riding."

No need for me to hurry. The bathroom would be occupied until she finished. I walked to the end of the room and looked out the gable window. I could hear the squeals of children splashing in the shallow waters of Oconaluftee River. A fisherman in waders headed upstream in the shallows, his wet line shimmering in the afternoon sun as he flicked it over the water.

It seemed summer vacations started ahead of time this year. Earlier, when I gave Johnny the keys to his car, he said his lodge didn't have a single opening next week.

I went down the stairs and banged on the bathroom door. "Hey, shake a leg in there."

"Sure, sweetie. You got a problem?" The door opened and a thirty-something with streaked brown hair and red lips dressed in a waitress uniform came out.

The look on my face must have been hilarious. "I'm sorry. I thought Sybil . . ."

"Na, she's already in the dining room. Said to tell you she'd meet you there."

I pushed my hand in her direction. "Hi. I'm Maddie."

"Joyce June Jacobs from Atlanta, Georgia." She took my hand and then put up her hands to block the next question. "Don't ask. It's a family thing."

I laughed. "Do I call you Joyce?"

"Over my mother's dead body. No, everyone calls me Joyce June."

"I'm pleased to meet you, Joyce June. Are you here for the summer?"

"Yes. Guess we'll be working together. When do you start?"

"Tomorrow morning at five."

"Not a minute after." We said in unison and laughed. Joyce June headed for the dining room.

"See ya."

I freshened up and followed her. Sybil sat at a window table with access to the river scene below. Her friend Ray sat opposite. They were in animated conversation. I decided not to join them but headed for a secluded spot near the stairs to an upper banquet room. Waitresses often ate there when not on duty.

Joyce June appeared with her order pad and a glass of iced water.

"Hi, sweetie. What can I do for ya?" She craned her neck around, looking at the seam in her nylon stockings. "Can't ever get the confounded things straight." She whipped her body so her back faced me. "Are they okay?"

The left one had a rakish angle as the stocking disappeared underneath her white skirt. "The left side is a bit off. If you adjust the seam, you'll need to unhook your garter belt."

"Does the angle look really bad?"

"If you move fast, no one will notice."

"Thanks, Maddie. What can I get ya?"

"Meatloaf, mashed potatoes, and fried okra."

"What to drink?"

"Sweet tea."

"I'll have your order right out."

After Joyce June left, I had a chance to look around the room. The restaurant's ceilings were twenty-feet high with huge pine log beams holding the open rafters. Four huge posts—actually, tree trunks—positioned at fifteen-foot intervals in the center of the room, held the roof at the highest point. Rows of windows ran along the riverside.

On the end where customers found parking, windows sat on either side of the large stone fireplace. The glowing logs added warmth to the yellowish-brown interior. The side facing the road contained several intimate booths holding six people each. A glowing kerosene lamp above each booth provided lighting. The final end opened through doors into the office, gift shop, and hallway to guest rooms and stairs to upper lodging. Swinging saloon doors opened into the kitchen area.

I looked up as Johnny Raintree appeared from the office. "Maddie, can you use some company?"

I nodded. He always kidded me about getting married. His wife had been dead several years from a flu epidemic that ravaged the area.

He pulled a chair from the table, sat down, and looked around the room. "I see Sybil's got a friend. Starting early this year, isn't she?"

"She hasn't changed in the years I've known her. My mission in life is to keep her feet on the ground and head on her shoulders. Sometimes a hard proposition. I cringe to think what may happen if she really gets interested in one of her men friends."

"How about you? I don't see a ring on your finger. Is there still hope for me?"

I grinned at him. He had my greatest respect, but not an ounce of the kind of love he wished for. Not that he wasn't handsome. With his black hair and twinkling dark eyes, brown skin, and wide toothy grin, I wondered why he hadn't gotten remarried. With these characteristics and plenty of money, any girl with an ounce of sense should jump at him. I knew they had, but Johnny didn't want *any* woman. He intended to have the best.

"Hope springs eternal." I used my standard answer.

"I may not be kidding." His face looked serious.

I felt a flush of warmth. "Sure, and cows fly."

Not hearing the answer he wished, he laughed and changed the subject. "I'm in the process of building a new home off Paint Town Road. I'd like for you to see the place before you leave this summer."

"When would you ever stay there? You're married to this place."

"My son will take over in five years. I plan to travel—see the rest of the world. I enjoy my visitors, but my desire is to be one."

Thoughts of his son—Junior, we'd named him, flicked through my mind. He'd never impressed me with having his father's drive.

"I love traveling—new places, historical places." I thought of my future trip to the New York World's Fair.

"You see. We have something in common."

Joyce June interrupted the uncomfortable conversation by unfolding a food stand and tray by our table. "Meatloaf, mashed potatoes, and okra, sweetie." She sat the food on the table with a flourish, including the sweet tea. "Johnny, do you want something?"

"I'll have the same—looks like a good combination." He looked at Joyce June towering above him and winked.

"He's a lady's man, Maddie. Better watch him."

We all laughed at her comment. I knew she was partially right, but Johnny Raintree kept his distance. Somehow, I felt when he talked to me, the distance shortened.

25

The next morning, at one minute to five, Sibyl and I entered the dining room through the employee entrance. Dressed in new, white, shirtwaist uniforms with slate-blue, ruffle-edged aprons and a matching blue hanky in the shirt pocket, we picked order pads off the dessert counter, placed them in our apron pockets, and started filling glasses with ice and water. Within minutes, breakfast at the lodge buzzed like a beehive.

Sybil's friend, Ray, came in the door at seven o'clock with the other salesmen at White Feathers, including Chief Big Foot and someone I didn't recognize. Ray motioned at Sybil and Joyce June led the five men to one of her empty tables.

"Miss, I'd like another glass of water." I removed my gaze from the spectacle unfolding across the room, took the glass held toward me, and attended to my guest's wish.

"Sorry, I didn't realize you were out." I set the full glass before an elderly gentleman and his wife.

"Harold drinks two full glasses at the end of his meal," his wife volunteered. "Thinks the water is good for his health."

"I'll remember tomorrow," I promised the customer, who drained his second glass with loud gulps. "What's on your site-seeing list today?"

"We're heading for Newfound Gap. How long will the drive take?" Harold asked, putting his empty glass on the table. He put his fist to his mouth to cover a large burp.

"Plan on two hours to the top and two hours back. That'll give you time to stop at pullovers and take in the view along the road. Be sure and take your camera. You should be back in time for a late lunch."

"This is my wife, Adrienne. She wants to get in some shopping this afternoon. Can you recommend a good shop?"

"She sure can," a male voice behind me answered. I turned around to see Chief Big Foot at my elbow. He continued, "White Feathers is four doors down from the lodge. I'll be glad to wait on you. Name's Abbott Kendall. Do you have grandchildren? I work in the children's department."

"We do—have grandchildren that is. I was thinking moccasins. I hope you have a good selection."

I managed to keep from laughing. "Moccasins—yes, they do."

"Our choice is the best in Cherokee, and we have a large collection for adults." Abbott Kendall looked at me as if to make a point. His eyes twinkled with laughter.

I turned around and headed for the dessert counter to figure Harold's ticket, leaving Abbott to chat with my customer.

When I came back, he'd gone to sit with those at Sybil's table. I guess he didn't want to push his luck.

"What a nice young man. Says he knows you," Harold's wife took the ticket from my hand. "Where do we pay?"

"You'll pay in the office as you leave, and I don't know him very well." I flicked my eyes in his direction and met his gaze. My customers got to their feet and prepared to leave.

"Should I take a coat to the mountain top?" Adrienne stood.

"Yes, the wind blows and the air can be chilly this time of year."

"Maddie, I believe you should get to know your young man better."

I grinned at her. How did she know my name? Sybil, the chatterbox, to Abbott, of course. He'd asked to know.

I wanted to say he wasn't my young man. "I hope you'll sit at my table this afternoon."

"You can count on us."

I hurried to take orders from another table of visitors. This time, when I happened to look in Sybil's direction, Abbott smiled and nodded his head. I turned, ignored him, and tended to my customers.

The morning lull between breakfast and dinner afforded rest for everyone but the waitress on schedule who covered the slack period.

I heard Sybil before I saw her. She bounced into the attic room, took off her shoes, and flounced onto her bed.

"Whew. The first part of our first shift is over." She leaned down and rubbed her feet.

"Yes. We were busy."

"Did you see the men from White Feathers? Ray introduced them. Well, everyone worked there but one."

"Which one?"

"The tall guy with blond hair and the most wonderful eyes I've ever looked into—a blond, blue-eyed Clark Gable." Sybil rolled her eyes, grabbed the pillow on her bed, and gave its feathers a hug.

"Sounds like Ray has some competition." I shook my head, thinking here we go again.

After going to Atlanta to see the movie *San Francisco*, Sybil had gushed for months over its star, Gable. Then, last year, she grew infatuated with Errol Flynn, who starred as Robin Hood. She tended to go from one man to another. She'd find something wrong with Ray, and he would be history. "Where do the men live? Are they from North Carolina?"

"Kentucky. They all live in the Bluegrass State. Smiley and his cousin live in East Kentucky. Ray and his friend, Charles Roberts, live in Western Kentucky. I think Smiley has a crush on you."

"Who's Smiley?"

"You know, he's the one who spoke to you at breakfast."

"Ah, I believe his proper name is Abbott Kendall, alias Chief Big Foot."

"What do you mean by that?" Raised eyebrows accompanied the question.

"Private joke, friend."

"Ray's coming for early supper. We're going for a walk after work. Want me to get him to bring Smiley? We could make our stroll a foursome." She looked at me out of the corner of her eye with a sly smile.

"No!" I said, hoping my word contained enough force to be convincing. Sybil had a way of ignoring my wishes.

"Okay. You don't have to be so loud and hateful." She curled her mouth into a pout and sniffed.

"I'm sorry, Sybil. I wanted to make an impression, so you wouldn't forget." I changed the subject. "Do you like Joyce June?"

"Yeah. She'll be fun to work around."

"I like her too. I'll need someone to go places with, since you'll be dating Ray. She's from Atlanta. We might look her up the next time we go to a movie premiere."

"Sure, sure." Sybil turned over and closed her eyes to rest and dream about Ray.

26

My first week of work exhausted all my energy. On Saturday, I wanted nothing more than to put my feet up and relax. During the lull in the morning's work, I went into the office to stretch out in one of several padded, wicker chairs—feet on an ottoman and shoes off. The reception area's colors of green, white, and yellow cooled and refreshed my aching body.

Johnny gave me a smile. He stood behind the checkout desk with a visitor before him. I put my head back and watched the blades of the ceiling fan rotate in a slow circle. Joyce June came from the dining room, pulled up a chair, and sat down beside me.

"Sybil's not happy today," she observed, leaning in my direction. "She's too quiet—not smiling."

"I noticed. Did Ray come in this morning?'

"Come to think of it, he didn't show, but the others were at her table."

"Oh dear. Wonder what's with those two. I'd conked out by the time she got home last night. We didn't talk. She didn't move a muscle when I got up to come to work this morning." I pulled in a lungful of air and let it rush out my nose as the customer went out the door.

"I heard." Johnny stretched out in a third chair he placed next to me. "How long did this one last?" he said, grinning his handsome smile.

"Seven days."

He put his hand on top of mine. "I wouldn't worry too much. She'll have another man friend before the day's over."

"She does this a lot?" asked Joyce June.

"*Modus operandi* confirmed," Johnny said.

She leaned toward him. "What does that mean?"

"Means yes. Her method is to love them and leave them." Johnny looked at the door as a tinkling bell announced another customer. "Uh oh. Another checkout." He stood, stretched his arms, and hurried to wait on the man.

"I'd better go talk to her. See what's happened." Leaning over, I pulled my black shoes onto my protesting feet and tied the laces.

"Are you coming back?"

"No. If she's handling everything okay, I think I'll take a small walk."

"Do you mind if I go with you?"

"You're always welcome."

I headed down the short hallway to the dining room. Sybil's occupied tables had dwindled to one. I caught her at the kitchen door.

"Hey, friend. What's wrong in your life? You're too quiet."

She rolled her eyes at me. "I sent Ray packing last night. He won't be back."

"And he did what?" I leaned against the dessert case and waited for an answer. The best way for Sybil to get over her problem and smile again was to talk about it.

"Oh, the argument isn't important." She tugged at a lock of hair behind her ear. "He's not the man for me, and I told him so. Told him not to come back." She paused. "We didn't have much in common."

"I guess he's not *the* one."

"No." Sybil smiled at my bit of sarcasm. "I've got my eye on another of the men."

"Sybil, Ray's not even cold."

"Doesn't matter." She winked at me. "The other one's got a car, and he's interested and interesting."

"Is that the problem with Ray? He didn't have wheels?"

"He told me he did. He shouldn't have lied."

I looked at her. "I believe you're gonna survive."

"Of course. I always do." Sybil's nose turned upward as she tossed her head.

"Joyce June and I are going for a short walk. We'll be back by eleven." I stood erect and took some steps toward the office.

"Don't be any later. This place will start buzzing by then," Sybil called after me.

The office contained several people waiting to check out.

Joyce June saw me come through the door. "Ready?"

"Yes. Come on."

The outside air smelled of dust, river water, and exhaust fumes as we walked down the boardwalk in front of the Waltzing Bear. Cars traveled in both directions on the street. Hard to believe we were in an economic depression.

"The sun's rays are brilliant today," Joyce June remarked, looking into the sky at the white, puffy clouds and swinging her arms. With each arc, she clapped her hands together with a popping sound.

"Oh look! There's Chief Standing Deer." Joyce June exclaimed. The chief stood on the opposite side of the street in his feathered headdress. He wasn't a Cherokee Indian. They didn't wear feathers. We waved.

"I'm glad to get away from the odors of cooking food."

"Amen to that," my companion exclaimed. "What did Sybil say?"

I explained the situation to Joyce June. "She'll have another boyfriend by noon tomorrow—mark my words."

My last comment placed me in front of White Feathers. Abbott Kendall rushed from the store to join us as we walked.

"Good morning, ladies."

"Abbott, isn't this day just perfect," my Georgia companion exclaimed.

"It is now." Abbott looked at me with a deeper meaning. "Aren't you talking, Maddie?"

For a week, he'd come into the restaurant, speaking in passing but not imposing his presence on me.

"Mr. Kendall. Nice to see you," I said in response, stiff and unsmiling. Uncharacteristic of me. Why did he rub me the wrong way?

Joyce June glanced at me. "You two have a problem?"

"Seems that way. Although I've tried to apologize, Maddie's not forgiven me."

"Maddie, I can't imagine anything Abbott's done being so bad. He's such a nice young man. I wish I were ten years younger. Come to think of it, would you be interested in an older woman." She laughed, poking fun at me, but looking at him.

"You two. Guess the time has come to call a truce, but I warn you, Mr. Kendall . . ." I pointed a finger in his direction.

With a swift motion, he got in front of me and walked backwards. "Whatever I've done or will ever do to aggravate you, I'll apologize right now."

"Don't ever mention feet in my presence again. The next time I won't be so merciful." I grinned, dropping my hand to my side.

"The word f-e-e-t is forever banished from my vocabulary." Abbott bowed and showed his almost dimples. Mercy, he was good looking.

He continued to talk as I looked into his light-brown eyes. Liquid, transparent, almost as if I could see into his soul. I felt a connection.

"Maddie," Joyce June said. "Didn't you hear what Smiley asked?"

"What? I'm sorry. My mind was somewhere else. What did he say?"

"He asked if you're doing anything tomorrow. He has the morning off."

"Yes. I'm going to church at the Protestant mission across the river. Don't guess you'd be too keen about going, Abbott."

"You think I've never been to church?"

"Have you?"

"Yes. My grandfather preached many years at a small church in the Kentucky foothills—until he died. What time?"

"Nine thirty. The church service starts at ten."

"I'll be waiting for you at the front office." Abbott stopped and stepped to the side. "I'd better get back to work."

"We'd better do the same, Maddie." Joyce June and I followed Abbott down the walk.

The next morning at breakfast, I watched as Sybil's friendliness to Charles Roberts increased. His appeal—a magnetism enhanced by perfect good looks not seen in many males. What comment had Sybil made? A blond, blue-eyed Gable? My woman's intuition said he realized his attractiveness to women and exploited their vulnerability. Could he spell major trouble in the future?

I changed clothes after the morning rush. Checking my hat in the attic mirror, I hurried to the front office. Abbott sat in a wicker chair waiting on me. Johnny sat beside him. Both men jumped to their feet when I appeared.

Johnny spoke first. "I understand Smiley's going to walk you to church this morning. Good. I worry about you going through the short alleyway before you get to the bridge." He knew I always cut through to shorten the trip. "Young bucks like to congregate at the end, causing mischief."

"It's Sunday morning. They're recovering from last night's debauchery. I've never had trouble before," I said as he put his arm around me in a protective or possessive motion. Protecting me from what—the young bucks or Abbott? My shoulders twitched at his overprotective touch.

I glanced at Abbott, noticing his eyes widen at Johnny's action.

"There's always a first time, Maddie."

I walked away from his embrace to the door. "Ready, Abbott?"

Outside on the sidewalk, we headed north to a wooden bridge spanning the Oconaluftee River. Rain two days prior caused the water to jump and splash over the rocks as we crossed.

"Whoa. Slow down, Maddie. Are you going to a fire?"

We hadn't said a word since leaving the lodge because I trudged along in front of my companion, determined to leave looming problems behind.

"Sorry." I stopped on the bridge, and Abbott stumbled not to run into me.

"You got problems?" He grinned his disarming smile—the reason for his nickname. His brown eyes serious, questioning.

"Forgive me for hoofing it. I wonder about too many things happening around me."

"I'm a good listener."

"I'll figure them out myself. I always do."

He inclined his head, understanding the discussion of the subject ended and grinned again. "Do you go to church every Sunday? Sybil doesn't go? I asked her."

We continued our walk, heading up the road paralleling the riverbank. "Yes. I go, and Sybil doesn't. At home, our family walks if Dad's working."

"What does your father do?"

"He's a policeman with the county. He may become a guard at Alcoa."

"What's Alcoa?"

The questions came rapid fire. "Aluminum Company of America. The biggest employer in Blount County since the tannery burned and Little River Lumber Company shut down."

"Alcoa is a good place to work?"

"Yes. The employees make good money."

"What's the name of your church?"

"We're thinking Union or Grandview. The church is a small one, getting organized."

"Are you a member?"

"Not yet. My parents are. I'm a member at Red Top in Chilhowee, Tennessee. It's Primitive Baptist. My grandparents go there. That's where I surrendered my life to Christ in January several years past. They baptized me and my cousin Iris in Abram's Creek with snow on the ground. I almost froze to death." I shivered in the warm sun thinking about the experience.

"Do you follow Christ's teaching?"

"For many years. How about you? You sat under your grandfather's preaching."

"He died after I turned twelve. I don't remember going to the altar. I do believe in the Holy Bible—that it's God's word. Times were tough after Grandpa passed away."

"Did you and your family continue in church?"

"Pops never went to church again."

"Why not, if you'd always gone?"

"My father worked seven days a week to support his family. My brother's medical condition needed expensive medicine and care. He never went without."

"What did your father do for a living?"

Abbott hesitated. "Whatever a Kentucky man can do back in the Cumberland Foothills to make money."

He left his explanation with those few words, and I didn't feel the need to probe further.

We were at the small mission. A tiny cross atop the gable identified the building. From inside, the congregation sang "Shall We Gather at the River." Appropriate, I thought, for the location.

27

The afternoon lull between dinner and supper sometimes afforded the waitresses a chance to take a nap, especially during the week. We alternated these breaks.

Fridays, Saturdays and Sundays, the restaurant stayed busy from dawn to dark—except for the Sunday morning lull, when I went to church.

The following Wednesday after Abbott accompanied me to church, Sybil and I stretched out in our slips on top of our beds in our attic room. Both windows at the end of the two gables were wide open, and a breeze blew through the loft. Without the wind moving the air, our bedroom became hot and stuffy.

"Charles has offered to drive us to Asheville to catch the train to New York," Sybil gushed, then yawned.

"You know Johnny's supposed to take us. How do you intend to tell him?" My words bounced around and through the rafters where I watched a wayward wasp working at establishing a home. Relishing my prone position on top of my bed, I decided I'd handle him later with the swat of a newspaper.

"I thought you'd take care of the task. You're his special friend, aren't you?"

"Friend is all." I turned on my side, getting a better look at her questioning face.

"Are you sure he feels the same?" Sybil rested on her stomach, head on pillow, and turned toward me, kicking her legs in a slow arc.

"I'm sure he doesn't feel the same, but I'm discouraging him the best way I know."

"How's that?"

"By avoiding him as much as possible."

Sybil giggled. "Shunning never works. Makes men more interested. Remember, I tried the same method last year with the guy from Maggie Valley. He drove me crazy—the egghead."

"He turned out to be four years your junior and slightly nuts."

"Well, not seeing Johnny Raintree won't work. He's going to press his case. He's not getting any younger, and I believe the new house is a statement of his intent—he's building something you'll like. Mark my words, he needs a wife, and you may be his first choice."

"Hurting Johnny isn't a prospect I'd enjoy, but he doesn't get my hints and refuses to understand." I ran my fingers through the waves of hair on my head and patted the tresses back into place.

"What about Smiley? He's a swell guy. If I didn't have Charles, I'd go for him in a heartbeat. What shoulders he has—and beautiful eyes."

"I admit, Abbott's interesting, but I don't know enough about him to form an opinion. I can't make snap judgments like you."

"What do you mean snap judgments?" Sybil's eyebrows rose. I felt a pout coming on.

"You size people up in a hurry and either accept or reject them. I'm more cautious, preferring to interact over a period of time to decide their fate. I'm not saying your method is wrong. I don't operate the same way." The pout became more noticeable. "In other words, my friend, we are two different people with different characteristics and modes of selecting friends, and this is okay." I tried to explain without getting into the real details of our difference in selecting people for our inner circle. The one standing out being, Sybil looked on the surface. I looked into the person.

"For a minute I thought you were putting me down." The pout started to fade.

"Not at all." I could have added more words but decided not to dig my hole any deeper. I couldn't be Sybil, and she couldn't be me.

"Can you believe we leave for New York in a week?" Sybil's manner changed from pout to excitement. She pounded her bed with her fists. "I think I'll get my luggage and start packing." She made no effort to carry out her statement. If I knew her, she'd be throwing clothes in her suitcase fifteen minutes before we hopped in the car to leave.

"I can't wait to see the Trylon and the Perisphere." Everything I'd read in the newspapers throughout the year indicated the Trylon stood seven hundred feet tall and looked like an obelisk, reminding me of the Washington Monument in America's capital but much taller. Sybil and I had visited Washington D.C. after graduating from Maryville College and knew the memorial well. The Perisphere would be a huge round globe. Together they represented The World of Tomorrow—the fair's theme.

The exposition's organizers intended for the fair to put the Depression behind America's growing population, even though rumors of war clouded its future.

Sybil's response brought me back to earth. "Do you think we'll see the queen?"

"Supposed to," I replied. "Unless she and the king cancel their trip due to concerns for their safety or England's position in the war on the continent."

"Charles says there's talk of bringing back the draft. He's not for it."

"I've read about the likelihood in the paper. If it happens, many of our college friends will be called into service. My Uncle Dwight went to Europe after being drafted in the First World War. Daddy signed up. The government felt his job helping build dams for producing electricity in the South to supply aluminum war materials was more important. Mama didn't regret him not going. She prayed and worried each day about her brother. They were close in age."

My friend pulled in a load of fresh mountain air and released her filled lungs through pursed lips. "I don't want Charles to go," she stated flatly. "Something dreadful might happen to him." She said the words about her new boyfriend, but I knew who she worried about the most.

If Sybil thought beyond her own self, I found the act unusual, although she could be very generous to me. Our friendship started in the freshman year at Everett High School. The acquaintance continued in college. She became my earthly support when pneumonia took two of my closest siblings, both high school students who died within a month of each other. We graduated from college together and obtained subsequent teaching positions at Walland School.

She was funny and fun to be with. Exuberant and poutful. I loved her, although she could be exasperating. I'd learned to live with those instances.

A knock on our door announced Joyce June. "Maddie, you've got a visitor downstairs."

"Who is it?" A shot of adrenalin went through my body. I hadn't gotten over thinking the worst when unexpected visitors came my way.

"Smiley, of course."

"Ah, ha!" Sybil's unnecessary and loud exclamation caused me to jump.

Joyce June went into gales of laughter.

"Tell him I'm indisposed—whatever that means."

"You were perfectly well this morning at breakfast when he ate with us." Joyce June continued to laugh.

"Get out of bed, Maddie. Your handsome knight has arrived to take you away from all this. Better take advantage of the opportunity."

No use in arguing with Sybil. I dressed and followed Joyce June downstairs. Abbott waited in the dining room.

"I took a chance you might not be busy. I have an hour to walk . . . or talk." He held out his hands in a whatever-you-want attitude.

"Walk."

Abbott turned toward the office.

"No, this way." I lead him down the hall past the lodge rooms entrance and out a back exit so we didn't have to walk through check-in. "Fire escape for the employees," I explained as I took the ten steps to the ground behind the kitchen. We walked to the river and started upstream on a well-used trail.

"Maddie, do you ever get a day off?"

"I'm sure I could forget work for a day, but I'm here to toil and make money. Helps with extras during the school year."

"What extras?"

"Clothes . . . besides white waitress uniforms." I tugged at the skirt of the shirtwaist to make my point. "Trips to Nashville, Atlanta, and Washington D.C."

"Wow. What do you do on your trips?" Our hands brushed on the narrow path. Abbott intertwined his fingers through mine.

"Sight-see and go to movie premieres."

"Do you like movies?"

"Yes. We have a theater at home. Don't you go?"

"No. Money's tight, but that's not saying I wouldn't like to. Maybe I can visit you in Maryville, and we can see one together."

Screams from the river caused us to stop and check the origin. A father led his child into the cool water. The smiling child splashed the water with her free hand, resisting his efforts. No one needed to be rescued, so we walked on.

"What about the movies, Maddie?"

"I thought you didn't have a car."

"I can borrow one. Or I can ride the train to Maryville, and we can meet at the station. Is it far from your home?"

I shook my head. "That's a possibility. The station's about two-and-a-half miles. Not far to walk."

"Can you get off this week or next? I need to see more of the Smokies."

"There isn't much time. Sybil and I leave in a week for New York City. We're going to the World's Fair."

Abbott stopped on the trail, bringing me up short with his hand. "You're leaving me?" His eyes sparkled as he grinned. My heart skipped a beat.

"We'll be gone five days."

"I'll bet Johnny likes the idea of you being gone. What's with you and him?"

"Nothing's with us. He's my employer and we're friends, that's all." I bristled at his question and pulled my hand away.

"Ah, hit a sore spot, didn't I."

"We'd better turn around."

"Sorry. I seem to have a knack for irritating you. You have to admit I didn't mention f-e-e-t." He spelled the word and bent to look me in the eye.

I grinned. His manner disarmed me. "No, you didn't, so I guess I'm still speaking to you."

Abbott seemed satisfied with my reply. "You haven't answered my question. What about a day off?"

We walked in silence as I pondered his question. I had to admit, Johnny's obvious attraction caused a problem with the decision.

If I remembered this morning's conversation at breakfast, he intended to drive to Asheville next Tuesday afternoon. He'd be gone until late in the evening. "A day's impossible, but next Tuesday we might have some time in the afternoon to drive to Newfound Gap. The view from the parking area is marvelous. I'll clear the exact time with the girls. They'll need to cover for me." Checking with the waitresses was only a formality. We helped each other if one needed time off.

"Let me know in the morning at breakfast?" he asked

"Sure." We were back at the fire escape steps. I moved to the first one.

"See you then." Abbott tiptoed and kissed my cheek. He hurried away toward White Feathers before I could admonish him for taking liberties.

Inside the building, I thought about our time together. He did seem nice. Not like some of Sybil's friends who gave the impression of mirroring her shallow depth of worth or makeup. We were on the same level intellectually—both college graduates. Beyond this I knew little about him, and his lack of spiritual commitment bothered me. Tuesday would give me more time to get to know him.

Loud voices and the crash of a table came from the dining room. Shocked at the noise, I ran to the sound.

A frightened Sybil stood crying, “Charles, Charles don’t.”

The scene in the dining room told the story. Sybil held Charles. Her boyfriend’s fists were clenched to strike again—a large, red welt appeared on his cheek.

Johnny stood in front of him—hands raised in a stop, don’t do it gesture.

On the floor, Ray pulled to his elbow and rubbed his chin with his hand. Disoriented, blood streamed from what looked like a broken nose.

“Okay, Charles. Back off if you want to enter this establishment in the future. Ray’s down. I think you’ve proved your point.” Johnny’s stern command demanded respect.

“I didn’t start the fight, but I’ll finish this battle if you’ll get outta the way,” Charles blustered, playing to his girlfriend’s notice.

“No more fighting today. Sybil, take him across the room.” Johnny turned to see me standing behind him. “Maddie, help me get Ray to the office.”

I moved to assist Johnny with getting Ray to his feet. He took a wobbling step. We each took an arm and shouldered him toward the front entrance. Once in the office, I went for wet napkins, handing them to the battered man.

“Thanks, Maddie. You’re the most levelheaded waitress I have. You can return to work. Ray won’t be welcomed here again.”

Back in the dining room, I watched Sybil fawn over Charles who played the wounded warrior to the hilt. Disgust—the emotion I felt for both. This man now posed the biggest threat to my friend—the greatest one in our years of acquaintance. What did she know about him? The web he’d started to weave must be resisted with logical actions and plain words, but would Sybil listen.

“Maddie, I need to talk to you.” Sybil sat on the edge of her bed fingering the lace running down her nightgown’s front. She sounded serious.

I'd gone to church with Abbott earlier in the day, then filled in for Sybil so she could take some time off to be with her lover boy.

"What's goin' on?" I put down my cold cream and wiped my face with a tissue.

"I don't think I can go to New York."

"What are you saying?"

"Charles needs me to stay here."

"Sybil, Charles is a grown man—far older than any man you've ever dated. He can take care of himself."

"Maybe Joyce June can go with you."

Did she hear a word I said? "Sybil, I don't want Joyce June to go with me. I like her, but I don't know her. You and I've been planning this trip for months. You need to go. Charles Roberts will be here when we get back."

"I just don't know." She ran her finger through her hair, still damp from her late-night bath, and looked at me.

"Well, I do. You're going, because you promised me first. You've always kept your promises." The one thing I demanded of her. "Remember? And, anyway, don't they say absence makes the heart grow fonder. Think of your reunion when we get back." I despised my last remark.

"Maddie, I really do want to go."

"And I want you to go." I gave her a hug and got into bed. "You gave me a scare." I reached for the lamp on our nightstand. "Are you ready to go to sleep?"

"I think so."

I didn't want to continue the conversation. Any energy I had left from the day disappeared with her first shocking statement. Reminding my longtime friend of her promise to me seemed to do the trick. She would go.

"Goodnight, Sybil."

No response.

I turned on my side and looked at her. She slept, or did she? No matter. Tomorrow she'd cope with telling Mr. Roberts the news she'd been keeping from him.

28

Abbott negotiated the curves to Newfound Gap with an expertise that impressed me.

"You've had lots of experience navigating Kentucky curves," I stated, hanging on to the seat as he rounded another sharp one, rocks flying from his back tires.

"Helped with my father's business." He made haste to change the subject. "You're not getting sick, are you?" He glanced toward me, checked my face, and returned to watching the rock road before us.

"You forget. I've lived in the foothills of the Smokies all my life. Curves are rooted in my life."

He laughed. "That's not the only place they're imbedded." As soon as the words came from his mouth, he started apologizing. "Maddie, don't blow your wig. I shouldn't have made such a stupid statement."

I gave him my most condemning look, but my insides were grinning. He thought I was a looker—a real tomato. I decided to let him sweat. "Abbott, I'm beginning to believe we weren't destined to be friends."

"Oh," he said in a gush of air. "It's my mouth. You're such a doll. You take my breath away. Or maybe it's my senses. Anyway, my mouth and mind aren't geared together when I'm around you.

"Now that's a revealing statement. Next you'll say I drove you off your rocker. You'll blame all your troubles on me, make tracks for the speakeasy, and drink enough rotgut to drown your sorrows."

He took a quick, uncomfortable look in my direction. "Maddie, I don't drink."

My laugh came forth as a short tinkle. "I didn't think you did."

"Aren't you a teetotaler? What do you know of alcohol?"

"Enough to not drink. I had an uncle die of gunshot wounds because he discovered an illegal still on his property in Happy Valley. My parents hung his bloody overalls in our garage's workroom—a fitting reminder of one consequence of the intoxicating swill."

"I'm sorry about your uncle. This happened some time ago?"

"Yes, several years, but the overalls are still there. On purpose."

Abbott rounded another sharp curve. "Are we close to the crest of the mountain?"

"A couple more curves should get us to the top."

"Great. You're not angry at my statement."

"What statement?"

"About someone's beautiful c-u-r-v-e-s," he said. He pulled into the parking area at Newfound Gap, switched off the engine, and turned toward me.

I laughed at him.

His brown eyes bored into mine. "You're toying with me like a cat with a mouse."

"I believe the cat's intention is to eat the mouse. I'm after what's in the picnic basket Joyce June fixed for us. Smells delicious."

I opened the door and hopped out, grabbing the basket from the back seat of Johnny's convertible.

Abbott hurried to help me. "Where do you want to spread our feast?"

I pointed to a spot on the rock wall. "Sybil, her father, and I sat there and ate when we crossed over headed to Cherokee. I love to swing my legs over the side and eat drinking in the view."

The gravels crunched under our feet as we walked to the wall. Several other cars sat near ours, and people milled around the area. I shook out the checkered table cloth and placed in under our picnic basket.

"What's going on at the end of the lot? Looks like the men are building a raised dais?"

"They are. President Roosevelt will dedicate the Great Smoky Mountains National Park next year."

"Really? He's coming?" Abbott stopped to get a better look.

"Yes." I pointed to the side of the platform. "See the small, wooden sign next to the stage? The new hiking trail to Charlie's Bunion begins there. The route is part of the Appalachian Trail."

"Why's the area called a bunion? Hurts me just to think about one."

"Because the Bunion is a chunk of rough rock bulging from and hugging the mountainside. The stone isn't very big. I've sat on the side and eaten a bag lunch more'n once. The feeling is like sitting in the vastness of space—nothing's around you. And the drop-off? Let's just say you wouldn't want to fall."

"Sounds like some place I'd like to see. Could we walk there?"

"Eight miles is too far for an afternoon. The trail is strenuous but worth it for the view."

"Is it better than here?"

"Every view in these mountains is breathtaking." I turned around and sat on the rock wall. He joined me.

We pulled fried chicken, potato salad, grapes, and cooked apples from our basket. China, glasses, and a quart jar of sweet tea came from its wooden depths.

"Food always tastes better with a view to ease it down," Abbott observed, pulling chicken off a thigh. He picked up his fork and filled the tines with apples. They disappeared into his mouth. "Didn't realize I'd worked up such an appetite. Musta been all the c-u-r-v-e-s." He looked at me out of the corner of his eye.

We sat looking at row on row of rounded gray-green hills, seeming to never end. Above us, mounds of gray-white clouds rushed across the sky, chasing the shadows they made on the hilltops. A gust of colder air pushed hair into my eyes. Before I could raise my hand, Abbott used his finger to replace the stray lock.

"In Kentucky, clouds like those," he pointed to the ones coming from the west behind us, "mean rain and colder weather."

"They mean the same thing here."

We ate the rest of our dinner watching the vacationers pull in and out of the parking lot. Squealing children ran among the cars with parents calling their caution.

Abbott wiped his hands on a cloth napkin. "Are you ready to go? I want to find some water—rinse my hands. Maybe we can take a shorter hike on the way back to Cherokee."

We packed the picnic basket and replaced the empty container in the car. Press looked at the threatening clouds. "I think we'd better put the top up, just in case it rains on our drive back to Cherokee."

If I didn't like my friend's driving coming up the mountain, the drive down and the sharp curves caused my wavy hair to curl even more. The car slid on the loose rocks, throwing gravel and dirt from the tires.

"Did you have a reason to drive curves this fast in Kentucky?"

He looked in my direction, a question in his eyes. "We did do some practicing to see who could negotiate a favorite set in our neck of the woods."

"I bet you won."

"No. I didn't.

"Then I wouldn't want to ride with the other guys."

"Do you want me to slow down?"

"I'll tell you a story, and you decide. Daddy and a friend on company business lost their brakes going down toward Cherokee from Newfound Gap. Urged by the driver, my father jumped from the runaway truck. He didn't break any bones, but being stove-up pretty bad, he stayed prone in bed for two weeks from the fall."

"What about the other man?"

"He managed to stop the truck a mile down the road by running up a hillside. Turned the truck over on the right side where my Daddy had been sitting."

Abbott slowed down, and we continued in silence until the sharp curves turned into more gentle ones and the road leveled somewhat.

"Abbott, we're coming to a historic mill—Mingus Mill. How about exploring the area? I've been at the entrance but haven't been on the road to the property."

"You mean there's someplace in these mountains you haven't seen?"

"One, anyway," I replied smiling and adding, "You can rinse your hands."

We turned onto a gravel road and drove a little piece to a parking lot. A short walk revealed the whole unpainted milling building, which had several windows. I looked at the edifice and frowned. "Where's the wooden water wheel? This one's not like Cable Mill in Cades Cove."

"I think I can solve the mystery." Abbott and I strolled beside the millrace. Water from a creek nearby flowed in the wooden conduit. The structure rose higher and higher on its underpinnings, towering over us and dropping water through cracks in the planks, watering myriad ferns growing on the ground below. Stepping closer, Abbott stuck his hands under a falling liquid ribbon and rubbed them together. "Feels much better." He slung water from his wet hands.

I followed as he circled to the back of the building.

"I can tell you how the mill operates. My father built one like this—metal turbine and grinding wheels for flour and cornmeal. You don't need a wooden wheel with the turbine. The metal blades inside the housing move in a circular motion when the water hits them, and turn a rod attached to the gears inside the building."

Abbott pointed to where the rod disappeared. "Come on." He took my hand. We walked around to the entrance and entered the mill.

Weekends, the park supplied people to give talks on its various attractions. "Being early in the week no one's here to explain the operation or give its history." I told him.

"I can't explain the history, but the operation is straightforward and not different from your local mill. The gears move the rocks to crush the wheat and corn. I'm sure you know the milling process, so I won't explain the operation."

"Your father is a miller?"

"Yes," he added, "among other things."

We explored an upper floor, looking at grinding wheels and stirring with our fingers the fine, powdered flour that covered everything.

Abbott helped me descend the steep steps from the second story. "Are my eyes deceiving me, or has nighttime arrived?"

He laughed. "No, I believe the clouds are getting ready to pour rain."

As predicted and before we could exit the building, a flash of lightning and loud crash of thunder affirmed his statement. Large droplets of water were followed by a downpour. We stood watching the water beat the ground with our car only steps away. More lightning and thunder.

"Should we run for it?" I asked, holding my hand out to catch a few drops.

"Mountain storms are known to pour one minute and the sun to shine the next." He craned his neck from the door to take a quick glance at the overcast sky. "I don't pretend to judge this one." Pulling his head back inside, he raked a drop from his eye.

Another flash was followed by loud thunder. Was the storm concentrated just over us? "Did you know there's and old Cherokee story that calls thunder the Destroyer? And, if I knew the Cherokee formula for calming a storm, that phrase, when repeated seven times, would rid us of this problem."

We waited ten minutes, gave up, and made a dash for the car. He opened my door. I jumped in and he ran around to pile into the driver's side. He laughed as water dripped from his hair.

I turned in my seat to open the top of the picnic basket, retrieving the napkins on top. I offered them to him. "Sorry, this is the best I can do for a towel."

As we turned onto the main park road, the sun came out and the last sparkling drops of rain cleared. "Wouldn't you know this would happen?" Abbott indicated the road in front of us—dry as a bone.

"Smoky Mountain weather. Always changing."

"Speaking of changes, you're leaving for New York tomorrow." Abbott kept his attention on the road where traffic picked up as we neared Cherokee.

"Yes. Sybil's boyfriend will drive us to Asheville tomorrow night. We'll catch the night train to Washington D.C. and change there to continue on to New York City. Should be really exciting. I've never slept in a berth on a moving car."

"I'm going to miss you."

My hand lay on the seat between us. He covered mine with his. In a low voice he said, "If I can get off early, do you mind me going with the three of you?"

"Why, no," I said, feeling the warmth of his hand. "I don't mind. Charles Roberts should be at Waltzing Bear at six."

"Won't you arrive in Asheville really early?"

"Yes. But better early than late for a train."

"If I'm not there at six, don't wait for me."

"Okay. Abbott, do you know Charles Roberts?"

"No. He's more of a friend of Ray's, who, by the way, doesn't care for him now."

"I can understand the reason. How's he getting along?"

"Don't know. He quit White Feathers. I think he's working somewhere down the street. Come to think of it, I haven't seen him since Sunday."

"I'm worried about Sybil and her relationship with Mr. Roberts. He's mysterious. Unknown."

"I can't help you, but I'll keep my ears open. Should I hear anything, I'll tell you.

I looked at Abbott out of the corner of my eye. I had to admit, bit by bit, he was inching his way into my life.

29

The porter on the swaying Pullman-Standard car stood in its doorway. "I'm Matthew. If you need anything, please ask." He bowed—a small, quick dip from the waist—and led the way down the lighted, carpeted aisle to our seats. "Ladies, are yo' ready to make yo' berth into beds, or do yo' wish to sit and watch the outside lights go by?" Our train was the night one to Washington.

"Matthew," someone called from a berth toward our car's front. He hurried to respond.

"Maddie, I'm bushed. Sleep sounds good to me."

"Who's takin' the top bunk?" I said, still troubled by the actions I'd witnessed before we boarded the train.

"I am," said Sybil, looking at the ceiling where her bed was attached. "What a grand adventure to sleep upstairs on a moving train. Charles will be surprised. He thinks I can't stand heights." She grabbed her train case from the lower bunk and hurried to the bathroom at the end of our sleeping quarters. The door clicked shut.

"Hmm." She must have used her "incapable and delicate woman" scheme on him. What had he used back? No, I didn't trust Charles Roberts, and Sybil's actions were a worriment to me as well. What should I do? Shaking my head, I looked at the top berth, glad she'd volunteered.

When Matthew returned, he didn't need to make Sybil's bed. Pulled from the ceiling of the sleeping car, the mattress had sheets already installed. "Excuse me, miss. Let me see to this gentleman's quarters." He indicated a man in his pajamas standing in the aisle only a few feet away. "I'll wait until yo' friend returns and make yo' bed."

I scooted under the overhead berth and sat on the velvet cloth of the bench seat marveling at the diamond tucking in the seat's back. Our couch at home had arms and back tufted in the same style.

Sybil returned. She came down the swaying aisle holding on to the edge of unmade bunks. "Nice hot water. I wanted to jump into the sink for a good bath."

Matthew hurried to take her arm, and she promptly climbed the ladder to her bunk.

"Good night, Maddie. Sleep tight. Don't let the bed bugs bite."

Our porter responded. "Miss, we don't have no bed bugs on my train."

"Sybil's kidding, aren't you, sweetie?"

She giggled, pulled the sheets up to her chin, and yawned. "See ya tomorrow."

Our car continued to sway from side to side with the sound of the wheels going clickety-clack on the rails and an occasional unexplained jerk. Though muted, the sounds could still be heard.

"Miss, I'll make yo' bed now." I watched Matthew pull the seat cushions into a twin-size bed. With an easy motion, he pulled linens to cover the top from the next berth and expertly tucked each corner so the sheets would stay put. My pillow rested atop, put there and fluffed with an unmistakable grace and expert hand. Matthew loved his job.

"Miss, yo's ready for a good night's sleep. Pull the curtain for privacy." He demonstrated this maneuver, flashing a white-toothed smile in his dark face.

"Thank you, Matthew."

Clad in a white jacket and black pants, he disappeared down the aisle toward another customer.

I looked at Sybil. Her deep breathing meant she'd fallen asleep as soon as her head hit the pillow. How could she fall asleep so quickly? I admitted my wish would keep her asleep, because she had a tendency to get sick on curves and during erratic movements.

I passed several berths with curtains pulled as I took my train case to the bathroom. Snoring came out of at least two.

The spaciousness of the train's lavatory took me by surprise. I looked around at two side-by-side vanities with lighted mirrors and chairs in front. A commode sat in one corner.

Sybil's statement about hot water hit home. Steam rose from the wash basin. A clean face cloth from those provided meant welcome relief from the strain of the day's activities. I buried my face in mine, heaving a huge sigh, and rubbed more water on my arms and neck. The warmth felt heavenly.

After changing into my nightgown and robe, my train legs carried me down the swaying aisle to my berth. I deposited my train case under the bed. A quick duck of my head and I scooted onto my mattress and pulled the curtains. My pillow was perfect. The sheets smelled of soap as I snuggled between them. But I found myself wide awake, reliving the scene as we boarded the train.

I shook my head again remembering the sight. Even Abbott had seemed shocked and disgusted. In a display, outrageous even for her, Sybil had thrown herself into Charles Roberts's arms. He didn't refuse her advance. For minutes the couple seemed melted together, oblivious to their surroundings—kisses were searching, long and deep.

Embarrassed, Abbott and I had turned and walked toward the boarding steps where another passenger with her umbrella and purse stepped into the Pullman car.

"I'm sorry about that," I'd said, indicating the scene behind us with a resolute waving of my arm. Annoyance at Sybil's display rose within me.

"Don't be embarrassed. We'll ignore them." He'd turned his back and continued. "I hope you have a pleasant trip into Washington. I've been to Lynchburg, Virginia—not too far from the capital. There's lots of trees and hills in the area."

"I'll miss seeing the country since we're traveling in the dark. I love watching the scenery pass the window. Sybil reads books—romance novels, of course."

"I couldn't have guessed," he teased, glancing back at the couple. "Tonight's ride will take you through the foothills of the Appalachians and into the flatter coastal lands. The train's movement should make you sleep like a baby."

Abbott had handed me my train case. Opened up, the small piece of luggage revealed a mirror and contained my cosmetics and other items needed for my morning toilet, when Sybil and I arrived in D.C. tomorrow. My other suitcase, labeled with our berth number, was already onboard.

The final whistle had sounded with a shrill, earsplitting noise. Speaking loud enough to disturb their private tryst, I had turned to call my fellow traveler and said, "Sybil, time to board."

"Abbott, see you when I get back."

"I'll look forward to your return." I didn't object when he leaned over and kissed me—a gentle tap on the lips. "It's catching," he said, his voice sounding sheepish.

If I hadn't been so angry at Sybil's display at the train station, his kiss would have dominated the night's thoughts. It had been tender. Not demanding.

"Sleep like a baby," he'd said as I stepped aboard.

I nestled my head in the pillow. Tomorrow I needed to have a talk with my best friend. See how far her relationship with Charles Roberts had progressed. Try to reason with her.

That was tomorrow. Tonight, the rails and gentle movements of the swaying train must relieve my anxiety for my friend—put me to sleep.

My resolve to talk to Sybil had lessened by the next morning. The last desire I had was a pouting companion for the next four days. When the porter announced breakfast in the dining car, Sybil bounced from the overhead bunk with train case and clothes in hand.

"I'm going to the bathroom to wash. Shouldn't take long."

While she performed her morning activities, I put on my day clothes and pulled the bunk and window curtains aside. The morning sun streamed through the window, causing me to blink at its brightness. The robin's-egg-blue sky didn't have a floating cloud within sight. What a glorious first day on our journey.

Sybil returned wearing a yellow dress almost as bright as the sun's rays. She was ready to eat.

"Hurry." She giggled. "I'm as hungry as our waltzing bear."

I always appreciated Sybil's sunny disposition in the morning. She bounced out of bed, and she never arrived late. I couldn't say a word to her—not now.

"I won't be long." I walked down the aisle way as she climbed upon my unmade bed and sat, legs crossed and mirror in hand.

The dining car sat to the middle of the sleepers. When Sybil and I walked in we saw several tables on each side of a center walkway—each positioned before a window. White tablecloths, white china, and silverware sets graced each one. Filled with customers of every description, the padded seats were covered with green, sculpted damask.

A dark-skinned waiter in white jacket with towel over his arm came forward to greet us.

"Ladies, will yo'se follow me." He continued to a table about midway in the car and held our chairs for us to sit. "Will yo' take coffee, hot tea, or orange juice to start yo' breakfast?" He said this as he placed menus on the table before us.

"Coffee with sugar and cream for me," Sybil stated, picking up the menu.

"I'll have orange juice, please."

"Yes, miss." He appeared gracious but businesslike, taking his towel to flick a bit of imagined lint off the table.

The waiter disappeared into a cubby hole at the end of the car but soon returned with our drinks. "Will yo' have the bacon an' eggs or our sausage, gravy, an' biscuits? Both is excellent. And this mornin' we have fried potatoes an' onions." The last must have been a delicacy on board from the passion with which he said the words.

Sybil ended up with buttered toast and jelly, and I ordered the sausage, gravy, and biscuits, hoping theirs would taste something like my Mama's. She always drilled into her children, *There's nothing more terrible than pasty gravy.*

"I thought you were hungry."

"I am, but the constant jiggling of the car and the thought of fried potatoes and onions, which Charles would love, made me reconsider." She looked out the train window at the trees whizzing by as we hurried to our destination. She glanced back at me and crossed her eyes.

The waiter brought our food. The smell made my mouth water—not so much for my eating companion.

"Do yo' need anything else?" he asked, setting gravy in a bowl beside my plate where sausage links and bread rested. He placed a large serving spoon next to the gravy.

"Yes. Coffee with cream for me."

"I'm good," Sybil said, waving her hand at him. When the waiter walked away she leaned forward and added in a low voice, "Ugh. Food. How much longer until we get to Union Station?"

"I think about an hour."

We busied ourselves with fixing our food and eating. My gravy was excellent. The waiter returned with a coffee decanter to freshen our cups.

He stood over me. "It's nice to be waited on for a change." I told him.

"Yes?" he looked at me.

"We work as waitresses in Cherokee, North Carolina in the foothills of the Smokies."

"Lots of tourists this time of year?"

"Bumper to bumper. We work twelve- to fourteen-hour days."

"Days is long on this train too—mornin' to night." He smiled.

Sybil spoke, "Waiting tables is our second job. We teach school in Tennessee. We use our money waiting tables to travel."

"I'se don't have no second job. Does yo'se always travel together?" he asked, looking from Sybil to me.

"We do on long trips," I replied. "Will we be getting into Union Station soon?"

Our waiter bent and looked through the window. "I'se think about one hour. Time fo' you to finish eatin' breakfast and get back to yo' berth."

When we finished our coffee, I left the waiter a tip. Sybil never left money. This mystified me, since we loved picking the coins off the table after a customer disappeared from the Waltzing Bear dining room.

She never sat long after eating. Today, she hurried back to our car. I rushed to keep up with her.

The sleeping berth's sheets were gone with my cushions transformed into seats and Sybil's bed locked to the ceiling, assumedly with new sheets installed. She and I sat side by side as the train sped toward Union Station. The houses grew more plentiful, and the traffic at railroad crossings thick, backed-up several cars deep on side streets.

We pulled into our station only a few blocks from the Capitol Building. Between the buildings and trees, we caught glimpses of the white-domed building as we arrived.

Union Station was a large, bewildering place if you'd never been there before. The cavernous entrance for our train opened on the lower level.

I tipped our porter.

We gathered our luggage and disembarked into a vast area where several train lines unloaded passengers. Our layover time allowed us a trip to the elongated, upstairs lobby where six statues towered over us in the great classical hall with arched ceilings over ninety feet high.

I imagined myself being high above Athens on the Acropolis in Greece. Surely this would have been a fitting prelude to seeing Athena's temple called the Parthenon—white marble, gold gilt, and granite everywhere—like our Nashville replica.

My companion didn't appreciate the architecture around her. She instead said, "I'm thirsty. Let's get a cola and hotdog."

My soaring imagination fell back to reality with a jar. How could she not appreciate the beauty of the room? "Something to drink sounds good. Sure you want a hotdog though? We're getting ready to board another moving, jerking train?"

She bought one anyway and two sodas. "Here's one for you—tip money." She grinned and handed me the paper cup full of ice and brown, sparkling liquid. I felt the cold drink slide down to my stomach.

"Do you realize our next meal will be in New York City?"

"I'm so excited." Sybil took the last bite of her hotdog and threw the paper wrapper and napkin in a trash can.

"We'd better find our train." I said heading for the steps to the lower boarding area. I hoped she'd left Charles Roberts behind.

"We've never ridden on the Pennsylvania Railroad."

"No. Being part of the Congressional Limited Express, we won't make many stops. We'll arrive in New York in three-and-a-half hours. When I bought our tickets, the agent said we'd approach speeds up to one hundred miles per hour, and the Pennsy runs electric powered trains instead of the steam engines we rode here and those at home."

"Pennsy?"

"Everyone's nickname for the railroad."

30

New York City. The minute my feet hit the ground—or, rather, concrete—in Grand Central Terminal, I knew the site and its town would be special.

"Can you believe this place?" Sybil exclaimed after walking the ramps to the main concourse. She stood looking at the ceiling. "And you thought Union Station took the prize."

I looked up. Up through smoky vapors to the ceiling, rising higher than the one in Washington. "I suppose New York couldn't let the District of Columbia get ahead of it. Where's the mural?" I craned my neck and swiveled trying to see the whole upper area.

"What mural?' Sybil followed my actions.

"The one of the night sky painted by Paul Helleu."

Sybil continued to gaze at the ceiling. "I don't see anything except painted plaster. Are you sure the ceiling had—"

"Yes, I'm sure. The constellations were reversed as if seen by God from the heavens."

"I swear, Maddie, you're a walking encyclopedia."

"I can't help loving history, art, and reading informational books—and I enjoy knowing facts of the places I visit." How often I wished she did too.

"What did you do? Go to the college library and research our trip?"

"Yes," I admitted. "Guilty as charged."

Sybil pinched her nose with her thumb and forefinger. "I don't read smelly, old books with lots of headache information. I love romances."

"Romances are fine—ones like *Jane Eyre* or *Last of the Mohicans*—something with a story, moral fiber and charming or unique surroundings instead of empty heads, mushy kisses, and muscle-bound men."

"Ugh. Books you have to think about. No, Maddie, I read for pleasure. I'm trying to remember—what's the Charlotte what's-her-name book I read last year?" She snapped her fingers. "Uh, *My Secret Fantasy*. That's the one."

"Come on, Sybil. Let's get outta here and take a taxi to our hotel. The Empire State Building is on our agenda for this afternoon."

Getting a taxi from the line of yellow cabs outside the terminal proved to be easy.

"SkyView Hotel on Tenth Avenue," I told the driver, who puffed cigarettes one after another. I noticed yellow tar on his fingers as he flicked ashes from his open window and packs of unopened smokes on his dashboard.

"Sure," he replied, glancing back at us in the rearview mirror while pulling from the curb. His mouth opened wide in a grin, showing a chipped front tooth. "Where you dames from?"

"East Tennessee," Sybil said, smiling back.

"I couldn'ta guessed." He grinned broader, if possible, and cut left into a line of cars, nudging between two limos. "I like seein' 'em cringe," he explained, waving his arm at the other two drivers. One responded with an obscene gesture. "Don't often get two limos that close together in this traffic."

Our short ride went through Manhattan—the business center of New York City. Busy streets, red lights, and honking horns mixed with exhaust fumes and close encounters with our driver's cigarette smoke made the ride anything but enjoyable.

SkyView Hotel sat on Tenth Avenue within walking distance of Central Park. I soon found "walking distance" meant a hike the distance of some Smoky Mountain trails but on flat ground.

Sybil and I checked into our hotel and took the elevator to the eighth floor. A room with two twin beds, a desk and chair, and large window facing the mottled brick wall of another hotel would be our resting place for two nights.

"The room's serviceable but not elegant."

"It's not the Barclay."

"No," I laughed. Sybil and her family stayed at The Barclay Hotel on one of their trips to New York. Barclay's site at Grand Central Terminal attracted visitors, and its location made seeing some of the sights in the city an easy walk.

"Where's our luggage stands?" Sybil asked, looking around the room.

I trudged over to a small door, which proved to be the entranceway to a small elbow-rubbing bathroom with tub and shower.

"How about the floor?" I said after coming back empty handed.

"I can do that." Sybil placed her suitcase and mine side by side on the wall under the window, which she had opened. "Guess we're unpacked."

"According to my city map, the Empire State Building is southwest of Grand Central Terminal. We need to take the subway or another taxi."

"No subway for me. You know I don't like dark enclosed spaces. You won't catch me travelin' underground like a groundhog."

"We were underground at the train terminal."

"I didn't *notice*, Maddie," she explained in short clipped words.

I sighed. Time to change the subject before she yelled or cried.

We took a taxi to the Empire State Building. "Will you ride the elevator to the observation deck?' I asked her.

"Sure, no problem. How many feet to the deck?'

"However many eighty-six floors turns out to be."

"Oh."

I almost didn't hear her.

She stood close and clutched my arm as the elevator jerked on its ascent, and when I looked at her ashen face, she'd closed her eyes, which didn't make sense at all—dark is dark whether underground or eyes shut.

The New York skyline was breathtaking from the observation deck. Sybil chose not to approach the rail, but I walked the three hundred sixty degrees, soaking in the sights. At this height, only the whistling wind or other jabbering witnesses to the city's glory broke the silence.

Alone and looking up, I imagined King Kong climbing to the top with blond beauty Ann Darrow in his clutches. Airplanes circled the tower as actress Fay Wray watched with pity the big, hairy ape fight for his life. The last words of the movie came to mind. "*It was Beauty killed the Beast*," I murmured.

"I'm thinking the same thing." I turned to look at a gray-haired woman dressed in a below knee-length red dress and matching hat with jaunty, black feather. She smiled.

I laughed a self-conscious giggle as I looked into her olive-green eyes. "Did you see the movie *Love Affair*?"

"Yes, every minute of it—more than once," she said. "I cried when Charles Boyer waited for Irene Dunn's appearance on the observation deck, since I knew she wouldn't show."

"I did too. Oh, how I wanted her to come," I said, only a little embarrassed by sudden emotions arising with my statement. I felt tears sting my eyes.

We paused to watch an airplane to the east. "Are you visiting, yes?" she asked.

"My girlfriend and I are here to see the World's Fair. We're goin' there tomorrow."

"Where are you from?"

"East Tennessee. Below Knoxville."

"Really? I have friends in Johnson City. Do you have supper plans?"

"No."

"Then let me take you to my favorite restaurant. Wonderful Italian food." She kissed her fingers to her lips. "Mama mia."

"I'll need to check with Sybil."

"Sure, okay."

We headed back toward the opposite side of the circle where Sybil stood close to the exit.

"What do you do in East Tennessee?"

"We're school teachers."

"I might have guessed."

"How?"

"Call it women's intuition." She continued, "I come here at least once a week, sometimes two, and sizing up a person is one of my pastimes."

"Your trips must be expensive," I said, remembering the cost of a ticket to the top.

She laughed. "No. My brother ran one of the tower's elevators. He died. They know me, so I go upstairs whenever I wish." She looked at a corner where the Chrysler Building rose in the distance. "My husband worked in the tall building to the south of the Chrysler Building. But we're talking another story, and I'm hungry."

"Maddie, I thought you'd gotten lost." Sybil's furrowed brow meant she was peeved.

"Sybil, this lady is . . ." I looked at my new friend.

"I'm Karina Mills." Assessing the situation, she looked at Sybil and added, "I'd like to take you both to dinner. How does Italian sound?"

"Good. I'm starved." Sybil's forehead smoothed, and she managed a smile.

I breathed a sigh of relief. Sybil's stomach had come to my rescue.

Four blocks from the Empire State Building, the three of us walked into a small restaurant tucked into a corner on the ground floor of an office building. The red lettering on the window read MAMA MIA'S.

Inside, several tables with red, checkered tablecloths were filled with patrons eating their fill of delicious smelling Italian food.

"Looks like the place is full, Mrs. Mills," I observed.

"Not quite," she said. "And call me Karina. I'm not an old lady yet." She winked. I had to agree as she headed toward a glassed counter full of pastries and indicated one empty table close to the kitchen entrance. "My table," she said and smiled.

"They keep a table reserved for you?" Sybil asked, seating herself.

"Yes. I eat here almost every day."

A middle-aged man came through the swinging kitchen door. He wore a white apron wrapped around his bulging middle. Seeing our new friend, he said, "Hi, Mama."

"Tony, I want you to meet my new friends, Maddie and Sybil."

My mouth framed a silent, "Oh." She was the Mama of the Mia.

"Let me guess. You met at the Empire State Building, no?" He looked back and forth between us, nodding his balding head.

"Anthony thinks he can read my mind." Karina huffed a puff of air.

"Okay, let me ask the ladies this question. Where did you meet my mother?"

"Enough. Get to work." Karina waved her hand to dismiss her son. "Go. Your customers are waiting. Pull up your apron," she ordered, "and bring three menus."

Anthony left laughing and returned with the menus. He leaned down and gave his mother a kiss on the cheek.

"Mama, you know I love you."

Mama stuck her miffed nose into the air. "Come back for our order."

31

Meeting Karina Bonacelli Mills started a chain of wonderful events and afforded us a tour guide for the next two days. She took two mountain girls from Tennessee under her wings and showed us the sights of New York.

The next morning, before the sun appeared over the Atlantic Ocean, we grabbed a taxi and hurried to the restaurant.

"Hurry, eat your breakfast. We're going to the Empire State Building to watch the sunrise. Can't miss seeing the view from the top of the tower," Mama Karina ordered. We were her new daughters. She intended to mother us as she'd done her own children. She filled our plates with enough food for two people. I put my hand over mine and begged her to stop.

"Guess that's the first place the sun hits America in the morning, being so tall and all," I said while eating bacon. The eggs were scrambled with sautéed onions and green peppers—delicious and filling. I watched Sybil eat with relish.

"New Yorkers would like to think so, but the actual place to see the sun first in America is Cadillac Mountain at Acadia National Park in Maine."

"Really," said Sybil. "I can't believe that's true." She turned toward me. "Maddie, you didn't know?"

"The sun's first rays on America isn't uppermost in my mind, although I also find the news hard to believe."

"Believe it." Karina blew the steam off her black coffee and took a cautious sip. "My husband and I went to Maine on purpose to verify the information." She waved her hand—a favorite gesture of hers. "There's no Cadillac. Just this big rock, small bushes, no trees. You sit on top with a blanket wrapped around you. Course, George and I snuggled together." She paused, remembering an experience from long ago with a man she obviously loved with all her heart.

Horns from the street blared as restaurant employees opened the front door. "We serve breakfast, lunch, and dinner," Karina explained. "Come on. We need to hurry."

"May we help with the mess?" I indicated our table as we arose.

"No, no, no. Trust me. The dishes will disappear." Karina nodded her head.

Breakfast over, we loaded into her sedan and drove among New York's early risers to the Empire State Building and took the ride to the observation deck. Mounding clouds over the Atlantic Ocean turned from gray slate to a deep rose, continuing through coral pink to yellow as we watched. The sun barely peeked over the horizon before it disappeared. "Mother nature's putting on a spectacular show for you ladies," our hostess observed. "But she may be forecasting drenching rain later today," she predicted. We turned to leave.

"I doubt I'll ever stand here at this time of day again," Sybil said, yawning. She copied her former visit and stood back from the rail.

"Come on. We need to go." Karina chauffeured us down the elevator.

We drove south through Manhattan's busy streets and crossed the Brooklyn Bridge over East River. Our trip continued across Brooklyn to Queensborough and stopped at Flushing Meadows where the fair's grounds were located.

Sybil and I didn't pay the seventy-five cent admission's fee. At the gate, the attendant touched his hat and waved us on. "Don't we need to buy a ticket?" I asked as Karina proceeded to drive through.

"No," came her short reply with no other explanation. "I have connections."

We were early. The place was empty except for shop owners, street cleaners, and maintenance people.

"The World's Fair site is huge—hundreds of acres. You can walk for three miles in one direction," Karina explained as we drove down a back street and pulled into a parking area already half full of cars. "Employee parking," she explained.

"How can you park here? Are you an employee?" She continued to be full of surprises.

"We have a booth." Karina opened her car door and waved her hand as if her gesture explained everything.

Sybil and I looked at each other and shook our heads. She whispered to me, "How could we be so lucky?"

"I heard that," said our guide, who then laughed. "Blame our meeting on the Empire State Building. 'Twas fate brought us together—like King Kong and Ann Darrow."

"We're thinking something different," I responded.

"What?"

"Divine intervention, the Creator, or the King of the heavens and earth."

Karina looked at us. "You believe in God?"

"Yes, I do—uh, we do," I said.

"So, do I. Let's go see George Washington—a man God placed in the Colonies to help secure and give steady leadership to a new, budding nation. The fair celebrates the one hundred fiftieth anniversary of his presidential inauguration." We walked toward a sign that read FOOD ZONE as Karina continued to talk. "Do you know his official residence while in New York?"

"No." I said, watching Sybil take quick shortcuts to peek into the windows of the buildings we passed.

"Cherry Street. The swearing in ceremony took place at the Federal Building. I've heard the pages and guides give this information so many times during the last few months, I can recall the words from memory."

We followed her, walking at a fast clip through the Food Zone. She pointed to her booth with attractive red-and-white lettering and red-and-white checkerboard motif as we passed without slowing down.

"We must walk fast to see the sights in two days." She did make a brief stop so we could purchase a guide book with the Trylon and Perisphere on the front.

"Hard to believe we're standing on New York's old garbage dump. Doesn't smell bad today nor will it ever again."

Washington, standing sixty feet high and clothed in his inaugural robes, faced the future represented by the two symbols on the front of our booklets. Directly to his rear, the Lagoon of Nations led to the Government Zone. Down each side of the central avenue where he stood were other zones with hundreds of buildings, booths, and an amusement park sitting on over fifteen hundred acres. Without the map provided in our tour guide and Karina's help, Sybil and I would have gotten lost in the maze.

After seeing George in all his glory, we headed for the symbols of the fair. Moving walkways took us through the Perisphere and the display of the City of Tomorrow. We traversed the Helicline and entered the Trylon.

By lunch, my overall impression of the fair was one of statues, flowing fountains, and pools of water with a relocated quarry of marble and granite constructed buildings. White—lots of white—except the colorful banners lining the streets and fronts of the pavilions and the painted outgoing walkways with progressing colors paling as you left the central area. The companies, countries, and productions became a hodgepodge of experiences. Our evidence of visiting each one was pins collected and fastened to the lapels of our dresses and a paper bag filled with free samples or purchased souvenirs for those back home.

Intermittent clouds kept the heat from being severe. By four o'clock we were three wilted women back at Karina's car, carrying our new straw hats in our hot, sweaty hands.

"The nighttime light show is spectacular, but I think you've had enough for today, no?" she asked before opening her door.

"Yes." Sybil and I responded in unison.

"We'll travel a different way home—a little north and west across the Queensborough Bridge into Manhattan. You'll see more of the New York skyline. Tomorrow morning we need to arrive early so you can get a good place to see the king and queen. Do you know what time they're arriving?" She pulled into bumper to bumper traffic.

"I wish we knew," Sybil complained, rubbing her feet. "We might not have to stand so long."

"Why don't you try to get the information from someone after we park tomorrow—a policeman perhaps," Karina suggested.

"Good idea. We'll all try. There's more of the fair site I'd like to see. Karina, may we bring our luggage to your restaurant in the morning. We'll have to check out of the hotel since we're headed to Washington on the afternoon train."

"Of course. Do you want to eat supper at Mama Mia's tonight? I don't want to monopolize all your time."

"I sure don't want another hotdog." I punched Sybil in the ribs. Hotdogs were her idea of dinner for the past three days. "I do hope to eat New York cheesecake while I'm here."

"My suggestion is Mama Mia's famous spinach lasagna for supper followed by a trip to Sardi's at Times Square for cheesecake. The atmosphere is wonderful with caricatures of famous people by Alex Gard. Do you know the story?"

"No." I wasn't sure what story she referred too.

"About Sardi's or Gard?" Sybil asked, voicing my thoughts and shooting a question at me with her eyebrows—*you didn't know this?*

"Gard," Karina responded. "Mr. Gard came to America as a Russian refugee and offered to draw a picture for a meal a day. The walls are covered with famous people. Afterwards, we can walk around in the Theatre District."

"Think we could take in a show?" I asked.

"We'll see, but I doubt it. The good ones will be sold out."

"Maddie, we can't go to a show. I told Charles I'd call him tonight at eight. He'll be in his room. Don't let me forget."

I hadn't thought about home except to buy souvenirs at the fair. Charles Roberts was the last person on my list of things to remember, but I promised to remind Sybil.

Because of Sybil's appointment with the telephone, our group rushed through the spinach lasagna and the Sardi's cheesecake.

Rain dropped from the sky and became a torrent as we hopped into Karina's car to go back to our room. She pulled into the stream of night traffic and navigated the wet streets toward our hotel.

At eight o'clock, we sat at a red light. The streets of New York were transformed by night into a fairyland of garish neon lights—some flashing in red, blue, and yellow. Raindrops falling on the windshield were dashed off the glass to the roadway, reflecting the colors of the rainbow.

The blue-canopied entrance of SkyView Hotel appeared toward the end of the rain-washed block.

"Karina, you've been so kind to us. How can we repay you?"

"Maddie, I don't want your money. I don't often get the chance to take two beautiful, young ladies from my husband's home state under my wing. All the reward I need is your companionship. My children are grown and very busy."

"Your husband is from Tennessee?" Sybil asked.

"Yes. Johnson City."

"When you said friends, you meant in-laws." I stated, remembering our earlier conversation.

"Yes, I did. Here we are." Karina pulled the car to the curb. "Remember, girls," our friend cautioned, "be at Mama Mia's by seven thirty. Our drive will not take long."

The elevator to our rooms carried two beat New York tourists. "I feel like I've been run over by a road grader. My feet are dragging." To prove this point, I stumbled crossing the threshold into our room.

"The bed looks wonderful." Sybil crossed the room, kicked off her shoes, and dropped purse and paper bag as she went. After opening the window, she fell across her bed, gulped a large portion of smoky, New York air, and closed her eyes. "What time is it?"

"Time to call Charles Roberts."

"Why do you always say his full name?" she asked, irritation showing in her voice. Sybil tended to be cross when tired.

"I don't know. I just do. The pay phone is in the lobby. Do you want me to go downstairs with you?"

"No." She heaved her carcass from the rumpled bed and grabbed her purse. "I can handle it." She flounced toward the door.

I called after her from the bathroom doorway. "Have you got the room key? I'll be in the tub when you return."

Sybil tried for two hours to reach Charles Roberts. At ten o'clock she gave up. "I can't imagine where he is." Tears streamed down a face knotted with hurt. "He assured me he'd be in his room."

I felt for her. "I'm sorry, Sybil. Something must have come up to detain him. Call tomorrow from Union Station before we board the sleeper train. I'm sure he'll have a good excuse. Now go take a long, hot bath. You'll feel so much better."

Sybil left for the bathroom, happy to hear words of encouragement, but still long of face.

Defending Charles Roberts left a bad taste in my mouth. How did I know what kind of problem he might be having? When we left, he promised to meet us in Asheville on our return. Should he not be available, Johnny Raintree or one of our bosses' friends would need to be called.

During breakfast the following morning, Sybil hardly said a word.

"What's wrong with your friend," Karina asked out of Sybil's earshot as we prepared to leave.

"She tried to call her boyfriend last night. He didn't answer, so she's tired and depressed from tossing and gettin' little sleep."

"Having a man around can be a big problem." She glanced over at Sybil. "Maddie, don't you have a boyfriend?"

"I have a friend—no one really special."

"Could he be?"

"Maybe," I smiled, embarrassed. "Isn't it time to go?"

We arrived at Flushing Meadows at nine o'clock and headed for the center of the fair where we hoped to see someone who could answer our question about Britain's king and queen's activities for the day.

"Where is everyone?" Sybil asked. "Usually this area is a beehive of activity with people waiting to direct you."

"There's a girl marshal." Karina pointed to a uniformed girl on the far side of Washington's statue. "I'll go see if she has any information."

Sybil and I sat on a marble wall and watched her as she approached the young lady. I heard my companion pull in air and let it rush from her mouth.

"Charles Roberts still on your mind?"

"I can't help but wonder." She sighed again. "I'm going to the bathroom." Sybil got to her feet and left in a hurry—her mood as gray as the cloudy skies. I figured she didn't want me to see the flood of tears that were sure to come after she left my sight.

I turned my attention to Karina. She talked to the girl who motioned with her hands and pointed to a location toward the end of the central mall—the International Zone. I saw our friend nod her head. She turned and headed back to me.

"Where's Sybil?"

"Gone to the bathroom to cry."

"Oh." Karina looked toward the area where Sybil had disappeared.

"She'll be all right. Needs to get her problem out of her system. Maybe crying will do the trick." I had little hope this would happen. "What did the marshal say?"

"She said the best place to get a clear view of the royal couple is from the Helicline as they enter the fair site." She waved her hand in a negative motion. "No chance of a place on the ramp, because you have to have a pass. But, if we hurry, the International Zone will have good spots available."

"What time will the entourage be there?"

"She thinks around noon."

"Will we have to stand for three hours to get a good spot?"

"Looks that way."

I'd been keeping an eye out for Sybil as we talked. She appeared from the alleyway where the bathrooms were situated.

"Here comes Sybil."

"A much-changed girl, I must say," Karina commented.

My blond-headed friend's face appeared wreathed in smiles. Her blue eyes sparkled with bright highlights even in the overcast skies.

"What mouse did you catch?" I asked.

"A handsome New York cop," she replied with a toss of her head, obviously happy her charms still worked. "Look here." She held toward us a piece of paper—a pass to the Helicline.

"Mama mia!" Katrina exclaimed. "How did you wheedle this out of him?"

"I blinked my baby blues and said a few kind words. He said it's the best place to see the king and queen and to come about eleven thirty."

"So it is," Katrina replied. "I just told Maddie the same thing. Now we won't have to stand in a crowd for three hours. I'll admit the idea didn't thrill me. What would you Tennessee girls like to do till then?"

"I want to see Carrier's new air conditioning system in the large white igloo—sounds interesting . . . and cool."

Sybil said, "I want to float the Life Savers parachute tower."

I looked at her. "Have you lost your mind?"

"Nope. I feel good."

I shook my head, amazed at the change in her attitude from the morning.

Karina led the way. "Let's go and have some fun. My suggestion is the tower first, before the sun gets overhead, and then a cool down at the Carrier exhibit. We'll have time for dinner at the café close to the House of Jewels."

"Is the House of Jewels what I think it is?" Sybil asked.

"Yes. You'll need a chinstrap to keep your mouth closed—diamonds, rubies, and emeralds set in gold, silver, and platinum. Millions of dollars' worth," informed Karina.

"Let's go. Our day's adventure waits," I said as we approached the parachutes floating 250 feet from the top of the Life Savers tower. "Sybil, are you sure about this?"

"Absolutely." To prove her point, she bought both our tickets for the ride.

Karina grinned at us. "I see legs showing on the downward descent," she observed as she held her head back at a crazy angle to get a better look.

Sure enough. Skirts flew into the air revealing white skin to the hip. "Oh, Maddie. Showing a little leg won't kill you."

I shook my head and mounted a seat held by the attendant for the ride to the top. "Have you lost anyone on former trips?" I asked him.

"No, ma'am. You'll be fine.

A strap around my middle kept me tightly in the chair so I used my free hands to hold my skirt together and enjoyed the spectacular view and the feeling of weightlessness as we floated down.

Sybil screamed, closed her eyes, and showed her legs to the hips.

Seeing King George VI and Queen Elizabeth became the highlight of our day. Once on the Helicline, we waited only minutes until the black, four-door car with glassed sides drove by—its coming announced by loud cheers from the crowd. The vehicle, lined on both sides by policemen and motorcycle cops, drove slowly through the entrance to the fair and down the avenue. The crowds were kept twenty feet from the car.

The king, dressed in a spiffy, dark suit, looked toward the raised sidewalk where Sybil and I waved furiously. He didn't raise his hand but gave a weak nod of greeting. The smiling queen, clothed in a light-colored dress and hat, stared straight forward, balancing a large bouquet of flowers in her hand. Mayor LaGuardia sat in front of the royal couple waving at the large, roaring crowd.

Later, on Karina's car radio, we heard that during the reception for the famous couple, the Commissioner of Italy refused to shake hands with the king and queen. He raised his hand in a Nazi salute—his way of putting a damper on an already misty, drizzly day and reminding everyone of the fighting in Europe.

Karina drove us straight to Grand Central Station from the fair. We said a tearful goodbye, and she promised to visit us at home in the future.

Sybil and I carried our suitcases to the waiting area for the Congress Express. The train arrived on time. We boarded and headed for Washington D.C. with one question on our minds. Would Charles Roberts meet us in Asheville? This question would be answered with my friend's phone call at Union Station.

32

Since we arrived at the end of the workday, Union Station buzzed with activity. Our one-hour layover gave us time to stretch our legs and call Sybil's boyfriend. She headed straight for a telephone booth.

I could see her plainly from the wooden bench where I sat. The longer she stood with the receiver at her ear, the more her shoulder's drooped. Her face went from animated to deadpan. Charles Roberts wasn't answering his phone. What problem did he have? I wanted to wring his neck. The musical clink of coins returning meant Sybil had given up. I dug into my purse for change to use for my call to Johnny as she approached.

"He didn't answer?"

"No. I can't imagine what's happened."

I stood. "I'll call Johnny."

She nodded.

I walked toward the telephone booth thinking the sleeper car back to Asheville would be a godsend. Sybil would not be social on the last leg of our trip home.

Charles Roberts did not show on Monday morning at breakfast, but Abbott did.

"Hi, beautiful." He gave me a hug and kiss on the cheek. "I missed you. How'd your trip go?" He sat down at his usual table. I placed napkin and silverware before him and went to get a glass of iced water before I answered.

"Great time. We met a lady who showed us the sights of New York and even took us to the fair." I pulled my order pad and pencil from my apron pocket. "The usual?"

He nodded his head. "Did you get to see the royal couple?"

"Oh yes. They were in a long, black limousine with large glass windows."

"I want to hear all about your trip. Can you get off work today?"

"Johnny's not going to go for any time off since Sybil and I've been gone for several days. I'll still go to church on Sunday. That's your only chance to catch up." I looked at him and smiled. He looked handsome in a brown, striped shirt, which matched his eyes.

He reached for my hand, looking deep into my eyes with meaning more serious than I wanted to admit. "I'll take what I can get." He smiled.

Other customers entered through the archway of the dining room, looked around, and sat at a table close to his.

"Same time."

"The fire escape?" he said, raising his eyebrows.

"Yes. I'll turn your order in to the kitchen." When I returned, I brought him a cold glass of milk, aware of his eyes on me as I waited on my new customers.

The couple was from Philadelphia. I took their order and brought cups of hot steaming coffee with a cream pitcher. The husband stopped me to talk.

"I'm Jake Butler and this is Janie my wife."

"Pleased to meet you. I hope you're enjoyin' your trip."

"We are, but could you give us some pointers on places to see in the mountains? We have five days so we must squeeze into our time as much as possible." The husband looked at me waiting for an answer.

"Knowin' the mountains as I do, I'd drive over the Gap to the western side and tour Cades Cove—see the area as it looked when taken over by the park."

"How do we find Cades Cove?"

"Go left at Sugarlands and follow the road to Townsend. Stop at the gas station, and they can direct you to the area. That will take a morning. Come back to Elkmont for lunch at the Wonderland Hotel—great food served family style."

"Have you been there to eat?"

"My uncle often treats me to dinner in the dinin' room. We sit on the porch enjoying the view of Blanket Mountain from the white rocking chairs—sometimes eatin' blackberry cobbler."

Jake wrote down my instructions. "We'll definitely do the hotel."

"No trip to the Smokies is complete without goin' to Gatlinburg to shop for souvenirs. Be careful and don't walk your legs off. End here for supper and tell me about the part you found most interesting."

"That's one day?" Jake asked.

"Yes. A busy one, for sure."

"What else to do on the western side?"

"Hike to Mt. LeConte or maybe to Alum Cave Bluffs. The Bluffs is shorter, if you don't want to spend all day. Take a food basket to the Chimneys picnic area and come back to Newfound Gap."

"What's Newfound Gap?" Jake looked at a map he'd opened at the table.

"I can help you with that." Abbott, who'd been listening from his table, joined into the conversation. "Go get my food," he mouthed.

Jake and Janie looked at him.

"Abbott Kendall. May I join you?"

"Please do," Jake motioned to a seat at their table.

As I left, I heard him explain, "Maddie's my girlfriend."

The Butlers and he were in deep conversation when I returned with Abbott's food. Newfound Gap, Clingman's Dome, and Mingus Mill were explained and pointed out on the map. I heard him offer to go with them if finding the places proved hard.

Abbott waited at the fire escape on Sunday dressed in a navy-blue suit and white shirt I hadn't seen before. I stood on the bottom step looking at him.

"You look beauti—I mean, handsome." I said stumbling over the words.

"You're the gorgeous one." Before I could stop him, he pulled me from the step and into his arms, kissing me soundly. When he drew away, I started to giggle.

"I hope you have a handkerchief. Unless you want to wear lipstick to church."

He hurriedly found a white square in his suit coat pocket and wiped at the red splotch on his face, smearing the lipstick even worse.

"Here, let me wipe it off." I swiped at the red blob.

"If it weren't for messin' up your makeup, I'd kiss you again," he threatened.

"Don't you dare." I stepped back to arm's length.

Abbott threw back his head and laughed. "Don't worry. I won't."

Reassured, I asked, "How's my face?"

"Lovely, charming, and dear to me."

"Answer my question."

"You'll need your mirror to touch up."

I pulled my compact from my pocket and flipped it open, staring into the mirror. "My, you sure have made a mess of things."

"But, sweetheart, lipstick is fixable. Some problems are not."

After church, we lingered on the bridge overlooking the Oconaluftee River—watching rivulets sparkling in the sunshine. I told him about the trip to New York and gave him the coffee mug I'd bought with his name on it. He stuffed the mug in his coat pocket.

"Abbott, I think I need to tell you something. I don't do summer romances."

He looked at me. "Neither do I."

Back at the Waltzing Bear, I lingered at the steps into the lodge. Abbott kissed me goodbye. This time I embraced him, letting myself feel the strength and warmth of his arms. Feelings rose within me—emotions I'd never experienced before. I realized I was falling in love with this Kentuckian.

On Monday morning before breakfast, Johnny Raintree asked me to go for a ride in his new car. A four-door convertible—with all the trimmings.

At our morning lull, he came to get me.

"I'll need to get my scarf." I told him. The bell of the front office rang, and he left to service a customer.

Joyce June winked at me as I left the dining room. "Don't do anything I wouldn't do," she threw after my retreating steps.

In our upstairs bedroom, Sybil lay on her bed—a picture of rejection and gloominess.

I sat beside her. "You need to get out in the sunshine." I had an idea. "Why don't you come with Johnny and me on our ride?"

She turned and looked at me with red eyes, tears still damp on her pillow. "You're absolutely right. But, I'll not go with you. I'll walk over to Charles's room. It's time we settled this thing." She rose from her bed, determination in her eyes.

"Sybil, do you love Charles Roberts, and does he love you?"

She paced the room. "He told me so, and I return his affection. Maddie, you know I don't usually let a man get to me. He's the first one I've let into my heart. Why is he acting this way? What happened after I left? I don't understand what's going on."

"Then go find out. Resolve the problem. Get your scarf. Johnny can drop you off." The prospect of riding in our boss's convertible perked her up.

Johnny waited beside the car and held the door for each of us. "Don't get used to having the door held for you." We both knew he kidded us. Johnny was always a gentleman, holding the door for customers coming to the Waltzing Bear and ushering older women up and down the stairs outside the lodge.

His intention was to take Sybil outside the rooms her boyfriend rented when working in Cherokee, but she insisted he not turn down the street. We let her out at the curb.

"Sybil, are you sure I can't go with you? Johnny and I can take a ride at another time."

"I'll be fine." She turned on her heel and headed down the street.

Johnny steered the car in the direction of Soco Gap and drove the curves up the mountain toward Maggie Valley. "We'll eat lunch in the Rainbow Café."

"Really. You're not getting me back for the dinner crowd?"

"No. Today we're taking it easy and enjoying the beautiful sunshine and green mountains. Letting our hair down."

Everyone around town knew Johnny. He waved as we passed souvenir stands beside the road. Signs for woven baskets, blankets, photos with Indian chiefs, and advertisements for moccasins. My thoughts turned to Abbott. Chief Big Foot. I couldn't help but smile.

"A penny for your thoughts," Johnny said, seeing my smile.

"I'm thinking about moccasins," I said. Well, I told him half of the truth.

"Do you want a pair?" Johnny braked the car, preparing to turn at the next wooden stand, which had been placed precariously on a curve before us.

"No. No. I have two pairs already."

"Deva, my cousin, owns the souvenir booth." He waved at a beautiful Indian girl dressed in fringed-leather with colorful beading on the front. Her shining black hair hung in long braids down the front of her costume.

I loved the drive. He talked about his ancestors and the good times he had growing up on the Cherokee Indian Reservation. "My great-grandparents, Stalking Bear and Willow Leaf, hid in the forest when the soldiers came to escort the Cherokee to Oklahoma. My great-grandmother gave birth at their hideout in the mountains shortly after. They stayed in the forest for two years until any danger of being sent away subsided."

"Times were bad."

"Yes. My family has come a great way since then. We have no regrets."

"But not everyone feels the same way."

"True," he said simply. "Resentment remains."

After dinner, we headed back to Cherokee. I realized he had an ulterior motive for the trip when he turned onto Paint Town Road.

"I want you to see the house." We traveled by a gurgling stream, which threw water droplets into the air as it rushed around and over rocks that blocked its passage. Residents grew scarcer along the road. He turned, forded the now small brook, and started up a newly graded and rocked incline to the top of the mountain.

My enjoyment turned to uneasiness. Hurting Johnny Raintree was the last thing I wanted to do. His friendship I valued.

I gasped as he pointed to a large log cabin sticking forth from a hillside where rhododendrons, dogwood, and hardwood trees grew. Multiple windows mirrored the mountains on the side facing the road.

"Did you select the building site for the view?"

"Yes. The hillside overlooks the place where my family hid to escape the move to Oklahoma."

"Family history is as important to you as times past are essential to my family. My great-grandfather, John Jack Tipton, lived in Cades Cove. His great-grandfather, Colonel John Tipton, helped write the Tennessee State Constitution."

He pulled to the basement garage door and stopped the car. Running around to my side, he opened the door. "Come. See my new home."

A set of flat, river-rock steps led from the driveway to the side of the house where a full deck ran from one end to the other. Inside, the living room windows spanned the wall from ceiling to floor. A large fireplace with mountain stone chimney sat in the middle of the windows.

"You'll never be cold here in the winter, Johnny."

"No," he replied. "No person living here will worry about being cold or hot. I installed air-conditioning for the summertime." He grinned, showing his famous dimples. "I know how important being cool is for some people."

I got his hint, and wished I were back at the Waltzing Bear.

"Look at the kitchen. Some lady will be very lucky."

We walked into the kitchen.

"Armstrong linoleum," he said proudly as our shoes tapped across the floor. The gray-and-red color scheme of the floor accented the charcoal and red countertops. Very colorful and cheery after the drab colors of the recession years.

"I've bought all new appliances." He walked over to touch the shiny metal toaster and electric coffee pot. The newest model of KitchenAid mixer sat on one end of the counter with the instruction booklet lying beside it.

I leafed through the pages.

"I have all the attachments—juicer, meat grinder . . ." He waved his hand at the cabinet above. "Come look at the bathroom."

The home's bathroom contained the newest in styles. A copy of *Better Homes and Gardens* lay open on the sink countertop. A look at the page revealed the room came straight from it.

"You read *Better Homes and Gardens* to build your home?"

"Of course. Doesn't everyone?" The dimples showed again.

I shook my head, surprised by his thoroughness.

"There's more—three downstairs bedrooms and an upstairs loft."

We walked a short hall to a large bedroom containing furniture but no linens.

"Why haven't you put linens on the beds?"

"I'm going to let my wife decide the color scheme. I'm going to marry again, Maddie."

I shook my head, turned, and started toward the living room.

Johnny caught me by the arm as I headed toward the entrance door. "Maddie, you know I have the utmost respect for you, and I like you. I think we'd make a good team. You were the one I had in mind to choose the linens."

I looked at him. I couldn't help but smile at his quaint way of asking me to be his wife. This modern man who used *Better Homes and Gardens* to build a stylish home for his future bride. I couldn't be the one. I didn't love him.

"Johnny, I'm honored . . ."

"I hear a *but* coming," he said, stepping closer and pushing a lock of stray, wind-blown hair from my eyes.

"You're a man I look at with loads of respect. Here's the but: *but* I don't love you as a wife should love her husband. I could marry you and be satisfied, but I want more. I want to be loved and love completely the man I marry." I hushed because I needed more air.

Although I suspected what would come as soon as we turned onto Paint Town Road, hearing the actual words and acknowledging them was like being punched in the stomach—something my younger brother did to me when we were children. I turned and left the room.

Outside on the deck, tears ran down my face.

"Here," Johnny said, offering me his handkerchief. "I didn't mean to ruin your makeup."

"I wish I could grant your request."

"I do too. You're a woman who should be honored and loved. I understand this." He paused and then asked, "Is Abbott the one?"

I pulled more air into my lungs. "I'd like to think so. There's another but. I don't know. Maybe. We'll see, as my Mama used to say."

Johnny pulled me into his arms for an embrace—an embrace that lasted a little longer than it should have. A relinquishing goodbye to his dream.

33

"Sybil's happier tonight," Joyce June whispered loudly in my ear as we passed each other on our way to turn orders into the kitchen. The clamoring customers in the full dining room insisted on immediate service and expected to discuss the day's activities over their meals. "Have you had a chance to talk to her—find out why?"

"No. Customers have me running my legs off. I'll try later after work, if I survive. Where do you think these people came from?"

"The large woman in the purple hat and blouse said our service is famous in Cherokee. She and her husband came to find out."

"Guess we'd better get to work. Not let them down."

I started away with my pitcher of ice water. Joyce June grabbed my arm. "Wait. What happened on your ride with Johnny today? You were gone some time."

"We went to Maggie Valley, ate dinner, and drove to his new house."

"That's all?" Joyce leaned toward me, examining my face.

"Yes, that's all." Much as I liked her, I didn't feel the need to share everything, especially Johnny's proposal. Special. Yes, the day was one to remember.

I pretended one of my customers needed me. "Duty calls. We'll talk later."

Thinking about Johnny? No, I didn't want to tackle our earlier discussion. He'd been polite but quiet on our drive back to Waltzing Bear. How would his attitude change toward Abbott? Toward me? So many feelings and questions about the future—Sybil, Abbott, Johnny, and Charles Roberts.

"Maddie, you haven't had time to talk to us." My friends, Harold and Adrienne Hutsell, interrupted my thoughts, motioning for me to join them. I walked over with the ice water pitcher.

"Have I given you your second glass?" I asked, holding forth the pitcher and grinning at my regular customers. "I've been so busy tonight."

"You did. We wanted to talk to you. This is the last time we'll eat supper at Waltzing Bear. Adrienne and I head for home tomorrow. Our vacation has flown so quickly."

I eased into the chair beside them. "You'll be missed."

"And we'll miss you. Harold and I appreciate your kindness during our trip here. The instructions you've given us and the good food you've fed us will be remembered for a long time."

"I think this vacation is the best we've taken," Harold stated.

"I'm sure the beautiful Smokies had a lot do with your feelings." I looked around the room. I couldn't sit long.

"We both envy you. The privilege of living in such a wonderful area," Adrienne observed.

"I know you're busy now, but could we get together after you get off. We'd like to treat you to dessert somewhere—get you out of here. Let someone wait on you for a change," Harold said.

"Sure. What a lovely idea. I'll look for you." I rose from the table. "I'd better get back to work. See you later."

I headed for a table where an attractive man in a suit sat by himself. He looked at a menu. "Has anyone waited on you?"

"No. A gentleman found me a table and gave me a menu, but I've been avoided like the plague." His smile told me he'd waited patiently for service.

"I'm sorry. Musta been Johnny who sat you."

"Yes, that's the man. He's on the front desk."

"Are you stayin' at the lodge?"

"For a few days. I'm playing music at the Watering Hole." The Hole, a dancing and drinking establishment or nightclub, sat in the heart of the town. The doors opened late and stayed open even later.

I nodded my head. "I know the place. So, have you decided what you want from the menu?"

I took his order, brought coffee and silverware. "I'm sorry you had to wait. Sit at my table while you're in town. I'll make sure you get good service."

"What's your name?"

"Maddie. Maddie Whitehead."

"Well, Maddie Whitehead, you've got a customer. My name's Deke Moffett from Cincinnati." We shook hands. "Come and hear me play."

"I get up really early in the morning to wait tables, but we'll see."

Mr. Moffett left a nice tip.

The rest of the evening passed in a blur of full and empty plates, smiling faces and squalling children, hellos and goodbyes. The Hutsells came around eight and waited until I cleaned my last table.

"I need to change clothes," I said as I stripped away my stained apron.

"You look fine. In the dark no one will notice." Adrienne linked her arm in mine.

I waved at Sybil as I left the dining room. She knew about my outing with the couple. No one waited the desk in the front office, so Harold, Adrienne, and I walked down steps to the boardwalk and continued toward the main shopping district.

The sun had slipped below the western mountains hours ago and twilight made the lights of Cherokee bright against the semi-darkness. From somewhere, a disturbed mockingbird made a raucous catcall.

Outside White Feathers, Abbott waited.

"Surprise, surprise! Harold exclaimed. "We asked your young man to go with us." He and his wife continued ahead of us.

"Hi, sweetie. You look ready to drop." Abbott laced his fingers through mine and kissed my cheek.

"I am exhausted. I'd rather have gone to my attic room and collapsed." I couldn't help but sigh for my dog-tired body. Today had been an emotional rollercoaster.

"I'm tired too, but the chance to see you perked me up." He squeezed my hand.

He made me feel guilty. I stopped him, put my hand on his cheek, and gave him a light kiss on the lips—the first time I'd initiated such an intimate touch.

"Wow. Does this mean you love me?" he kidded. He put his arm around me.

"Hey, you two lovebirds. You're falling behind," Harold called. "Catch up."

Embarrassed, we laughed and walked faster. "Sorry," Abbott said. "We'll try to be better companions."

Harold and Adrienne turned into a local ice cream parlor. We followed them to the counter.

"How about a sundae or banana split with all the trimmings?" Harold pointed to a sign above the counter.

Abbott and I shared a banana split. He ate the strawberry end, and I ate the chocolate one. The pineapple-vanilla center we shared.

As we left the ice cream parlor, the piano strains of "Georgia On My Mind" could be heard faintly coming from the open windows of the Watering Hole down the street. Strange I'd never heard the music before. But, then, I went to bed at nine. Four o'clock came early.

"Oh, Harold, we didn't get to visit the nightclub." Adrienne turned to me. "Do you dance, Maddie?"

"School dances—not much." Truth be told, I didn't do any dancing. "My sister Edie loves to dance." With athletic ability, her grace on the floor made heads turn, but we didn't flaunt our actions before Mama and Daddy. They wouldn't approve.

"How about walking down and listening for a few minutes." Harold looked at Abbott and me, expecting a yes.

"For a few minutes, Maddie?" I heard the pleading in Adrienne's voice. She'd be disappointed not to go.

"Okay."

As our group sat at a table in the rear of the smoke-filled room, Deke Moffett finished playing "Georgia On My Mind."

"Are you having a good time?" he asked from his seat at the piano. A round of loud applause confirmed the patrons were enjoying the music. "Let's change the mood and do something a little livelier. I need you to stay awake. In 1930, Ted Koehler wrote lyrics and Harold Arlen the music for this song. We're going to really jazz it up." A few rounds of his nimble fingers up and down the keys of the piano, and Moffett tore into his rendition of "Get Happy." "Recognize it?" He grinned as people nodded heads and came forward to boogie their version of swing dancing. The young Indian bucks in their military uniforms lifted and swung their partners off the ground.

Harold stood and held his hand to me, "Maddie?"

"Oh, no." I shook my head. "You and Adrienne go. Abbott and I'll watch."

After they left, I turned to Abbott. "I don't know how much longer I can stay. Work comes early in the morning."

"I understand. We'll leave soon."

"For an old couple, Harold and Adrienne can cut a rug," I observed. When Moffett launched into another swing favorite, they stayed on the dance floor. At the end of the second song, Deke stood and approached the dance floor with the microphone in his hand. "I want to talk to this young couple."

Harold and Adrienne weren't young, but they beamed at his comment.

"You guys can dance."

Breathing heavily, Harold explained, "We went to dancing school. Got a diploma hanging on the wall at home."

"What's your name and how long you been married?"

"Harold and Adrienne Hutsell. Forty-five years and counting," Adrienne said.

"Are you enjoying your trip to the Great Smoky Mountains?"

"Oh, yes. Best vacation we've taken—such interesting history and nice people," Harold responded with Adrienne nodding her head.

"What's the one word you'd apply to the Smokies?" Moffett stuck the microphone in front of Adrienne.

"Relaxing," she responded.

"Great answer. Well, the next song is dedicated to you." Mr. Moffett shook Harold's hand and gave Adrienne a hug. He went back to his piano. "I sing this to my wife when I'm not on the road."

The music of "I'm Confessin' That I Love You" brought most of the clientele to their feet. The dance floor's boards gave off a soft shuffling sound with the slow dance.

Abbott pulled me to a standing position. "We're dancin' this one."

"I'm really not a good dancer." I protested as he led me to the floor.

"I'll hold you close. Move with me."

And he did—hold me close.

Deke Moffett played through the song, and then he added the lyrics to the music.

I listened to the words and wondered what Abbott was thinking. We hadn't said 'I love you to each other, but the sense of love was there. Our actions spoke of love.

Abbott joined him in a low tenor voice as did others in the room—singing to their sweethearts.

I closed my eyes, listening to the piano, beautiful words, and dreaming.

Abbott continued with his cheek on mine, whispering the words in my ear.

The last verse sent a chill through my body. Was there a possibility that this was a summer romance, and a dream to be given up in August? Was I just guessing that he loved me—would he leave me? Why did the song turn negative with such a question?

Deke Moffit played an interlude and finished—singing the last two sentences again.

The magical moment was broken by the last verse of the song. The minute the music ended, my energy left. "Abbott, I need to go back to the Waltzing Bear. I'm bone tired."

"I'll tell Harold."

"See you at the door," I said, turning as I made the statement.

When Abbott came back, our friends were with him. I protested, "You don't have to leave."

"Yes, we do." Adrienne continued, "There's still packing to be done."

We left Abbott standing in front of the steps to his room. "I'll see you in the morning, Maddie." A swift kiss on the cheek and he bounded up the stairs.

I said goodbye to Harold and Adrienne when we reached the lodge, then dragged myself upstairs.

Sybil slept soundly when I entered our bedroom—the only noise being the hum of the fan circulating warm, moist air. Asking her about Charles Roberts wouldn't happen tonight.

I sat at the dressing table, wiped a layer of cold cream on my face, and rubbed the excess off with tissue. The light from an almost full moon shone through the open window, illuminating the contents of the room.

Walking to the eave and looking out, I let myself reflect on the day's happenings. Johnny's proposal. My kiss for Abbott. The door to Johnny's heart I'd closed, but would the door to Abbott's be opening?

Over a month had passed since Sybil and I'd started work at the Waltzing Bear Lodge—a short time of possible life changes for both of us. Where would they lead?

Down below, I caught a dark movement under the trees. A mother bear and cub moved quietly toward town. She stopped to sharpen her claws on a tree. I jumped as Mocker squawked. Disturbed, the bird flew into the blackness of the foliage across the river. Tomorrow morning, garbage cans turned over with contents strewn over the ground would attest to the bruin's visit. I watched until the two moved from my sight.

As I crossed the floor to my bed, the floor creaked and Sybil moved. I eased between my sheets and breathed a quiet prayer into the darkness. "Lord, thank you for getting me through this day, and help me get out of bed in the morning. Amen."

34

At morning break, Sybil was stretched across her bed looking like the limp leaf lettuce and green onions Mama killed with hot bacon grease and vinegar. The humming fan gave some relief from the attic heat.

I sat on the edge of my bed. Sybil turned toward me on her side. "What time did you get to bed last night?"

"Almost twelve. I was bushed." I told her, extending my body full length on the bed. I concentrated on the wasp nest on the ceiling. I hadn't killed the original insect, and now six of its buddies made the nest larger. Enclosed larvae cells meant more were on the way. I needed to tell Johnny. Let him get rid of the stinging pests.

"I've been resting here, thinking about Charles and wondering when he'll get back."

"Where's he gone?"

"I'm not sure. His landlord said some kind of emergency. He left in a hurry. I want to know why he didn't call us. He had the number of our hotel in New York."

"He should've. Sure gave us some anxious moments." Maybe an emergency did excuse his actions. I relented, but only a little.

"There's a good explanation. I can't believe anything else. His employer expects him back within the week." Sybil yawned, closed her eyes, and ended the conversation.

Charles Roberts came back to Waltzing Bear on Thursday morning. An excited Sybil acted as if two weeks hadn't passed without seeing or hearing from him. His excuse—his grandfather died. I heard her exclamation of sorrow from the other side of the dining room.

Days managed to pass into weeks. On the second Sunday in July, Abbott stood on the first step of the fire escape with a long thin box. "Put this in the kitchen's refrigerator."

"What is it?" I pulled on the top, but the two sides were taped together.

"Uh, uh, uh." Abbott shook his finger and head. "After church."

I hurried to the kitchen and deposited the box.

The marquee at Mission Church announced "God is Love" as the morning sermon. The preacher dwelt on the thirteenth chapter of First Corinthians where Paul teaches the "more excellent way"—a subject I'd heard in church many times, from many angles. The three points of his sermon were God is Love, love works in another's best interest and is seeable, and love is the best gift of all.

Abbott started asking questions as soon as we left the church. "Maddie, I understand how love is shown toward another human being, how the evidence of love is demonstrated in your life. My father often carried my brother in his arms because he couldn't walk properly and any effort left him breathless. Often, when he thought we weren't looking, he'd give him the biggest hug. My mother always said it was a love hug."

"Love hugs. Huh. Were love hugs common in your family?"

"Not so much, and I think to be able to love is a gift. One a person must strive to attain and give. I guess I don't understand how someone dying a cruel death on a cross shows love."

We were at the bridge over the river. Since rain hadn't fallen in several days, the water moved quietly beneath us. Abbot leaned on the rail and looked down into the clear water.

I realized Abbott struggled to understand the Passion of Jesus and needed to know the plan of salvation. "It's not the agony of the death. No one can deny the pain Jesus suffered. Most important is the reason for the cross. Do you remember from your former goin' to church days hearing about Adam and Eve sinnin' in the Garden of Eden?"

"Of course I do."

"Because of their sin, the whole world is under the curse of death."

"What does the curse of death mean?"

"Means you and I will die—the earth and all that dwell within will perish."

"How does the cross rectify this?"

"It's the hope of the life God wanted his creation to have in the first place—eternal life full of love in his presence and his protection. Those wooden boards and the blood shed as Jesus hung there belonged to a plan formulated by God, the Holy Spirit, and Jesus before the earth and heavens came into being."

"I still don't understand why anyone had to die such a horrible death."

"When you realize His death, God's agonizing death, completed a plan for you to live again . . . I think it's clear."

We started walking down the path toward the Waltzing Bear.

I tried again. "Jesus came to earth with a message of hope. His own people rejected Him. He had to go to the cross. He needed to suffer, be raised up, where everyone could see him." I stretched my hands into the air as tears came to my eyes. "My sin and your sin, Adam and Eve's sin, caused his death. His blood is necessary because it shields sin from the Father's eyes. When Jesus rose from the dead, he revealed the Father's power to raise us, resurrect us, if we confess our sins and believe his Word. The greatest love shown to man is the death of God. The omniscient, omnipotent, and supreme Ruler of the universe laying down his human life for all mankind. For me." Tears rolled down my cheeks. I dashed them away with my hands.

"I'm sorry, Maddie. I didn't intend to make you cry." With those ten words, Abbott changed the subject.

I'm not a pusher, as my home pastor calls those who browbeat unbelievers into making a decision. He admonished his listeners to plant the seed of the Word and let the Holy Spirit breathe life into the utterance. With all my heart, I wanted Abbott to believe.

We were approaching the lodge. Habit led me toward the fire escape. A quick change into my waitress uniform and I'd be ready to work. "We go this way," Abbott said, steering me toward the front of the building.

"But, why?"

"You have the day off, and we're going to Fighting Creek Gap. Walk to the falls and eat at Wonderland Lodge. You've talked so much about the place, I need to taste the food."

"Have you spoken to Johnny about this?" After several days, Johnny had returned to his old self. Except, now, instead of cautiously suggesting he liked me and could we have a future, he kidded me about love lost.

"Sure. He's lending us his car."

"Wow. What did you promise him?"

"That I'd fill the tank with gas and wash her when we return. Come on, I need to get the keys." He ran up the steps to the office.

Joyce June sat in a wicker chair in the reception area. "I wish I were going," she said when our itinerary was known.

"Come on. Abbott won't mind."

"I do mind. Don't often get to be alone with my sweetie," he said as Johnny handed him the keys to his car.

Johnny addressed Joyce June with a grin. "You have customers I believe."

"Oh, shucks. Don't remind me." She hauled her body out of the chair and disappeared into the hallway.

"Maddie, he promised not to drive fast and to take the curves without slinging gravel. You'll police him, won't you?"

"Maybe I should drive," I suggested.

"No way. Let's go." Abbott tugged at my arm.

Johnny called after us. "Be careful. She'll break your heart."

For a second, I wondered if these two had discussed Johnny's proposal. Abbott had guessed Johnny's interest, but I couldn't imagine my employer telling Abbott the full story of his offer.

We were almost to the car when Abbott remembered his box. "The box?"

"Ooh! I put it in the refrigerator." I told him.

"I'll be back." Only minutes passed until he returned. "This box is important," he explained, tapping the lid.

I eased into a white rocker on the veranda of Wonderland Hotel.

"This is a perfect day," Abbott said, pulling a chair closer to mine and sitting down. He leaned his head back and closed his eyes, setting the rocker in motion. I copied his actions.

We were alone on one end of the busy shaded porch. Outside the main entrance and on the other end, more couples talked and children roughhoused. Through the green leaves of the surrounding shrubbery, two couples played tennis doubles. The sound of the ball hitting the racket grid and ground gave a hollow thump.

I relaxed and thought about our day—the leisurely drive over Newfound Gap, a stop at Sugarlands Visitor Center, and the romantic hike to Laurel Falls with brief stops for scenic viewing and kisses. Abbott's declaration of a perfect day rang true.

His soft kiss on the cheek brought me back to the present. "Maddie, have you heard the story of the Cherokee Rose?"

"The one associated with the Trail of Tears?"

"No. This one's about a Seminole warrior and a Cherokee maiden."

"I don't think so. How does the account go?"

"Early in the last century, the Seminole and Cherokee peoples were at war. The story says a young Seminole brave was wounded in battle and captured by the opposing tribe. The warriors carried him away to their village. The custom at this time included burning captured prisoners at the stake."

"Not the only tribe to do this, I understand."

"The Cherokee preferred healthy men to burn at the stake. Besides his wound, the young warrior became physically sick."

"Pneumonia?"

"I don't know, but what I do know is he fell in love with the young Cherokee maiden nursing him, and she with him. Days passed, and he healed."

"Is this another case of star-crossed lovers?"

"Maddie, just listen. The burning stake loomed before the Seminole man. He convinced his love to run off with him. She wanted to go. They left very early one morning, long before the sun came up.

"Realizing she wouldn't see her family again, the maiden took a cut of a beautiful white hedge rose to plant in her new home. That's how the Cherokee Rose started growing in Georgia."

"And became Georgia's state flower," I added.

"How did you know?"

"According to Sybil, I'm a walking encyclopedia."

"What's the Kentucky state flower?"

"Goldenrod."

"North Carolina?"

"Dogwood."

Abbott shook his head.

I laughed. "You can't win. We studied the different states adjoining Tennessee in our geography class this year."

"You have a good memory to retain so much information."

"I do. The statistics are fresh in my mind."

Abbott stood. "I'll be right back."

I watched him bound from the porch and go to Johnny's car. He came back with the skinny, white box. "This is for you." He slipped his finger under one taped side and loosened it. I took the box he held toward me. "Before you open the package, there's something I want to say to you."

"You're being so mysterious," I grinned as his hand held onto mine.

"Maddie, we haven't known each other long, but, during these weeks, I've fallen in love with you. I've never loved a woman before, so you're special—so irresistible, sweet, kind." He leaned toward me, giving me a gentle kiss. "You may open the box."

I did as told, the effect of his words sinking in. The red rose with a bit of fern had wilted in the heat of the day. I didn't care. "It's beautiful, Abbott."

"The Cherokee maiden wanted to remember her family. I want this rose to be something you'll remember me by. Do you know what the color means?"

"Red is the color of love." For the second time today, my eyes filled with tears.

"Maddie Whitehead, I love you with all my heart. You're my Cherokee Rose." He leaned forward on the rocker, his hand on my cheek.

I slid from my chair to the porch floor, my knees on the painted boards, my arms stealing around his neck, holding on for dear life. "I love you, too—so much. You're the first man I've kissed." I moved to put my lips on his in a token and seal of our uttered words.

Abbott continued. "I don't know what the future holds for me, but I'd like to think you might be in the plan."

"When the time comes," I replied, ignoring the stares of the other people sitting on the porch. He didn't propose, but his words came close.

Abbott lifted me from the floor to his lap. I rested my forehead in the crook of his neck as he rocked the chair in a gentle arc. "Guess we'd better go or I won't have time to wash your boss's car," he whispered in my ear.

I carefully replaced the lid on the box where my beautiful rose rested. Maybe some water would revive it.

We walked hand in hand from the porch to the car. The drive from Elkmont over the mountains to Cherokee gave me time to think. The logistics of our hopes and dreams depended on the Depression, which seemed to be ending with the promise of steady, future jobs, and the looming threat of global war. Where would the end of summer take us?

I couldn't think of a reason we couldn't be together, except his lack of spiritual conviction. After his questions this morning, I had reason to think he might not understand the biblical principles he'd been taught as a young child in Kentucky. "I'll pray for his understanding of God's Word."

"What did you say?"

I scooted closer to him on the car seat. “I agree with you. This has been a good day.”

Washing the car turned out to be fun. We worked at the chore together. After discussing our plans to drive to Maryville for a visit to my home toward the end of July, I headed into Waltzing Bear to change into my waitress uniform. On the top step, I turned, waved goodbye, and blew Abbott a kiss.

❦ 35 ❦

Sybil changed her *modus operandi.* After Charles Roberts's hiatus and return to Cherokee, she often joined him when our work day ended, coming quietly into our room late at night. More and more, she excused herself from Joyce June's and my society. Exhausted, she became unable to carry her workload. We covered for her.

"She's serious about this guy," my co-worker said one day in early August. She said this after carrying a pitcher to Sybil's tables to fill glasses with ice water. She'd cornered me in the hall coming from the bathroom.

"For the life of me, I can't understand what she sees in him. She's had other boyfriends—most put him to shame. All he's got goin' for him is good looks. Sybil's obsessed by him," I said to Joyce June.

"*Magnificent Obsession*," she replied, using the name of a recent book and movie.

"Maybe, but I think he's a user and not in the least as magnanimous as the main character in the book turns out to be."

"I find the phenomena strange indeed—fascinating even. How a woman tends to go after an exciting and often wrong man. Charles chain smokes and drinks."

"What? I knew he smoked, but drinking? I didn't know he touched the stuff."

"No wonder, Maddie. You avoid him like the plague. I don't smell the alcohol often, but . . ." She nodded.

"Her blond, blue-eyed Clark Gable," I said with disgust.

"Is that her name for him?"

"She called him Gable while she dated Ray."

"From what the magazines say about Clark, well . . ." One hand flew into the air in a you-should-know gesture. "I wonder if Charles Roberts is an actor like Gable. I get the feeling much of his grandeo—grandiosity is put on."

I laughed at her. "Where did you pull that word from?"

"Didn't know I possessed such a vocabulary, did you?" Joyce June gave a two-chuckle laugh.

"I hate to think my long-time friend would be hoodwinked by a shallow dandy such as him."

"Me, too. Don't get angry with me, Maddie, but sometimes I think Sybil is a little like him."

"What do you mean?"

"She . . . well, you know. She can put on airs and exaggerate. A bit. I think you look over her faults as a friend must."

Joyce June's comment made me take stock of my relationship with Sybil. I'd been around her so long, I did gloss over and ignore her character flaws. "Sybil's generous and vulnerable."

"Isn't the fact that she's at risk most of the reason for your friendship? You protect her from getting hurt. And Sybil doesn't get hurt because she loves 'em and leaves 'em before they can go. All except for Charles."

"He may hurt her for sure." I shook my head. "I hope Abbott's not in the same category."

"Oh, no. Abbott's a sweetheart. Calm, peaceful. If you don't marry him, I will," she joked. "But what are we going to do about Sybil? Is there a way we can help?"

"She's a big girl. Stubborn and unwilling to listen."

"Well, at the next opportunity, you should try to talk to her."

"Okay. I'll take your advice. But get ready for a huge pout."

"How about your trip home over the weekend? Did Abbott meet your parents?"

"Yes. They liked him, especially my sister Edie. She went gaga." I giggled, remembering Edie's comment about my boyfriend's physique. "Edie said Abbott's shoulders were as big as a barn door, and she intruded on our conversation at every opportunity. We took her to the movies with us."

"Is Abbott a summer romance or the real thing?"

"I don't do summer romances, Joyce June."

"I didn't think so."

The days of summer rocked on. Abbott and I continued to see each other at breakfast. Every Sunday, Johnny loaned Abbott his car, and we went riding in the mountains, covering many of the shorter hikes and playing in the cold streams running down the valleys. My life seemed filled with rainbows, bluebirds, and red roses. He brought me a flower each day.

"Johnny, could I speak to you for a minute?"

"Sure, Maddie." He continued to alphabetize his customer cards. "Junior doesn't do such a good job," he explained, looking up from his work.

"I want to thank you for not . . ." I couldn't continue.

"For not being angry with you because you turned me down?"

"Yes." I watched his hands move the rectangles in piles across the desk.

"Maddie, you're someone I respect. I couldn't love anyone or offer them my hand without first admiring their honesty. You've never lied to me. When you told me you didn't love me as a woman should love a husband, I accepted your statement. What you said came from your heart as the honest-to-goodness truth."

He did love me, even though he hadn't mentioned the word when he proposed. "You didn't have to let Abbott borrow your car."

"Yes, I did. I want what's best for you Maddie." He looked from the cards to my face. I saw a fleeting expression of hurt in his eyes.

"Thanks again," I said, then fled toward the dining room.

"Maddie," Johnny called after me. "What's wrong with Sybil?"

I turned and took a few steps in his direction. "You've noticed."

"Yes. I know she's not performing her work duties suitably. I've had a few complaints. So I've been watching her."

"Charles Roberts—he's the problem."

"Do you want me to get rid of him?"

"No. Let me talk to her first."

Johnny nodded his head, and I left the reception area. Sybil's blatant actions were a concern to everyone. I couldn't procrastinate any longer.

That night, two weeks before the end of our summer work, I stayed awake waiting for Sybil to arrive. The change in her work habits and association with her co-workers had become alarming. Tonight I intended to approach her about her lackadaisical attitude brought on by her obsession with Charles Roberts.

But Sybil did not come home.

The following day, she ignored me and spoke very few words to our co-workers and her customers. She walked like a zombie throughout the day. It was clear something dreadful had happened the night before.

Joyce June looked at me and rolled her eyes. "Maddie, I've heard some gossip from the other girls."

"Do I really want to know?"

"Probably not, since you've always thought Roberts was a scoundrel."

"Dear God, what's wrong?"

"It seems his grandfather didn't die, but his wife came for a surprise visit. He whisked her away to Maggie Valley for a romantic holiday. That's the reason he didn't pick you up at Asheville or call Sybil."

I sat in the nearest chair, my legs like jelly. "This is worse than I thought."

"You've got to talk to her before she makes a big mistake and ruins her life."

"Waitress." One of Joyce June's customer's called for her.

Was this the reason Sybil looked like death warmed over? I needed to confront my friend—tonight.

At midnight, the sound of the top step squeaking told me Sybil would soon be in our attic room. In the moonlight, I saw her go to the dresser, pull some clothes, and gather other items from the top into a paper bag.

"Sybil." I sat to the side of my bed. The strong acrid smell of cigarette smoke assailed my nostrils. She didn't smoke or did she?

The sound of my voice caused her to step back in shock. An article of clothing fell from her grasp.

"Maddie, you scared me half to death. I thought you were asleep." She bent to pick the dropped item from the floor.

"No. I've been waiting on you. We need to talk."

"There's nothing to talk about."

"Yes, there is, and his name is Charles Roberts."

"Charles isn't any of your business." In the moonlight, her chin jutted at the old familiar angle that came before the usual pout. Did I detect a slight quiver on her lips?

I wanted to turn on the overhead light, but the switch was on the wall at the door. Sybil continued to stand at the open doorway, ready to bolt at any moment. I needed to be as non-confrontational as possible.

"Sybil, we're all very concerned about you. You can't execute your job properly. You always collected the most tips because your customers fawned over your service. Now they're complaining. Even Johnny's worried."

"I'm a little tired, but things are going to change."

"How so?"

"Charles and I are going to get married."

"Sybil." My heart begged for her to understand my next words. Would she let me approach her, comfort her? I moved, and she cast a furtive look behind her. I stayed seated on my bed. "Sweetie, I don't know how to tell you, but—"

"Charles is married." She cut me off and finished my sentence.

"You know?"

"Of course I know. Charles tells me everything, unlike your precious Abbott."

Her words hit me like a slap in the face. "What do you mean by your insinuation?"

"Nothing. Just drop it. I need to go." She took a step backward toward the door.

"Sybil, we've been friends so many years. Can't I persuade you to take another look at this man? Don't you see anything wrong in your relationship with him?"

"I love him, Maddie. Charles will get a divorce, and we'll be married."

Her words sounded simple—an easy solution to the situation, but not likely to happen. "Does he have children with his wife?"

"Two, I think. But they can come and live with us. I won't mind. And we can have some of our own."

Sybil's mind could not be changed. That much I realized. She wasn't thinking rationally. "Where are you going?"

"To stay the night with him."

I shook my head. "According to all we've been taught in church, you'll be going against God's Word."

"We're going to be married, Maddie. It's okay." She continued to believe her lover's lies.

"Does Charles Roberts tell you that?"

"Maddie, I'm through talking. I need to go." She bolted for the stairs.

"Sybil, listen to reason." I jumped from my bed to follow her.

From the blackness of the steps below, I heard, "Guess this means you won't be my maid of honor." Standing there listening to the sound of her retreating footsteps, I understood something else. The odor of alcohol wafted in the air along with the cigarette smoke. Sybil had started drinking.

Sybil did not work the breakfast crowd. When I went for midmorning break, I found the reason. Her clothes and other personal belongings were gone from our attic bedroom. She'd moved—I figured into Charles Roberts's rented room.

At lunch, Johnny came to tell me quietly about her work notice. "She said they were leaving town."

I couldn't help but cry. "We've been best friends for ten years. She'll leave a hole in my life."

"Why don't you get Joyce June to move in with you?"

"Thanks for the offer, but you know what they say about losing man's best friend?" I sniffed.

"I assume you're talking about a dog, not a woman. Although . . ." he grinned, making a joke, trying to cheer me up.

"Yes. A dog. I've read you should wait to replace a beloved pet. Gives you time to grieve and get over it."

"I understand. Will you be angry if I say I'm relieved Sybil's gone? I didn't want to fire her, and I was on the verge. I've been trying to tough the situation out until September."

I nodded and went back to work. The dining room chairs were full of guests, and we were shorthanded.

The day's work over, I headed for the girl's bathroom to wash hands and face for bed. What a day!

While combing my short wavy hair, I had time to think about Sybil. I knew my friend couldn't claim to be without fault. She loved to play at love—until caught in a snare of her own making. She reminded me of a bug in a spider's web. Once there, the spider trapped it, and the more it struggled, the tighter the web was spun.

The Bible talks about enticing women. Should it have the same discussion about men? Were women always at fault? Ah. The wolf in sheep's clothing, that's where Charles Roberts fit. He was a liar, cheat, and adulterer—the devil himself weaving a mesh of deceit.

Love. What Sybil had with her man-friend couldn't be called love. Consummating desire, passion, or sexual attraction without marriage is not love. Thinking about the word, a deeper understanding came to mind. Love shouldn't be trifled with, because God initiated the term. True love comes from truth, not deceit.

Sorting through the issue, making sense of the situation, did not cheer me up.

After one last look in the mirror, I walked the stairs to my bedroom with lead feet. The room's emptiness surrounded me like a wet, cold blanket as I entered and went quietly to the window. Mocker's tune was mournful—somber. I turned from the window, letting the moonlight guide me back to bed. Physically and emotionally exhausted after a long day of work, I climbed in and cried myself to sleep.

36

"Whew!" Joyce June and I sat at a table in the empty dining room, our aching legs and feet stretched between two other chairs. "I can't believe the summer's almost over."

Pulling my skirt up over my knees, I leaned my face upward toward the rotating ceiling fan. The air stirred the damp tendrils on my forehead. "I don't know whether to be happy or sad so much has happened."

"You've had a rollercoaster ride. Have you heard from Sybil?" She sipped a glass of sweetened ice tea.

"No. Not a word. Her parents are devastated. They sorta blame me. I don't know what I coulda done different. I still can't believe she's gone—that she ran off with him."

"Do you think they'll get married?"

"He has a wife and two kids, and she came to visit him. They spent several days together in Maggie Valley. Doesn't sound like she's unhappy with the situation."

"Don't guess Sybil will be back next year. Will you come back, Maddie? We could room together."

I drew circles in the frost on my cold glass. "I'd like that, but my life depends on how my relationship with Abbott progresses."

"Has he said anything about marriage?"

"In a roundabout way. Nothin' concrete."

"But, you're expectin' him to."

"I think he will."

"Will you say yes?"

"What do you think?"

Joyce June laughed. "He told me he wasn't feelin' good this morning."

"I know. I may need to check on him. Not tonight, of course, but after breakfast tomorrow—if he doesn't show."

"Maddie, *Gone With the Wind* opens in Atlanta in December. Why don't you come down and stay with my mother and me? I'll get tickets, and we'll go to the premiere."

"Clark Gable—ugh." I couldn't think about a movie starring him without . . .

"Come on. I know the name leaves a bad taste in your mouth now, but four months should make a difference. I'll give you my address in the morning so we can write each other."

"Okay. I'm bushed." I stood and took a few steps toward the hallway. "Joyce June, if I don't get the chance to talk to you before I leave, I want you to know I've enjoyed gettin' to know you."

"Thank you. Me too. Let's don't lose touch."

Abbott didn't show for breakfast. I finished the morning's work, worrying he might be ill. As soon as possible, I pulled my apron off and went to find Joyce June. She sat in a chair inside the kitchen wrapping silverware with napkins.

"I'm goin' to check on Abbott," I said, walking over to the soup pot and dipping a bowl of hot cream-of-chicken soup ready to be served to the dinner crowd.

"I noticed he didn't come to breakfast."

"I hope he isn't really sick. He's supposed to take me home tomorrow morning." From a box of aluminum foil, I took a sheet and wrapped my partially full container.

"My mother always said, *sick men are such strange little creatures.*" She handed me a soup spoon from her stock, plus a cloth napkin and kitchen towel off a counter nearby. "You may have to feed him," she explained.

"That'll be the day." I grinned at her.

"Do you want me to go with you?"

"Somebody's gotta stay in case we have a customer. I won't be gone long." Placing the towel under the hot bowl and the napkin on top, I tossed my apron on the dessert counter as I headed past the office.

"Hey, Maddie. Where you goin'?" Johnny asked.

"Goin' to check on Abbott. He didn't show for breakfast. He may be sick."

"Better get an umbrella." He nodded at a tall container next to the door. "Looks like it'll rain cats and dogs any minute."

"Ah, I'll be fine. Don't have far to go."

"Remember I warned you. If he's bad sick, will you still need my car tomorrow?"

"I hope so. I may need you to."

"Now, you're talking." He grinned and winked.

I gave him a smirk and let the door slam behind me. I knew the noise would irritate him. Johnny didn't get ruffled often, but the door slamming annoyed him. I looked back thru the office windows, and he raised his fist in a mock threatening gesture.

Fifty steps on the boardwalk and a cold, light rain started to fall. From a distance, I heard the rumble of thunder. The bowl of hot soup felt good in my wet hands.

My summer job was finished—almost. Tomorrow, Abbott would take me home to Maryville. School opened shortly thereafter, and I intended to continue my position at Walland School. The thought of teaching again excited me, although without Sybil my enjoyment of the post would diminish somewhat.

White Feathers didn't seem busy. I climbed one step to the wooden sidewalk, walked to the side of the store, and stepped inside the covered entranceway to Abbott's upstairs bedroom. Setting the bowl of soup on a nearby window sill, I used the kitchen towel to wipe the water from my damp hair and clothes. The sound of men's voices came through an open door off the entranceway.

". . . sick as a dog. Something he ate at Waltzing Bear Lodge, no doubt." The voice coming from the store sounded like Abbott's cousin, a recluse who didn't often come to Waltzing Bear or go beyond his job as janitor and shelf stocker at the store. His casual remark about our food got my dander up.

"He's hoping Maddie will come and rescue him. Man, she's a real looker." Someone else laughed in response.

I grinned ruefully at this comment, took another swipe at my hair, and one step in the direction of the stairs while commandeering the bowl of soup.

"I told him a good bellyful of his Pa's rotgut would cure all that ails him." The cousin's statement accompanied a loud chuckle.

My smile froze on my face. What? Had I heard right?

"His father makes moonshine?" the unseen man asked.

"Biggest darn still in the eastern hills. Makes the best too. Abbott's carried the stuff to Knoxville, Tennessee, over to Asheville, and Lynchburg, Virginia."

"Pays taxes on his brew, huh?" The return comment held ridicule.

His companion's sarcastic response brought another rough laugh from the cousin. "Nope. Doesn't pay a dime's worth. Bribes everyone in sight—even some of the revenuers."

I'd heard enough. Abbott's father made prohibited alcohol, and his son hauled the moonshine to several states. No wonder he could manipulate mountain curves. Running an illegal product meant being fast—faster than the cops or the Ku Klux Klan.

Heading back to the Waltzing Bear at a near run, I broke into a cold sweat in the drizzling rain. Soup sloshed from under the aluminum foil, and the spoon fell to the ground. I didn't stop to retrieve the utensil, but turned into the alleyway leading to the back of the lodge, to the fire escape where Abbott and I often stood to say goodbye. Excruciating pain flooded my heart, and my throat constricted as I thought of our last parting—the sweet kisses and words of devoted love.

Sobs came with my tortured gasps for air. I doubled over and worked through the whole scenario I'd overheard. No. I couldn't be wrong.

We'd talked about his father. Some. Abbott never dwelled long on a conversation about him. I remembered Abbott's exact words at Mingus Mill when I'd asked if his father was a miller. *Among other things*, he'd answered. Other things meant a despised moonshiner. “Why hadn’t he told me then?” I murmured.

Deceit—the word I’d applied to Charles Roberts was a valid word pertaining to Abbott. I sat on the wet steps, dropped my head to my palms, and wept uncontrollably.

Finally drained of emotion, I got to my feet. The bowl of cold, diluted soup sat nearby on a step. I emptied the contents on the ground and watched dully as the white mixture coated the leaves of a dandelion and its yellow flower. Six steps led to the door. As I opened the door, a flash of lightning and loud thunder reverberated through the area. I turned around and looked at the sky. "Thunder, you *are* a destroyer, and I wish I knew the formula to get rid of you.” Could I blame my shattered heart on the weather? No, and there was no blueprint to heal my broken heart.

I headed for the bathroom. My hair dripped water, and my clothes were soaked. No need for Joyce June to see me. I dried my hair and clothes as best I could, then I climbed the stairs to the attic. The sight of Sybil’s empty bed made me cry again. My lovely summer had turned into a dreadful nightmare.

“Maddie, are you all right?” Joyce June’s hand on my shoulder woke me from a fitful nap.

I turned over, rubbing my sleepy eyes. “What time is it?”

“Almost twelve. Johnny’s worried about you. He’s waitin’ tables. Sent me to see if you were here. What happened while you were gone?”

I didn’t answer her obvious question. “I musta fallen asleep after coming back from White Feathers.”

“Your dress is wet, and you’re cold as ice.” She went to the clean dresses hanging on the wire line. “Here put this on and come down. We need you. We’ll talk at the afternoon lull.”

Being that I was typically as dependable as clockwork, Joyce June knew something must be horribly wrong. I appreciated her concern and let her boss me around, feeling good about not making the decision.

My afternoon talk with Joyce June didn’t include the conversation I’d overheard at White Feathers. I couldn’t bring myself to discuss the open wound. My bleeding heart ached thinking of the episode. It needed a Band-Aid. I distanced myself from the pain. I needed to decide on a rational course to resolve the difficulty. If Abbott came to pick me up tomorrow, our trip to Maryville gave me an excellent opportunity to confront him. What would he say?

A sliver of retained trust hoped he might be able to deny and explain the whole problem.

Abbott loaded my suitcases in the car while I stayed inside saying my goodbyes to Joyce June and Johnny. We stood in the office, watching the loading process.

"Maddie, you've got my address, haven't you?" Joyce June had her pocket hankie in her hand, dabbing at her eyes.

"Yes, I'll write you at the end of the week. You should get my letter by the time you arrive home." She intended to work one more week.

"Sure you don't want to stay until December, Joyce June?" Johnny asked. "I need someone to cover the leaf change. We'll be extra busy in another month."

"No. I don't think so. I need to recuperate. Anyway, I think I've got a job waiting tables in Atlanta in October."

"Will you come back next year? How about you, Maddie?"

"Have to see what the year brings," I said, going over to give him a hug. "I'll be back to see you, even if I don't come and work."

"I'm going to hold you to it." He pulled his lips into a thin half-grin and nodded his head. "I—I'll miss you if you don't return."

"Ditto to what Maddie said." Joyce June opened her arms wide for my hug, giving me a wet kiss on the cheek.

Abbott came in the door. "Maddie, the car's packed. Are you ready?"

If I answered the question according to how my heart felt, I would say no. Confronting him wouldn't be easy. But the time had come to go home. I was ready to see my mother and Edie.

Abbott held the car door and I slid onto the seat. Johnny and Joyce June stood on the boardwalk as Abbott entered and started the car. I kept waving until they were out of sight.

"I thought you'd come to check on me yesterday. I coulda used a hug and kiss."

Not wanting to answer him I asked, "And give me what you had, no doubt. How do you feel today?"

"Much better. Are you excited about going home?"

"Yes. I can't wait to see Mama and Edie, eat my mother's cooking, and sleep in my bed. You have two more weeks before you head home to Kentucky?"

"I do. Thought I might come over to Maryville and visit before leaving." He reached for my hand.

Instead of answering, I nodded.

"Maddie, I got some bad news yesterday. Looks like I won't have work when I get home. The teaching job went to someone else."

"What are you going to do?"

"What do you think about me joining the Army? If Congress okays the draft, they'll get me anyway. I'll have work and money coming in each month. Granted I won't get rich, but it's better than being on the dole."

"Abbott, everyone says the United States will go to war with Germany. You might get wounded or killed." I couldn't keep the concern from my voice.

"Would you cry over me, honey," He squeezed my hand.

"I'd cry over anyone who gets wounded or dies on a battlefield."

"I'll not get home often."

"I know." I decided to wait to confront him about his father.

Abbott continued to talk about his future plans. He stopped at Newfound Gap to take in the view. "Ole Smoky hasn't changed since the last time we were here."

Back in the car, he concentrated on driving the hairpin curves down to Sugarland Park Headquarters, where we again stopped for a bathroom trip.

"I'm glad to get out and stretch my legs. Driving curves like the ones we just came through make them ache."

“I thought you were used to driving curves. Had lots of experience at it.” My tone was lightly sarcastic.

He glanced at me but didn’t respond. Driving from the Sugarlands, he was quiet.

Abbott didn’t say anything until we topped the hill at Fighting Creek Gap. “Do you want to get a bite at Wonderland Hotel? We have memories there, Maddie.”

Yes, I thought. We’d spoken love to each other for the first time there. “Mama will have leftovers from dinner. Guess we’d better not.”

“Maddie, is something wrong?” The road straightened here, and he could turn to look at me.

Abbott had given me the perfect opening. So why was I procrastinating? “I’m tired from working and packing.” I gave him a weak smile.

“I have something for you in the back seat. Reach and get the package.”

The box was small and rectangular. “What’s in here?”

“Something to remember me by. I think you’ll get a chuckle from the gift. Go ahead and open it.” He went back to manipulating the curves.

I tore the brown paper from the box, tossing the shreds onto the back seat. The lid came off easily. Tissue covered a beautiful pair of white, leather moccasins with fringe and the Cherokee bird emblem beaded on the toe. Tears came to my eyes. “They’re beautiful, Abbott.”

“I thought you’d like them. They should fit your big f-e-e-t.” He held up his hand as if to protect his face from a blow.

I started to join him in his banter. Thought better of it.

We drove several miles, talking about Little River Lumber Company, Cades Cove, and my mountain heritage.

“You love these mountains,” he stated.

“I do. My family’s roots are here.”

We crossed the river at Townsend and headed downstream, passing Walland School.

“Is this a rock quarry?” Abbott asked as we went by a deep gouge in the mountains beside the road.

“Yes. The rock is used as fill on this road when Little River floods and washes the surface away.”

We were only minutes from my home. Maybe if he didn't say anything about a future together . . . *Please, Lord, I don't want to have this discussion.*

At Coulter's Bridge, Abbott pulled the car into a well-used parking area. Swimmers often congregated here in the summer to jump from the stone bridge into the deep water hole below. A seasoned cannon-baller sent water from one side of the river to the other.

He turned off the motor. "I have something else for you."

From under the driver's seat, he pulled with a flourish a long, white box—the exact copy of all the others he'd given me. "There's something inside besides the red rose." He slipped his finger under the tape holding the lid and offered the gift to me.

My heart thumped in my chest as I slowly opened the cardboard container, not wanting to guess the secret inside but knowing in my deepest being the possible contents. A small square velvet case sat at the bottom of the rose's stem. I shrunk from the discussion I knew would follow.

Abbott kept talking. "Maddie, you know I love you, and I believe you love me. Will you marry me? Not right now, but next year, after I settle down in the Army. I don't want to leave Cherokee without knowing you're waiting for me."

He reached into the box and retrieved the white case. The lid snapped open. A small, gold ring with three tiny, sparkling diamonds lay among the silk lining. He'd sacrificed several dollars to buy a charming engagement ring. Abbott held the ring toward me. "Maddie, I love you."

Tears of anguish flowed down my cheeks in a tiny river. My body shook with wrenching sobs.

Abbott made the wrong assumption about my tears. "Sweetheart, I'll be so proud to call you mine." He moved across the car's seat and took me in his arms, kissing my temple and cheek.

When he tried to move my face to his, the words I'd been hoping not to say burst from my mouth. "No! No! I can't marry you."

Instead of recoiling from the shock of my statement, his embrace became tighter—viselike. "Maddie, I don't know what's wrong. Tell me."

"You've deceived me like Charles Roberts did Sybil." I gasped between gulps of air. "You lied to me." My shoulder ached from his tight grip.

"Honey, I'm not married." He laughed. "Is that what you thought?"

"No, that's not what I'm talking about. Your father is a bootlegger, and you helped him run illegal alcohol. You know how I feel about both . . . what it's done in my family."

"Maddie, I did keep it from you because I knew how you felt about people who make the stuff and people who drink. But I haven't helped Pa since I graduated from college. I promise you not to help again. And the only time I touch the stuff is with rock candy as medicine. I'm sure your mother doses her children the same way."

He'd made a correct statement about my mama.

He relinquished part of his iron grip—enough for me to sit sideways so he could look at my face.

"Love can't be based on anything except the truth." I told him.

"Maddie, really. I didn't lie to you. I just didn't tell you the whole story. I promise that's the only skeleton in my closet. I love you. Please take the ring." His low voice cracked, and the tone contained the suffering he must have felt.

"I can't take it." I shoved the rose box into his lap.

"Now, honey—be reasonable. I thought you loved me. Didn't you tell me so?"

"Abbott, you lied to me. This action takes precedent over my feelings. Much as I care for you, I can't marry you."

"Then I'll throw the ring into the river." His emphatic statement caught me by surprise. Abbott never lost his self-control. He opened the car door and slid his legs from under the steering wheel, then headed for the water.

I jumped from the car. Followed him and grabbed his arm. "Don't do that. It's too beautiful to treat in this way. You'll be throwing your hard-earned money away."

"Then take the ring . . . or I will." He held the circlet toward me again.

I looked at Abbott, shaking my head slightly. This side of him I'd never seen before.

"I mean what I say, Maddie. If you don't take it, the river's its grave."

He placed the ring in my open palm. "This doesn't mean we're engaged," I said, not looking him in the eye.

"Okay." From the sound of his voice, I realized the discussion wasn't over.

The car hummed in perfect mechanical precision as we pulled into the driveway at my home—if only my life imitated its flawlessness.

When I opened the car door, I heard the clang of my father's blacksmith hammer. He was working in his shop in the field beside the house. My mother and siblings were nowhere in sight.

Before I could scoot to the ground, Abbott grabbed my arm, pleading. "Maddie, we need to talk. I've been thinking. Surely there's something I can say or do to change your mind."

The tears flowed again. "Abbott, you can't say anything to change what's happened. The moment's over—finished."

"I never knew you were so rigid. So set in your opinions."

"I haven't kept anything from you. I talked truthfully about my belief in God and my abhorrence of alcohol."

He dropped his hand to the seat beside him. Picking up the rose in its box, he placed it on my lap. I still clutched the ring in my hand.

"I won't give up, Maddie," he said. "I'll come in and greet your mother."

"No. Don't bother." I jumped from the car before he could detain me another moment. Instead of going to the front door, I ran into the breezeway between the house and garage. The workroom door at the back of the garage stood open, inviting my entrance. I eased the door shut behind me. The last thing I wanted was an audience.

The bloody overalls hung from the ceiling. I shivered as I passed them and fell into a dilapidated cane-bottomed chair near the electric wash tub. The strains of the song Abbott and I'd danced to ran around in my head—the words prophetic. But, my whole life did not depend only on Abbott, even though my love for him still remained.

Laying my head against the tubs cold, enameled surface, I continued to think about the last two days happenings. How quickly my life changed. Why? I didn't have the answer to that question. No, I sure didn't.

I didn't hear the car leave, but when I left the workroom, my suitcases, pocketbook, and the box with the white moccasins sat on the front porch of my home. I eased down to the top step at the end of the sidewalk—with the rose box in one hand and the ring in the other. I opened the box and retrieved the case, intending to replace the ring. Curiosity made me slip the ring on my finger. Abbott's ring sparkled in the sunlight with a perfect fit.

I pulled air deep into my lungs, letting it gush from my mouth. Snapping the box shut with the ring safely installed, I replaced it at the bottom of the rose stem. A piece of paper lay in the box's bottom—the address of Abbott's home in Kentucky.

"Maddie, it's good to have you home." Mama opened the screen door. "Let me help you with your luggage. Where's Abbott?"

As we went into the house, I explained that he needed to get back to work. "You know the businesses at Cherokee are short-handed this time of year."

37

May 8, 2006—Jenni

I stood on my mother's front porch with mixed emotions. Nothing of my confused mind pertained to her, but all focused on my stay in Kentucky. I wasn't prepared for the instantaneous change in my iron-gated heart. The whole idea of a man in my life was totally amazing. The poet's old line, *God moves in a mysterious way, His wonders to perform,* became an amazing conundrum in my life. What did He have in mind?

I pushed the lighted doorbell and entered before my mother could answer her door.

"Hey, Jenni. Come on in. Dinner's ready." I heard my mother's cheerful voice from the direction of her kitchen. "I've missed you."

"I'm in," I called to her.

I walked through the living room, past the formal dining room, to the delicious smell beyond. She came from behind the island, which held her stovetop range, and gave me a hug, waving an egg turner. "We're having fried yellow squash from your Uncle Stan's garden."

"Mmmm, smells like fried yellow squash." I stuck my nose over the steaming frying pan and looked at the lightly browned pieces of vegetable. "Mom, I'm glad to be home. Sort of."

"Now, what do you mean by a statement like that? Oh, hold that answer." She pulled the last of the squash from the pan and placed it on a serving platter. "Let's eat."

Carrying bowls of food, we went to her kitchenette and pulled chairs to the table. She murmured a prayer for my safe arrival and the food.

"Explain your remark, young lady," she demanded before filling her plate. "Did you leave your heart behind when you came home?"

My surprised look told her she'd hit the nail on the head. "How did you know?"

"Lucky guess, but you did talk about one young man a lot when I called. Come on. Tell me all about this lucky guy." She patted my hand and forked a slice of ham onto my plate.

I watched as she placed mashed potatoes, squash, and slaw alongside. Red, crunchy cinnamon pickles added color and flavor to the meal.

"I'm still attempting to understand what happened to me. I didn't go to Meadowview Stables to fall in love. You know my feelings regarding marriage. I've not been secretive about them, but, being in the presence of a consecrated man of God and his grandson who seems to be a good imitation of the older man, changed my heart and mind."

"Jenni, I'm absolutely thrilled. Haven't we been telling you this would happen? Wait until your Uncle Stan hears about your man."

"Mom, nothing's happened yet. Not one word of love's been spoken. So . . ." I picked my fork and knife from the table mat and cut a chunk of ham. "I'd prefer you not say anything until we see how my relationship with Abbott progresses. Doesn't this plan of action make sense?"

"If you say so. Have you told B.J.?"

"No. We eat on Thursday. I'll tell her then." I would share my secret. But, for the moment, I relished my undisclosed relationship, hugging it to me like my favorite baby doll, whose red lips and blue eyes filled my young heart with love.

Mom put down her fork and looked at me. "I still can't believe you've found someone to love—after all these years." She shook her head at the incongruous thought. "What about

Abbott drew you to him? What melted the iron gate you've always claimed guarded your heart? He must be really special."

What indeed? I'd been mulling this question all the way home from Kentucky, and there was no definitive answer. Abbott was a Christ-follower, although he didn't seem to exhibit the deeper commitment of his grandfather. He was good-looking physically, deep-dark, brown eyes, a charming smile. Even so, I'd known men of this caliber before. Peter Johnstein fit this mold. No, something in my new love's inner being called to a component of my soul, intertwined or meshed with this element without rejection. I looked at Mom and grinned. The explanation would be too complicated and ridiculous for her.

"I don't have a good answer for you. Our relationship is complicated. We just clicked." Those three words summed up our attraction without going into intricate details.

"Your explanation seems simplistic, Jenni. I was thinkin' earthquake or at least earthshakin' to introduce my daughter to love. How about Pops Kendall? What's he like?"

I drew a small sigh of relief that the subject had changed. The conversation continued with descriptions of Pops, the Milbern's, and the running of the Kentucky Derby. We went from eating at the table to washing dishes.

"I'm sure you're tired after driving home from Kentucky and unpacking, so you don't have to stay. Go home and rest." Mom let me off the hook of staying until dark.

"I do have a load of clothes in the dryer."

We said our goodbyes, and I headed home. As soon as I drove from her driveway, the words of a song from Mom's oldies-but-goodies station popped back into my mind. I'd dealt with this Frank Sinatra tune, *Love and Marriage*, coming home from Kentucky. The tune seemed very appropriate for my situation. My heart sang the song over and over again. "Jenni, you've lost your mind."

My heart answered. *No, you've only lost me.*

38

The quiet in my condo unnerved me. Being with Pops for two weeks and knowing he'd be around for companionship had spoiled me rotten. I longed to be back at Meadowview Stables. I missed Abbott. Although we talked each night, not being around him became harder with each passing day.

I settled into a routine of writing in the mornings and doing chores in the afternoon. Sometimes I'd write all day, not even changing my nightgown, just brushing my teeth and combing my hair. The story, flowing forth, filled my notebook.

Canceling my Wednesday lunch with Peter Johnstein came to mind, but I decided against it, electing to tell him in person there'd be no dates in the future. I drove to the hospital and took the elevator to the cafeteria. He waited at the door. After getting our food, we sat down to eat and made small talk. When we started talking about my Kentucky trip, I told him about Abbott.

He seemed genuinely hurt, and this made me feel guilty.

"Jenni, I thought we might have something permanent," he said, getting up from the cafeteria table and putting the dishes together on one tray. He walked me to the elevator but didn't ride down with me. I never expected to see him again.

On Thursday, I had dinner with B.J. We ate Mexican food at The Cantina. I loved the place—the same restaurant my mother and I'd planned to visit before the accident. The booths and tables were colorful with South-of-the-Border themes.

B.J. had worked late, so the customers were sparse when we arrived. The sign at the front entrance said to seat yourself. We chose a large, intimate booth where we could stretch our limbs and talk in private. Chips and salsa arrived soon after we settled onto our wooden benches. Chimichangas were on special. We ordered matching ones and leaned forward to talk.

"Jenni, I'm so glad you're home. There's been a big hole in my life with you gone." My friend glowed with happiness.

"Won't be long until Troy will fill the void completely," I suggested, smiling at her regretfully.

"A man can't take the place of a girlfriend. You know that. We'll always be going places together and talking on the phone."

"Troy's okay with that?" Women doing activities alone—even with members of their own sex—threatened the clingy, needy men in my family. There was always a woman in the mix, wife or not.

"He is. He plans to keep golfing and playing tennis with the guys. I wouldn't want to take him away from his interaction with them. You and I will have all kinds of time to run around together."

"I hope we can continue our Thursday dinners."

"I don't know why we can't. Let's plan on it."

"B.J., I have something to tell you."

"It's about time," she responded. For the second time this week, I looked at my dinner partner in surprise.

"What do you mean?"

"There's a man in your life."

"Have you been talking with Mom?" My mother had broken her promise.

"No, silly. Anyone who knows you and knows your feelings about men could figure this out. You've gushed about him on the phone. How is Mr. Abbott Milbern?"

"He's great," was all I could manage. When did I gush about Abbott on the phone? I didn't remember being so open and talkative about him.

"Are you in love with him?"

"We haven't used the word love. Our relationship is still in the beginning stages."

"But you think it's possible." B.J. leaned forward with the most wonderful smile on her face. "You do, don't you?"

"Oh, B.J., I've never felt this way about anyone before. I can't get him out of my mind, and every time I think of him, the old song about love and marriage and a horse and carriage comes to mind. Crazy stuff, huh?"

"You're gushing again."

"We've talked each night on the phone. For hours. He wants to come and visit. And soon. Says he misses me."

"No words of love, huh?"

"No. Is that normal?"

"He's careful, just like you. When he makes a commitment, it'll be a forever promise—no ifs, ands, or buts. Till death do you part, guaranteed. You won't be able to pry him loose with a crowbar."

"I wouldn't want to," I assured her. "I can't believe two weeks can make such a difference in my life."

"In my valued opinion, love has two methods of getting to you. It either creeps up behind you, or it slams you in the face. I believe you've been slammed, and I'd have guessed this is exactly what would happen." She chuckled. "What about Peter Johnstein?"

B.J. had no more than uttered the words when Peter appeared from a backroom with a stringy-haired blonde hanging onto his arm.

"Speak of the devil." I leaned forward and discreetly pointed my finger in his direction.

B.J. craned her neck toward the exiting pair. "That's him? With the blonde bombshell?" she asked, her hand over her mouth.

"Yeah. Said yesterday he thought we might have something more permanent." I scrunched into the corner of our booth, making myself small. They passed on the opposite side of the room.

Peter leaned eagerly toward his date, who chattered away. He didn't see me.

"What do you think of that? And I felt guilty about telling him I wouldn't be seeing him again."

B.J. hung out of the booth watching them as they proceeded down the aisleway. "They look pretty chummy. Guess this isn't the first time he's been out with her."

The couple rounded a corner leading to the entranceway and disappeared out of sight.

"Whew! Now I know why I had reservations about Peter. Funny how my intuition told me not to trust him."

"Do you have the same feeling about Abbott?"

"No, not at all. I'd trust him with my life and love. How about you and Troy? Would you do the same?"

"Absolutely, Jenni." We finished our meal. "I have an idea. Why don't you invite Abbott to the wedding? Have him come early to the rehearsal dinner."

"I wanted to ask you, but I knew money was an issue."

"Not when it comes to you and your special friend. In fact, I needed one more to round out the seating. Abbott will fit right in."

"Thanks. I'll ask him tonight when I talk to him. Only a little over a month until the wedding. Are you excited?"

"Definitely."

"Mom and I talked about your shower. We're looking at June second, two weeks before your wedding."

"I think the date's all right, but I'll check and let you know. Where?"

"Mom's. She has the biggest place, unless you have another suggestion."

"If I can get the fellowship hall at church, would you be open to that? Most people would be able to find our church easier than your mom's. What do you think?"

"Check and see. Mom's is available if the hall is booked."

"Speaking of books, how's your writing coming along? Did you gather much information from Mr. Kendall?

"Oh, yes. Pops Kendall is a dear, old pastor with experience in compiling sermons for Sunday delivery. He used his computer to record on hardcopy most of the information he shared, even researching some points."

"My guess is his input is especially helpful since he's lived the story."

"His memory is amazing. I have descriptions of the area, people, and customs of the Cherokee community. This is during the time period of his and Maddie's stay. Between his writings and hers, I understand the interaction between the characters and why they never married. My next step is to show my former writing teacher some of the manuscript and get her input."

"What would've happened if they'd gotten married?"

"Abbott would have been ecstatic, but my grandmother would have regretted the union. In the end, they would've been an unhappy couple with an unfulfilling marriage, much like some I know today."

"Why wouldn't your grandmother have been happy? She loved Abbott."

"Yes, she did." I paused to think. "Her life revolved around church activities, and she realized and planned for her husband to have this same commitment. Abbott went to church with her, but he didn't feel the same need. He didn't have Christ in his heart."

"But you just said Abbott Kendall became a pastor. Sounds like an ideal situation to me."

"Could've been. But that happened some years after their meeting in Cherokee. His epiphany came during the war. That's when he committed his life wholly to Christ."

"What a shame." B.J. felt the pathos of the doomed relationship.

"Not really. If they'd gotten married, we wouldn't be sitting here talking, and I wouldn't be in love with his grandson."

"Jenni, you're terrible."

"Maddie and Abbott were meant for each other, but circumstances in both of their lives pushed them apart, and they each learned to love someone else. I think their marriages were satisfying."

"Satisfying is not an exciting word when you apply it to marriage, Jenni."

"Maybe not, but I believe most marriages are based on being satisfied rather than excited. And maybe that's a good thing. After all, my Grandma and your Grammy were married several decades to the same man. Didn't seem to hurt them."

B.J. pulled a lungful of Mexican-spiced air into her lungs and exhaled. "True. How many women find the perfect man?"

"Only one."

"What!"

"Eve."

B.J. laughed. "And how did that relationship go?"

The cell phone rang as I dropped my nightgown over my head. I ran to my kitchen, picked the vibrating device from the counter, and headed for the den.

"Abbott, how are you?"

"Wondering if you'd had another accident or if someone had kidnapped you." He wasn't angry, just kidding me.

"B.J. and I were having dinner at The Cantina. I didn't take my cell with me," I explained, noticing he'd called twice before.

"I knew this, didn't I? You told me last night you were going and not to call early. Guess the info didn't stick. I'm bushed. Maybe I can use that as an excuse."

He sounded tired.

"Hard day at the dealership?"

"Not too bad. I didn't sleep much last night. Thinking of you, I suppose."

"Are you saying I'm a problem to you?" I pestered, smiling. I hoped I'd attained the station of big trouble in his life.

"No, you're a sweetheart—correction, my sweetheart. You are, aren't you?"

"Yes, I am, but causing you not to sleep . . ."

"My sleepless nights have nothing to do with you." He dropped the subject. "I miss you, Jenni. I'm thinking of getting in my car and making a flying trip to Tennessee to see you."

"I have a suggestion along that line."

He interrupted me. "You'll meet me at the welcome center and give me a great big hug and kiss. I'd like that. A real Tennessee volunteer welcome."

"No, silly. You know B.J.'s getting married."

"Yes, sometime in June—a June bride. Why do women want to marry in June?"

"Abbott, don't change the subject." My lighthearted chastisement worked.

"Okay, okay. B.J.'s getting married. Continue."

"She's extended an invitation for you to come, and she suggested coming early and attending the rehearsal dinner with me. The wedding's on Thursday, June fifteenth. Do you think you could take off from work on Wednesday, stay until Sunday? We'd have a long weekend to explore the Smokies."

"Miss Loften, you've come up with a perfect plan. I'll make arrangements with my father and plan on coming to the rehearsal dinner. He shouldn't mind since I've been covering the yearly holidays so he can forget work. Will I stay with you?"

"I-I don't know. Maybe Mom's. I'll finalized the details and let you know."

"Someone said to tell you hello."

"Pops?"

"Yes. Said his second biggest mistake in life was letting you go home to Tennessee. He's been lecturing me on not making the same blunder. He misses you too."

"Pops is a very special man. Someone easy to love. I admit, my condo seemed quiet and bare—no shuffling of a walker, no friendly morning greeting or busy rapport."

"He said you're a lot like your grandmother—looks, personality, and actions."

"I've been told the same thing by other people. When did you see him?"

"I stayed with him last night. Slept in your bed."

I laughed. "He's okay?"

"Oh, yes. We had a long talk." I heard Abbott grab a lungful of air. Its release made a shushing noise over the phone. "Jenni, I am tired, so I'll sign off, and we'll talk longer tomorrow night. Sleep tight, sweetheart."

"You too. Give Pops my love." His cell went dead.

I felt unfilled, discontented at the end of tonight's conversation. Abbott's demeanor, his tiredness worried me. And what caused this sleepless night? I should have asked him. Pinpointed the problem.

39

The following week, I caught up with Mrs. Rutherford, my literature and writing professor, at Maryville College. I remembered her favorite quiet place at Thaw Hall Library was at the end of the building whose façade included a long row of tall casements filled with panes of glass. I caught a glimpse of her through a panel as I walked the long, concrete sidewalk to the entrance.

"Jenni Loften, what a surprise." She flicked a smile in my direction. She sat at a heavy, wooden table among stacks and stacks of musty books, some extremely valuable since the building and part of its contents were around two hundred years old.

"I thought you'd be here, Mrs. Rutherford. Have you retired?" She hadn't changed a bit—gray-haired, serious demeanor, with steel-gray eyes that could drill into your soul and find the least of errors on your school papers. I liked her because she made me think and she sought to bring out the best of her students. Someone looking at her wouldn't guess at her natural cheerful personality.

"Yes, two years past. I still dabble in writing—novels and articles for literary magazines." She indicated several books strewn on the table before her. "What brings you to your old alma mater?"

"I need your help and advice."

"Please sit down. Tell me what's going on."

I pulled a heavy chair from underneath the table and sat beside her. "The writing bug has bitten me. I'm afraid I have a bad case of authorship."

She chuckled quietly. "You always did have a way with words. Just what are you writing about?"

"I'm working on a novel." My notebook with several chapters rested in my briefcase, which I'd placed on the tabletop. I pulled the blue, two-inch binder from its hiding place and pushed the manuscript toward her.

She opened the top and read the title. "What is this—fiction, non-fiction, biography?"

"The book is fiction, but it's based partly on a true story."

"What's the time period?"

"Before World War II, and takes place here in Maryville and in Cherokee, North Carolina."

"Does the novel include a love story?"

"Yes."

"Hmmm. It's a historical romance or somewhere around that category. I don't know enough to name the type with certainty. Where did the inspiration come from?"

"From my grandmother." I went on to explain the storyline and the amount of work I'd invested in the project. I told her about the many ideas I had gleaned from hearing people talk about old times in the mountains. "You see, there are many stories I can build upon to create future interesting books. You're holding my first attempt to put thoughts to paper."

"Ha! The bug has bitten you fatally." She sat silent for some seconds, tapping my manuscript with her finger. She leaned toward me. "Writing isn't the easiest profession in the world. Many people think we just sit down and put ninety thousand words on four hundred pieces of paper. They don't understand that research and interviews are involved to make sure our work is professional and accurate. And this is the easy part. Finding an agent to push the manuscript, editor to look at your work, and a publisher is an iffy proposition, especially if you haven't published before. Once this is accomplished, there's graphics and marketing, and somewhere down the road, your finished book. Years of work can go into one project. Do you understand what I'm trying to tell you?"

"Yes. The chances of getting published aren't great. But I believe I have a great story to share with readers."

"I didn't say those things to discourage you. I wanted you to understand the process of getting a book into print. Now, how can I help you?"

"I've got several pages done. I brought the first one hundred. These I've edited and gone as far as my limited experience in writing will take me. I hoped you'd check them, give me some pointers or even correct my mistakes."

She nodded her head. "Jenni, I remember you as one of my best students. If anyone can accomplish what you've decided to do, you can." She paused to think. "When do you need this back?"

"I'm not pushing, but my plans are to finish writing in July. Editing will take some time."

"Do you have an outline?"

"Yes, a rough one."

"Tell you what. I'll have this back to you the first week of June."

I grinned. "You'll edit my manuscript?"

She nodded her head. "I'll do this part."

"Oh, thank you. You can't imagine the fear and unease I carried into Thaw Hall along with my briefcase. I found it hard to ask someone to check my work."

"I know how you feel. I've been there too. The writing is your baby, and, although criticism is what you need, you don't want someone to hurt it—not fatally."

"But you're an English professor."

"Doesn't make any difference. Have you got your phone number on your work?"

"It's on the back page."

"I'll call you when I'm finished."

"Thank you, Mrs. Rutherford."

I snapped my briefcase closed. She had work to do, and I felt in the way. I waved goodbye as I rounded the first stack of books on my way from the library. Out on the concrete walk, I saw her open the notebook and start to read.

I worked even harder at my writing, trying to get countless thoughts down before I lost them completely. Sometimes I'd skip ahead and write whole scenes after an inspirational idea popped into my head. Then I'd weave the section into the manuscript at the appropriate place. Writing became a joyous experience with little writer's block.

One especially trying Saturday morning, the phone rang. Abbott never called this early in the day.

"Hey, girl," he said before I could say hello. "I wanted to remind you that Barbaro's in the Preakness Stakes tonight. Thought you might want to watch the second race in the Triple Crown since you saw him run the Derby. He stands a good chance of winning."

"I can't believe the race is tonight. Sure, I do. Want to watch, that is. I'm going to Mom's to eat. I'll twist her arm. She doesn't care much for sports."

"Every time I call, you're headed to her house for lunch or dinner. Be careful, you'll be as big as a horse, especially if she's a good cook."

"There's none better than her. She learned from my grandma."

"Guess I'll find out when I come down for the wedding. A little less than a month to go. I'm counting the days." He would stay the nights at my mother's.

"Me, too. I'm glad you called. I needed a distraction. My head's quit thinking."

Abbott laughed. "Jenni, that's not possible, or it's another version of brain freeze. Why don't you stop writing for a while? Go do something fun like clean house."

"Now you're talking. My favorite thing. No, not clean house, but you've given me an idea. I'll go have ice cream and have a *real* brain freeze. Maybe that will cheer me up and clear my head."

"I wish you were here. We'd go into Meadowview and have ice cream." I could tell he smiled at remembering our trip to the pharmacy. He added, "I'm watching the race with Pops at the big house."

"Is your mom cooking?"

"Yes. Hamburgers by the pool after the Preakness. I'm taking my swimming trunks. The house will be full of bed and breakfast guests. It's sort of a tradition for our family—the more the merrier."

"Sounds like a lot of work for your mother."

"You're right, but Sarah and her family are invited. She'll help. You met Sarah when you were here. She's got three kids and they love to roughhouse. We'll have fun."

"Yes, I remember her—delicious squash casserole."

"She's the one."

"I can't believe B.J.'s shower is only two weeks from today."

"I don't think I can—" He paused, and I heard the intercom at Milbern Ford announce his name.

"Jenni, gotta go. I won't call you tonight or Sunday. We'll talk Monday."

"Okay. Talk to you then."

Stuffed full of Mom's cooking, I reclined on her couch with my arm propped on a cushion. She rested in her recliner. The television announcer boomed the lineup for the Preakness a tenth time. The horses stood ready in the gates. Suddenly, one horse bolted the multi-gated network of enclosures.

"Isn't that Barbaro?" Mom sat forward in her chair, counting the gates.

"I think so. He's ready to run this race and win."

I watched as the handler worked to get the beautiful bay horse back into his stall. At the buzz of the bell, the horses bolted down the raceway. They thundered past the cameras with the crowd roaring in the stands. But then . . .

Something was wrong. Edgar Prado, Barbaro's jockey, pulled back on the reins. The horse slowed down until he stood motionless on the dirt track. Before he stopped, he appeared to be limping.

The announcer went on with the race, but the interest in the stadium was on the reddish-brown horse standing on the course with his head down, weight off his right hind leg. Prado jumped to the ground. The medical team from the track hurried onto the field. The race ended. No one cared who won, and almost no one left the stands. Everyone's attention riveted in one direction—Barbaro.

"What happened, Jenni?"

"I'm not sure, Mom. Something is terribly wrong with Barbaro."

"I saw him limping."

"Surely the track has facilities for dealing with injuries such as his. We'll hear more later."

Abbott called at nine.

"Did you hear, Jenni?"

"No. I saw what happened."

"Barbaro broke his leg. Several places. The prognosis isn't good."

"You mean he'll never race again?"

"Not likely, and that may not be the end of his problems."

"What's the worst that could happen?"

"Horses can't live without working legs."

"Oh, Abbott. He's such a beautiful animal." I felt tears stinging my eyes.

"Jenni, I want to see you. Meet me at the welcome center next Saturday."

I laughed as I wiped two tears from my eyes. "Silly, I thought you were kidding about meeting at the state line."

"I'm not kidding." He sounded dead serious.

"Okay. I'll plan on it. We'll discuss the time later."

"Jenni, I love you."

I wondered if he could hear my singing heart.

40

I drove several miles north beyond the welcome center at the Kentucky-Tennessee state line before I could cross the interstate, turn and head south to the brick building that housed the info center. The sidewalk rose gently to the entrance. From a kiosk in the center of the main hallway, a pleasant-looking lady asked, "Ma'am, may I help you? Do you need a map?" Tennessee is a state that loves visitors.

"No. Thanks anyway. I have a new one. I'm going to look around."

"Are you from Tennessee?" she asked as I reached for a brochure among many hanging on the wall.

"Yes, I am."

"Nice weather we're having." She pulled a new map from under her counter and turned toward another visitor.

"Just beautiful for the end of May." As I left the building, she was talking to the new arrival about Pigeon Forge and Gatlinburg.

The smell of freshly cut grass and the hum of a large mower came from somewhere toward the back of the building. I debated going back to my car or standing in the grass on the tree-shaded hillock in front of the glass and brick building. The hill won. Abbott wouldn't be able to see me sitting in the sea of cars in the parking lot. A small maple tree afforded me some protection from the sun.

This particular welcome center was always busy, being on the popular north-south Interstate 75, which stretches from Michigan to Florida.

Abbott and I hadn't seen each other for three weeks and our relationship had continued to grow. I wondered if the meeting would be awkward. My watch said eleven on the nose—the time we'd chosen to meet. Ten minutes later, he drove into the parking lot and stepped from his car onto the pavement.

I walked toward his vehicle. "You're late," I stated, pointing to my watch.

He never uttered a word but walked toward me with determined steps. Grinning, he gathered me into his arms and, to the amusement of those walking the sidewalk behind us, kissed me solidly. "Not good husband material, am I?" he said as he pulled his face from mine. His eyes twinkled and happiness covered his face. "Punish me."

I did. I lifted my face to his and gave him a kiss of my own.

He steered me toward his car. "Let's go eat. I'm starved. I kept thinking about biscuits and gravy all the way from Meadowview. I didn't eat breakfast."

"Really. Food was first on your mind?" I teased.

"Second to you, of course."

I poked him in the ribs.

"Ouch! That hurt."

"Good."

"Where do you want to eat?"

"I thought about Kentucky Fried Chicken. My grandparents made eating there a tradition when we traveled, but we stopped only one time each trip."

"So food was on your mind?"

"Second to you, of course."

He laughed. "Do you know where the restaurant is located?"

"Sure, follow me."

We decided to get boxed dinners to go. The server gave directions to a local park where we could eat without company or distraction.

Our table was shaded by a huge oak tree.

Unseen to us but heard, squirrels raced up and down its limbs, barking sharply at each other. Occasionally a leaf fell to the ground from their above-our-head antics.

"I feel like we're being dive-bombed," Abbott said as an acorn narrowly missed his head.

I took a sip of tea from my cup. "It's spring. Thoughts turn to love."

"I understand their problem." Abbott nodded his head and reached for my hand. "We should ask a blessing on the food and thank Him for safe travel.

After eating, we strolled around a small lake watching ducks and geese paddle through the waters of the spring-fed pool. The glassy surface reflected a few white, puffy clouds floating above the still waters. The air, warmed by the sun, blew fitfully.

"All we need is a boat to complete this scene," Abbott said, dropping my hand, kneeling and throwing a small stone in the still water.

"Why do people do that?"

"Do what?"

"Throw stones in water?"

He turned to look at me. "Because they can, maybe."

I nodded my head, accepting his answer.

He put his arm around my waist, and we walked to a bench close to our picnic table. The ducks came to eat biscuit halves we'd saved for them. When the bread disappeared, Abbott put his arm around my shoulder and drew me to him. I rested safely in his arms, head against his neck.

"Jenni, I love you," he said for the second time.

"Abbott, I never expected to love anyone. I've kept my heart in a lockbox. If I open my heart to you, you can't hurt me."

"You can trust me. I won't hurt you."

I pulled in a huge lungful of air, letting it rush out of my pursed lips. "Then I can say I love you. And I've never, ever spoken those words to another man."

"My sweetheart," he whispered, pulling me carefully to him and kissing me tenderly, as if I might break should he squeeze too hard. "Jenni, there's one thing I need to sort through before we talk future plans. I can't tell you the problem. Don't ask me.

Is it enough to know I love you? Will that suffice for now?" He looked at me, brow furrowed.

I tried to look into his soul, find the problem in the depths of his eyes. Had I missed a certain air or thought alerting me to his despair?

"Jenni, is my love enough for now? Will you trust me?" he asked again.

"Yes," I answered quickly. "We have forever."

We lingered over dinner at a small, local restaurant until we needed to say our goodbyes.

"I don't want you to be tired at church tomorrow. You have a longer drive than me." I stood in his arms with mine firmly locked around him.

"Yes, and I have a part in the service." Abbott confided.

"You do?"

"It's our emphasis on missions Sunday. The pastor wanted me to give a brief testimony about a trip the college group took to Montana last year. We went to a group of Lakota Sioux to refurbish the local church.

"I didn't know you participated in missions."

"I usually take one trip each year. The Bible tells us to take the Word all over the world."

"Yes, I know. Our church goes to New Mexico and South America. I've never been, preferring to stay closer to home."

"Would you go if called to a foreign country?"

"I don't know. I've never thought seriously about the prospect. I hope you do well tomorrow. I don't relish getting up in front of our church."

"I'm ready. I have notes prepared."

"Don't be late," I said, smiling at him.

"Never," he replied as he bent to kiss me one final time.

41

The next three weeks became a whirlwind of wedding activities and details leading to B.J.'s wedding. Most fell on me since she worked until the final week before the selected date.

"Jenni, thanks for coming on such short notice." B.J. looked rushed and tired as she pushed against the door to Jensen's Flower Shop. She carried a large shopping bag in one hand.

She stopped with her shoulder against the glass door. "My wedding is small. Can you imagine what kind of preparation one with six or seven attendants requires? All the hoopla that goes with it? Sometimes not having much money is a blessing." She scrunched her head and shoulders together and shook noticeably.

"I know what you mean. After helping you, I don't want a huge one either. But, just think, one week to go and the ceremony will be over, and you'll have a stack of thank you notes to write."

She laughed. "I already have one from the beautiful shower you and your mother gave me. People are *so* generous."

"You're a sweet lady. You deserve everything you receive."

She squeezed my arm. "Next Thursday I'll be a married woman—Mrs. Troy Donaldson. B.J. Donaldson. Sounds important, doesn't it?"

The cool, moist atmosphere and smell of multiple flower scents permeated the interior of the shop. Mrs. Jensen came toward us from behind the counter. "B.J., I'm glad you could come. How are you, Jenni?"

Before I could reply, B.J. said, "Running her legs off for me. But now I'm through work until after the wedding—a whole month to wear myself out and recuperate. Yeah!"

"Stella's been gushing all week about being a bridesmaid. She'll fly home Tuesday from Harvard." Mrs. Jensen's daughter was valedictorian of our class in high school. She was studying political policy and scheduled to get her doctorate degree at summer's end. I had to admit to being a bit jealous of her. All she had to do was don her dress and walk down the aisle, and she could do this very well, being blonde and statuesque with perfect features. When she walked into a room, heads turned and empty chairs appeared. Most of my dilemma concerning her dealt with the fact that she knew her charms and flaunted them. Most of her ego trip started after our school years together.

"Did you know she's been offered a job at the State Department in Washington D.C.? She'll be working in a division directly under the Secretary of State.

"No!" B.J. squealed. "I talked to her Saturday. She didn't say a word."

"She heard Monday."

"What wonderful news."

"B.J., I called because I've dressed a vase with the flowers you selected."

"Speaking of vases, Jenni and I have been combing garage sales and here are the white cups and bowls you asked for—thirty for ten tables." She held the shopping bag for Mrs. Jensen. B.J. expected at least eighty for the reception, but only twenty at the more intimate rehearsal dinner.

"Great. We'll make up these for the rehearsal dinner tables and use them for the reception at your church. White mini candles scattered among your flower arrangements will provide a glow and romantic atmosphere in a room with lights dimmed."

After placing the bag on her countertop, she walked to a tall, glassed case and pulled from the cold interior a flat, white vase with an arrangement of exotic flowers. "After looking at this grouping, I thought maybe you'd want to make a change to your selection. And I have a suggestion."

"What don't you like, Mrs. Jensen? It looks beautiful," I said, deciding to join the conversation. I put my hand under a delicate, pink rose, cupping the flower in the circle of my palm.

"That's a dusty rose. I was afraid the arrangement wasn't light enough. Maybe we should take out the brown-tinged echeverias. They look like dark blobs in the combination." She pointed to the plants in question.

"They look like my Mom's hen-and-chicks—only they're green," I replied.

"They're kinfolks," she said.

"What's the small rose flower?"

"Would you believe oregano?"

"The spice?" I asked in amazement.

"Yes," B.J. said. She'd been looking at the pot of flowers during this exchange. "What was your suggestion, Mrs. Jensen?"

"To replace the echeverias with a harmonizing daylily. I have those in my flower garden. That will lighten the whole effect and reflect the candles."

"You'll have to replace them for the reception. Daylilies bloom only for a day."

"Yes, but I don't mind the extra effort if I think the endeavor makes enough difference."

"Then I'm okay with your change."

"Do you want me to show you a sample of the alteration?"

"No, I trust you. Jenni and I are going to lunch. Would you like to go with us?"

"Oh, no. We have another wedding this Saturday. I have plenty to do to get ready. Thanks for asking."

"Tell Stella to call me the minute she gets in town," B.J. called as we turned to leave.

"I will," the owner said, carrying the vase back toward the refrigerated case. "B.J., I don't know what I'm thinking. Here—take this home with you." She walked toward us holding the arrangement. "My mind's in a tizzy. But don't worry, I'll be fine next week," she grinned, running her finger through her bangs and giving my companion a quick squeeze.

When B.J. and I turned to leave the flower shop, I felt a moment of dizziness—not enough to make me curious as to its origin though. I assumed I'd moved too fast.

We stepped into the bright sunlight from the cold store. A stab of pain in my head caused me to have an instant headache. I never have headaches, and the last time my head hurt was after the car accident.

"Where're we going to go eat, girlfriend?" B.J. asked as the door shut behind us.

"I think I'm going to have to bow out," I said, putting my hand to my head.

"What's wrong?" she asked, immediately concerned. She juggled the flowers into her right hand and put her left one on my shoulder.

"I don't know." I crossed my arms and rubbed them with my hands above the elbow. "Could be coming from the cold store into the heat." I pushed my fingers against my temples and blinked my eyes.

"Do you need me to drive you home?"

"No. I think I can manage." I opened my car door and threw my shoulder bag into the passenger seat.

"You go home. I'll go get Chinese takeout and meet you there. I don't have anything else to do this afternoon. I'll stay with you."

I was ready to let her take over our plans. "I'll leave the front door open."

The stabbing pain subsided as quickly as it came, but the headache continued. At my condo, I took two aspirin and went to my favorite couch corner. When B.J. arrived, the headache was gone.

"How do you feel?"

"A little weak." I didn't tell her I wasn't hungry, but, after taking the medication, I knew I should eat. We opened the Kung Pao chicken and settled down to chat.

She picked my favorite subject to start. "When's Abbott coming?"

I managed a puny grin. "He'll be here for lunch on Wednesday."

"When will Troy and I get to meet him?"

"I don't know, unless you have a crisis before the rehearsal dinner."

"I'll see if I can arrange that. We need to spend some time together before the ceremony," she grinned. "When do you think Abbott will propose?"

"I don't know." I wanted to tell my best friend about Abbott's problem. Since I had no idea of its origin, I decided not to include the subject in the conversation.

"So much has happened this year." She reminisced. "Who'da thunk it?"

We went back to January and talked about all the highlights of our lives.

"Have you been back to your grandmother's home?"

"No. Mom said the work is progressing—painting and yard work. She said the family will list the property soon. Clearing the house of Grandma's stacks of papers and books is the biggest problem. It seems I'm inheriting those too."

"Where're you going to put the stuff?"

I huffed one short chuckle. "Good question."

"I feel like a nap." She yawned. "Your condo is too quiet."

"If you're serious, there's a throw and pillow in the bookcase next to the fireplace."

"I am." B.J. got to her feet to retrieve the throw. She settled down, wrapping the warm coverlet around her. "Be nice to have a few minutes of peace." She yawned again.

42

"Jenni, Abbott's here. He arrived earlier than we planned. You've certainly picked a dreamboat," my mother whispered on the other end of the phone.

"Do you approve?"

"Absolutely. When will you get here?"

"I'm ready except for makeup. Give him a hug for me."

The drive across town took forever. I caught every red light. A stalled truck blocked one intersection, and an ambulance with siren's blasting didn't help my progress. The only noise louder than the siren's wail was my beating heart at the sight of Abbott's car in Mom's driveway.

I pulled in beside the vehicle and grabbed my purse from the seat.

The driver's door flew open, and he pulled me into his arms.

When I could catch my breath, I stated, "We've got to quit giving the public a scene from a mushy screen romance."

"Never," Abbott exclaimed. He bent to kiss me a second time.

I came up laughing. "It seems you were on time this trip."

"Most important, if a beautiful woman loves you. I couldn't wait to get here." Holding my hand, he guided me through Mom's garage into the kitchen, where the smell of roasting turkey breast and green beans wafted from the direction of her stove.

"Hey, you two. Sit down. I just put the potatoes on to boil. We have a few minutes to talk." She rounded the center isle in her kitchen and followed us to her den.

"I've been helping your mother cook." Abbott picked a spot on her couch and pulled me down beside him. I sat, firmly held in the circle of his arm.

"He's a good helper. Peels potatoes very efficiently."

"It's nice to know he's useful. But I knew this already. He fixed my breakfast one morning at Meadowview."

"Well, when you're single and dependent upon your own expertise, you cook if you eat. Everything did seem to work okay—no cold eggs or burnt toast." He rubbed my arm, using the hand resting on my shoulder.

"I ate every bite."

Mom changed the subject. "We watched the—uh, what's the name of the race, Jenni?"

"The Preakness, Mom."

"How's the poor horse who got hurt?" asked my mother.

"Barbaro?"

"Yes."

"News is he's progressing nicely. The bones are starting to heal. Long range, his doctors will need to watch for laminitis."

"What's laminitis?" Mom asked. I wanted to know too.

"Put simply, when a horse favors one leg, he puts more weight on another. This may cause an inflammation in the second hoof, or laminitis. It's a very painful condition. I'm hoping his condition doesn't deteriorate to that point."

"The television cameras showed a closeup. Such a beautiful horse. I hope he's going to be all right." Mom put her feet on the ottoman in front of her chair

"I can truthfully say every racing fan in the world wants the same."

"Jenni says you're a champion swimmer."

"No, not me. My brother is the champion. He almost made the Olympics in '96. I do like to swim."

"Our clubhouse has a swimming pool, if you get the notion while you're here."

"I believe Jenni will probably keep me busy."

"I have another item you two can put on your list." She looked at me. "Your grandmother's papers are boxed and sitting in her garage. While you've got Abbott here, maybe he can help with moving them. Some of the boxes are heavy."

"Sure, we can do that," Abbott looked at me and nodded his head. "I'd like to see where Mrs. Ryeton lived. Pops said the mountain view from her backyard is exceptional."

My mother pulled her forehead into several rows of wrinkles. "Your grandfather came to Maryville—visited my mother?"

"I'm sorry, Mom. I forgot to tell you. We were out of town when Mr. Kendall and Kathy visited. Remember when we went to Uncle Jerry's and followed the Natchez Trace clear to Vicksburg? We ended up in New Orleans for boiled crawfish."

"Your graduation trip after finishing high school. Some years ago," she stated.

"Yes. We both needed a vacation. Grandpa was gone, and we stayed with Grandma for months until we felt sure she'd adjusted to life without him."

"How did Mr. Kendall know my father died?"

Abbott spoke up. "After my grandmother died, he subscribed to your local newspaper. Your mother often wrote letters to the editor, and she participated in your genealogy meetings. He loved reading about her. After your father passed, he sent her a card of condolence with a note inside. She wrote him back."

"She never said a word. What a sneaky, old . . ." Mom ended by shaking her head at her mother's ability to keep her relationship to a former love secret. "To think we knew nothing about Mr. Kendall."

"My family has known about your mom for several years. Pops told my mother a couple of years after his wife died. Not everything all at once, but over several years. Until she knew most of their connection."

Mom stood. "I smell my pecan dressing in the oven." She left the room.

"Jenni, Pops sent you an addendum to your conversation in Kentucky. He said it's *the remainder of the story.*"

"How could there be more? I thought we covered everything."

"You'll see. He filled me in on the details."

Mom called from the kitchen. "Guys come and help me put the food on the table."

Mom graciously released us from helping with the dishes. "Go on. I know you have lots to do today with the rehearsal this afternoon and dinner tonight."

Abbott followed me to my condo. We spent a few minutes so he could look around and approve my home.

I left my car in the garage, and we headed to my grandmother's.

The sight of the FOR SALE sign in the yard shocked me. "I guess, more than anything else that's happened since she passed, the sight of a sign announcing the sale of her house brings a feeling of finality to her long life."

"I'm sorry, sweetheart. I know this visit must hurt." Abbott reached for my hand as he held the door for me to exit his car. He unlocked the front door with the key I'd given him, and we walked into the foyer.

A quick glance at the staged living room and den gave me a feeling of her presence. The furniture had been reduced, but not totally eliminated. The bookcases, empty, except for a few knickknacks discreetly placed for show.

"Jenni, I forgot something in the car." Abbott left the room.

I walked down the hall to the three bedrooms. The first was empty. I looked quickly at mine and glanced at hers. The hospital bed had been removed. Her bedroom furniture sat in the same familiar places I remembered. I walked over to the bed and ran my hand over the comforter.

"Jenni, where are you?"

"I'm coming." I took two steps to leave, but, turning back, I whispered to the empty room, "Grandma, I believe you would approve of him."

Abbott stood in the den with another batch of neatly stapled papers and a manila envelope. "He finished these last week. He said the story of Abbott and Maddie ends here."

I took the papers from his hand, wrapped my arms around them, and pulled them to my chest. What could I say? And what would they say?

"Sweetheart, I'll look around. Why don't you sit down and read what Pops wrote."

"Thanks, Abbott." I kissed him on the cheek.

The lift chair had disappeared, leaving a big hole in the corner. Another fireside chair with a lift-up leg rest sat awkwardly in its place. I went to it and made myself comfortable.

Turning the first page, I became lost in the words Pops had written.

43

May, 1994--Maddie

The motor of the lift-chair hummed as it gently lifted me to a standing position. Using my walker, I headed for the foyer. Just as I turned the lock to open the wooden door, the insistent doorbell rang again.

He stood there, his hair as white as snow. The man I called my first love. I remembered the smile as our eyes connected—welded together. The earth and all its trappings disappeared.

"Abbott."

The face was an older, wiser countenance than the one I'd known in Cherokee or after the war.

"It's been a long time."

"Almost fifty years, Maddie. I counted them on my fingers. We saw each other when I came back from fighting in Europe. I wanted to tell you of my decision to follow Christ and make sure you were all right. You were married, of course."

"What a shock it was see you standing on my porch with no warning." On his visit years back, he hadn't called or written to inform me of his coming.

As I continued to reminisce on that last visit, he continued. "Jerry followed you to the door, and you carried a beautiful blond girl who looked a lot like you. I recall thinking they could have been my children. May we come in?"

"Oh, I'm so sorry. Where are my manners?" Caught up in the moment, I'd forgotten to welcome my guests inside. I unlocked the screen door.

"Please, Kathy, go ahead." Always the gentleman, Abbott held both car and entrance doors for females. His daughter walked into the foyer.

"Mrs. Milbern, so glad you've come."

"Kathy, please. I wouldn't have missed this meeting for anything. Pops, can you make it?"

Nothing separated us except space. Abbott walked forward, pushed the walker to the side. He enveloped me in his arms. His kiss on my cheek sent me swiftly back to the fire escape at Waltzing Bear where he'd taken the same liberty. I wanted to chide him for this action—in a joking way—but the sweetness of his being in my presence prevented any negative words.

I looked at his daughter. Tears threatened to make two curvy trails down her cheeks.

With his arm around my waist, two tottering old folks made their way into my comfortable den. My heart beat fast at being so close to him. My mind cautioned, *slow down—might be unhealthy at your age. Watch your blood pressure.*

Kathy pushed the walker in front of her.

"I'm sorry, Kathy. You'll have to look over us old people."

She looked at me. "I intend to do that. If you two will excuse me, I'm going to the front room—let you have some privacy. I have a book to read." She pointed to a satchel big enough to carry several. "When lunch time arrives, I'll drive you to the restaurant of your choice. We'll have some time to share while we eat."

"Are we going to Waltzing Bear Lodge and Restaurant?" Abbott asked, laughing. His chuckle, so familiar, rang in my eager ears.

"I'm afraid it's not there, Abbott. Karen and Jenni drove me to Cherokee three years ago. The building is gone and a new, modern motel stands in the same place."

Kathy responded. "We took Pops with us to Biltmore Castle and took a side trip to Cherokee. This was after Mom passed. Pops showed us White Feathers, and we drove by the lodge. The building stood in a neglected condition—boarded up."

"They tore it down. Nothing remains the same—even the people," I replied.

"Hearts and minds don't change, Maddie. The same feelings and thoughts come back over the years."

"I'm going to disappear." Kathy waved and left the room.

Abbott sat next to my lift-chair. He leaned forward with my hand held tightly in his. "You occupy a corner in my heart, Maddie. Over the years, I've entered and swept the area clean of cobwebs, revisiting our love and the many wonderful memories we made in Cherokee."

"Hard to forget a first love," I mused, my heart filled with joy at his presence. "I still have your ring." I held my hand for him to see. The gold circlet no longer fit my ring finger. I wore it on my pinkie. "When I see the gold band, I remember our first kiss. Do you remember where we were?"

"The train station in Asheville. You were headed to New York City for the World's Fair. You took my heart with you. Interesting how we can talk about such intimate details without being embarrassed."

"We're too old to be coy or uncomfortable."

"We'll, as the young people say, 'let it all hang out.'"

I laughed with him. "You haven't changed much."

"Neither have you. You're still my beautiful Maddie."

Minutes turned into hours as he and I reminisced about our summer in Cherokee. I told him Johnny Raintree had died.

"What about Sybil?"

I shook my head. "Never heard directly from her again."

"But you did hear something."

"Yes. Her brother told me she didn't marry Charles Roberts, but latched onto an older, wealthy man. I believe they did marry and have a child."

"It's so strange to suddenly cut a long-time friend from your life."

"A mystery I haven't been able to solve. I didn't approve the lifestyle, but my love for her didn't stop with her leaving or bad judgment."

"And Joyce June?"

"We went to the premiere of *Gone With the Wind*, and I stayed a week with her and her mother. For several years we corresponded. Then the letters ceased. While on a vacation trip to Florida, Charles and I stopped at her home. The young couple who lived there knew nothing about our former friend or her mother."

At this point, Kathy came from the front room. "Aren't you starved? I am."

I looked at the clock on the mantle. "One o'clock. Where has the morning gone?"

"Yes, and I'm off my schedule." Pops stood.

Over our meal, I learned more details about the Milbern family. Although Abbott and I corresponded regularly, being in each other's presence brought forth many facts too numerous to mention in letters. We laughed as we shared family secrets.

After lingering over lunch, Kathy, Abbott and I headed for her car.

"Do you drive, Maddie?" Kathy pulled into the traffic and looked briefly in my direction.

"Only to the store and bank. They're both close. I'm thinking of selling my car and giving the money to the children. Being a burden on them is my only reservation."

"Sometimes Pops drives into Meadowview. We worry about him." She looked into the rearview mirror at her father.

He pretended not to hear her.

"Pops, when we get back to Maddie's house, we'll only have an hour before we need to head home. You'll be exhausted and asleep, and I don't want to drive after dark."

The rest of the day passed too rapidly.

Abbott pulled a recent picture of Karen and Jenni from an end table. "Maddie, you know my namesake is about your Jenni's age." He raised his eyebrows, looked at me, and smiled.

"Are you suggesting . . ."

"I'm just saying maybe." He spread his hands in an open palm gesture. "We'll have to think of something to bring the two together."

"I'll work on it."

"I do have an idea."

"What's that?"

"Have you given any thought to marrying again?"

"What!"

"You and I, Maddie."

I sat astounded, my mouth open. We were both in our eighties.

I laughed—a short tinkle full of delight. "I'm honored by your suggestion." I shook my head as I replied. "Much as I would like to be your wife, it's too late. I don't want to leave my life here or my house. Guess I'm too set in my ways." I looked around at the familiar items in my den. "But that doesn't mean I don't love you. Always have."

I pulled the ring from my finger and offered the gold band to him. To my surprise, he took it and smiled a little bit mischievously.

"I have a suggestion. I tried to give this to you before. Maddie, I'm going to ask you to marry me . . . again. If you say yes, we'll be permanently engaged for the rest of our lives. Do you understand what I'm saying?"

I don't think I'd ever smiled as big in my life. "Yes, I do." I wanted him to ask with all my heart. Abbott had become a man I could admire and respect. He loved the Lord and shunned alcohol—the two problems, keeping us apart so many years ago. The barrier to our continued relationship had disappeared.

Abbott managed to get down on one knee and still sit on the couch. "Maddie Whitehead, you've been in my thoughts and prayers since I made the mistake of talking about your big f-e-e-t in Cherokee. I've loved you so many years, I can't stop now. Will you marry me?"

I looked at him. I didn't see the wrinkles in his face or the white hair. I saw a young man with dark brown hair, almost dimples, and eyes like sweetened iced tea. "Yes, Abbott. I'll marry you?"

"Sweetheart, I've waited so long to hear you say those words. That's the response I always wanted." He couldn't kiss me from where he knelt, but he kissed the ring he pushed on the finger of the hand he held firmly in his.

Minutes later, Kathy came to say goodbye.

Abbott and I followed her to the door.

"I'll be outside on the walk, Pops." She left, holding a lilac-and-blue afghan I quickly pulled from a couch in my living room.

Standing in the doorway, knowing I might not see him again, I couldn't help but cry.

"*Parting is such sweet sorrow*," Abbott quoted from Shakespeare. He brushed the gray hair from my temples, running his eyes over my face.

"We'll keep writing."

"Of course, we're engaged now."

I wondered if my face reflected the distress I saw in his.

"Abbott, this hurts too much."

"I know, sweetheart. Maddie, I'm going to kiss you—not a peck on the cheek, but a real one. One I'll remember until . . . well, you know."

Tenderly, lovingly, he pressed his lips to mine.

The door closed behind him and sorrow descended like rain drops from a Smoky Mountain cloud. Gentle at first, then hard, heavy. Pressing my forehead to the cold, wooden door, I stood in the hallway, sobbing.

44

June 14, 2006--Jenni

"Jenni, are you okay," Abbott's voice brought me back to reality. "You've been crying."

Lost in the words on the pages in my lap and dreaming of the many-years-ago encounter, I'd soaked a tissue pulled from a box on an end table nearby—the one he casually half-sat on. "I'm okay." I dabbed at my eyes. "They had such a sweet love. They might have . . ."

Abbott put his finger on my lips. "Don't cry over spilt milk. They weren't meant to be. The time wasn't right," he said. The finality of his words hit me hard. "Things turn out that way sometimes.

I pulled in a sigh. "We mustn't—"

"There *are* no it might have beens with us, Jenni." He leaned down and kissed me. "We *will* be."

"Is it actually possible to love someone your whole life? The couples in my family seem to miss any such target."

"I know," he nodded. Their actions might make you think so. Could be a little fire burns where you can't see it."

"I'd like to think you're right."

"You know what I think? I think your grandmother and Pops are a perfect example."

"But they never married."

"That's true, but I believe their love wouldn't have changed if they had been."

"Really. I've wondered about that. The fact that she loved your grandfather doesn't mean she didn't love Grandpa Charles. She did, and stayed with him for fifty-five years."

Abbott nodded his agreement. He turned his attention to the room. "This is a huge house—early seventies, ranch style."

I followed his gaze. "Yes, my grandparents loved this place. After my grandfather retired from the hardware store, his greatest joy was using his woodworking tools to make tables, lamps—any idea his family brought to him. He grew wonderful vegetables in his garden and took basketfuls to church. They traveled to all fifty states."

"Somebody liked to read."

I knew Abbott was referring to the many bookcases in the house, which were almost bare, the books packed in boxes and sold at garage sales or given to our local library. "They both loved history, autobiographies. And grandma loved women's fiction. Plus genealogies and books on marriages, deeds—you name it."

A large, framed picture of a church in the mountains hung on the brick over the fireplace with the room-warming insert still installed below. The anniversary clock with glass globe and mantel candles remained on the wooden ledge. Afghans and comfortable cushions waited on the couches to be used. "The rest of the house's rooms are formal," Abbott observed. "Even stripped, this one feels comfortable. Did your grandmother utilize the fireplace?"

"The boys did when they came to visit. She couldn't start a fire."

He stood to look out the den window. "The view from your grandmother's den is spectacular. Does that range of mountains have a name?"

"Yes. The Chilhowee Mountains. Nestled in them is East and West Miller's Cove. Beyond them, the Smokies' foothills begin. They're riddled with scooped-out valleys called coves."

"Are those apple trees?" He gestured toward my grandmother's backyard.

"Yes."

"Let's go look at them. I think I see evidence of this year's crop growing on the branches."

I held one more piece of paper in my hand. "I'm going to finished Pops's letter. I'll be with you in a sec."

"Okay, but don't take too long. I might not remember who you are."

"No chance of that. I'm going to make a pest of myself."

"I look forward to being pest control." He grinned and walked through a door leading to the back porch. His shoes rang on the short flight of metal steps to the concrete walkway below.

The piece of paper I held in my hand was handwritten, unlike the rest of Pops's information. I soon found myself reading an addendum meant for the present day.

My dearest Jenni,

We've covered the relationship between your grandmother and me in detail. Let me say something else. Maddie was right to refuse me. She stuck to her Christian roots by not marrying someone who wasn't a servant of God. Of course, I didn't understand this at first. But, as I studied the Bible and got to the meat of the Word, I admired and loved her more for her decision.

She didn't sign a paper like my grandson Abbott did. She didn't need a piece of paper or pen. Your grandmother was a strong independent woman. She made her commitment directly with her Savior. Her pledge remained in a sealed compartment of her heart. When a situation such as our love arose, she examined the circumstances by that oath. I came out lacking, and I should have.

Abbott's made the same decision, which is the reason he hasn't married.

Jenni, Abbott loves you. We've had many discussions about his feelings toward you. You can trust him with your love and life. He's good husband material—even if he's late sometimes.

I hinted to you that someone in the family might carry on my life's work. Abbott's struggling with a commitment. I can't tell you more than that. It's a secret, you know.

I love you, Jenni, my newest "sweetheart." Please marry Abbott. Even if he weren't my grandson, I'd think he was the one God picked for you.

I can't wait for you to come and visit again—sit on our loveseat.

Pops

I pulled another tissue from the box on the table and blubbered into its softness. I wanted to marry Abbott with all my heart. A future was implied, but Abbott hadn't asked me. And this secret or commitment, how would it affect our relationship? I stood and looked toward the mountains. Abbott had gone to the chain-link fence and stood looking over the farmland adjacent to my grandparent's property. He turned. Seeing me in the window, he waved and motioned for me to come.

45

B.J.'s wedding didn't have a single glitch. After two very intense days of festivities, Abbott rode home with my mother after the reception. Exhausted, I fell into bed at my condo. The next morning, he came for breakfast.

"You made a new friend last night," I stated as we washed the dishes.

"The bacon and eggs were delicious. Did you make the blackberry jam?" Abbott asked, ignoring my statement.

"The answer is yes. Mom and I picked them ourselves. You ignored my observation."

"If you're talking about Stella Jensen, I think I was pursued. Every time I moved away from her, she seemed to follow with another question."

"Men usually run *after* her."

"Do I detect a bit of jealousy in your inquiry, little lady." Abbott dried his hands with the dish towel and took me into his arms. "That's a no-no." He shook his head back and forth. "I have absolutely no interest in Stella. I have exactly what I want in these two arms—the most beautiful girl in Tennessee." He hugged me. "I thought you and she were friends."

I pulled away and turned back to the task at hand. "She's more B.J.'s friend than mine. In school, she struck me as being too smart, too beautiful, too . . ." I struggled with a kind word.

Abbott finished my sentence. "Too egotistical?"

"Well, yes. B.J. never seemed to get her."

"She's a charmer. Do you think her actions cover a deep-seated inferiority? That she's actually afraid of screwing up and people finding out the true Stella?"

"Huh? Guess I didn't get her either."

"Cut her some slack and feel a little sorry for her, like I do." Abbott changed the subject. "I like B.J and her new husband. I never asked where they're going on their honeymoon."

"Big Bend National Park, since both are hikers."

"I've never heard of the park."

"It's in Texas someplace, down near the Mexican border. Troy's been there with his buddies. I believe they've got a rafting trip planned on the Rio Grande."

"Now I could handle whitewater rafting."

"I believe the trip's tamer than shooting rapids."

"You have rafting trips here in East Tennessee and North Carolina, don't you?"

"Yes."

"Haven't you been?"

"No."

"Not very adventurous, are you? We need to put a little excitement in your life."

"You're all the thrill I can stand." I elbowed him.

"What's on the agenda for today? I'm ready to ride with my sweetie. Be nice to be alone with you all day—no distractions, no loud talking."

The dishes were clean and stored in my cabinets. "We're going up to Clingman's Dome, the highest peak in the Smoky Mountains, and walk to the tower. Down to Gatlinburg or Pigeon Forge for lunch and shopping. We'll finish with a nice, quiet sunset trip around Cades Cove where my ancestors, the Tipton's, lived."

"I can't wait."

"Did you bring a jacket?"

"I did as you asked."

"Mine's on the bed in my bedroom. Will you get it?" Abbott left, and I rinsed the soapsuds from my kitchen sink.

"We're ready," he said when he returned.

As we walked to my garage, I asked, "So you don't think much of Stella?"

"I didn't say any such thing. She's beautiful and—"

"Abbott!" I punched him in the ribs.

"Why do you do that," he complained, grinning.

Being with Abbott was like basking in the warmth of the sunshine. He loved learning new things. When we got to Sugarlands Visitor Center, I had to pry him from the place. We watched the movie commentary in the theatre, and he bought several books to read, including some I recommended.

We drove the curvy road to Newfound Gap. I explained the park's dedication occurred there, on the dais built into the side of a hill, with President Roosevelt the guest speaker.

"Maddie and Pops were here when the platform was in the construction phase. They sat on the rock wall surrounding the parking area eating fried chicken from Waltzing Bear Restaurant. Being here, in a site special to them, makes me cherish the story of their love even more."

"We need to sit on the rock wall and do the same someday—eat chicken, gaze at the everlasting hills." Abbott waved his hand in an expansive motion. "I know. We'll celebrate the publishing of your book. How's your writing coming?"

We walked back to my car and Abbott drove toward Clingman's Dome. "I've finished the rough draft. Now, I start reading the chapters and putting more meat on the bones. Add and edit description and action." I went on to explain what I had in mind, giving him some descriptions of my work. "I can see a month, or maybe two, before I send in a proposal."

"What are the chances your book will be published?"

"Not good for an unknown first-time writer with no platform."

"We'll pray about finding the right place to send your hard work."

"I'll need all the prayer I can get."

The Dome parking lot had several rows of cars, but we managed to find a space.

"Are you ready for this?" I asked as we started the half-mile walk.

"Piece of cake," he replied.

A few minutes later, we both huffed and puffed as we walked the steep route to the concrete incline which led to the covered overlook. Abbott loved the view. He spent some time, walking the elevated concrete circle, reading the information concerning the vista from each direction.

"Maryville is there." He pointed to the southwest. A steady wind blew his hair onto his forehead. He held the stray locks with his hand. "Let's go," he said. "I see why we needed our coats." The jackets kept us warm in the cool, mile-high air.

Back in the car, I turned the heater on briefly. We cruised down the mountain into Gatlinburg.

"Are you game to drive through Gatlinburg to Pigeon Forge?" I asked as we stopped at one of many red lights on the main drag, which was packed with store-to-store shopping and people.

"Sure. Walking sidewalks looking at t-shirts with only elbow room doesn't appeal to me at all."

"How about snow skiing?"

"Sure, but not in June."

"They have pecan fudge and turtles."

"Now you're talking. I am hungry. Haven't you heard my stomach growling?"

"Then we'll go to a place next to the old mill race and eat. They have superb corn chowder, and the meals are great. When we head back to Cades Cove, we can take the spur and bypass the traffic here in Gatlinburg."

"Isn't Dollywood in Pigeon Forge?" Abbott asked as he stopped to let pedestrians cross the narrow street.

"Yes, but we don't have time to visit today."

"I'm a little old for carnival rides, and most theme parks are two-day trips."

"Dollywood's no different, but old mountain ways are showcased there. You might learn something."

"You forget my roots are dug deep in the Kentucky foothills where Daniel Boone and many other mountaineers lived. I'm not unfamiliar with making soap, grinding meal, and blacksmithing. I'll be glad to take our children one day."

I glanced at Abbott. He made this statement as casually as talking about the weather. But he still hadn't asked me to marry him. Did he assume he didn't have to? The thought made me uneasy and the presence of an unknown problem in his life added to my troubled reflections.

46

On Saturday, Mom planned a cookout on her back deck. Uncle Jerry and Aunt Bonnie were in from Nashville to do paperwork on grandma's estate. Uncle Stan and Aunt Marilyn intended to come. Steve, his wife, and the twins weren't coming for lunch, but promised to attend later.

I arrived at ten o'clock. "Where's Abbott?" I asked Mom, who scurried around the kitchen in a tizzy.

"He's on the back porch," she said without elaborating.

I walked through the French doors leading from Mom's hallway to the redwood deck. Abbott had a rag and dishpan. "What are you doing?"

"Seems your mother doesn't use her deck furniture enough to keep the dust and dirt from the cushions and framework. I made the observation and somehow volunteered to make them user friendly."

I laughed. "That's Mom for you. Have you got an extra cloth?"

"How about a drying towel?" He indicated one hanging over a banister nearby.

I pulled the towel off the railing and started drying the cushions of the chairs he'd cleaned.

"Did you sleep well?" I asked.

"Dreamed about you." I stood close enough for him to kiss me lightly on the lips.

"What time will you leave tomorrow?"

"I'll be here for church services and leave after lunch." He slapped his rag at a piece of leaf on a deck chair and slopped soapy water on the vinyl cushion. The water ran onto the dusty deck. "Guess I'll have to spray the deck with the water hose. Wonder where she keeps it?"

A pang of aloneness hit me. "I hoped you'd stay longer."

"Pops and I are scheduled to attend church services in the evening. Mom and Dad have a prior commitment and can't take him. Pops never misses."

"I admire him for his dedication."

"Jenni," Abbott stood and looked at me. "I don't think he'll be going to the evening services much longer. I can tell he's slowing down. I wonder if Maddie's passing has anything to do with his sudden frailness?"

"They supported each other. I think you may be right."

"I've been thinking. You need to come for the Fourth of July. We shoot off a few fireworks at Meadowview, and you need to see Pops. He misses you. Stay for a month with us."

"A month—I don't know."

"Good. Then it's settled."

I laughed. "I'll think about your proposal."

There was the unsettling word, once more.

"I'd better go check on Mom." I put the towel on the railing.

"I need a see-you-in-a-minute kiss."

Abbott sat his work tools on the deck table, took me in his arms, and gave me a wonderful good morning buss. Any reservations I had about the future melted away.

Uncle Jerry and his wife arrived at exactly eleven thirty. After introductions, Abbott joined my uncle in the den, and Aunt Bonnie and I helped my mother in the kitchen. I could hear the drone of voices from the other room but couldn't distinguish any words.

Uncle Stan and Aunt Marilyn were fifteen minutes late.

"It wasn't my fault," my uncle said to Mom. "I sat in the car at fifteen after eleven."

Aunt Bonnie, anticipating the argument to come, headed discreetly for the hall bathroom. She detested arguing. Moments later, I heard the unmistakable sound of water running in the sink.

Aunt Marilyn shoved a bowl of potato salad onto Mom's cupboard. "If he'd gotten the ice from the downstairs refrigerator and the cooler like I asked him to, we wouldn't be late. But no, I had to climb a ladder to get the cooler and wash it out in the laundry tub. The ice had become one big chunk, so I beat it with the hammer, cut the end off, and dumped it in the cooler. Then I had to lug the heavy thing up the stairs, put my potato salad inside, and take the two to the car where my husband sat listening to the radio." She didn't take a discernable breath during this barrage and ended by glaring at my uncle.

Uncle Stan rolled his eyes. "I didn't hear her."

"You hear what you want to, Stan." Another glare.

"We weren't driving that far," her harassed husband protested. "She didn't need a cooler and ice. The doggone po-ta-to salad," he spat out the syllables and continued, "wouldn'ta got warm during the ride here."

I couldn't help but think it was just another beautiful day in the Ryeton family. Nothing had changed—except Abbott, of course.

"Okay, okay." My mother jerked the wrap off the potato salad and leaned over the counter. "Marilyn, this smells delicious."

My mother was a whiz at diffusing the squabbles between those two. And Marilyn loved being praised for her cooking.

"Uncle Stan," I decided to help. "Abbott and Uncle Jerry are in the den."

"I'm gone."

After our lunch, Uncle Stan cornered me as I put his wife's po-ta-to salad in Mom's refrigerator.

"Wow, you've snagged a dreamboat, Jenni."

"You approve, Uncle Stan?"

"I do. Makes my last suggestion look sad. Have you set a date?"

"He hasn't proposed."

"Why's he waiting? Do you want me to nudge him?"

"No, uncle," I said, horrified. "Give him time." Secretly, I wished someone would nudge the love of my life.

"You do love him, sugar?"

"Yes, for the first time, I love someone I can marry."

"I'm happy for you." Uncle Stan gave me a little squeeze.

We walked back to the deck where a discussion of race horses was in progress. Uncle Jerry was saying Andrew Jackson raced horses. "We were at the Hermitage and attended a meeting where a gentleman was discussing the former president's stable of racing horses. Jackson's horse, Indian Queen, raced in the first official horse race in Tennessee. In fact, in the late 1700s and early 1800s, Tennessee thoroughbreds were superior to other breeds in the United States."

"Are you saying their blood ran orange?" Steve asked, who'd arrived with his wife and twins.

"I doubt the color orange was the state color at that time," my uncle concluded.

"How do you retain such detailed information? Do you have a photographic memory?" Abbott asked.

Uncle Jerry laughed. "No. We just wrapped a one-hour documentary on Andrew Jackson, during which we chronicled his love of horses. He wasn't the only president or politician who kept a stable of the racing breed. Even George Washington raced horses, and he loved Arabians. Used the sturdy breed when fighting for our nation's independence."

"I heard George loved mules." Steve had two of these animals. He used them to pull a wagon around his new eighty-acre farm.

"Yes, I ran into this info while researching articles for the Jackson story. Maybe we'll do a future documentary on how he acquired the first ones to come to America."

Abbott walked over and put his arm around my shoulders, giving me a little squeeze. "Jenni's coming to Meadowview in July. She started riding lessons on her last trip."

"You, Jenni?" Uncle Stan exclaimed. "I'd never have guessed."

"I'm in the same boat with your uncle." My mother looked at me with new admiration in her eyes.

"I wasn't very good."

"She was too. I kept her on the horse too long. I'll try to be a better teacher when she comes back for her July visit."

"How long are you going to stay?" my mother asked.

"She's going to stay a month," Abbott stated. "Pops misses her."

"Who's Pops," Uncle Jerry asked.

My mother chimed into the conversation. "While you're discussing Abbott's family, I'll put a pot of coffee on to perk and get our dessert ready to eat." She headed for the French doors into her hallway.

"What are we having?" Uncle Stan asked, always ready to eat his favorite part of a meal.

"Devil's food cake with vanilla ice cream and drizzled chocolate syrup over all. I may even put a maraschino cherry on top to add color." She looked at the twins, knowing they loved the red orbs.

"We'll help, Aunt Karen." The twins disappeared behind her.

"Is it time to go home?" Abbott asked. His arms surrounded me as we stood in my garage saying goodbye.

"Afraid so. Time passes so quickly."

"I enjoyed meeting your family yesterday. Uncle Stan and Aunt Marilyn got along well."

"Yes, one would think I made up their squabbling. Probably tried to put on a happy face with you here."

"Uncle Jerry is fascinating. His business must be really interesting."

"Lots of pressure, I'm sure. I went to Nashville and stayed a week with them. He let me go on a shoot. There musta been twenty people scurrying around putting up lights, checking set details, and working the cameras. After ten takes for a single scene, and this done multiple times during the day, I got bored. The movie business is monotonous and very tedious. Detail oriented."

"I can't imagine you being bored, sweetie. We'll try to keep you occupied when you come to see us in July."

"Abbott, I haven't said I'd come. I'm sort of a homebody."

"But you traveled with your Mom and your grandparents and loved it."

"We took one or two-week trips. I've never been away from home a month."

"Might as well get used to being gone now."

"We'll talk in the next few days."

"Okay, I'd better hit the trail. I'm going to miss you."

He didn't linger over goodbye.

I stood in my garage after he left wondering why I hadn't realized my life would change drastically when he and I married. I'd been so enamored with our new love, I hadn't thought about the consequences of our future together. But don't couples discuss these matters after the proposal?

Abbott needed to settle his problem, and we needed to either become engaged or cease our connection. The latter caused my insides to shudder. Could our relationship end? He'd said I could trust him, but this lingering . . .

I pulled in some hot air—unusual for June—and let it gush from my mouth. My arms had chill bumps.

47

"Mom, I need to talk to you about something." In B.J.'s absence as a sounding board, I decided to confide in my mother.

"I wondered when you'd break the silence. Do you realize we've sat ten minutes without saying a word? The television isn't on, and we don't have books to read. You've been staring into space, and I've been looking at you," she laughed. "What's on your mind?"

After eating dinner, we sat on her deck with the light from her hallway casting shadows on our seating area. Crickets chirped in the darkness beyond her railing. A dove cooed to her young in a nearby tree.

"How long did you and Dad go together before he proposed?"

"Is that it?" She slapped her hand on the chair arm. "Why do you ask such a question?"

Immediately, I felt silly. "Abbott hasn't proposed."

"Jenni, aren't you rushing this situation. You've only known him—what, three months?"

"Going on. But, he's talked about a future. I'm sure he'll ask me. I want my life settled."

"I've never thought of impatience as one of your behavior traits."

"Am I maturating or morphing into another being?" I grinned in the darkness.

"I hope not. I liked the former Jenni. But, to answer your question about your father, we dated for eighteen months and waited another three before the wedding."

"Eighteen months! That's a long time. Abbott and I can't wait so long."

"Why not? You want to make a good decision—not rush into a life-changing choice. After all, a year and a half didn't help me.

"Five years wouldn't have helped you, Mom."

"No, it probably wouldn't have," she said turning serious. "Walter's troubles started with his father, and maybe farther back than his generation."

"You felt sorry for my dad? His family situation?"

"Yes. But what about you? What's your hurry, besides having your life settled?"

"Mom, have you ever been in a circumstance where you just knew your inclination or decision was a right one. You didn't need any other information or time?"

She nodded. "When I married your father?"

"Mooom."

"Okay. I've told you before I had reservations even on the day of our wedding. I never felt what you just intimated."

"I couldn't marry anyone with doubts in my mind. I'd run fast in the opposite direction, especially after waiting so many years for Mr. Right to come along. Right means right one."

"I should have run but didn't. You see, I think you, my dear daughter, were meant to be. And I wouldn't switch one day of my life if the time meant not having you."

"Thanks, Mom. I love you too."

"Sorry I changed the subject. Let's get back to Abbott."

"He is the one. There's no need to wait. I don't want anyone else. And we aren't getting any younger."

"Man, you've come a long way. From an emphatic young woman who didn't intend to get married to an emphatic young woman who does."

"I have, haven't I?" Now I laughed.

"I thoroughly approve of him. His demeanor exudes confidence and steadfastness. Good qualities in a husband." She paused and added, "Hang in there. He'll come around. When I asked him how he felt about you, he immediately confirmed he loved you. Didn't hesitate a sec."

"But, he didn't mention marriage?"

"Jenni, it's necessary to love someone first."

"Okay, Mom." My chest heaved a huge sigh.

"Is there anything else?" She looked at me. "*Whaaat?*" She opened her palms and fingers in a tell-me gesture.

My mother could read my actions like a book. "One reason he's not asked me pertains to a mysterious problem he's struggling with. Pops even mentioned Abbott's dilemma."

"You didn't ask him?"

"No, I wanted to press him on the subject. He gave me the impression he wouldn't know the answer if I asked."

"Then wait for him. Pray for him. Abbott's worth every bit of your endurance and patience. Are you going to Kentucky for a month?"

"I think so. Pops is such a wonderful influence. A lovely man. Maybe you could come to visit—meet the family."

"We'll see. I'm going to miss our jaunts around the country. We had some great times, didn't we?"

Before leaving for Kentucky, I needed to do one more thing. I headed back to the cemetery where several members from my family were buried.

There's something solemn about the quietness of a graveyard. Today the smell of freshly mowed grass permeated the air. A lawn mower still hummed from somewhere in the distance.

I paused at Grandpa Charles's and Grandma Maddie's graves. All the dates of birth and death were finalized. I bent to touch the last one—my grandmother's date of passing.

"I wish I'd asked more questions of you two—especially you, Grandpa," I murmured. "You were always so secretive about your growing-up years. You preferred to live in the present and forget the past. Did you know you were my favorite Grandpa? I'm telling you now, but you aren't the reason I'm here."

I walked over to my father's grave. After all the change the last months had brought in my life, I felt I needed this time with him. What would I say? I stood looking over the area, biting my lip and collecting my thoughts.

"Dad, I need to talk to you. You hurt me. Not physically, but emotionally. I never saw you hit Mom. The sound was enough. I heard her crying, and it wounded me as much as it injured her." The tears started to flow.

"I wanted to speak the words I'm going to say now while you lay in the hospital—when I saw you the last time. They wouldn't come. The moment wasn't right. Just as the time of Maddie and Pops's meeting and commitment didn't work in Cherokee. I know now God's plan didn't include a match between them. His scheme intended for a wedding two generations later. Isn't that exactly how He works?"

I shook my head at these thoughts, and the wonder of an omniscient Father filled me with joy.

I continued to look at my earthly father's tombstone. "I-I forgive you, Dad. I forgive you for hurting me and Mom. She had to endure a marriage no one should suffer. Did you just hear her say she's okay with that? Is there any greater love than this—to sacrifice for another?"

My thoughts turned to the greatest Sacrifice. "Jesus paid for your sins here on earth. He forgave you when He went to the cross. I must too."

There. I'd said the words I came to say. But, had I spoken all?

"Dad, I love you."

48

The sight of Meadowview Stables made my heart sing. I drove straight to the garage and parked my car. Kathy was in Lexington, and Pops expected me. Abbott planned to join us for dinner after work.

The afternoon sun beat down without mercy as I exited my car.

Someone called from the house. "Jenni, how are you?"

I turned around to see Sarah standing on the concrete patio with a broom in her hand. She waved.

"Hi, Sarah. I'm fine."

"Kathy wanted me to tell you the front door to Pops's home is open. Just go right on in. Oh, and Abbott said he'll help you with your luggage when he comes this evening."

"Thank you. I'll see you then."

I walked the rock drive to Pops's cottage carrying my overnight case and laptop. Instead of knocking and disturbing the sleeping occupant, I gently opened the door and went to my former bedroom. Nothing had changed. Peace reigned. I felt at home. A large vase of freshly cut roses sat on the dresser, a note attached.

The card read, *To our sweetheart—Pops and Abbott.*

At four o'clock the sound of a golf cart crunching the gravels on the front drive caused me to put down the book I read and walk to the front door. Abbott entered and took me in his arms.

"Sweetie, I'm glad to see you. I've been counting the minutes. Got off work early."

This was the extent of the conversation until our kiss was finished. "Ready to get your luggage?"

I nodded and added, "Thanks for the roses. They're beautiful. Are they out of Pops's garden?"

"Yes. He insisted I cut them yesterday. Can you picture him standing at the kitchen window pointing out each one to cut?" Abbott laughed—a carefree, lighthearted chuckle. He seemed different. More relaxed.

I didn't get a chance to inquire as to his cheerful spirit. He grabbed my hand and pulled me toward the cart. "I can't believe you're here for a month," he said as we went for my luggage.

Pops stood in the doorway as we returned.

I waved from the driveway. "Pops, I'm here."

"I see you are, Jenni, my dear one. I thought I heard you. Come into this house out of the July heat."

"Go on," Abbott said. "I'll put everything in your bedroom."

Rushing to the open doorway to embrace the gray-haired old man, I noticed his eyes were a bit more sunken than my last visit in April, his walk to our loveseat a bit slower. He leaned more heavily on his walker. His weakening condition wrenched my heart. I wanted to reach over and steady this lovely man as he sat heavily on a soft cushion. I didn't. I knew he wouldn't appreciate any action to help on my part.

"Pops, you look tired today."

He leaned toward me, putting his hand on mine. "I am. Didn't sleep well last night. I don't often have those times. I'm so happy you consented to visit. You light up this old man's home with your presence."

We looked up as Abbott walked into the room. "I certainly agree with you there, Pops." He came to the coffee table in front of our seat and sat on the corner. "What's this?" he lifted my heavy manuscript from the surface, looking at my cover sheet underneath the front plastic pocket of the notebook.

"A story I think Pops will want to read."

"Jenni, is this . . ." Pops reached for the four-inch binder.

Abbott stood. "Here, I'll put this tome into your lap. Weighs a ton."

I laughed at Abbott. "You're exaggerating, of course." I turned to Pops. "It is heavy, though. Be careful."

Pops rubbed his hand over the surface of the notebook. The pages included the edited version from Mrs. Rutherford, my college English professor. "I see you've titled the story *The Ring and the Red Rose.* Why?"

"Because those were the key items in the box Grandma gave me. But don't get comfortable with my heading. Publishers often change an author's ideas."

"They won't change your story, will they?"

"Not if I can help it. You'll find I've taken some liberties with Grandma's and your narratives, but I did this to make the story more readable and keep the reader interested. The skeleton of your story remains true to yours and Grandma's notes. I hope you'll approve."

"I have faith in you, Jenni. We both knew you must embellish the narrative somewhat. Whatever you did will beautify and enhance a wonderful love story—one ordained by our heavenly Father. If not for Maddie, I might not have accepted the Lord's call on the battlefield in Europe fifty-one years ago. One never knows when we plant the seed of the Word if it will grow and come to fruition. In my case, Maddie's words pointed me to the very decision God wanted me to make. I praise Him for her."

Abbott cleared his throat and leaned to kiss me lightly on the lips. "Dinner time." He pulled me to my feet. "Come on, Pops. Your chariot waits."

"Like Elijah?" Pops asked, looking up at his grandson with a twinkle in his eyes. He let Abbott help him to his feet while I recalled the passage from Old Testament Kings where Elijah went to heaven in a chariot of fire.

Abbott shook his head and laughed. "No heavenly fire or whirlwind associated with a golf cart."

"But possibly a mantle?" the old man said.

The men looked at each other, sharing a moment of understanding. I didn't get the mantle part, but, before I could ask its meaning, Abbott shepherded us out of the cottage. At the main house, he drove to the dining room door, which opened from the patio.

I left the back of the golf cart as Abbott hopped from the front. "Pops, sit still. I'll get your chair."

Chair? I stood next to the cart and waited. The sight of the wheelchair shocked me. Pops's health *had* deteriorated more than I could have imagined. I *should* have helped him sit on the loveseat.

I hurried ahead and opened the patio door, familiar with the routine of maneuvering an awkward wheelchair through small spaces.

Kathy came from the kitchen hallway with a tray of food. "Jenni, I'm happy you've come. Will you help me set the food on the table? Joe will be here momentarily. He's washing his hands. Pops, how are you feeling today?" She sat the tray on the buffet. Rubbing her hands on her apron, she came to give me a hug and kiss. "Come help me with the drinks and ice."

When we returned, she carried another tray of coffee cups and glasses filled with ice, and I carried tea in a pitcher and a carafe of coffee. Abbott or his father had arranged the food on the table. The men stood opposite Pops in his wheelchair, and the conversation had turned to fireworks.

"Let's eat before the food gets cold," Kathy suggested.

"Can't sit until I kiss my *future* daughter-in-law," Joe said. He took the coffee from my hands and placed it on a hot pad on the table. He turned and gave me a kiss on the cheek.

"Dad, she hasn't said yes—yet," Abbott admonished.

I pointed a finger at him. "You haven't asked."

"Oh," Joe said. "Guess I've got the cart before the horse." He laughed, raking his fingers through his sparse hair and looking a little bit uncomfortable. Slapping his son on the back, he continued. "Time's a-wastin'." With those words, he went to the head of the table and sat down. "Abbott, my *slow* son, will you say a blessing on our food?"

Everyone laughed. The sudden tension in the room eased.

“Is the dealership closed tomorrow?” Pops asked of his son-in-law.

“We’re closed in the afternoon. Decided to let my employees enjoy part of the Fourth at home.” He turned to Abbott. “The Moore couple will be at the showroom in the morning. They called after you left.”

“Great. What car did they decided on?”

“The blue Explorer.”

“I’ll get the car cleaned and start the paperwork as soon as I drive on the lot.”

“Are the fireworks arranged for tomorrow night?”

“Yes. Everything’s in order.”

“Joe, I’ve invited several from the church and Meadowview.” Kathy continued, “We’ve food to serve to our guests.”

“Food—does that mean hotdogs and all the trimmings?”

“Yes, and I’ll need the grill lit and managed by someone.” She looked from Abbott to his father. “And chairs on the patio. Lights too.”

“Don’t worry. We’ll manage, won’t we Dad?”

49

All day, a barrage of trucks and flurry of activity could be heard from Pops's cottage. After Pops left for his afternoon nap, I walked to the horse barn to see the setup for the fireworks. On the highest hill to the left of the barn, in a cleared field, several banks of wires, tubes, and tables were taking shape. Most of Meadowview would be invited or parked on the highest roads around the stables or on the grounds to enjoy the show.

My walk back home went through the woods to the far left of the display area. I wanted to visit the rock and trickling stream where I'd first understood my love for Abbott. He was at the main house, helping his mother with plans for tonight. I knew he'd arrived to help. Every sense in my body affirmed his coming.

In the sun's dimming rays, the lights in the swimming pool gave off a soft glow. The citronella patio lanterns' flickering flames reflected on the water's surface around the pool. The faint smell of burning lemon oil wafted from the open blazes atop the tall, portable lamps. The mood produced by the lights was romantic and malleable. Those in attendance spoke in low tones—their laugher low and steps noiseless.

Pops sat dozing in his chair, covered by a chenille throw, as Abbott and his father doled out hotdogs to the last guests.

When the last bun was filled, Abbott put down his tongs, came toward me, and whispered, "Sweetheart, I know Pops is tired. I'm going to wash my hands and take him back home. There's a special place we can be alone to watch the fireworks. We'll go there."

I looked around at the crowd. People sat in every conceivable place and cars lined the rock road leading to Pops's cottage and beyond—all the way to the barn and in the surrounding fields. Even the volunteer fire department's engine sat in a field close enough should they be needed. I couldn't imagine where we'd find such a place.

When Abbott returned, he knelt in front of Pops, placing his hand on a knee. "Grandfather, are you ready to go home?"

Pops started awake. "Yes, son, I'm ready—readier than you think."

Abbott stood, looked at me, and shook his head. He and I both knew Pops wasn't talking about the cottage.

We pushed his wheelchair to the golf cart sitting at the edge of the patio and helped him onto his seat.

Abbott turned to me as we headed for Pops's home. "I'll help him to bed. Give you time to freshen up. We'll take the golf cart to the barn."

Several minutes passed before Abbott appeared. "Sorry. He's really tired. We shouldn't have kept him up so long. I thought about letting him sleep in his clothes, but he insisted on a pair of pajamas." Abbott pulled me into his arms. "Have I told you today that I love you?"

"No, and I'm really upset. How are you going to make this up to me?"

"Come on, I'll show you."

The ride to the barn took longer than Abbott planned because people along the road stopped us to thank him for the show to come. Finally, we pulled into the horse barn. Rows of tack hung from the walls. Straw for the stalls, which were located on the far end of the barn, appeared to be stacked to the ceiling. The smell of horses, leather, and straw blended together. Even a sightless person could guess the use of this facility.

Caleb and his family sat in an open doorway looking toward the fireworks display area.

"Mista Abbott, can I get you somethin'?" he said and jumped to his feet.

"No, no, Caleb. Sit down. Enjoy the fireworks." Abbott waved to his wife and children as we rushed past them.

"Where do we go?"

Abbott led me to a corner behind the straw, where a set of metal, circular stairs led to the loft of the barn. "We start here."

The barn's copula had narrow benches—enough for four people to sit in comfort. A perfect place to watch the show. Abbott switched on a light as we entered.

"Shouldn't we leave the light off to watch the fireworks?"

He looked at his watch. "We have fifteen minutes."

I sat down. Instead of sitting beside me, Abbott sat opposite. His face looked serious. What on earth had happened?

"Is something wrong?"

"No. Everything's just perfect." I watched him pull air into his lungs and start talking as he exhaled. "Jenni, I love you. I've told you so many times, and you've told me the same thing."

He reached for both my hands. It was then I knew he would propose. My heart said yes, yes, yes.

"I also told you that I needed some time to work through a problem in my life. I've done so, and the answer will affect our future relationship. Pops and I've been talking about my decision. I've been making plans."

I remembered Pops saying he didn't have a son to carry on his work—but there was still a chance. And the brief mention of a mantle. Elijah had passed his on to Elisha. Did Abbott plan to be a minister? How wonderful! I could be a minister's wife.

But Abbott was saying, "I'm going into fulltime foreign missionary service. I've already contacted the mission board of our church association for details, and Heritage Chapel will sponsor me. I never thought I could face the challenges of leaving the States and learning a new language. Pops has convinced me otherwise. We prayed about my misgivings. This is the right choice—God's desire for my life. You have no idea how relieved I am to acknowledge His leading."

A chill came over me as I listened to him, my mind racing with thoughts. He was talking about leaving the States for a foreign country, staying gone for years at a time. I loved traveling in the United States, but I never shied away from coming home. I loved Abbott with all my heart. Could I sacrifice my comfort, home, and family to be with him?

"Jenni, will you be my wife? Love me in whatever circumstances we find ourselves—here and abroad?"

My mouth opened, but the words he wanted to hear didn't come. "Abbott, this is a shock. I need to think about what you just said. I do love you. I love you so much it hurts." He moved to take me in his arms. My head rested on his shoulder.

"I know I've hit you with something you weren't expecting. I know I didn't make up my mind in minutes. Take some time and pray for His guidance. I'm going to be praying too. I have no doubt that God has brought us together. But, I'll say no more."

At that moment, the boom of the first volley of firecrackers lit up the sky. I jumped in his arms. Abbott held me gently for the show.

He left me at the cottage door with a kiss. I clung to him. I didn't want to lose him.

"I'll wait, Jenni. As long as it takes."

I didn't sleep. I paced the floor. I went to the kitchen for ice water. I got on my knees and prayed at the loveseat where Pops and I spent most of our time. In the morning, I wasn't any closer to an answer.

Pops took one look at me and asked, "Jenni, you didn't turn Abbott down?"

I started to sob uncontrollably and fled to my bedroom.

✠ 50 ✠

Pops didn't come after me. He let me cry until I was calm. When I felt strong enough, I left my bed and went to join him. He sat on our loveseat, reading my manuscript and looked up as I approached. Closing the book and placing it on the table before him, he reached his thin arms toward me. I ran to him and fell into them. I needed his godly wisdom.

"Oh, Pops, what will I do?"

"Tell me your problem."

For the first time, I unloaded my life to him, not keeping anything back. I told him about my parents' marriage, my family's problems, and my wish never to marry. His comments were few but to the point, leading me to understand the necessity of letting the past and its troubles remain history.

"Jenni, in First Corinthians, the thirteenth chapter, Paul says, *when I was a child, I talked like a child, I thought like a child, I reasoned like a child. When I became a man, I put childish ways behind me."*

I sat up and looked into the eyes of a man filled with years of wisdom that came from studying his Bible and loving his Lord.

Pops continued. "As a child or youth, you reasoned or gained an immature perspective from the family turmoil happening around you. As an adult and a Christ-follower, it's necessary to look at your former surroundings through His

Word. This enlightenment should change your viewpoint—should make you understand according to Romans that in *all things God works for the good of those who love Him.* Now this may be for edifying today or in the future."

Pops continued. "Don't let the distrust, uncertainty and fear from the past influence your future. You're here and there's a reason you are here. The iron gate is gone and there's a new Jenni—one who can love in a way she's never loved before."

"Oh, Pops. I feel so much better getting that load off my chest."

"We find altars in the funniest places. Even in an old man's arms. I've been praying that God would let me help you break the bonds of the past on your life and decision making. How do you feel now?"

"Better. Empty. Swept clean."

"Let's don't bring back the old family stuff. We need to concentrate on new—a new future family. Abbott asked you to marry him."

"Yes, he did."

"What did you say?"

I shook my head. "I didn't answer him because his decision to become a fulltime missionary took me by surprise. I wasn't expecting . . . I suppose in my heart I thought car salesman's wife for the rest of my idyllic, secure life."

"Jenni, it's easy to let our former lives influence our future. Once we struggle through those problems and put them in proper perspective, as you've just done, we can make good decisions without the past influencing them. Do you agree?"

"Yes." I'd listened to my tirade as I unleashed the words on Pops. Nothing I said made sense if I believed the Bible.

"God gives us power to overcome all obstacles, including the hurts of the past."

"I agree that He does. How could I not believe this? I gave my life to Him."

"Do you love my grandson?"

"With all my heart. And knowing all I just told you about love and marriage in my family, those four words say a lot."

"Yes, they do. So, what are the obstacles to you marrying Abbott?"

"There aren't any now."

"How do you feel about his decision to become a missionary?"

"With God's help, we can lick tigers."

Pops laughed and squeezed me in a hug. "I hope you don't have to literally lick tigers."

"I need to call Abbott." I made a move to get off the couch.

Pops grabbed my hand. "He's coming. He'll be here tonight to help me to bed."

"Then I'll wait. Oh, Pops, surely God has been directing both our families these many years.

"Yes, He has."

"I'm hungry, Pops."

"By now your breakfast is cold."

"I'll see what I can salvage."

When I went into the kitchen I felt remarkably calm for the first time in my life, and I knew the answer I'd give to Abbott. Happiness bubbled from the depths of my soul and my heart was glad.

51

Abbott and I decided to have the wedding on the first Sunday in October. Pops couldn't come to Maryville, so the ceremony would take place at Heritage Chapel in Lexington.

After the morning preaching service, we would provide a catered lunch at the church for those who wished to attend, and we'd say our vows following the meal. An invitation-only reception for family and close friends was planned at Meadowview Stables when the ceremony ended. We felt, due to Pops's declining health, getting our special day bundled into one short period of time would be best.

During the two months before the ceremony, my mother and I made several trips to Kentucky, helping Kathy with the arrangements.

"Jenni, don't be concerned about the preparations. I have everything under control," Kathy said over the phone two weeks before the ceremony. "I'm actually enjoying working through last minute glitches. Have you got your dress?"

"Promised for tomorrow. B.J. and I'll pick it up after she gets off work."

"I know you're excited. I am. Soon you'll be my daughter."

"I wish my grandmother could be present. She would've loved this occasion."

"Are your uncles coming?"

"Yes. Uncle Stan said he'd be there with bells on—whatever that means. Uncle Jerry promised to video the ceremony."

"I'll make sure he has a good seat in the front—right beside your mother. Uncle Stan can sit behind him."

"I'm glad we kept the ceremony simple but elegant." Although I could have asked several women to participate in a larger ceremony, B.J. was my only attendant as my matron-of-honor. Abbott's father was best man. His brother, Earl, and my cousins were ushers. His brother's granddaughter, Lily Milbern, would act as flower girl.

"Jenni, you'll love the flowers and candelabra and unity candle. The florist showed me a computer-generated layout of their suggestion. Come to think of it, I'll get them to email you a copy."

"Great." I continued, "Kathy, I sure wish I could be there to help. You've got most of the work on your shoulders."

"Ah, this is my last wedding for years to come. I'm enjoying the excitement immensely. How's your book proposal coming?"

"Done, except for taking my pages to Mrs. Rutherford to check. I didn't realize the time involved in gathering so little information. Thank goodness for the Internet."

"I understand its benefits. Although, sometimes, I long for a good telephone book with pages I can leaf through for local numbers."

"Mrs. Rutherford suggested submitting my manuscript to an editor she knows who publishes historical women's fiction."

"Your book is on my prayer list."

"Mine too."

"Today's the day for final arrangements for the catered reception here at the house, and my appointment is in one hour. Guess I'd better hang up and get going."

52

H*urry, hurry, and hurry again*—familiar words of the past week's unending preparations. Like falling into a rushing river and swimming frantically so I won't drown.

"Don't anyone take my blood pressure," my Mom joked as we walked from the catered luncheon down the hallway at Heritage Chapel.

Nor mine either. The arrangements were over, but the pressure wasn't.

The excitement was palpable as I stood in the bride's dressing room at Heritage Chapel. I draped my wedding dress over the high back of a fireside chair. The pearls and sequins nestling among the embroidered bodice flashed in the overhead lights.

My busy mother unzipped the new wheeled carry-on case she'd bought for my honeymoon. She pulled toilet articles, shoes, and other items from its pockets and then scurried around the room placing and replacing her bridal clothes on a nearby couch. She ended by nervously picking at my wedding dress on the chair—working its folds just so, checking a minute thread sticking from an underarm seam.

I watched in amusement. "Mom, take it easy. We have a whole hour. You'll have a heart attack if you don't slow down. Catch a breath."

She stopped in her tracks. "I want your special day to be perfect." She smiled and approached me. "Abbott's such a wonderful man. He'll be a loving husband and father."

"Whoa, now. Let's get through the wedding before we start discussing children."

She laughed and kissed me on the cheek. "Jenni, I'm so proud of you—happy you're my daughter. I love you, dear." Tears appeared in her eyes. She gave me a hug.

"Mom, I couldn't have picked anyone who's supported me as much as you have. You've been a steady anchor in my life. I love you back."

The poignant moment passed as the door burst open. Mom and I turned to see B.J. rushing into the room. She carried her own suitcase and held her deep-rose attendant's gown over her arm.

"How's it going?" she gushed. Without waiting for an answer, she continued. "I just saw the bridegroom in the hallway. He's gorgeous in his white tux with the dark-rose cummerbund and bowtie. He's headed to entertain the guests in the fellowship hall, and I sent Troy with him. He said to give his bride a kiss." B.J. gave me a buss on the cheek.

"Not that kind of kiss, I'm sure," Mom said.

We laughed, easing the tension in the room.

"Where do I put my dress?" B.J. asked. The gown rustled in its plastic bag.

"In the bathroom—there's a small rack."

She came back from hanging her dress. "Never saw a refrigerator in a bathroom before."

Mom grinned at her. "The bouquets are inside. Keeps them cool, exactly the way I'm not feeling at this moment."

Kathy came through the door. "Last chance to see the auditorium before guests start filling it up. Abbott's promised to stay away. He's eating lunch now. You should see him with a bib tucked under his chin." She laughed, holding the door open.

Avoiding Abbott had its challenges since we usually sat together in church. We'd decided to keep the tradition of the bridegroom not seeing the bride. He hadn't come to church services or been present at lunch. Not being around him when he was close by felt like part of me was missing.

We hurried to the open door. As I passed through, Kathy said, “He said to give his soon-to-be bride a kiss.”

I pushed my cheek toward Kathy while Mom and B.J. giggled.

Kathy continued. “And your Uncle Jerry’s started making his video. He’s coming here in about ten minutes.” No photographer for Abbott and me since we’d have a professional video with sound at no charge.

“Hurry,” Kathy said. “They’ll start seating guests soon.”

During last night’s rehearsal, the candelabra were in place with ivy intertwined in the metalwork. Some of the side aisle and entrance flowers were installed, but most of the flowers arrived after today’s preaching service, being set up as we ate.

The four of us walked across the hallway to a double-door entranceway. Kathy pulled one door ajar to let us enter. I looked in shocked wonder. The email hadn’t done justice to the real thing, or Kathy had made last minute adjustments.

She confessed, “I made a few modifications at the last moment. I added more urns to give a wraparound effect to the wedding party—tall to short. I hope you don’t mind, Jenni.”

“Not at all. The whole effect is breathtaking.”

We walked to the front of the auditorium. The white runner I’d walk on down the aisle lay rolled up before the first altar step. Behind it and up the altar steps, the unity candle stood on the pulpit platform overlooking the ceremony below.

“I love the roses, all colors, and the greenery brings out their delicate hues,” Mom said, touching a pink flower and bending to smell the blossom.

“What’s this one?” B.J. asked, pointing to a small, delicate cupped bloom.

“Sweet pea. And the large flower is clematis. Ranunculus is used for fill-in.” Kathy looked at her watch. “We have to get back to the bride’s room.”

We walked past the pews with white net and a single red rose tied at the end. I hugged Kathy. “I feel like a princess marrying a prince.”

“Good. That’s exactly what I intended. It’s time to dress the princess.”

"Mom, I believe I hear my music." Played on the church organ, the strains of the "Bridal Chorus" swelled through the halls of the church.

"Yes. Are you nervous?" She opened the door of the bride's room.

"A little." It was an understatement. I pulled the long train of my white bridal gown through the narrow doorway and headed down the hall to where B.J. stood. Three large gulps of air didn't stop the panicky feeling. "Please, Lord, help me through these next few minutes," I whispered and felt some better.

Kathy waved. She directed traffic for the processional into the main church. Lily Milbern, my flower girl, disappeared through the auditorium entrance carrying her basket of rose petals.

"I'm so excited," B.J. said. She stood ready to head down the aisle. "Did you feel this way at my wedding?"

I nodded.

Since my father couldn't accompany me on my walk to the front altar, Mom insisted on performing this honor. She would walk on my left side and Kathy on my right. They both wore long dresses the color of B.J.'s.

B.J. disappeared through the door. Mom and I walked forward and waited for the musical entrance cue.

A noise to my right caused me to look in that direction. Kathy wheeled Pops from an open doorway to my side. "He insisted on going down with you." She shook her head.

"I think that's perfect." I leaned down and whispered to him. "You are full of surprises, but I love you still."

"I wouldn't miss the opportunity of escorting my Maddie's granddaughter for a pot of gold at the end of the rainbow. I do this in her honor, and because I love you too. I wish I could have performed the ceremony, but this will do. Ah, there's the trumpets. Ready?"

We stepped into the doorway. Mom and Kathy positioned the train of my gown. "Mom, take my arm." I winked at her and pointed discreetly at Pops.

"Oh," she mouthed, understanding my signal. The rustle of people standing blended with the music.

I put my free hand on Pops's shoulder. He covered it with his. Together we walked slowly down the aisle as Kathy pushed her father in his chair.

Abbott stood before the altar. His full grin and easy-to-read face loudly proclaimed his love for me.

At the front pew, we stopped. I bent to kiss Pops. Kathy locked the wheels on his chair, gave me a hug, and slid into her seat next to her father. I took Mom's arm, and, together, we walked to our designated place before the minister.

When the pastor of Heritage Chapel asked, "Who giveth this woman to be married?" my mother replied, "Her brothers and I." She sat down next to Uncle Jerry. I gave B.J. my flower bouquet, and the pastor put my hand in Abbott's.

"Here we go," Abbott whispered to me.

Our ceremony was a traditional Christian ceremony. We exchanged vows and rings. Abbott helped me up the altar steps to the unity candle. The lighting of the candle and the following pastor's prayer ended the ceremony.

Abbott and B.J. helped me maneuver my dress down the steps to the church floor.

We stood in front of the minister. "Abbott, you may kiss your bride."

He did, soundly.

"May I introduce Mr. and Mrs. Abbott Milbern."

Those in attendance clapped with some whistles thrown into the mix. B.J. handed me the bridal bouquet as the sounds of Mendelssohn's "Wedding March" reverberated to the rafters. The audience stood for the final time.

Abbott walked to Pops's side. Leaning over, he gave his grandfather and then his mother a hug and kiss. We moved to Mom's pew, and he did the same.

The wedding party headed to the bride's room.

Abbott and I arrived first. "Mrs. Milbern," he said as he pulled me into his arms, "your first official act after our wedding is to give your new husband a kiss—a really good one."

In the midst of the "really good one," the door opened, and we were joined by B.J., my Mom, Kathy, and many of our families.

"Where's Dad?" Abbott asked.

"He's taking Pops home. I don't think he'll be joining us for the reception. Past his afternoon nap, you know," his mother responded. She stepped closer to Abbott and whispered. "He's very tired. All the starch is gone."

"Hey, everyone," Abbott said over the noisy crowd inside the room. "If you don't know the way to Meadowview Stables, throw yourself on the mercy of someone who does and head to the reception. Jenni and I will leave here to join you as soon as we can collect our things."

My mother opened my carry-on.

"Mom, I can do this. You go with Uncle Stan—be his guide to the reception."

The room cleared as if a magic wand had been waved over it. "Good job, sweetheart." I grinned at my new husband.

"At least we can breathe. I'll go get my things and come back for you. They're already packed."

The minister stood at the side doorway to the church—one not frequently used by those attending services. He grinned. "Your car seems to have suffered a bit of abuse."

"Oh, mercy!" Abbott exclaimed. The vehicle had streamers, tin cans, and writing on the side and rear windows.

"Your Sunday School class, I presume."

"No doubt, pastor."

"Abbott and Jenni, I wanted to congratulate you and say I'll be supporting and praying for you both during your next months of preparing for the mission field."

"Thank you. We realize our lives are changing, and we look forward to the work ahead—following Jesus' command to take his message to the world."

The pastor nodded his head. "I know you need to get going. I won't keep you longer. Don't hesitate to ask my help, if you need anything—anything at all."

He held the church door as my new husband and I went to the car. I waited as Abbott placed our cases behind the front seat. I reached for the door handle.

"No. Don't ever do that."

"What?"

"Open the door yourself."

"Why?" My hand fell from the lever. "I open car doors all the time."

"The rule is never let your wife open the car door. A husband always opens it as a sign of respect." Abbott pulled on the metal handle.

"Who made up that regulation?"

"Pops. My grandmother never opened a single one."

"I remember you admonishing me before, several months back. I wasn't your wife then." I scooted onto the leather seat.

"No, but I knew you would be."

"Really." My amazement at his comment was evident on my face.

"Yes." Abbott stuffed my wedding gown around me, while giving me quick pecks on the lips as he worked. "I loved you the minute I laid eyes on you—hit me like a ton of bricks. All I had to do was hook you and reel you in like a fish. Did a pretty good job of it, I must say." He shut the door, went around the car, and slid under the wheel.

"Well, husband, I wouldn't pat myself on the back for fishing prowess, especially if the fish couldn't wait to take the bait." I grinned at him as he started the car.

"Aren't we a fine kettle of two fish?" he said, and we both started laughing.

"I hope we never stop laughing at and with each other. Come to think of it, the ability to accept another's blunders or habits with amusement or grace might be what's lacking in my family's relationships."

"A very perceptive statement, my love. I'm married to a psychologist as well as a writer." Abbott pulled from the church parking lot.

"They go hand in hand. Writers put their experiences down on paper—whether learned from personal experience or gleaned from studying those around them."

"Am I to walk on tiptoes, carefully watching every step and word?"

"No, silly. You aren't fair game—well, unless . . ." I let the subject drop. We drove in silence for some minutes.

"Wife, this is the first day of our married life."

"Now that's an insightful observation." I teased continuing, "Will we grow old together?"

"If I have anything to do with making it happen, we will."

"I love you, Abbott. I meant what I said in our wedding vows. I'll follow you to the ends of the earth."

"You may have to." He grinned.

I poked him in the ribs.

"Why do you do that?" he said, grimacing.

We were stopped at the crossroads at Meadowview preparing to continue onto Cameron Road. He leaned toward me, cupping my cheek in his hand.

"I'm going to kiss you."

"You'd better hurry. The light's turned green."

53

A large sign hung over the entrance to Meadowview Stable. The banner read *Congratulations, Jenni and Abbott.*

"Someone's been busy," Abbott exclaimed, stopping to get a better look.

"It's got notes and signatures written on the surface."

Abbott ducked his head, trying to read some of the messages. "Can't tell the words, but I'm sure we'll get the chance to read the comments after our honeymoon." We planned to spend our first night at his apartment—wind down from the pressure of the weeks before the wedding and the finalizing of my book.

Abbott placed his hand on mine. "One more official duty and we can go home, little wife. Are you ready?"

"Are you promising me rest and quiet?"

He put the car in drive. "As much as possible and a warm fireside so you can snuggle in my arms."

"Hmmm, I like the heavenly picture you paint."

When Abbott stopped our car at the entrance of his parents' home, several people rushed from the door to escort us into the house. The beautiful flowers from the church were positioned in the foyer and on the terrace, where swimming was forgotten and the reception took center stage.

Two large tables, laden with traditional hot and cold hors d'oeuvres, rested under a white screened tent. A punch fountain hummed near the middle of the enclosed area. Pink liquid streamed from the top. The bride and groom's table sat in a front corner with the wedding cake nearby.

Abbott and I, along with our parents, stood at the entrance of the tent and welcomed our guests inside.

Seventy people, some I'd never met, went through the line and past the goodies on the reception table. The "serve yourself" affair proceeded as planned.

After greeting the last participant, Kathy whispered, "Abbott and Jenni, you need to cut the cake."

By this time, I'd become an expert at maneuvering my wedding gown. Abbott gathered the train and we followed Kathy to the table. She rang a crystal bell to get the attention of our guests.

"Abbott and Jenni will cut their cake."

Uncle Jerry came from the group to video the cutting. Abbott leaned toward me and spoke in a low tone. "He's been taking pictures when we haven't noticed. Wonder what he's recorded and what we've been saying?"

"I noticed him a couple of times at church. I confess, I haven't paid much attention." I pulled the handle of the knife into my palm. "Are you ready?"

"Yes. You aren't going to smear wedding cake in my face, are you?"

"Would I do that?"

I didn't, and he didn't. We were too old for such shenanigans.

"Abbott, I could use some punch." I sat at our table and watched him walk to the punch bowl. He got two cups.

The blinding headache started instantly. I closed my eyes and put my hands on my temples. The top of my head felt like it was caught and being closed in a vise. The pain moved downward into my neck and shoulders.

"Jenni, are you all right?"

I didn't see him set the cups of punch on the table. I felt his hands on my shoulders and heard his voice full of concern.

"Jenni, what's wrong?"

"I have a horrible pain in my head, and I feel sick. Get me out of here to the bathroom," I whispered.

Abbott helped me stand. Concerned family rushed to our side. Other guests hung back in alarm.

"Can you walk?"

"I think so."

Kathy and Mom cleared the way for us to leave. We walked past Kathy's husband, my uncles, and their families, and toward the house.

I kept my eyes shut as much as possible. The light hurt. Noise in the tent behind us diminished, and I was grateful for the silence of the house and Kathy and Joe's large bathroom.

"Get a facecloth," Mom ordered. She dipped it in cold running water. I sat on the commode with my face in my hands. The cold against my forehead caused me to feel nauseous. The next move produced projectile vomiting. I made an effort to hit the tub.

"Abbott, get Dr. Wright. Your father will know him. He's riding horses at the stable."

"Mom, I need to lie down—get onto the floor. I still feel sick at my stomach." The stench of vomit didn't help my situation.

"We'll put her on my bed." Kathy's hand slid under my arm.

"No, no. On the bathroom floor, please. I'm going to throw up again." I pushed away from Abbott's mom and hung my head over the edge of the tub.

From the bathroom floor, I heard them discussing the situation. "We need to get her into Lexington to the hospital."

Mom said, "I'm with you." She wiped my face with a warm, wet cloth.

"I never heard Jenni complain of headaches."

"She doesn't have them. I can't remember any except for after the car crash earlier this year. Her head hurt from the concussion."

"Could this be related to the accident?"

My mind was asking the same question. I couldn't piece the conversation together, but I remembered Peter talking about complications. I cleared my head of any thoughts. It hurt too much to think.

"Wonder what's keeping Abbott?"

"Nothing, Mom, we're here. How is she?" Karen and Kathy moved aside as Abbott walked over and knelt beside me, leaving room for the doctor to do the same.

"Quiet the last few minutes," Kathy answered.

Dressed in his riding clothes, Dr. Wright asked, "Do you have a blood pressure monitor?"

"Of course, we keep it for Pops."

From a distance, I heard the results. "Very high. This is not good, and I don't like her symptoms. Call an ambulance, Abbott." He paused in thought. "We don't want to lose one minute waiting for it. Tell them we'll be leaving here on our way to the hospital." He followed Abbott from the room, shouting orders staccato fashion as my husband dialed 911. "Give the drivers a specific route. We'll update them by cell phone as to where we are and where to meet." He returned to the bathroom. "Ladies, help me fold her dress."

"Should we take her gown off?" Mom asked.

"No, we mustn't move her more than necessary. I wish we didn't have the bouncing trip into Lexington. Come with me." Dr. Wright scooped me from the floor and hurried down the corridor leading to the front door. Finished with his call, Abbott helped me into the backseat of his car.

He and Dr. Wright jumped into the front seats. Mom started to get in with me. "Mom, I can't stand to have my head elevated."

"Karen, go with Mom and Dad. Meet us there," Abbott instructed. "We'll take good care of her."

54

I don't remember much of the ride into the hospital. We stopped once, and I felt the sensation of floating in the air. Then, from a distance, the vague noise of a siren and someone sticking a needle in the back of my hand.

I awoke with the stringent smell of hospital disinfectant invading my nostrils. *Deja vu.* The sight of emergency room equipment made my head ache even more, if that was possible. Instead of the beautiful pearl-and-sequin bodice of my wedding gown, I felt and saw out of my half-open eyes the smooth cotton of a hospital gown. A white sheet covered my torso and legs.

"Please turn off the lights," I asked.

I heard Abbott tell someone, "Go to the nurse's station and get Dr. Wright. Tell him she's conscious."

An attendant in a smock hurried from the room. Opening my eyes caused the nausea to return. "Abbott, I'm going to be sick."

He held me until the episode ended. "My head—the pain—what's the problem?"

"Darling, we don't know. You're scheduled for a CAT scan and an MRI." Hopefully these will pinpoint the trouble." He wiped my face with a wet cloth.

"Where am I? How long have we been here?"

"You're in the emergency room at Lexington General Hospital. We've been here only a few minutes."

"What happened to my wedding gown?" He still wore his tux. The rose cummerbund and bowtie were gone.

"Your mom and mine took the dress off. It's safe in my car."

"Abbott, I threw up on it." Tears rolled from the corners of my eyes.

"Don't cry, sweetheart. That's the least of our worries at present."

Dr. Wright came into the room. "The neurosurgeon is on rounds. He's been paged. I'll give him ten minutes and we'll page again."

At nine minutes, Dr. Clifford walked into my room. After introductions, he started asking questions.

"No, I had no history of migraines."

"Yes, I had a concussion a few months before."

"Yes, writing a book and planning a wedding has caused me some stress."

"No, I didn't sleep well last night."

His questions ended with a detailed description of my present symptoms. "I understand the emergency room doctor ordered a CAT scan and an MRI."

Dr. Wright responded. "Yes, he did."

"I'll see that we get Jenni to these tests immediately." Dr. Clifford left the room.

"He's very thorough, Abbott. I believe you're in good hands." Dr. Wright bent over me. "Jenni, I'm leaving now. I'll request prayer for you tonight at church services."

"Thank you, Dr. Wright."

After the doctor left, I asked Abbott to dim the room's lights and close the door. "The pain is excruciating, and my neck feels like a muscle spasm that doesn't quit." I shut my eyes. Semi-consciousness returned.

For the next few hours, I alternated between being conscious and unconscious—and every level linking them.

During one period of lucidness, I heard the doctor telling Abbott, "We're giving strong pain medicine and something to calm her in the IV."

Another time, he said, "The tests so far indicate a small brain bleed."

"What exactly is a brain bleed, and what causes it?"

"A brain bleed is a hemorrhage of an artery. Your wife's bleed is in the frontal lobe of the brain. As for what causes one—could be genetic or the stress of the wedding, which caused the high blood pressure. The accident might have aggravated the problem, or she could have had an aneurysm of the artery."

"This is such a shock. We were laughing and enjoying our wedding reception, and now she lies here, holding on to life."

"Be thankful she's still here. A larger one and your wife wouldn't have made the trip to the hospital. Abbott, there's one more test I want to do—an angiogram."

"Why?"

"We need to determine what caused this problem and see if the bleeding has stopped. We might need to do surgery to correct it. I need to caution you. There can be complications with the procedure."

"What complications?"

"We may worsen the bleeding or cause a blood clot to loosen. That means a stroke—death may occur. We'll need you to sign a release."

"What if I don't agree to the test?"

"The same thing may happen as you see here or she might get completely well. I can't give you a prognosis without the test."

"I'll sign the papers."

"Does your wife have a living will?"

"We haven't discussed one, so I doubt it."

"I'll have the nurse bring one in. We may catch her in a coherent moment. In her medical condition, she needs one. You do too."

I heard Abbott move across the room and sit down. "Father, be with Jenni as she undergoes this examination."

I couldn't understand the rest of his words, but I echoed his prayer.

I awoke in the intensive care unit. The terrible headache and projectile vomiting continued. I lay in the semi-darkness of the room—no television and no visitors except for visiting hours.

Without realizing the change, I started to feel better.

Three or four days after the first tests, I had another CAT scan and MRI. Dr. Clifford delivered good news. The bleed had sealed itself. There was no leakage. My head still hurt, but not as badly.

By Friday, I felt good enough to sit up in a chair. On Saturday, I walked down the hall past the nurse's station and back. Mom came and helped me wash my hair.

On Sunday, I woke with a blinding headache and projectile vomiting. Was the artery bleeding again? For the first time, I felt fear. It surged from my innermost being and overwhelmed me. I wanted to sob, but sobbing caused my head to split open. I lay alone in my sterile room with tears rolling from my eyes, the hair covering my ears soaking wet.

Dr. Clifford ordered another angiogram for five thirty on Monday morning and asked for the family to be present on Sunday night for his discussion of the procedure. The doctor explained he would install a metal coil to facilitate the flow of blood.

"Will that take care of her problem?" my mother asked.

"If I find what I think I'll find, the answer is yes, but let me discuss the risks." He went over the long list of possibilities.

Dr. Clifford came to my bedside. "Jenni, I'll see you in the morning. Get some rest."

I nodded and a sharp pain shot through my skull.

Slowly, my family said goodbye. Some had tears in their eyes. Mom lingered over me. "I'll be praying all night, sweetheart, and I'll be here for lunch tomorrow."

I held hands with Uncle Stan who waited until last. "Sugar, when you get out of here, we'll go horseback ridin' at Meadowview Stables." He bent and kissed me on the forehead and disappeared through the door, swiping at his face.

The nurse came into the room with a syringe. "Pain medication and something to help you sleep." She injected the liquid into the IV.

She left, and Abbott and I were alone. "What's going to happen, Abbott?"

"I wish I could answer your question." He came to my bedside, sat in a chair, and leaned his head on my exposed arm.

"I'm afraid."

"I am too," he said quietly. "We must remember we serve a loving God, who is the Greatest Physician. He cures all sicknesses."

"Fear is a human emotion hard to overcome."

"I'm reminded of the verse from Psalms, *God is our refuge and strength, an ever-present help in trouble. Therefore we will not fear*. And then there's the passage in James about the testing of faith developing perseverance. Jenni, this may be a trial that tests our faith in Him. It may be a precursor to our future situation, wherever we are in this world."

The fear I harbored said there might be no future to experience.

Abbott continued, "In Peter, the apostle says, *Cast all your anxiety on Him, because He cares for you.*" He laughed—a low chuckle. "Am I helping or hurting?"

"I love Bible verses. Go on," I drowsily replied.

"John says, *Peace I leave with you; my peace I give to you. I do not give to you as the world gives. Do not let your hearts be troubled and do not be afraid.*

The last verse I remembered as I fell asleep was, *You who fear the Lord, praise Him.*

55

Was it raining? In my dazed state, I reached my unsteady hand to my cheek and wiped moisture from my skin. Then I realized Abbott's face hovered over mine. The rain was tears—his tears.

"Jenni, come back to me. I love you."

The bed moved, and his face disappeared. As the attendants wheeled me down the hall, I tried to remember the verses Abbott quoted the night before. I couldn't. One word seemed embedded in my mind. The word *praise*. Praise Him.

Dr. Clifford told me later that I sang at the start of the procedure, while the nurses secured me to the table so I couldn't move during the insertion of the catheter and movement of the soft tube through my arteries. He said I sang just above a whisper. I didn't remember singing.

I will sing praise, I will lift my voice. I will sing praise, I've made my choice.

I will sing praise in all I do. I will sing praise to You.

He said I repeated the verse, seemingly hesitant to go to the final one. Then, without warning I sang the last part of the song loudly enough for everyone in the room to hear. He said, surely the Holy Spirit was in the place. From that moment on, he never doubted the outcome of the angiogram.

No matter the storms that come my way. No matter the trials I may face.

You promised that You would see me through. So I will trust in You.

So I will trust in you.

The last verse, I sang once.

I do remember the procedure hurt. There was a hot sensation. At times, a white brilliant light flashed in my head and slowly went back to blackness. Perhaps I only dreamed this.

I went to the recovery room and back to my original place in intensive care.

Abbott waited for me in my room.

My eyes opened.

"Jenni," Abbott said, "Dr. Clifford will be here in a moment. He's at the nurse's station filling in paperwork." He bent to kiss my parched lips. "How do you feel, sweetheart?"

"My head still hurts, but I'm not nauseous," I said doing a quick self-examination.

He applied Vaseline to my lips. "Would you like some cold water?"

"Maybe a little. I'll be glad when I can sit up and eat. I'm tired of lying flat on my backside."

Abbott looked amused and happy. "Well, you are feeling better. Wait until I get you home. I'm going to really baby you."

"I'm sorry about the honeymoon. Didn't plan on spending our first days apart in an invalid ward."

"We'll take care of that problem with a delayed one. I have a plan."

Dr. Clifford came into the room. "How's my patient." He was smiling.

"She still has a headache, but the sick feeling is gone. She's beginning to sound like the feisty lady I married. How did the procedure go?"

"Everything looks great. The coil did its job to stop the bleeding. We'll take it slow the next couple of days, and see how she progresses. I'm reducing her meds, and if she does as well as I think she will, we can release her next Sunday or Monday."

I asked the question I'd been dreading. "What's the prognosis?" Abbott took my hand in his.

"Okay, here goes. You could have a headache from now on. There's a possibility of seizures and mobility issues."

"What kind of mobility issues?"

"Minor things like stumbling more than usual. She doesn't have any mental impairment. I believe she's one lucky lady."

"God is good," Abbott said.

"Yes, he is," Dr. Clifford stood up. "I'm heading home. This has been a long day."

Abbott followed him from the room. When he returned, he said, "Dr. Clifford thinks you'll move to a regular room in two days. I know someone who's been anxious to see you."

"Pops?" I said. My eyelids felt like lead weights were pulling them down.

"Yes. Once he knows you're in a private room, wild horses won't keep him away."

I smiled weakly. "Has my family gone home?"

"All but your mother. She's coming in the morning. She said to remind you about lunch."

"Oh, we missed lunch today. Tell her I'm." Sleep overtook my words.

From a distance, I heard Abbott praying. "Father, thank you for bringing my Jenni through her operation. Losing her would have been almost too hard to bear. Keep her safe through these next days and continue to apply your healing powers to her body.

I renew my commitment to you—one she shares with me. Work through any complications that would deter our future in missions. I accept your wisdom. Amen."

For the first time, the question of our future in missions hung in the balance. The song that had enveloped my mind all day returned. I sang it in my dreams, especially the last verse.

56

On Sunday, Abbott drove me home to his condo. A cold wind blew and the skies were gray. "Do you smell snow?" I asked as we got out of his car in the driveway. He'd insisted we park there instead of the garage so he could carry me over the threshold.

"Maybe." Abbott laughed. "But our nest is warm and cozy, little wife."

He unlocked the front door and pushed it open. His face reminded me of the man standing before the altar at our wedding—happy, full of love, and smiling.

"I'm ready, dear."

"No swift movements," I cautioned, knowing full well my admonitions were unnecessary. "Don't bump my head."

Carefully lifting me into his arms, he negotiated one step and carried me through the entrance. The welcoming sign that had been hung over the entrance to Meadowview Stables was strung on the wall leading to the kitchen.

Following the initial shock of seeing the ten-foot banner gracing one wall of his living room, I said, "Your décor has taken a decided turn for the worst."

Instead of stopping inside the door and putting me down, he continued to a couch in front of his fireplace.

"It's not 'your' but *our* décor, sweetheart. And you are welcome to change *our* interior decoration however you want." Abbott said this as he lowered me carefully onto a soft cushion.

"This has been a bachelor pad for too many years." He pulled a soft throw from the back of the couch. "I don't want you getting a chill," he explained, giving me a kiss. "Get comfortable. I'm going to close and lock the entrance door."

When he returned I said, "Something smells good." I pushed my nose into the air and sniffed the delicious odor of food not cooked in a hospital.

"Potato soup. My mother's recipe. I normally bake cornbread to eat with my delicious potage. But, today, we'll eat crackers. I understand they're easier on your stomach."

"You're reminding me of my problem with nausea. I've thrown up enough to last me a lifetime."

"Are you hungry?"

"Yes, but sit down." I patted a couch cushion. "I want to talk to you."

We hadn't discussed our future, and I needed to know if plans had changed.

"I promised you a fire." He stooped to light a match to wood and kindling waiting to burn in the fireplace. "Give me a sec to check on my soup."

I heard a spoon stirring inside a pot and running water in the kitchen. He returned, poked at the fire, and, coming to the couch, he gathered me into his arms. "This is what I've been dreaming about, sitting here with you beside me." He pushed my hair off my forehead. We looked at each other. "I love you, Jenni."

"I love you, Abbott." Our lips met.

"What did you want to talk about?" he asked after our moment of intimacy.

"Abbott, what is our future in missions? How does my problem affect our prospects for service?"

His face looked serious. "I've been thinking we'll wait for Dr. Clifford to release you. See if the prognosis changes at that time. We need to let some time pass before a definite decision is made."

"I still want to go—anywhere."

"My intention hasn't changed either. I'll call the mission board and talk to our consultant. See how your illness will figure into the picture. I've applied to the seminary in New Orleans.

They have a master's degree in evangelical missions or church planting."

"Have you decided which one God's leading you into?"

"No."

"So, you'll be going back to school to complete the courses necessary to be a missionary—get a master's degree. Our mission board expects its personnel to be well equipped for service."

"Not only me, but you'll take courses also. Our mission board wants the wife to be prepared as much as the husband."

"Sounds like we are in a wait-and-see mode."

"This is true. I thought we might use this period to study former missionary's lives and read some books relating to the mission field."

I nodded, agreeing with him.

"Do you see that pile of books on the end table?" he pointed to one close to where we sat.

"I'll start tomorrow."

"Until we can determine our permanent destiny, I'll continue with Dad at the dealership, selling cars."

Three months later, Dr. Clifford released me. "Every CAT scan and MRI we've done since you left the hospital indicates there's been no more bleeding."

"What's the possibility this problem could happen again?" I asked.

"I don't expect a brain bleed such as the one you experienced to ever happen again. I can't promise this one hundred percent."

Abbott and I got up to leave.

"God bless you," he said as we left his office.

Abbott and I both welcomed the good news. "Let's celebrate," he said, pulling his cell phone out of his pocket. "Pops, we're coming to get you for lunch." There ensued some discussion of the weather, which threatened snow. In fact, the weatherman predicted two inches.

When he hung up the phone, I asked, "Is he going and where are we going to eat?"

"Yes, and The Horse Hair Café, of course."

Pops sat across from us at the restaurant. He looked frail in a thick sweater pulled to his throat and buttoned down the front. He pulled knitted gloves from his hands and placed them neatly on the top of the booth's table. His hands looked like bones with skin pulled tautly over them—lumps indicating arthritis defined each joint. I recognized these hands, looking unmistakably similar to another set I'd observed not long ago. The aura surrounding him and smile hadn't changed. If anything, both were enhanced. I could imagine a halo around his head.

Engrossed in my observation of Pops Kendall, I jumped when Abbott said, "Hey guys, I'm going to the restroom." He scooted out of the booth. The restaurant manager stopped him on the way.

I moved around to sit next to Pops, placing my arm around his shoulders and giving him a kiss on the cheek.

"Jenni, what good news you received from the doctor visit."

"Yes, God is good."

"I've kept you and Abbott in my prayers, asking the Father to undergird you with his power and healing. I believe He's answered my petition."

"He's the author of miracles, and I believe I received one. I wonder why me?"

"God keeps people alive for a reason. The Bible's full of examples. Take King David, who encountered and overpowered a lion intending to have a sheep and maybe him for a meal. He killed Goliath and became Israel's king."

"So, do you think I'll have to fight Goliath one day?"

"God has prepared you by bringing you through a medical crisis. David didn't fear Goliath, because he'd already fought the lion and won."

"Are you preaching to me?" I gave him another hug.

"Ministers never quit. Have you heard any news on your book?"

"The publisher is considering my novel for publication."

"Hey, you two." Abbott interrupted our conversation. "Pops, are you trying to steal my wife away?" Abbott waited for me to move from his grandfather's side to my former seat next to him.

"Now, Abbott, you know that's against my moral and biblical values," Pops kidded with a twinkle in his eye.

"Jenni, you remember Barbaro, the horse who won the Derby?"

"Sure. How is he?"

"The manager told me Barbaro is experiencing more problems with his hooves. Damaged tissue was removed from the left hoof, and realignment of bones is necessary by adding a new cast. He said the prognosis isn't good."

"Medicine works miracles these days. I hope he makes it," I said, remembering his thundering finish at the Kentucky Derby.

We ate our lunch and took Pops back to his cottage.

It started to snow on our way home—a few flakes at first, then heavier.

Abbott put the car in the garage and went to the mailbox. He came back to the kitchen with several envelopes in his hand.

One, he'd ripped open.

He sat at the kitchen table reading a single page of printed words. I went to look over his shoulder. "Jenni, the seminary in New Orleans has admitted me for the summer session." He looked at me, his face a mixture of happiness and joy. "We'll be eating crawfish in Louisiana, sweetheart."

"Abbott, what wonderful news."

He pulled another envelope from the stack and waved it in the air. "From the mission board." He placed the rectangular piece of paper on the table.

I looked at the letter and got quiet. It contained the results of our application for the mission field. "I think we'd better pray over its contents."

Minutes later, Abbott opened the envelope. I read the contents along with him. We were accepted on a provisional basis, pending a medical clearance and the completion of his studies at the seminary. Then we would start our missionary journey as three-year apprentices and be assigned permanent status after this period on the mission field.

Abbott leaped from the table and took me in his arms. We joined hands and danced around the kitchen, laughing and praising the Lord.

"I'm going to call Mom." I left the room to find my cell phone.

When I came back, Abbott was on the phone to Pops.

I sat at the kitchen table and rummaged through the other envelopes. My heart jumped when I saw one from the publishing company, the one looking at my novel.

Okay, Jenni. I believe good news happens in threes. I opened it. The page was signed by my agent.

Ms. Loften,

We have carefully considered your manuscript for publication. At present, we must reject the novel. We suggest you find someone to edit the book thoroughly, and we will happily consider it again.

Don't quit writing. You have talent.

Jane Winston

"I'm sorry, darling."

I sat for some seconds before answering, but I couldn't think of anything profound to say. "I'm okay. Maddie's story has been written, and we won't change one single word."

"Why don't we self-publish?"

"Maybe so. Let me get over the disappointment of rejection. Writers have thick skins. Regret doesn't last long."

Abbott took off his coat. "I'm going to make a fire in the fireplace. If the snow continues to fall, we can go outside and make a snowman."

"And snow ice cream," I added.

He left the room.

I folded the paper and pushed it into the envelope. I remembered thinking, when the boxes contents were exposed, that this was the end of my grandmother's influence on my life. No, not really. In writing about the Tipton family, I'd relived some of the times we'd spent together, and, most of all, I thanked her for telling me the story that had changed my life.

The best story I'd write would always be hers.

ACKNOWLEDGMENTS

My thanks:

To Sue Marsden and others who read the manuscript and made productive comments and corrections.

To Robin Swayney at the Museum of the Cherokee for her time and interest.

To Nancy McClemore for accompanying me to Churchill Downs and outside the Lexington area.

To Sam Venable for suggesting getting your family's memoirs.

To Jessica Everson, Ken Raney, Robin Rhyne Greenlee for editing, book cover and background photo.

To Kristen Veldhuis of EA Publishing for her good work.

To Joshua Duke for his help in securing the permission to publish copyrighted, I Will Sing Praise.

To Betty McKenzie for sharing a traumatic event in her life.

For three-quarters of a century, Reba Rhyne's home has been in East Tennessee. During this time, she was married for 25 years, had a daughter, and established a business of her own. Writing began as a hobby, while she spent months on clients' locations as a consultant, developing prototypes for boat upholstery.

Writing in the style reminiscent of Laura Ingalls Wilder and Janette Oke, Reba Rhyne, tells stories based on real history, much of it inspired by her own Tipton ancestors. Her books are Christian-oriented and suitable for teens and adults. Her first novel, Butterfield Station, was published earlier this year.

For sixty years, she has been a Christ follower who believes her responsibility is to follow the Great Commission found in the Gospel of Matthew. Retired?, she lives in the Smoky Mountain foothills.

Made in the USA
Columbia, SC
04 September 2018